"Stay With Me."

Grania gasped softly as Niall lifted her off the floor and laid her on the pallet.  resist him, at least mak keep him at he eine from her breast.

His belly was wa . . .

"Have you bew ssed a kiss to Grania's earlobe.

She writhed against him. "I made no charm." Her voice was ragged.

"Liar." Niall's mouth covered hers with a hard, grinding kiss. Grania arched up to meet him. His mouth withdrew.

"Please," she gasped. She'd make any promise, deed him anything. He was a fool to fear her; it was she who was his slave.

BLAINE ANDERSON

HEARTSPELL

WARNER BOOKS

A Time Warner Company

WARNER BOOKS EDITION

Copyright © 1992 by Blaine Aislinn Anderson
All rights reserved.

Cover illustration by Gregg Gulbronson
Cover design by Anne Twomey
Hand lettering by Carl Dellacroce

Warner Books, Inc.
666 Fifth Avenue
New York, N.Y. 10103

A Time Warner Company

Printed in the United States of America

First Printing: January, 1992

10 9 8 7 6 5 4 3 2 1

Dedication

To my beautiful daughters,
Anna and Jillian,
who fill my every day with magic.

Author's Note

Scholars of Irish history will no doubt recognize *Heartspell* as the story of the Irish high king Domnall mac Aed and his foster sons, Cellach and Congal Claen. Although some character names have been changed, it is my hope this will not offend the historians among you but rather make this wonderful piece of Irish history breathe and live for you as it does for me.

Blaine Anderson

My love is a thistle,
It is the four quarters of the earth,
It is the breaking of a neck,
A drowning in water,
A race towards the sky. . . .

From the ancient Irish Tales

INISFAIL (IRELAND), A.D. 628

Prologue

The Inaugural Hill of Tara, A.D. 628

Today, on an ancient plain thick with mists and priests, Grania would watch a man die. The hideous thought soured the venison she'd managed to force down for breakfast. Yet something else sent a clammy spark crawling like a roach down her spine. As she waited to witness the O'Neill chieftain Connor risk his life to claim Inisfail's high kingship, the magic of the old Druid ways seized her. It was the druidhect—and it was starting to work through Grania like honey soaking a bees' comb.

The magic came with spine-stiffening chills, often bringing the Sight, with its glimpse of the future. Grania never welcomed this witchery when it possessed her—and she wanted it least of all here and now.

She roughed her palms against her wind-numbed cheeks—if she warmed herself, there was a chance she might escape the grip of the druidhect. Grania cupped her numb fingers around her mouth and blew on them, then yanked the folds of her *bratta* tight, as if the woolen cloak alone could stop her from shivering. It was useless; she was freezing. She could only hope the magic could be stayed until this gruesome O'Neill spectacle was finished.

She squinted, searching the circle of raised plain; it was soft and wet with morning mist. Wind pushed and pulled the fog, congealing it into a white wall one minute, thinning it into milky vapor the next. Grania drew a stiff, buttressing breath, but it didn't help; the dawn chill sank like lake water in her lungs. Her eyes fluttered sideways, clinging to the flickering tongues of a beacon fire. Day was just starting to pulse on the dark horizon. Grania closed her eyes and felt the sun's warmth tingle her cheeks. The frigid tightness in her chest loosened a little, then returned as she heard her father's measured footsteps come up behind her.

"You shouldn't have worn that."

Grania turned to face Brian, her hand rising to clutch the dragonstone that hung from a leather thong around her neck. Her father stared in accusation at the lumpy neckpiece, and Grania felt the chill pour back into her.

"If you are to be one of us . . ."

"I am *not* one of you," she said, too quickly and insistently. Grania dipped her face, embarrassed at the razored tone of her voice. She had no wish to stir up her father's anger; if anything, it would serve her better to appease him. Then, perhaps, he'd give up his notion of making her live with his Christians and let her go back to the Druids at Uisneath. Grania's mother, Emer, had been a Druidess— leaving Grania half of two things, whole of nothing. Even with the Druidesses at Uisneath, she never felt a sense of true belonging. But she belonged there more than in this cross-cursed place.

"I knew there was a risk in sending you to foster with your aunt in the Druid mists. But what else could I do when your mother died? I'd hoped one day to bring you back to me. Now I need you here."

Brian wouldn't have bothered with her if his second wife, Fea, hadn't died; but Grania refused to ease her father's grief. "I could have been yours for the summoning." *Fourteen years*, Grania thought bitterly, remembering how the time lost between them made Brian nearly unrecognizable when he'd come seeking her among the Druid priestesses. *He'd waited fourteen years to claim her. Now it was too late.*

"I wish to make amends."

"Send me home, then." Grania's voice was as calm and implacable as her well-schooled features.

"This is your home," Brian answered softly. "I've missed you."

Her father's honeyed words were self-serving lies. Brian had been quick enough to pack Grania off when her mother had died. There was, after all, no reason to keep her. She had a dark, Druid face—a face that surely would have embarrassed him.

"I'd hoped, in bringing you to Tara, you could come to know the part of you that is my blood, too."

Grania's gaze rescinded to a distant green. Her father's eyes looked less human than like agates set in his broad, large-boned face. Everything about Brian proclaimed their differences: his sunlit complexion, his brightly pied *bratta*, worn to mark him as bard to the great O'Neill chief.

Her father was tall and glistening and towered over Grania's dark, small frame. In a way, she was glad for their differences; for just as Brian had refused her, Grania now meant to refuse him.

"Will you force me to stay here?" She'd been too afraid

to ask until now. Her aunt Maeve had warned Grania to go easy with Brian if she meant to come back to Uisneath. Grania had hoped, once Brian saw how much she looked like Emer, saw how badly she fit here, that he'd give up keeping her. But, incredibly, he wanted her still. *Goddess*, Grania prayed silently, *let him set me free*.

"I've missed you," Brian said as if that excused the chasm of time that lay uncrossed between them.

"My heart's no changeling."

"Have you no hope of loving me?"

It was a preposterous question, considering Brian's neglect. Grania's silence gave him a firm, icy answer. She threaded her arms over her chest and turned her face away. Everything around her was another reminder that she didn't belong.

Strange sights and sounds warred on her senses. Droves of nobles made a thick ring around the edge of the plain, their voices clotting into a low rumble capped by the tinkling of bards' bells. Chieftain's *brattas*, the cloaks brilliantly colored to befit their high station, bloomed like tufts of spring on the sod, shaming the unbleached linen of Grania's simple *leine*.

Cracks of sunlight shimmered off the men's gold crowns and neck plates, doubling their brightness. Tribal standards snaked and snapped high above her, like loud tongues chiding the copper sky.

Christian priests—Grania had never seen so many— speckled the throng with their grotesque faces, their eyelids blackened with alder berries, their heads half-shaved and shining in the tonsure of their faith. Their jeweled staffs rose like defiant spires over the crowd; the clappers of their priests' bells seemed to beat against the inside of her skull.

Mercifully, Brian kept silent. And there were welcome distractions to draw her eye. Circling the plain was a huge earthen wall cut with one wide gate; it was through this opening that the O'Neill Connor would enter, driving his chariot with its unbroken team. Grania's gaze followed the chieftain's planned path into the circle's interior, then widened as she stared at the limestone pillars, whose thick white shafts were still smudged with night.

The stones rose up to twice a man's height, then tilted inward to meet in a dull collision, as if they'd been pushed together by a great, angry hand. There was a triangular opening between their sides and the sod below, and it was through this dangerously small space that Connor would try to drive his team. And then, though Grania could not imagine him surviving this first test, the O'Neill would levy his sword against a third stone, the Lia Fail. Even Grania had heard of the touchstone of destiny. If Connor were meant to rule, the Lia Fail would scream beneath the strike of his blade. So the O'Neills made their kings—and slaughtered pretenders.

Grania closed her eyes, picturing the miserable sight. "Why must I see this?" she mumbled.

"A kingmaking is a rare, honored thing." The voice came up suddenly behind her. It was so full and resonant that it seemed to issue out of her own head. Grania whirled around, her *bratta* loosening. A huge, looming man shadowed her child's height. Grania's mouth and eyes waxed wide, and she felt like a pup in thrall to a new master. Whatever she meant to say was forgotten under the intensity of the chieftain's stare.

"Niall, this is my daughter, Grania."

"I see you've kept secrets, Brian. This is the first I've heard of a daughter." Niall peered down at her, making Grania wish she were taller and lighter, less conspicuous among these snow-skinned O'Neills. Her unusual appearance didn't escape him. "Were you raised in a fairy hill, little girl?'' The stranger laughed loosely, a broad smile lighting his leonine face.

He was golder than sun. A soft crease cut his brow, and thick shanks of hair, the color of summer bark, arced toward his dark, cobalt blue eyes. His shoulders, already broad-beamed, were squared to extremes by two huge, studded brooches. A wide, jet-laid necklace flattened the top half of his *leine*, which was cut shorter than Grania's shift but was more richly embroidered.

He had the hard, pithy look of a champion. Well centered, well full of himself. But he wore a mark of low caste—his face was clean-shaven, like a cow chief's. He stared down curiously, looking as though he were trying to decide whether Grania was a child or a woman. She shrank under his scrutiny, then lifted her chin to him, rocking onto the balls of her feet to make herself taller.

''Is she mute?'' The chieftain's brow rose in a taunt.

''I . . . I . . .'' Grania's fear caught in a stutter.

''Leave her be, Niall. It's no day for teasing nurselings.''

Grania's eyes shot to a second man; she'd been too spell-bound by the first to see him until now.

His head was nearly as black as her own and he looked like a condensed, darker version of the other, equally mus-cled but more compact. Grania gasped as her gaze struck his left eye. The iris was all white and the lid was crudely twisted in a mockery of sleep. He was worse than ugly; he was beauty damned.

''But then you've seen kingmakings before,'' the darker man said, his voice curling like smoke on the words. ''Your father Maelcova's—and then again when Sweeney stole his crown away.''

Grania watched the taller chieftain's fists clench; with obvious difficulty he stilled them to his sides. She took a step back from the kindling fight, expecting blows, but there was only tense silence.

The light-haired chieftain was still for a long moment, then his face broadened slowly into a grin. With no warning, he reeled back and thumped the smaller man between the shoulder blades. The blow knocked out a blast of breath, making him cough. "Aye, Fergus, let's to the kingmaking."

The men's stares met, then unlocked as they strode off, mismatched in everything except the moment's purpose. Grania felt the weight of Brian's eyes on her and she squirmed, drawing nervous circles with her slipper in the sod.

"Connor's foster sons," Brian offered as if Grania had asked him. "The maimed one, Fergus, is prince of the province of Ulster. He was sent to Connor as a boy to ally their tribes. The other man, Niall, is Connor's nephew— and chosen to succeed him as the next high king." Grania imagined the young O'Neill's chance would come soon enough—likely today.

A trumpet's shrill blast rent the air and the crowd hushed, its circle tightening. In memoried ritual the chieftains turned toward the opening in the sodden wall. Connor's silhouetted chariot lurched into sight. The cart's body moaned and rocked behind its restless team.

Dawn shot coral-colored shafts of light through the wheel spokes; white steam belched rhythmically from the horses' nostrils. Their reins slacked and snapped like black ribbons on the face of the rising sun, each strike feeding the animals' frenzy.

The chariot pitched and rolled, and Connor rode it like a sea god on storm waves. He swiveled his eyes around the circle, then raised a huge gloved hand to set his leather helmet in place. Throwing his head back, Connor gripped the reins tight to his vest and howled the O'Neill battle cry. "Red Hand to victory!" His whip sectioned the air and the chariot exploded forward, churning up clumps of sod.

Grania felt the earth rumble as the team surged toward her. She could see the horses' bridles, red-dripped with enamel, making their mouths look to bleed and their tails, stained purple, flying wildly beneath the levy of the O'-Neill's whip. The chariot's bird's-wing awning hummed with wind; its wicker body shook with seam-splitting force. Wheel-mounted scythes whirred through the air, and as Connor squalled past, his *bratta* snapping furiously, the team's hooves threw earth up wildly. Grania spit out what she could and wiped the rest off her lips.

Connor drove as if nothing in heaven or on earth could stop him. When he was two team lengths shy of the stones, sunlight broke through, lighting the mists blinding white. Grania blinked back the glare, moments ago unwilling to see, now unable to wrench her eyes from the horrific sight.

It was then the druidhect came again, like a miserable hand choking her throat. Her spine spiked rigid and she had to think hard to breathe. She bent over, slumping her head into her hands, blinking and taking in air with deep, open-mouthed gasps as she struggled not to faint. She was only vaguely aware of the distant sound of cheers. Something—maybe metal striking stone—screeched. Still shivering and shaky, Grania rolled slowly upright and blinked her watery eyes.

Against all odds, Connor had driven his team through the opening between the standing stones. And the Lia Fail, the stone that made the O'Neill kings, had proclaimed him its own. Connor floated above the thick mist, hoisting his gleaming sword to the sky.

"O'Neill! O'Neill!" The crowd's call swelled to a deafening roar.

The roar of Grania's own blood in her ears drowned out the cheer as the druidhect levied its full power through her. This time it brought the Sight, which filled her brain with a cold, clear voice: *Brian would not make her stay here.* Before Grania had time to be relieved, a second swell of magic came over her. *She would choose to live in this cursed place.* Grania felt as if her blood were turning to ice in her veins.

CHAPTER

1

Niall flew off the gelding's back like a slung stone.
Thwack. He fell onto a cold deck of sod, teeth clacking, as
his head ricocheted onto a limestone boulder.

His brow was slick and warm, but there was no time to
check the extent of his bleeding. The cougar was dead on
him—and, from the look of its straked ribs, keen for a
meal. Niall scrambled to his knees, his unfocused eyes
wheeling wildly over the sod for his sword. He saw it—
lying impossibly far away.

Niall spun back, but it was too late; the cat's claws caught
his thigh like fire on dry spunk, shredding his striped wool
legging in one easy swipe. A quartet of ruby wakes oozed
up through the fabric's slits, then fell in crimson glops to
the sod.

The animal recoiled with a hiss, its ears nailed flat on
either side of its small head. Its eyes shrank to amber coals

while its tail slapped up columns of dust. Lean, hungry shoulders punched like bats' wings through the cougar's dirty, mottled fur.

Niall's leg sang with pain and his head banged like a drunkard's drum. Every ragged, hard-won breath hinted at one fractured rib, maybe more. He had ridden out scouting alone while his party broke camp. The distant whinny of Niall's horse Murchad confirmed his worst fear: Niall was orphaned in this deadly fight.

The cougar froze in a crouch, its tail switching in rhythmic, lethal intent. Black cores pulsed in its waspy eyes as it took on the unblinking, pitiless look of a warrior.

Niall set his teeth, steeling himself with what breath his splintered rib could bear. He dragged himself slowly backward, his wounds conspiring against him. Pain forked down his left arm, and the clawed leg gained weight. Even the earth itself thwarted him; Niall's woolen *bratta* snagged like silk on twigs of bracken.

Grunting and gasping, Niall slogged on obstinately, sweat and dirt quickly coating his brow. Black pinpoints pocked his sight, and he teetered on unconsciousness. He glanced at the cat from his hard-won path—all his misery had bought him precious little distance. The cougar, still watching and waiting, could have him in one easy bound.

Niall's head whirled like a weaver's distaff; the cat softened and blurred. Niall's head lolled sideways as he heard the cougar growl. He saw a fuzzy image of the animal's gullet vibrating.

Something else gurgled; Niall stole a quick look behind him and saw that a stream brooked through a butterwort field. Niall couldn't see much of the glimmering water, but it looked too narrow to stay the cougar. Still, Niall would try.

He muscled, gasping, over the turf, working his arms till

they shook and stung. Five, maybe six more pulls and he'd have the stream. The cougar snarled, his whiskers scrunching up to expose stained yellow teeth. There was no mistaking: the animal was hauling in to spring.

With no weapon, Niall improvised. He yanked the heavy gold collar off his neck and, pushing up on his good arm, reeled back. The fractured rib froze him with pain, but with a gut-sprung yell, Niall missiled the neckpiece dead on the cat.

The collar flew with a champion's eye—the cougar shrieked and shrank as it struck him. Then the cat rallied, swiping a slow paw over its face. Fresh fury filled its slitted eyes, and with no other warning, the cougar lunged and recoiled again; now Niall's calf matched his thigh.

Niall felt the stamina leaching out of him. On the next spring the cougar flew and Niall ducked, slamming back with a dull thud as his head struck the turf. His locked arms shot up, catching the cat's sinewy throat.

Suddenly there were two cats, then three and four, their teeth a snarling kaleidoscope. Niall's arms trembled shamelessly and his vision ebbed; still his hands held like a vise on the cat's gullet. One of them would die before he let go. Everything waxed black; when the cat went limp, slipping and sinking, Niall could only guess the wetness soaking his chest and neck was blood. He hoped it wasn't all his.

Niall's brain congealed to a tight, dark knot as his arms thumped, slack, on either side of him. With his last conscious thought, he knew he was dying.

Grania stared at her unconscious charge and wondered what had moved her to drag Niall from the clearing to her hut on the Druidesses' lake. She leaned in closer than she would have dared had he been awake and stared intently at his badly bruised face. Even wounded, he looked finer and brighter than the day they'd met at Connor's kingmaking. His arms were roped with smooth, tanned muscles, and his golden hair glimmered even under a dark mat of dried blood. Niall's large hands balled into loosely formed fists; even unconscious he wore a warrior's ready mien.

It had been five years since she'd met the O'Neill on the plain at Tara. One week was all it had taken for her father to realize how much she hated him and his way of life. Perhaps it was that Brian had decided his daughter's dark looks and Druid blood made her too unseemly to keep. Grania didn't care why he'd let her go; she was home to stay.

Yet her fears of her father's rough-edged world dogged her. Asleep and awake, the druidhect still seized her. And the magic's message was always the same: Grania would choose to leave Uisneath, choose to live among the O'Neill. She couldn't imagine inviting such misery. But neither could she have imagined this half-dead chieftain, lying here, his huge feet dangling over the end of her bed.

She went back to mashing the mallow and plantain leaves. The sooner this O'Neill was freshly poulticed, the sooner he'd be healed—and gone.

The hut's door creaked, and the small room shivered with light. Grania popped up like a hare out of a wet burrow, her mortar of medicine banging to the floor. The other priestesses at Uisneath could sense a visitor coming, but even after all her years here she still couldn't anticipate their startling arrivals.

"Let me help you." Her aunt Maeve gave her an apologetic smile.

Maeve bent down, but Grania patted her hand, refusing her offer with a gentle shake of her head. Picking up what she could salvage of the half-finished poultice, she shot Niall a sour glance. From the moment she'd found this hulking O'Neill, nothing had gone right for her.

Her shoulders still ached from hoisting his leaden bulk onto Uisneath's sole mare. And Grania wanted her bed back. She should have left him bleeding in the field; with luck, a second cat would have finished the work of the first. Grania resolved glumly that the best she could do was heal and dispatch him.

"Will he die?"

Grania puckered her face. Niall was too damn strapping to die. "He has a cracked rib and a gouged leg. Along with that goose egg on his hard O'Neill head. He'll live to fight again."

"O'Neill . . . you know him, then?" Maeve didn't appear surprised; Grania knew she'd been acting sullen ever since she'd dragged the bloodied O'Neill in yesterday— and she knew her strange behavior had not escaped her aunt's keen eye. Grania plucked the pestle off the floor and thumped back onto the stool, sighing. "I know his kind. This one will be the next high king."

"Is he Connor's son?"

Grania shook her head. "These O'Neill disclaim even their own blood kin to strengthen their political alliances. This one's Connor's nephew—and his fosterling."

Maeve stared at Niall, nodding. Grania could tell her aunt too recognized the royal look of him. Niall's torn, dirty *leine* was edged with gold fringe, and his collar, which Grania had plucked up from the clearing, shimmered with expensive white gold as it lay on the bed stand.

"It's been five years since you went beyond our mists to see your father. Yet still you know this O'Neill—'tis a long remembering." Maeve cocked a brow at Grania.

Grania shook off her aunt's stare and focused on the

plantain leaves, grinding the rosettes with irritated vigor. They both knew it was less Maeve than the O'Neill who unsettled her. "I've put my prayers on the poultice. If this one dies, his priests will lay it on our witchery."

"If he dies, it will be the Goddess's doing."

Grania clucked her tongue; years cloistered in the Druid mists had left her aunt naive. "Connor will hardly believe that. Their O'Neill world is a dangerous, bloody place. Full of weapons—and men eager as boys to wield them."

"You were born of that world as much as this one. It pains me to see you disclaim it."

"It was my father who disclaimed me." Grania's eyes snapped up, then softened a little. It was Brian, not Maeve, who deserved her anger. "I've no bond with their sword-lust or their kohl-faced priests."

"But your father's blood still runs in you."

"Thin and weak compared with that of my mother."

"Emer would want you to claim both your legacies— Druid and Christian."

"She would not bid me live with her murderers." Grania's stony eyes drifted with old, painful questions. Emer had died in childbed, overbled by a zealous Christian physician. Grania missed the hundreds of things she would never know of her: the pitch of her voice, the shape of her eyes, the small things that would have made Emer smile.

"Emer loved your father."

"Then perhaps it is better I did not know her." Grania's features lightened as she smiled. "I need no mother but you. You kissed my skinned knees. You taught me to cipher clouds and rain."

Maeve pressed a hug on her, but even as they embraced both women knew Grania would never claim a full place at Uisneath. Even here, where she fit best, she didn't fit well. She lacked the full Sight, and her magic was embarrassingly unreliable. Her mother's Druid legacy bloomed in Grania's healing skills, but the half of her that was Brian left her in want of the quiet peacefulness of the other Druidesses. Her sisters were polite and kind to her, but they too knew the truth: Grania didn't belong here. She didn't belong anywhere.

Maeve drew Grania's head against the soft folds of her summer *leine*. "You are as bronze—stronger because you are fluxed of two fine metals. There may come a day your mixed blood may serve you. The Druids are Inisfail's past, not her future."

"Then I choose the past. For all their bloody kind has to offer—" Grania levied her finger at Niall, who was starting to fret in his sleep.

He let out a baleful moan as his head flopped over onto one flushed cheek. Grania arced over him, instinct ruling inclination as she pressed her hand to his brow. He was tacky with fever; despite her tireless ministrations, the infected leg was already poisoning the rest of him.

Grania peeled the linen dressing off his thigh and jockeyed loose the old poultice. As she fingered his raised flesh, a cold spark ripped down her spine. The druidhect. Why should this bruised warrior stir the magic in her?

Her eyes flew to Maeve. Her aunt's features danced slyly. "So it comes."

"It was a chill, no more."

Maeve nodded, closing her eyes. "As you say."

"I'll heat a new poultice. The sooner healed, the quicker he's gone."

Grania finished the fresh medicine with practiced efficiency, cleaning and packing the leg, then laid a cool cloth on Niall's sweat-beaded brow. The compress revived him; the O'Neill's eyes cracked open slowly.

"I see you'll live," Grania said.

Niall startled and arced off the pallet, then slumped back in obvious pain; Grania wondered he could move at all with the split rib. Niall rolled his head sideways, staring at her.

Grania squirmed on the stool as his eyes ran down her. His mouth hinted at a smile—but the pleasure slid off his face as he found the blue moon crescent tattooed on the top of her breast.

"Pitag!" Grania knew the word well; it was the Christian epithet for "witch." Again Niall hurtled off the bed, his eyes shining pinpoints of terror. Grania raised her palm and pushed him back effortlessly. The cougar had bled Niall better than any physician, leaving him weak and defenseless.

"Yes . . . *pitag.*" Her eyes and mouth eased into a vexing smile. She hadn't saved his life to have him insult her. It was clear he didn't yet recognize her; Niall's face was filled with fear. She and the O'Neill had come far from the warrior who'd teased a frightened child on Connor's plain.

Grania's new role as captor pleased her—until Niall's blue eyes took *her* captive. Grania was relieved when he began to scan the room with frantic urgency. He studied every beam, every corner of the small, staked-wall house, as if he were trying to decide where he was, trying to see if there was some way out. Confusion clouded his eyes, and his jaw hung slack with shock. Grania could hear his breath quickening. Few Christians would even recognize the structure as a Druid crannog hut, a shack built on an island in the shallow part of a lake. But Niall seemed to know.

The ceiling's fire hole and one tiny window were the hut's only openings, and both drew air badly, leaving the interior air choked with peat smoke. But from the look of fear on his face, Niall smelled something more telling. His eyes flinched and his nostrils flared, as if he caught a strange jolt of wind; Grania knew it was the scent of magic. Even mortals could sense the druidhect in places where it was strong, like Uisneath. She watched Niall's hands comb the pallet wildly, seeking his sword. Grania had purposely left it in the clearing.

"Is this fairy land?" Niall's eyes widened and his voice was unsteady.

"Is that what you think?" Grania stared down ingenuously.

Niall's fingers flew to his brow, then recoiled with a sharp gasp. He felt the bump he'd gotten on his head from the fall off Murchad, this time more gently. Grania could see he was relieved that the blow was still fresh—it meant he hadn't been here long. In fairy land a lifetime could pass as a day.

"Where am I?" Niall's eyes scanned the small room.

"Uisneath," Grania answered, knowing the truth would unsettle him as well as any lie.

"No, I've been to Uisneath," he said, his head shaking. "This is another place."

"You've been to the village. Beyond the mists' end, on the lake, there are things even an O'Neill can't see." Grania stirred the smoking hearth fire until it flamed.

"I was less than a day from Connor's fort when the cougar came. I demand to know where I am!" Niall's shout startled her so badly, the fire poker clattered out of her hand to the floor.

She'd heard that O'Neill mothers gave their babes first food on a sword tip, to accustom them early to the feel of the fight. From the look of this one, she didn't doubt it; Niall was brimming with bravado.

"I'm not your hostler, O'Neill," she snapped, her hands snatching up angry fistfuls of her leine. "Any more of your insolence and you'll taste my magic. I could turn you into a fat pig. Or thieve your mind with a madman's wisp. The proper spell could even wither your manhood.'' Niall's hand wound down to his crotch, then flew back as he flushed in embarrassment.

''You needn't worry,'' she said, calming a little. ''I've no plans to keep you.''

''But *you* brought me here?'' He looked a little calmer too, as if he reasoned that she wouldn't save him to murder him so soon after.

''A mistake, so it seems—'' Grania realized there was no point in antagonizing him; Niall was contentious enough already. ''Eithne saved you.'' Grania nodded back over her shoulder.

Niall squinted into the darkness; his eyes widened as they found a massive she-wolf curled up inside an ellipse of firelight. Her muzzle rested on huge silver paws, and a thick bush of a tail wound up like a third leg through the wolf's haunches. White eyes, sharp as icicles, riveted on him.

Niall crossed himself. Grania was pleased to see he was afraid. Well he should be. Wolf pups still in milk teeth could gut a full-grown stag. The killing urge was bred into them; Grania had even seen wolves eat bloodstained snow.

Grunting with pain, Niall pushed onto his elbows, his eyes keeping a steady vigil on Eithne. ''Get that beast away from me.''

''That beast saved your life. Eithne killed the cat that was sharpening its claws on you. If you had any breeding, you'd thank her.''

''And you, too, I suppose? What do you want with me? Do you plan to ransom my hide? Or slit my throat in some Druid rite?'' Niall said it jestingly, but his eyes took on a blankness, as if he considered that the possibility might not be so farfetched.

Grania's eyes screwed down to match her tight mouth. The Druids hadn't sacrificed humans for centuries; right now the decision struck her as ill advised.

"If I'd wanted to kill you, there were easier ways." The logic seemed to calm him. "It's not our practice to turn a blind eye to suffering. No matter whose," she added flatly.

Grania picked up her mortar and siphoned hot water off the fire kettle, then finished mixing the fresh poultice. "I'm no murderess," she pronounced. "Not like those who suckled you."

Niall's anger was fast up. "And what would a little *pitag* know of the O'Neill?" he asked, his eyes flashing. Again his gaze combed over her, but this time more coolly. "You," he said slowly. "You're the bard's daughter. Brian's."

"I am a priestess of Uisneath," Grania said tonelessly, her mind scrambling. She tried to think how she would act if she were telling the truth. Disinterested and relaxed. She stiffened, coughing nervously.

"Liar." A smile lurked in his voice. "How did you come to be here?"

"Lie down," she ordered, lifting the steaming mortar high over his face, knowing he was unlikely to take on a woman wielding scalding water.

Niall paused for a long moment, then thumped backward, grunting indignantly. Grania peeled back the blanket covering his leg as he shifted to make room on the pallet for her. "I would have expected a *pitag* to be uglier," he muttered, his eyes glazing on the light hole overhead.

A peat turf thumped off the hearth pile, hissing as the flames licked at its wetness. Grania strained the water off the mashed herbs and sat down as far away from him as she could manage without falling off. She wound a linen rag around her fingers and dragged them through the poultice. None too gently, she began to lather dollops of medicine into the raw tracks sectioning his thigh.

He mumbled something unintelligible, and Grania smiled as she heard his breath notch with pain.

"Is it too hot?" she asked sweetly.

"It's fine," Niall said, sliding his clenched fists under his buttocks so Grania wouldn't see.

CHAPTER

2

Dreams of fatted calves and pig sausage assaulted Niall like loose women, making his mouth water. The glimpse of sky framed by the overhead smoke hole had cooled from dawn's orange to the pale blue of morning; it was well past breakfast, but still no meal came knocking. He wondered if his *pitag* jailer had decided to starve him.

He felt stronger than yesterday; at least he felt hungrier. Vengefully so. He'd go mad if he kept on thinking of flesh meat. A haunch of goat or a joint of badger—any reprieve from the anemic leek soup the little Druid kept ladling down him—would do him fine. Niall's throat hitched as he stared at the thin leavings in last night's bowl.

He jammed the heel of his hand against the leather band trussing his cracked rib and heaved himself to a breath-stealing sit. Pain forked through his chest, and his clawed leg began to shriek. The calf caught by the cougar's swipe was almost bearable—not so the thigh.

Niall loosened the crusted linen bandage, hoping the wounds would look better than they felt. They didn't. The gouges were red as a finch's breast and puffed up in tight, bloated ridges. But he had suffered worse and fought out the day. And he had to relieve himself. He'd get up with or without her.

Rocking onto one hip, he pushed up, shifting his weight onto his good leg as he clenched his teeth. The bad leg bowed like green birch and he thumped backward, cursing, onto the sweaty, blood-soaked bed.

Broadswords of pain parried through him. Every gasping breath broke the rib anew, and the knot on Niall's brow began to throb in time. Every movement made him shudder. The little witch had heaped too much ash on the turves to stretch their burn through the night, and the hut's air was thick as mud. He could feel the peat smoke coating his face; he could taste its soddy must. He breathed through his mouth, trying to keep his lungs from convulsing under the thick, oily smell.

Niall sank back into the damp pillow, his hands tightening to fists as he remembered that while he rotted in this miserable bog jail, Fergus was rallying his warriors in Ulster to thieve Connor's throne. His one-eyed fosterling had warred against Connor before, four years ago. That time Connor had beat him—and foolishly, he'd let Fergus live.

But now rumors of fresh insurrection curled like first smoke over all of Ulster. Surely Connor would put an end to the province's uprising—once he knew of it. But with Niall here, trussed like some Christmas goose in a god-lost lake, who would tell him?

Niall tried to rise again, but his head was slogged with exhaustion and his blood felt thick as porridge. He decided to rest, just a bit; then he'd try again. He resettled his head on the pillow and closed his eyes. He wouldn't have bet the scream was in him. Eithne, flying onto the foot of the pallet, raised it easily.

Niall twisted wildly, trying to slither onto the floor, hoping he could shield himself from the wolf by rolling under the pallet's frame. But the animal was too swift for him; she pinned his legs effortlessly under her warm, solid weight. Niall shielded his face with his hands. It was a woman's defense, but he had no weapon, and what else could he do?

The animal inched up his leg, whining. Niall blinked down incredulously; the wolf's ears smoothed to her head, and her tail whumped happily on either side of his thighs. She licked him. Sweet Jesus.

She probably wouldn't make him her breakfast—she'd already have taken a bite of him if she'd had that in mind. Niall decided to try befriending her; maybe then, if the wolf dropped her guard, he could manage to slip free. He stretched out his palm, ready to recoil at the first growl, the first glimpse of sharp teeth. Eithne licked him again. He could almost swear the wolf's lips curved into a lupine smile.

The hut filled with light as Grania rounded the windbreak. Kicking the door closed with her heel, she balanced a steaming bronze bowl in front of her. *Not porridge*, Niall prayed.

Grania stared at Niall and the wolf at his hand. "She seems to like me," he said, giving a small, game shrug.

"Eithne!" The wolf bounded off the pallet, and gave Niall a look of apology as she circled and settled on the floor. "She doesn't know better," Grania snapped, wincing as broth slopped over the bowl's handles onto the backs of her hands. Niall saw her suck on one especially bright finger; he was sure she'd been burned, but she dropped the hand back to her side as she saw him watching her.

"That thing's as tame as a dog."

"Here's your soup." Grania yanked a bullock's horn off the side table and dragged it through the foaming tureen. She didn't bother to wipe the sides as she thrust the container at Niall with rude, straight arms.

The smell was terrible and all too familiar; it was last night's grim fare all over again. Warm or cold, it made no difference—Niall would starve before he'd drink more of that witch's piss.

He shied his face sideways, and Grania took the gesture to mean he was too weak to rise. She hooked his nape with her hand and hiked his head up briskly. Niall's eyes rolled back, whitening with pain. He wriggled free, plopping backward and raising his palm to Grania to protest her further aid.

"I imagine that dog eats better than I do."

"Eithne's a wolf. And she eats as I do. Without meat."

Niall lifted a doubtful brow. "A wolf that refuses flesh-meat?"

"Not every predator chooses to kill." Grania could see from his tight, flat mouth that her point wasn't lost on him.

"I'd heal faster with a loin of venison."

"It would thicken your blood. Clear broth sieves the poison."

"That concoction you call soup is the poison."

Grania splashed the meal back into the kettle. "Fine. If you starve, it'll be your fault, not mine." She realized she was foolish to have expected better from an O'Neill.

"You shouldn't have bothered to save me if that's all I get," Niall muttered, nodding at the tureen.

Grania nudged the pot sideways on the floor with her foot

and turned to stoke the fire. She wasn't usually this brusque, but for some reason Niall combed up the worst in her.

The truth was, he scared her bloodless. Everything from Brian's hard, cold world worked a chill down her spine. Ever since the Sending at Tara, the fear that something would tempt her—or more likely drag her—away from Uisneath lay like a weight on her heart. Every pleasure, great or small, was only a delight to be lost, every sadness a hint of what might yet be. And if the premonition about her future among the O'Neill were true, who could say how the instrument of fate might work her? Might it not come in as unlikely a guise as this handsome, odorous man sprawled on her pallet? Grania could feel Niall staring at her; she concentrated on the peat fire, trying to wash all the expression off her face.

"You still haven't told me how you came to be prisoner here."

"I'm no prisoner, O'Neill, but here by choice and right. My mother—" Grania stopped, her breath catching mid-word. He had no right to know. She gave her head a quick, angry shake.

"So it's *her* dark coloring you wear," Niall said matter-of-factly. "I could understand if your father were Druid, too. But Brian has none of the old blood. You could be kept in comfort by him. Why choose life in this peat-choked place?"

Grania heaved the soup tureen onto the hearth hook and spun to face him, squaring her shoulders and planting her hands on her hips.

"I—and my sisters—serve the Goddess Danu. Who ruled here long before St. Patrick brought the new god to Inisfail."

"And your men too follow this Mother Goddess?"

"We have no men. Only our high priest the Regaine."

Niall's mouth said "Ahh" wordlessly. A pagan nun. That explained it; women were always cross when they lived without men.

Grania picked up the foul bandage Niall had dropped on the floor. The piece stank too badly even to consider washing it. Holding its edge with her fingertips, she flung the wrapping straight into the fire. "Your leg needs a week to heal. Leave it bound. And stay off of it."

Niall's blue eyes bristled. He'd never taken orders from women—not even before he was breeched. His mother, Finnabair, called him the perfect O'Neill child: large, stubborn, and contentious. But he hadn't much leverage here with the *pitag*.

"As you say." Niall's jaw twitched, betraying his thin effort at politeness. "But if I'm to keep to bed, I'll need a pot." He gestured toward his groin.

Grania flushed with embarrassment and reached under the pallet, then flung up a brass jar. "There. I'll wait outside; call when you're finished."

"And then?"

"The leg—and the rest of you—needs a bath."

Niall didn't wonder he was an affront to her nose. He had a bath drawn daily at Aileach. Counting the day lost skirmishing with the cougar, it had been three since his last soaping. "I see no bath trough." His eyes circled the room.

"There's a warm wellspring in the forest beyond the lake shore."

"I thought you said I should stay off the leg." Niall's stare raked her slight frame as he lifted his brows. "You don't look much built for carrying."

"I'm built for things you know nothing of, O'Neill." Grania left the room so quickly that she slammed the hem of her skirt in the door. But she wouldn't give Niall the pleasure of reopening it; she'd wait.

She leaned her head against the door's wicker stakes and remembered how easily he'd mortified her when they'd met at Tara. And again, as had happened that misty morning, a flurrying, like dry snow, began to swirl in her belly. At first she thought it was the druidhect, coming to seize her again. But this stirring was of flesh, not of magic. And it was no raven's cry but her thoughts of Niall that brought on this bewitching.

Her hands balled to fists; was this all her devotions and training at Uisneath had taught her—to be so frail, so human, that a surly O'Neill could set her stomach spinning?

Grania was relieved when he called her, though less so when she realized there was no hope Niall could hop, much less walk, without her helping to lift him. With a loud groan, he swung his legs over the pallet's side and reached his huge arms out to her. Grania took a step closer and ducked down her head so the O'Neill wouldn't see the hot flush working her face.

Niall was warm and heavy as she wedged her shoulder under his armpit. With surprising efficiency she pulled him to a stand, listening to his breath notch with pain. Niall yoked his left arm awkwardly over Grania's back, his fingers tense in the air as if he didn't want to grab her accidentally.

He'd expected Grania to be bony and angular. But she was soft and pliant, feeling as much woman as witch. And she was stronger than he had imagined. Her back was willow slim, but stalwart as a baby ox's. At first he wondered if she'd used magic to lever him; then he decided it was simple resolve, tempered, no doubt, by her obvious distaste for him. Together they left the crannog hut without speaking, hopping and lurching like a gangly, three-legged beast.

Outside, the crisp wind made Niall's cheeks tingle, and the morning sun, polishing the blue plate of the lake, stung his eyes. It felt good to be alive.

He shaded his brow against the glare and looked back at the strange, staked hut. Its roped roof squatted on short wicker walls; another identical house stood alongside it, the both of them perched on a scrub-and-sod island peppered with gray rocks crushed nearly to scree. The ground underneath felt as loose as a bird's nest: he hoped the water below was shallow.

Nine, maybe ten similar huts dotted the lake. Clusters of white-robed women flowed in and out of them, occasionally raising their hands to each other in some silent, secret greeting. A woman on the next island looked up and stared briefly at Niall, then returned to her business as if he were only an unusual lake bird. Grania was right; this was no place for men.

A slight wind scored the gray water, and a small school of dabchicks swam by languidly. Sun slithered over the lake, crashing into a white wall of mist that rose like steam off the arc of the shore.

"There is a lake near Connor's palace at Fort of the Shields. Is this the same?" he asked. Grania nodded silently. She kept her gaze to the water, trying to ignore the pleasant warmth of Niall's breath on the crown of her head.

"What business have you here?" She half expected him to say he'd come to fetch her.

"I mean to warn the king that Fergus betrays him." Niall's voice grew distant and lean. He stopped and stared out distractedly toward the mist-fogged shore.

Grania unshouldered him and rubbed the spasm starting in the side of her neck. "Is Fergus not your brother—your fosterling with the wizened eye?"

"He is brother to me no more."

"You speak with hate."

Niall turned to face her. His eyes were achingly blue and so intense that Grania had to fight the urge to step back in retreat. But she held her ground; she would not have the O'Neill see how the mere look of him could make her tremble.

"My father, Maelcova, was once high king. The usurper Sweeney thieved his crown, then killed him. Believing Connor would reclaim his brother's throne, Sweeney exiled my uncle to Pictland. Fergus went with Connor. When at last they returned, it was Fergus who killed Sweeney."

"Then you are in Fergus's debt."

"Killing the bastard was my right. Always Fergus thieves what is mine—" Niall stopped, then snapped his eyes to Grania. "Heal me quickly, witch."

Grania ignored his obvious irritation as she continued questioning him. "Why would Fergus rail against Connor when the high king fostered him?"

Niall sighed, exasperated, but he apparently decided the only way to silence Grania was to answer her. "Connor promised, once he was crowned, to give Fergus the Airghialla. It is a ribbon of land on Ulster's western edge; it belonged to the province in ancient times. But the Airghialla would not abide by Connor's decision. They refused him, and they promised to war against the O'Neill if we made Fergus their master."

"So now you war with Fergus?"

"He has raised his blade against us before. This time we will take his head."

The Christian world was as violent as Grania remembered it. War was all they knew. "The leg needs the wellspring," she said curtly, offering Niall her shoulder, thinking only to rid herself of him all the more quickly.

Niall leaned down on her. Together they lumbered toward the water's edge where a hollowed oak trunk, hulled with hides, lay tethered to a small, spiked stone. A second rope was strung from its stern to the shore so the boat could be retrieved from either land or island. Grania slapped her leg, and Eithne bounded up from behind them, landing with a thump in the rear of the boat.

Grania drew Niall close to the gunwale before she unshouldered him. She lifted her *leine* over the boat's shallow draft and stepped in.

In a decision he'd rue, Niall didn't wait for her hand; he hiked up his good foot—and discovered the injured one couldn't bear his weight. The leg spasmed and buckled, sending him toppling like a millstone shearing free of its fastening. He thumped headfirst into the boat. On top of Grania.

She lay pinned helplessly under him, her back belling into the soft scoop of the hull. She could hardly breathe. "Get off!" she gasped, giving his chest a rough shove.

"Please—" The fall had angled Niall's rib into a fresh, sharp puncture; his breath came in explosive rasps. "The rib . . ."

Grania realized he would move if he could. There was nothing to do but lie there, miserable, dying under the weight of him. Niall's mouth pressed, panting and warm, against her cheek, and Grania wrenched her face sideways, but it was a weak improvement. Everywhere, absolutely everywhere, his body covered her.

His warm breath sparked gooseflesh down the side of her neck. His muscular chest flattened her small breasts like oatcakes. He managed to push up onto his elbows, but his legs and hips still pressed intimately against her.

Niall tried to get up again, but as he shifted, the cracked rib canted out, punching through its truss. Grania felt it break free—and poke through him into her.

"Mother . . ." It was all she could think to say.

"Are you—all right?" he asked, coughing and gagging.

"I should have . . . bound the rib tighter." Grania was panting, too.

"It's . . ." Niall's voice trailed to nothing. He spent all his strength pushing a little higher off her. "It's fine." His face contorted in pain as he eased up, then sank back, moaning, against the gunwale. Grania rocked back onto her knees and breathed a sigh of relief. She could still feel the hard impression of Niall's long, muscular legs on her own, of his wide chest pressing against her breasts. Other disquieting sensations joined the swirling in her belly: her fingertips felt hot, as though they'd been held to a griddle, and the air seemed too thin for her to catch a full breath.

She squinted an angry indictment at Niall—what gave him the right to work this misery on her? Rib or no rib, they were going to the spring. On the Mother's moon, she wouldn't nurse this O'Neill one day more than was necessary.

"We're here." Grania shrugged Niall onto a large flagstone and sat down with an exhausted groan. She cringed as she caught the smell of her *leine*. She reeked of him.

Her shoulder bore a wet saddle of his sweat, and her back, which had been fulcrum for his weight the past endless mile, ached as if he'd beaten her. Grania snapped her hands in ablution down the skirts of her *leine*. It was useless— inside and out, she was completely undone.

Niall leaned back, taking all his weight off the aggrieved leg and digging tired circles with his fingertips in the shadows under his eyes. Except for his rasping breath, he suffered silently. Complaining, Grania imagined, must be another O'Neill shame.

She'd underestimated him—his endurance, his skill at

infuriating her, most certainly his weight. He was broad as a weaver's beam and only half as personable.

"That's it?" He nodded at the tiny pool in front of them.

"That," she replied calmly, "may well save your leg."

"Save it?" Niall hadn't considered losing it. Panic hiked up his voice. How could he fight Fergus if he lost the leg? He mumbled something, his eyes distracted and drifting. "Is there a physician—or a house of the territory?"

Grania bolted to her feet. "I wish I had taken you to your filthy hospital. By now your herb leech would have bled the life out of you."

Niall wheeled his eyes around the clearing, ignoring her. Chieftain trees—oak and yew and holly—enfolded them like a dark, full womb. Moss sheathed their branches, dripping green over the blue-black pool. The water lay set like a jewel in the forest's midst.

He eased off his sandals, and Grania watched him silently, unable to wrench her eyes away even as he hoisted his hips from the flagstone and unhooked the thongs of his leggings. Before she had time to blink, Niall sat naked from the waist down directly in front of her. Grania jerked her head sideways; she was relieved to hear the lop of the water as he entered the pool.

The pond wasn't as frigid as it might have been—scattered shafts of sunlight pierced the oak and yew canopy, heating small pockets of the water. Niall tenderfooted over the round, slimy stones, then, not trusting their uneven surface, let himself fall forward where the pool was deep enough for him to half float and half stand.

Grania turned in time to see him sink like a stone. A shrinking dimple marked where he'd gone down. She hiked up her skirts and dashed in up to her knees, her eyes combing the water's surface in frantic horror.

Niall bobbed up like an acorn, a stream of water arcing

out of his mouth. Grania would have dived in and held him under until he drowned if he hadn't been such a damned sight. He was sleek as an ocean seal; the water glistened like Kerry diamonds on the contours of his chest and shined the lean, strong planes of his face. Sunlight partnered him everywhere; how dare he look so bright, so beautiful?

Again he threw her that infuriating, unnerving smile. Grania realized he was pleased she was staring at him. When he sank again, she was grateful. And when he came back up, she was submerged all the way to her waist.

"Are you joining me?"

"Be still." Grania knew if she told him the truth, he'd never believe her. Instead she'd just press on, using her magic to warm the pond and heal his leg.

Water flung like gems off Niall's dark, wet hair as he tossed his head back, laughing. When he brought his head forward again, Grania's eyes were closed and her hands oddly twisted. She stood silently, leaning over as she trailed her fingers over the pool's surface.

A sound, like the whirring of mill paddles, began to surround him. Niall's eyes waxed huge as the tepid water began to turn frigid. God almighty—the little *pitag* meant to freeze him to death with her magic! He struggled half back to shore before a cold bite of current seized his calves, then raged up his whole body. His legs went numb and he couldn't breathe—at all. He sank without so much as a word, and this time he didn't come back up.

Grania didn't need to open her eyes to realize the magic had gone awry; she too had felt the water turn to ice. She dove in, flailing her arms until they caught Niall's thick, limp shape. Kicking and gulping, she dragged him in, the both of them wheezing with cold and shock and exhaustion.

Niall was infinitely heavier wet than dry. Grania dropped him the moment his mouth cleared the edge. Still half-submerged in the frigid pool, Niall stared up, baffled, his eyes newly respectful.

"I'm sorry." Grania was, genuinely so, but she doubted Niall would believe her. "Sometimes the magic—well, sometimes it just doesn't work the way I intend it to."

CHAPTER

3

Fort of the Shields

The little *pitag*'s medicine had worked. Less than one week after the cougar attacked him in the meadow, Niall's leg and rib were healed enough for him to ride. He slid off Murchad as quickly as his leg would allow and, deeding the reins to Connor's stable boy, limped over the courtyard toward the raucous noise of the mead hall.

Inside was a teeming mass of bobbing heads and hoisted horns. He sank his weight onto the oak branch he'd whittled into a crutch and breathed in the familiar, happy sounds of the *feis*, the ancient gathering convened by the high king once every third year. Bone dice clattered, cheers spurred a chieftain crowing about his war feats, and a harp *gantree* silked through the smoky air. Niall smiled; this was his true ken, not some damp, lost lake. It felt good to be back among men.

A staggering brehon, his judge's cloak splattered with red wine, gusted past Niall. He knocked him sideways against a pine puncheon of hazelmead, routing the breath from Niall's lungs. Niall pushed off, groaning, from the barrel's sticky planking; the rib was not yet ready to take a blow.

The raucous room hardly hinted that the gathering was as much business as it was bawd. The *feis* of old had its origin in funeral games, but the centuries since had added an official agenda to the wares market and the blood-pumping races churning up dust on the game plain. Laws were promulgated and read aloud for the illiterate, land disputes were arbitrated, and bards dueled each other with poems and the O'Neill genealogies.

Official business, however, was dispatched quickly. After two days of the week-long celebration, the island's chieftains and their wide-eyed attendants had already abandoned the legal discussions in the smoky confines of the judges' huts for sweeter pleasures.

Niall stared down the length of the banquet hall at the bright yellow tunics of the Fena, Connor's standing militia; the men's vests glowed like burning brands under the hall's flickering torch lights. The army had been billeting in the countryside for most of the summer, and every O'Neill tribe's flag hung on the wall. Each crest was different, yet the red hand signifying O'Neill marked the corner of each banner.

Connor's door steward safekept the warriors' broadswords; there'd be fighting aplenty when the soldiers left next week to do battle with the Leinstermen pressing the O'Neill's southern flank. For now, the Fena's business was drinking and women and dice.

It was only noon, but already drunkenness ruled the day. Men lay sotted with too much mead, headaches brewing, their feet sticking out from under the hide-draped tables. Niall shook his head in disgust; it would hearten Fergus to see this sloppy disarray.

Niall's eyes scanned the smoky hall; Connor was nowhere to be seen. He edged down the clogged center aisle, elbowing toward the fist-size king's candle proclaiming Connor's place on the dais.

Huge silver trays of food streamed past him. Beds of steaming watercress tumbled with scallops and oysters, and spencers' knives clicked as the king's carvers went to work on a platter of grilled salmon and half of a boiled bullock. The air was soaked with the thick, sweet smell of butter.

A pert-nosed serving maid slopped clustering cream on Niall's *bratta* as she raced toward a pile of wheaten bread stacked like stones against the wall. An older woman followed her, headlocking a wicker horn, its mouth bursting with a wanton arrangement of quickenberries. Cup bearers spoked out from the casks of wine and mead that were the center of the hall, splashing trays of drinks to the loud, impatient guests.

"Niall."

The voice was as familiar as the fit of his sword. Niall turned. "Brother." Niall winced as his sore rib met Cuanna's bone-bruising hug. His fosterling was half-witted, as dumb and friendly as an oversize dog. Yet of all the men in Connor's mead hall, Cuanna alone had recognized Niall.

Niall didn't wonder, considering his ransacked look. Grania had begrudgingly washed the bloody trousers, but she'd staunchly refused to mend their tears. And Niall's *bratta* was hopelessly muddied from the fight with the cat. For lack of a razor, his face even hinted at a beard.

Cuanna grinned broadly, spittle oozing out the corners of his mouth. He'd spent less than a year of his fosterage with Connor before it became clear his mind wasn't right.

Still, Connor loved him—and would have kept him, had a chieftain of his standing not been forbidden to foster an idiot. So Cuanna had been returned to his own kin.

"Have you seen our father?"

"The king?"

"Have you seen Connor?"

"There." Cuanna wagged his finger down the hall, then danced off, swallowed by the jostling crowd. "Have some wine, Niall," he shouted, tossing his head with a laugh. "It's from Poitou!"

Niall squinted through the fire smoke and swaying bodies. Connor's blood sons, Oengus and Lucan, stood side by side on the dais. They too had been fostered out from seven to seventeen, gone to live with high chieftains in the western province of Connaught. Their wide brows and strong chins echoed the powerful planes of Connor's own face, but beyond that resemblance they were little connected with the man who had sired them.

A sword hilt glinted in the firelight, and Niall knew Connor was close by; weapons were forbidden in the cups hall, except to the king's guards.

The knot in Niall's throat loosened as he caught sight of his foster father. Connor was two score three years, but still looked the yearling. His forearms were hard and lean hewn, though web-worked with battle scars, and his full black hair shanked in neat plaits to his shoulders, unmarred by gray. His face was as strong as a weapon: a clean blade of a nose, eyes focused as sling stone eyes, and a dangerous, daggering mouth.

Niall worked his way toward the dais, dodging stacks of tribute piled on the floor rushes: mother-of-pearl chess-boards, copper cauldrons, carbuncled drinking horns. There was even a mail coat said to have been sent by the Mercian king, Penda. A pure gold bridle with a matching charioteer's headband lay flung at the pile's base, as if the priceless piece were a trifling. A pair of huge wolfhounds, their collars marked with the insignia of Connaught, slept chained to the wall, oblivious of the clamor surrounding them.

Connor's king's mien melted as his eyes found Niall's. He pushed toward him, staring at Niall as if he were rarer tribute than all the wealth at his feet. Connor drew Niall's head to his breast and held him, silently.

Tears banked in the corners of the king's eyes. "Niall." Connor's voice was husky with relief. For a full week he had refused to mourn Niall, sure he'd only been waylayed en route from the northern O'Neill fortress at Aileach. Connor had silenced his priests, saying there would be no wake for a son who still lived.

"Ehh . . ." Connor pulled back, cuffing Niall's cheek in mock dismay. "A king's a fool who rides without his guard. You look the worse for it."

Niall nodded. Connor's eyes flew downward and flinched on his bandaged leg.

"A cougar bested me. 'Twas an herb leech who healed it." Niall would explain the whole story to Connor later. First there was Fergus.

"I have news, Father, from Ulster."

"Fergus." The name came wistfully on Connor's tongue. He shouldered Niall gently onto the dais and ushered him to a crimson couch at the platform's rear. "Fergus," he repeated with a sodden voice as he sat down slowly. "He turns his cheek to my gifts; silken cloaks and gold collars come back refused as if they were worthless things."

Niall had not seen Connor in nearly a year. But his fosterer had not changed—neither the proud, angry look of him nor the soft bent of his heart. "You bribe Fergus even as he readies to war against you."

"Has he mounted more cattle raids?"

"He still hungers for the Airghialla. He has not forgotten the promise you could not keep."

Connor snapped his narrowed eyes up to Niall. "And has Fergus forgotten why? If I deed him the land, the Airghialla will war against me. Their blood is O'Neill. I cannot spill it."

"Then drive out the hound that preys on our herds. Fight Fergus."

Connor leaned forward, his huge hands resting on his knees. "I cannot raise my war banners against my own Airghialla. But neither can I level my sword on my son."

"Fergus raises his to you. Again, Father."

Connor closed his eyes as he spoke. "You think me weak because I did not belt his head last time. But there are debts I owe. . . . You know it well, too—it was I who blinded him."

"It was a wasp maimed his eye."

Connor roared up to his full height, his fists clenching. "It was I who sent his nurses home, thinking the boy would be more of a man without them. Perhaps, had I let them stay—"

"You cannot do penance, Father, when you've committed no crime."

"I hold the crown; that is crime enough for him. The kingship has not always belonged to O'Neill. Princes of the four other provinces have taken their turns. Who could say Fergus might not have claimed the throne but for his injured eye? And yet when Sweeney banished me to Pictland, Fergus loved me. He came with me in exile. When we returned, he killed the usurper to make me high king. How could you whet your blade on the bones of such a foster brother?"

Niall could do it easily if Connor would let him. Still his father refused to see. That the guilt Fergus had used to make

Connor take him to Pictland had left Niall with a legacy of shame.

Five years Niall had suffered at Aileach with Sweeney, paying bitter homage to his father's murderer. Trying to believe Connor's reasoning: that no one was better suited than he to keep watch on the new king, that Sweeney would not suspect Connor while Niall stayed to serve him. Connor had made Niall heir to the throne to repay his obedience. But it was not enough.

Still Niall heard his men whisper. . . . Had Connor left him and taken Fergus because Niall stood weak in the fight? Was that weakness he saw in the boy still present in the man? Fergus had worked Connor well—and as long as Fergus lived, Niall would be yoked with shame.

"Niall." Niall shifted his eyes back to Connor. "It is my throne, not yet yours, that Fergus challenges. This is not your fight."

"I would not see any man make you a fool, Father."

"There is no shame is seeking peace. It is love, not weakness, that stills my sword against Ulster."

"And will you sue for peace when Fergus raises his blade to you, his army swollen with bought men? He seeks aid from the great isle to the east, from the kingdoms of Deira and Northumbria."

"Are you sure?" Niall nodded. Connor shuffled over the dais with leaden feet. "I'd prayed otherwise."

"As Fergus lives, Father, the O'Neill throne shifts on sand. If you mean to keep the Airghialla—if you mean to keep the crown . . . Fergus must die."

Connor closed his eyes with a great, tired sigh. But still he would not say what Niall would hear of him. Still he had no words of war.

A trumpet sang out, heralding the arrival of new tribute.

The courier, bearing the yellow standard of the O'Neill tribe Conaille, scurried to the dais's base. He bowed, his eyes downcast obeisantly. Gently he set down a carved yew chest, unlocking the latch and pulling out a large, sheathed dagger. Connor's guards seized him instantly, ripping the knife from the Conaille's hands.

Connor's arms stiffened at his sides. "It is a death offense to come weaponed into the king's hall."

Hands pinioned behind him, the messenger stared at the blade and began to sputter. "The dagger is our gift to you, O'Neill. From the clan Conaille."

Connor plucked up the swordlet and unhinged its sheath. With a swift *whoosh* he pulled it free, stilling the hall's clamor to silence. This was no yew-handled meat knife. Its candescent bronze had been sweated with sun.

Connor rotated the weapon in front of his eyes, then gave the dagger a small toss in the air, sizing its gold hilt in the wide fit of his hand. Firelight galvanized the dagger's planes into snakes of light, and Connor's eyes became enormous as he studied the blade.

Sea horse teeth were struck in the handle, and the sword-smith had sheathed the rivets with garnets as bright as new wine. An etched serpent slithered down from the cross of the hilt. Niall's breath snagged at the sight—he'd seen the design: on the lintel over the door at Uisneath.

"Release him." Connor's guards dropped the Conaille with a thump to the floor. "The blade is cut with fire." Connor's voice was wondrous and his face wide with delight.

"The Conaille are happy it pleases you, lord."

Connor offered Niall the sword. Unwillingly, Niall's hand homed to the hilt. He trailed his thumb down the edge of the blade but misjudged the angle—a line of blood oozed up on his finger. The sword would split hair blown by wind.

Niall would have dropped the dagger if Connor hadn't seized it. Connor's eyes slid to the Conaille. "Who made this?" Coaxing metal from stone was the province of magic; swordsmiths were considered nearly as suspect as Druids. Niall sucked the blood off his thumb and waited, watching Connor.

The courier's gaze skittered unsurely, too frightened to climb Connor's full height. "As I said, lord, the Conaille."

"The Conaille are farmers, not metalsmiths. Who made this blade?" Connor leaned off the dais, shaking the dagger in front of the man, who was shaking to match it. "Shall I loosen your tongue by cutting it free?" Connor hooked the tip of the knife under the messenger's chin. The crowd gasped; murder at a royal *feis* was a forbidden thing, even for the high king.

"A Druid, lord." The man mumbled the answer so softly, Connor made him repeat it.

"The sword came from Uisneath."

"The Conaille of Uisneath are farmers, not metal-lurgists —"

"There is an enclave of priestesses—beyond the mists of the lake."

Niall let out a relieved sigh; Connor had no tolerance for followers of the old faith. He would order the man and his cursed knife gone. Niall was sure of it—until he saw how intently Connor studied the blade.

"Could a sword be made to match this?"

"Father."

Connor silenced Niall with a lean, leveling stare. "Tell me, Conaille."

"Aye, lord, I believe another blade could be made." The messenger's voice was low and tremulous; Connor's over-keen interest was clearly more than he'd bargained for.

Niall felt a dark miasma choke the room. Foul things

were aborning. "Father, surely other swordsmiths can copy the blade. . . ."

"I am high king!" Connor boomed in a voice that made no mistaking it. "It's not your right, Niall, to question me." He turned to Niall and tipped the knife upright between their faces. "Perhaps . . . if Fergus knew of this, he would be too frightened to fight. Such a sword might bring Inisfail peace."

"Father." Niall's eyes implored him as his hopes stumbled. And yet his father's plan might work, if inadvertently. If Fergus retreated at the sight of the blade, it could be to Ulster's shame. But more likely Fergus would rally even stronger—and then Connor would see the fathoms of his traitorous son's hatred. Niall clamped his hand over Connor's on the dagger's hilt, and the high king smiled.

"Go with the Conaille, Niall. Bring me a sword to match this."

Niall looked up, astonished. He'd never have encouraged Connor if he'd realized he wanted him to fetch the blade. He had no desire to go fishing back through those mists.

"But Aileach—who will stand the fort's defense if I leave? Fergus's raids dare farther west every day—"

"Your brother Cael will defend Aileach; I bid you to Uisneath."

Niall stared at the dagger. The thought of Uisneath and the dark little *pitag* chilled the marrow in him. But if the sword could somehow finally bring Fergus to justice he would go beg the Druid blade.

"As you wish, Father." Niall nodded at the Conaille. But as he stepped off the dais Niall caught sight of an unsettling face in the rear of the room. The eyes froze him, the man's stunned look mirroring his own distraction. It was Connor's bard, Brian. Once again a dark wind seized Niall's heart.

* * *

It was an apple of a fall day, crisp and golden and shining. Even the kiln smoke smelled sweet. Grania pitched her head back, balancing on the forge bar as her feet pumped a fast trot on the goatskin bellows. The O'Neill was gone; life was fine again. She closed her eyes, swimming in the sounds of metal being made: the whir of birch coal burning, the soft chink of Maeve's peen hammer as it struck and molded, the *whoosh* of the bellow bags driving the flames.

Forges were important; whole towns sprang up around them. Metallurgy was a man's domain in the world of the O'Neill. But at Uisneath it was Maeve who was brazier and smith, working brass or iron with equal ease. Grania's aunt bargained with the Wicklow miners for tinstone and sweated brittle blue chunks of copper into precious red metal. She repaired broken colters and scythes and etched beautiful detail on the priestesses' gold neck plates.

Maeve said pulling metal from stone was the highest of all magic. Today, her calves tingling with heat from her dance on the goatskins, Grania believed it; she felt the Goddess course like a blood current through her.

In the open shed just back of the kiln, Maeve worked a bronze mirror. Grania glanced back; a shower of sparks arced off Maeve's hammer as it struck the anvil, the fire's embers dying against her deerhide apron. Her aunt had been working the piece for a week, repeatedly heating the mirror, then quenching it in a water trough. She'd been careful to blend its flux and copper properly. This morning Maeve had laid the mirror between vellum and a bone mold and hammered its final design.

"Bring me another bag." Grania's voice was breathless as she called to Maeve; she'd worked the bellows so hard today that she'd already burned through two sacks of charcoal. More hung like hams off the shed's rear wall. Maeve

quenched the metal again and flung the bag with a soft
thump at Grania's feet. She handed the still warm mirror
up to Grania.

"As always, Mother, your work is beautiful."

"It's a gift—for you." Her aunt's voice was thin and
strange.

Grania handed it back down, shaking her head. "I've
done nothing to earn a present so fine."

"My sweet child." Maeve's eyes crinkled softly. "The
mirror is a gift of parting."

"I've no plans to leave you." Grania's quick smile sobered when Maeve didn't return it.

Maeve set down the mirror and made a Druid hand sign
for Grania to stop working. The bellows bags sank with a
whoosh to the sod as Maeve cupped Grania's small, damp
face with her cool hands. "The Sight has come to me. As
it came to you."

Grania had told no one, not even Maeve, of the frightening vision that had seized her on Tara's plain. She jerked
her head free and began to pump again, double time.

"I know not what you speak of—"

"We both know your fate is not here at Uisneath." Tears
clotted in Maeve's eyes.

"Mother," Grania said, her voice full of fright and her
smile false and fragile, "if this is more of your silly worry
about our future . . . I'm not afraid. I belong here."

"This decision is not mine." Maeve said the words
slowly, as if to give them weight. "You must leave Uisneath."

"Has my father demanded me back again?" Of course
—this was it. Brian wanted her returned to him at Connor's
court. "You cannot think I could be happy there, after all
this time? I'll tell him that I'm grown, that it's my right to
choose—and I choose to stay here."

"This is not Brian's bidding." Maeve paused. "It is the Mother's."

Disbelief stormed over Grania's face. "The Goddess would drive me from Uisneath?" Her head sank down as she realized. "Is it that I am only half-blooded?" The fear was no new one to Grania. She'd never truly belonged here; but neither had she considered that she would be forced away.

"Your fate is with Niall."

The name knocked Grania's chin back, making her feet freeze on the kiln pedals; the hide bags hissed as they sank flat under her. "I've no more business with him," she said tonelessly, her eyes moons of fear.

"You're to marry him."

A violent chill spiked Grania's spine, squeezing a nervous laugh out of her. "You shouldn't tease me so cruelly."

"It's no jest, child. Your destiny is bound with the O'-Neill. Uisneath's fate depends on it." A terrifying clarity suffused Maeve's face and poured more ice down Grania's spine.

"Uisneath—how could Niall help Uisneath?"

"There are things even I cannot see," Maeve answered softly. "But I know this: that you must go to him."

"Please, Mother, you're frightening me."

"It is the O'Neill banner, not the Mother's moon, that rules Inisfail's skies," Maeve said.

"The O'Neill would lift his hand only against us, never in aid. We are safe behind the veil of the mists. What need could we have of him?" Grania was near dumb with fear and confusion. Her eyes combed the sod as she mumbled a string of half-formed protests. "He sleeps with his sword. . . . I'm sworn to the Goddess, to chastity. . . . Niall would never have me . . . nor I him!"

Grania set her hands back on the forge bar and looked

up at Maeve with steely eyes. "The Mother would not ask something this vile of me!"

"It is a great test of faith to follow even when we do not understand."

This was the best explanation Maeve could give her? It wouldn't do. Grania would never leave Uisneath, especially not to beg the hand of a man she loathed.

"I want you to speak no more of this," Grania said with a voice she had never before dared use with Maeve. She stepped off the bellows and plopped onto the wet edge of the quenching trough. Maeve sat beside her, brushing a loose strand of hair off Grania's tight face.

"You can't think it was an accident the O'Neill came to us?"

"Well, yes," Grania said, none too credibly and, from the flushed look on her face, knowing it. She'd never agree. What if Maeve knew of her vision—it was all some strange mistake. What else could it be? And yet . . . even if Grania could deny the force of the magic, she could not deny that Niall combed up an odd mix of emotion in her. Ever since the first time she'd seen his despicable, glorious face. But marry him? Never.

"Through your father, you too have O'Neill blood." Maeve was calmly relentless.

Grania's hands rose up in useless petition. "I won't make my bed with a blood thirster. You cannot ask me."

"It is not I who asks you."

Grania bolted to her feet, grabbing a piece of oak to stir up the kiln fire. But she caught the wrong end and the stick burned her palm. She rushed back to the quenching trough and thrust her hand into the water. She had the sinking feeling that her situation was only just starting to worsen.

CHAPTER
4

"The hostel's a cock's crow that way." Niall turned away from the old woman and stared dejectedly down the dusty road. Even the worst hostel would offer him a horn of mead and a pallet. But he had to resist the sweet temptation— there was still light left.

Damn the Conaille man; he'd been as quick to disappear as the Druidess who'd made the sun-hewn dagger. He would have to find the priestesses on his own in order to keep his promise to Connor.

The field hag didn't look to know anything. She hunched over ribs of red earth, stuffing handfuls of woad plant into the pockets of her muddied *leine*. The hem of her skirt was hitched over her girdle to keep her feet free, and her gray hair was tightly plaited, then caught efficiently under a loose, ragged cowl. Her cheeks were ruddied from over- much wind, and her hands were as mottled as gull's eggs. Harvest was hard, hot work for a woman her age.

Niall scanned the huge stretch of field. Scraps of daylight sculpted the bogland verge in a progression of shadow. But even this late in the day, the sod teemed like a living thing.

Harvest sickles hummed, flattening wide swaths of red wheat. Men bound the gleanings into thick sheaves, wrestling them upright until they stood like tuft-headed sentries. Women and boys scurried in the men's wake, tucking mint sprigs into the wheat to ward off mice. The smell of summer casting off washed over Niall; it was the full, ripe smell of chaff and loam, of the seasons turning. Come snow, there'd only be what had been worked and nothing to do but regret what had been left undone.

Niall shifted his leg to a less sweaty spot on Murchad's withers. In the past three days on the horse, he'd tried a thousand times for an easier position, always failing. It had been two weeks since he had ridden, and Murchad felt as hard as a monolith. The cracked rib wouldn't tolerate anything faster than a trot, and at this old maid's pace, he expected to be healed before he found what he was looking for.

The woman uprooted the woad, stuffing it into her pockets in an efficient blur, making no pause as she hawked and spat into the field. Grunts and breath came out of her simultaneously. She spared a sidelong glance up Murchad's jigging legs.

"O'Neill, eh?" She squinted at Niall's bossed neck torque and his bright blue *bratta*.

"I'm looking for Uisneath. The enclave of the Druid priestesses." The woman turned her pockets inside out, shaking her harvest into a large wicker basket propped near the base of an oak tree. Soon the woad would be processed into blue dye; if the woman bargained wisely, the profits would buy her a new milk cow. Niall watched her set her hand in the small of her back and guessed that today the woad bought the old woman only a backache.

He waited less out of patience than fatigue. This ghost chase was a woman's job, an insulting assignment for a prince of the O'Neill.

"Do you know the road to Uisneath?" Niall pricked the edge of the woman's hood with his sword tip, pushing it back off her face. The woman rolled her spine straight, her faded eyes winnowing; Niall could see she'd have nothing to tell. He guessed most of these simple folk didn't know the way through the Druid mists. And if they did, they wouldn't say.

He'd have to keep going, a town farther, a day longer. What did he expect of these doltish farmers? Even *he* couldn't retrace the path back to the lake.

"Mark the hilt." Niall completed the tired litany, pulling the dagger out of its sheath and angling the handle toward her. That day alone he'd shown the etched serpent thirty times, always to shaking heads and vacant stares.

The woman's lips parted slightly. "I see," she answered, her eyes barely touching on the weapon before they froze on Niall's face. "Been there, have ye?"

Niall straightened, his voice rising with hope. "You know it, then?"

Her face softened as she studied him. "Who does not know the serpent's mark? Some say Uisneath's that way." She levied a finger down the winding road.

"I've just ridden there. That's not it."

She shook her head slowly, her weather-scored lips spreading. "Then ye may not find it. It's not really on the road, ye see." Her hand fluttered, fingers drumming against her breast bone. "It's here."

Niall stiffened impatiently. Stones would bleed before

these simpletons would deign to help him. He clucked Murchad on down the road.

"O'Neill!" Niall pulled up sharply, twisting a look back over his shoulder. "Past the next hill, there's a deer mark on an oak tree. If the mists will have ye at all, it's there. I ken take ye no farther. The wind with ye, O'Neill."

Niall stared back, wondering if the old woman played him for a fool. Well, what had he to lose? "Wind to you," he called, urging Murchad to a painful canter.

Niall had passed the deer mark before, unaware. This time, believing he would find it, he did.

Oak and ash bowered the trail. Niall raised his arm up to push back their sagging branches; if he squinted, he could see an ember of sun sinking behind the blue eskers that rolled over the horizon like large, inert waves. The day was dying; he would either find the Druid smithy soon or go back and find the hostel and try again on the morrow.

The mist came up without warning, catching Niall and Murchad like the fingers of a begging wraith. It was a palpable, breathing thing, spindrifting around Murchad's hooves. The horse reared back, pitching his head as if he caught a strong, foul odor. Niall patted his withers, calming him, assuring the both of them against the unknown.

The trail narrowed impossibly, succumbing to a tight chute of hedge. Niall cinched his wounded thigh up higher on the blanket to clear the spindles. He doubled back the foot on his uninjured leg, flattening his toes against the horse's warm flanks.

The wilting light warped what little he could see. The trail, barely more than a cow path, deteriorated to dark, twisting turns. The twilight played trickster; tree knobs watched him, and everywhere shadow took on human form.

Disembodied sounds rose up, then fell away, smothered

before they began. A jackdaw *tchack*ed for its mate; some small creature scrambled, squealing, through the thick undergrowth. The voiceless wind became visible, bullying the mist into delicate, lacy swirls.

Dusk pushed toward darkness, and a hunter's moon popped up suddenly, bathing the tree leaves in cool, silver light. Now the path was too narrow for Niall to turn Murchad; all they could do was keep going.

The trail spilled unexpectedly into a small meadow. Niall made a useless, quick search for water—Murchad had gone miles without stopping, and foam dripped off his bridle bit.

The horse's ears perked and Niall heard it, too: the tinkle of an apple branch. *Druids' bells*. Murchad threw his head as Niall fought off a shiver. Something cold and forceful seized his throat, nearly choking him. He knew he'd found Uisneath.

He slid off Murchad, tethering him to the low branch of an ash tree. He could see a second narrow path sprouting off the clearing's far end, but before he began toward it he checked his wallet; there was only one soggy oatcake, but it would be enough to mark his trail. He ground the biscuit to crumbs in his palm and crept toward the tinkling, hypnotic sound.

Light flickered at the trail's end. Niall wound toward it like a moth drawn to a flame. He kept expecting to hear the lap of the lake or see the thatched hats of the crannog huts, but nothing felt familiar. Yet the acrid smell of magic hung in the cool air.

Niall crouched down as the path opened into another clearing, this one larger than the first. Squatting behind a hawthorn bush, he looked up and went slack-jawed as he stared at what no God-fearing man should ever see.

White-robed women, twenty, maybe more, wheeled in slow ceremony around the hub of a roaring fire. These were the priestesses he'd seen at Uisneath—but he'd never seen them like this, in the midst of their foul rites. A jolt of quicken smoke singed his nostrils, and he knew it was the rotting smell of men changing to beasts, of demons blackening the sunlit skies.

Niall drew his sword from its sheath, preparing to fight —to fight what? Fire shadows taunted him; still crouching, he pivoted left, then right. There was nothing. Breathless and feeling foolish, he let the blade slump to his side and sat down.

The bonfire's flames rioted against the ebony sky, sparking stars off the women's gold crowns. Their clasped hands rose, twisting in magic, their voices climbing to an angelic, unearthly keen. Niall realized that whatever the priestesses' worship, this was no time to come begging a favor. He'd return tomorrow, when this witchery was through.

He stood up to leave, but his feet were as heavy as stones and wouldn't move. He stood like a paralyzed dreamer, unable to fight or flee, and when he opened his mouth to make sound, nothing came. Yet the priestesses seemed to sense him. One at a time they nodded at Niall as their circle turned. But none stepped toward him—except Grania. When she saw him she slipped out of her place, her priestess sisters closing rank behind her.

The moon churned whitecaps on her black hair and kindled the dragonstone that caught fire on her pale breast. As she crossed the clearing, Niall could see, even from a distance, that every ounce of her was shaking with rage. Her hands were fisted, set akimbo on her slender hips, and her short legs overreached her furious gait.

"You." She hurled the word like an epithet as she came to a stop in front of him. "You have no business here."

Niall started to explain, to ask for the sword, but the sight of Grania struck him dumb as a beast. She was so beautiful she made him ache. Her eyes shamed the fire in the drag-onstone, and the quicken heat made her *leine* cling like second skin to her damp breasts and waist.

He wanted to draw her close, to bury his face in the nest of her black hair, to feel her flesh against his fingertips— it looked so luminous that he was sure it hummed and burned. He wanted to taste her small, full mouth and to sheathe himself inside her.

Then he realized—she'd bewitched him! It was a sor-ceress's trick; the little *pitag* wasn't beautiful—she wasn't even real.

"Why are you here?" Grania was rigid with fury. She'd purged every prickly thought of Niall from her mind for a fortnight. She'd shaken herself awake from dreams when his face rose up in them. She'd bolted from her hut when Maeve mentioned his name.

Finally, blessedly, her aunt had let her be. Niall had been consigned to an unsettling memory. Until tonight.

Her eyes dropped to the trussed rib. He was a fool, too —she'd told him the bone needed a full month's resting. But he wasn't, as she knew, a patient man.

"I've come with an offer for you."

"I seek nothing you have." Grania wove her arms across her chest, and when Niall still made no move to leave, she shook her finger at the path back out.

"Do you know this?" Grania lurched backward as Niall unsheathed Connor's dagger. "I mean you no harm," he said, seeing he'd startled her.

Grania didn't believe that. Just the fact that he was here meant trouble for her. She slivered her green eyes to match the threat of the blade. "Your weapons have no place here, O'Neill. Neither do you."

"Look closely." He thrust the hilt toward her face.

Her breath choked on the etching. The serpent—it was

the same design Maeve had made on her mirror. There was no mistaking her aunt's skilled hand. Why did her fate with this O'Neill keep thickening?

"What is it you want of me?"

Niall smiled as he saw her eyes claim the blade. "Then you admit to it."

Grania shook her head in rapid beats. "The Goddess deals in life, not death."

"Yet she makes a dagger for a king. A Conaille brought the blade as tribute to Connor. He swears the weapon came from Uisneath."

Grania felt a flood tide of fear surge up in her. It wasn't just that Maeve had made the blade; her aunt's intentions were plain to see. It was that Niall had managed to pierce the mists. Who . . . or what . . . had helped him through?

"The sword is not Druid."

"Little liar."

Grania pushed the hilt aside rudely and stepped close, her chin tilted up in defiance, her eyes reading Niall's surprise that a tiny unarmed woman would breach a warrior's honor space. "Careful, O'Neill. The druidhect is thick here tonight."

The warning sobered him. Already the *pitag's* Druid Goddess had made stone of his feet and turned a sour-faced witch into the most beautiful woman he'd ever seen. It seemed likely that Grania *could* wither his manhood with a spell.

He stepped back, relieved and surprised to find he could move again. He lowered the blade. "Will you swear to know nothing of this?"

"I owe you no oath." Grania pitched her head in exaggerated instruction for Niall to leave.

"Which of your sisters works the anvil here?" Niall fixed

his eyes on the fire circle, which was still turning, oblivious of them. He should have known better than to take this matter up with Grania. Clearly someone else had made the blade; he would barter with the metalsmith.

"This is a perilous place for you, O'Neill. What's so valuable that you'd chance losing your life in the mists to find it?"

"Connor bids me find a sword with the same brilliant blade. Without it he will not war against Fergus."

Grania clucked, shaking her head. "So you think to make me an accomplice to your blood thirsting?"

"There will be war, with or without you. But if Connor stands weak against Fergus, many men—maybe even your father, Brian—will die."

"You have no right to speak of him." Grania's green eyes widened until they were nearly all white.

"Connor will pay you well for the blade." Niall's brows rose with hope.

"Do you think everything can be bought, O'Neill?"

"You too must have your price, priestess."

Grania glowered at him, her words hissing out through clenched teeth. "The sword is not of Uisneath. Whoever told you otherwise lied."

There were lies aplenty, Niall thought—all the little witch's. Especially her dark, silky face. It took so much concentration just to see past her beauty. Niall was half-relieved she wouldn't help him. He'd return tomorrow—and find another, more tractable priestess to deal with.

"I'll be back."

He vanished into the thicket and the night. Grania shivered, gathering her *bratta* tight to her chest as she listened to the fading crunch of Niall's feet.

There was no mistaking that Maeve had worked the dagger and bade Niall here tonight. But only the Mother could part Uisneath's mists. It was only another undeniable Sign. As Grania fought against tears, she turned back to the quicken fire. Niall offered her meaningless wealth. But fate—that was a harder bargain for her to refuse.

CHAPTER

5

Grania waited in the clearing the whole next day for Niall to return. He was nowhere to be seen. She wondered if he'd taken her warning to heart and abandoned his quest for the Druid sword. Or perhaps he'd been lost, unable to make his way back through the mists.

Why ever he had failed to appear, Grania now had the unenviable task of finding him. For she had no strength left to deny her fate: she'd decided to ask Niall to marry her. *Marry her*. Even thinking the words made her heart feel like a stone. She was nineteen, spinstered by O'Neill standards, and going to beg the bed of a man she loathed . . . with nothing but a sword to seduce him.

It wasn't that Maeve's strange vision made any more sense to her than her own. Uisneath was safe behind the veil of the Druid mists; what need was there for some O'-Neill to protect it? But the argument the druidhect raised when it leveled through her was indisputable. Often when she thought of Niall the magic seized her still. At least Grania thought it was magic—what else could make her stomach pitch and her chest tighten that uncomfortably? She was miserable—and willing to pay the price of wedding Niall if it would bring her relief.

Perhaps this sending of her to Niall's bed was only the Mother's way to test her faith. Perhaps, if she went to him, if she followed the path blindly, she could prove her devotion to the Druid ways. And having done so, perhaps Uisneath would finally, fully become her home. But Grania would only see Uisneath again if Niall refused her.

The prospect that he might agree to her proposal was absolutely numbing. If she'd misjudged him, if, for some unfathomable reason, Niall wanted to marry her . . . Grania couldn't bear to think of it. The horrible intimacies a husband might rightfully demand of his wife made her face flush.

She'd heard the priestesses whisper of men and women coupling like animals in the harvest fields at the rites at Beltane; she'd seen the sloe-eyed courtesans winking and smiling as they plied the drunken soldiers at Connor's kingmaking. Grania was sure she wasn't at all suited for this kind of thing; she was a healer, sworn to serve the Goddess—not some irascible man.

She clung to one other hope: that even if Niall accepted her offer, he would settle for a marriage in no more than name. Grania remembered how he'd squinted at her, bracing himself as he lay on her pallet in the crannog hut, his hands balled, ready to strike out if she came too close, as if she were some horrible, leprous thing. Surely the last thought on his mind was to bed her.

On foot, it was a six-day journey from Uisneath to Aileach, but Grania had made it in four. Her horrible sentence, she thought, was better dispatched quickly, like a beheading. Now, for better or worse, she was here.

Aileach loomed in front of her like a huge stone fist. Ever since she had left Uisneath, her brain had been turning topspins imagining Aileach's stone walls, all dark and foreboding. But the O'Neills' northern capital shone bright as a morning star. Sun lit its limed walls to wildest white, giving it a proud, resolute look—just as Grania remembered Niall to be.

Grania stared out wearily at the vast, upland moor that unfurled around Aileach's feet. The land was hard and lean compared with Uisneath's soft, dimpled hills. Gray sedge grass and heather mantled this thin soil, as if even the land mourned her strange fate.

Grania yearned for her mists, for the sweet, wet smell of the lake. She longed for the lap of water when she lay down to sleep, for the familiar lilt of her sisters keening. Here there was only the sound of the howling wind, disembodied like a ghost wandering in off the north sea. It made her eyes water and snapped her skirts until they raised painful welts on her legs.

Grania sensed the Mother in all things, in the flight of a goshawk as much as the flash of the quicken fire. But this barren hinterland was the realm of the cruel Christian God. Grania wondered if the Goddess, having delivered her fate, had abandoned her to it.

She knelt down, looping her arms around Eithne and nuzzling her head against the wolf's soft coat. The animal was her only comfort in this miserable destiny. If Niall took her as wife, he'd have to take Eithne, too. That was one thing she wouldn't barter.

She pressed on with a stiff breath, winding past a wooden hostage house flying bright tribal flags and a trio of stone cottages, smoke curling out of their tiny roof holes. Huts for hounds, a small cow barn, and horse stables clustered at the base of the fort's outer earthen wall. A total of three sod banks ringed Aileach, each twice a man's height and capped with a thick crown of heather. Apple trees, their boughs bent low with fruit, made a brilliant red splash against the outer wall's base. A small group of women sat bowered by the orchard.

The O'Neill women's kohl-smudged eyes followed Grania dispassionately, the way women watch their lessers. Grania trained her gaze forward, but out of the corner of her eye she could see the women's white hands with their stained crimson nails and their blond, cornsilk hair, braided with bells that tinkled in the soft morning breeze. The women smelled of rose and lobelia, and their obvious charms buoyed Grania's hopes: surely Niall would never pick a dark Druidess over these sweet, sunny trifles.

But the Mother would expect her full commitment when she went to ask him. So Grania yanked her hands through her wind-knotted hair and wet her fingers to wipe the dirt off her mouth and her eyes.

Her *leine* wasn't fixed so easily. Its bodice was splotched with mud from yesterday's rain and the skirt's side had been ripped by hedge spindles. Well, she mused glumly, at least Niall wouldn't think she'd come lusting for him.

She walked through the outer rath gate, her feet slowing as she passed a well capped with a high cross. But as if to remind her that she too had rights here, a granite monolith jutted up farther down the grassy enclosure. From its markings Grania could tell the stone had been raised by the Dedannans—the ancient Druids.

The innermost wall was cut with a huge wooden gate, its white, limed door bearing the red hand that was the mark of O'Neill. Grania pulled the yew knocker gingerly out of its wall niche and gave the bell a soft strike.

A swarthy warder popped his head out the window in the door's center; looking to deem Grania no threat, he creaked open the gate. His cheeks and nose were as pink as a hound's tongue, likely from overmuch mead, and his leather vest looked as if it might have fit him when he was younger and leaner.

"I wish to see your lord Niall."

The man's eyes ran down her dirtied *leine*, then widened on Eithne.

"She's tame as a milk goat." Grania smiled and petted the wolf's head, barely staying a growl. "I've come to see Niall of Aileach," she repeated intently.

"What business have you?"

"Tell him Grania of Uisneath is here. He'll see me," she added hopefully.

The man's faded eyes gave her a hard roll, as if he were trying to gauge her harlot or thief. "What's that?" He stared at her woolen-sheathed sword.

"A cross. A gift for your lord from our village priest."

The guard paused, then gave her a terse nod. "I'll tell 'im. But keep that sharp-toothed thing chained."

Grania pulled Eithne tighter against her leg. They'd be lucky if they both weren't served up as middle meal. The guard cracked the door only a touch more, making Grania angle sideways to squeeze through. Her face nearly collided with his raised hand as she entered. He halted her as though he were staying a dog. "Wait here."

He disappeared up a narrow stone staircase that snaked up the interior of the fort's thick, battered wall. A sunny house, called a *grianan*, perched at the steps' summit. On either side of it a catwalk curled around the stone wall's perimeter.

The courtyard in which she stood was a miniature village. A bread kiln's chimney smoked invitingly, and a kitchen rattled next door to it, its sweet smells nearly drowned by the earthy scents of nearby cow stalls. Hounds milled at the door of a small wooden dog hut, whining and yanking their chains, and a familiar pinging sang out of Aileach's smithy, which stood in isolation to safekeep its sparks from the stock's flammable hay.

Warriors of Aileach swarmed everywhere. At the enclosure's far end, some played a stone slab pegged for gaming, while others honed their sword blades, talking and laughing with thickly accented voices. Smooth-faced boys, liming their masters' shields, sat cross-legged in front of small wooden lean-tos that backed up to the white wall. Awnings thatched of birds' wings shaded them, and chalk flew up like dust off their hands as they worked.

The sweet strains of a harp *gantree* floated down from somewhere above her. Women, gowned and groomed as fine as those in the apple orchard, stood near another small stone well and stared impolitely at Grania.

She'd heard that Aileach and its attached lands quartered close to three thousand men. There were certainly more people here than she'd seen in a lifetime—but only one of them frightened her.

Grania felt the weight of eyes on her grow. Finally she took a deep breath and backed up against the rough wall, palms flat and her eyes closed.

"It is an interesting piece."

Grania jumped at the startling touch, her eyes popping wide. A priest's bony hand clutched the dragonstone that lay on her breast, stretching it outward until the pendant's thong cut her neck. The cleric opened his eyes, blackened with kohl, wide; they looked like dry eggs stuck in soot.

"It is a luck charm," she chirped, her voice cracking. The priest's expression played her; he knew well it was a serpent's egg. A Druid stone.

He loosened his grip, letting the dragonstone thump against her breastbone. Then he burrowed his hand back into his huge, loose sleeve. "I am Ossian, abbot of the monastery at Derry. What's your business here? Lady," he added, the insult *pitag* not far from his lips.

Grania stepped away from his rude, burning stare. "I come to speak with your lord Niall." Her hands tightened until she could feel her nails carving lines in her palms.

She waited for more of the priest's questions. But there was only silence, and when she turned to face him she saw that the priest had left—and Niall stood in his stead. She was toe to toe with the huge O'Neill; his eyes lit brightly as they slid down to her sword bag. A phantom smile teased her. How she wanted to wipe the cocky grin off his O'Neill face.

"You didn't come back to beg for the sword at Uis-neath."

"I tried," he said, then mumbled something Grania couldn't quite catch about "wretched mists." She saw Niall's shoulders loosen as his eyes relaxed a little. "But there was no need. It seems you've come to me." He looked as pleased as a cat with its paw on a mouse. Grania could see his smug hopes rising.

"I've come—" Her well-practiced words died in her throat. Just like her first glimpse of Aileach, Niall stole her breath away. He was dressed as heir to the throne now, his neck hung with a massive gold torque, his large fingers shining with jeweled rings. His beam of a chest belled out under a saffron *bratta*; brightly colored leggings emphasized the contours of his long, muscled thighs.

Grania's eyes retraced his face—she'd almost forgotten the expectant brows, the mouth quick as a scythe, his eyes, as dark and explosive as storm sky. He looked more hale and rugged and more of a man than she'd ever seen.

"Have you reconsidered my offer?" His face hardened to stark, serious planes; Grania could see he still wanted the sword. She nodded dumbly, no voice left in her.

"What will you bargain for? State your claim." Niall's eyes tightened; Grania said nothing. "Have you come all the way from Uisneath to stand mute in front of me? Name your price, woman!"

"I . . ." Grania's heart stammered to match her voice. She couldn't say what she'd come for, not here, with half of Aileach watching. Niall seemed to sense her uneasiness, and with a loud, disgruntled sigh, he grabbed her wrist and dragged her, stumbling, up the stone stairs to the *grianan* house perched on the top of the wall. He slammed the door behind them and leveled a lean gaze on her.

Grania rubbed her stinging wrist. "It wasn't necessary to . . ."

"Well, at least you can talk now."

Grania slumped backward onto a crimson couch to hide her wobbling legs. The last thing she wanted was to marry this insolent man. But duty drove her. If Niall meant to refuse her, it would not be because she hadn't tried.

But he looked so prickly, so unlikely to agree. Grania decided to show him the sword first; that would whet his need, make this all go easier for her. She unwound the wool casing and held the weapon out on flattened palms. Niall's eyes glazed on the blade.

Even Grania was impressed with the metal's fine workmanship. The sword was double the size of Connor's dagger, and its blade shone twice as brightly. The hilt bore the same delicate serpentine etching.

"Yes," Niall breathed, approving. Grania let him take the hilt in his hand. As he smoothed his fingers down its edge, the depths of his blood-lust came clear to her; he caressed the sword as she imagined he would hold a lover.

"What is it you want?" His languid, wide eyes still stuck to the blade.

"I—" The words stung on her tongue. "I want you . . . to marry me."

"Marry you?" Niall's eyes glared in astonishment at her. For a moment that seemed to go on forever, he said nothing. Then he fell backwards onto another couch that faced Grania's and doubled over the sword blade, holding his sides as he burst out laughing. "Marry you? That's all?"

The waggish expression slid off his face when she didn't answer him. "You're serious."

"Aye."

"You mean you'll give me the sword if I promise to share my bed with you?" Niall's voice hiked a notch higher with each word. Grania slowly nodded.

Niall set the sword down on a table and splashed out a horn of mead, drinking it in one quick tilt. He ran his fingers through his hair and squinted down at her, as if he were taking a fresh look. "If it's my services—as a man—that you want . . ." His eyes shot to his groin, then volleyed back up to Grania. "That can be arranged. There's no need for anything so permanent as wedding me."

"I want you to *marry* me," Grania answered stonily, so embarrassed all she could manage was to stare at the floor rushes. Niall was going to make her beg him.

"I thought you were married to that virgin Goddess of yours," he snapped.

" 'Tis she who bids me to you."

"To me?"

Grania understood his incredulity. Even she could hardly believe her outrageous proposal.

"I think your Goddess makes sport with you."

Grania stared up with blank, calf eyes. He was going to refuse her, just as she'd prayed. She should feel relieved, even jubilant—but she didn't. Still the Goddess drove her.

Niall shifted the hilt from hand to hand as he shook his head. "I didn't think that you were . . . disposed to me."

"My feelings for you have nothing to do with it."

"Indeed they do!" he blurted, his chin receding into his neck like a turtle's. "I'd no plans to marry anyone."

Grania felt her cheeks start to blaze. "I won't argue the offer with you. It's a simple trade: the sword for me."

Niall's brows crashed down over his eyes. "I have the weapon in my hand. What's to prevent me from keeping it, from sending you back to Uisneath without it?"

"The sword was sweated with the druidhect. If you were to dishonor our bargain . . ."

"We have no bargain!" he shouted.

"The blade would turn to ash in your hands." It was a lie, a child's argument; but from the look of him, Grania had guessed correctly that Niall would believe it. "And," she added, smugly pleased with the afterthought, "I thought O'Neill were men of honor." Again she'd reduced him to silence.

"I want no wife," Niall said after a stunned pause. His voice was slow and deliberate. "Look here." He snatched Grania by the elbow and pulled her to the window. For a moment she thought he might push her out of it. But instead he took her chin in his hand, training her eyes down on the land below. There was a commanding view of the apple orchard—and the women she had passed sunning and laughing.

"I could have any woman. *Any* one," he added as if he wished the emphasis to be particularly hurtful. Grania jerked her face free of him.

"I could be useful to you," she said with soft determination, her eyes clinging to the floor. "I'm a skilled healer and . . ."

Niall took her skull between his flattened palms and raised her face into the hard beam of his stare. "Don't shame yourself—"

Tears glistened in Grania's eyes. She had shamed herself even by thinking to undertake this mad, doomed mission. Even the Goddess wouldn't ask the impossible of her. She heeled Eithne in and plucked up the sword, then stormed like a gale toward the *grianan* door.

"Wait." Niall rushed after her, his huge hand clamping down on her shoulder. "I still want the weapon. Surely there's some way—"

Grania gave him a slow, stonewalling shrug.

The indecision in Niall's eyes made her die all over again. "No," he answered, his head making slow, furious passes. "No wife." He wanted the sword—but not badly enough to strike her wild bargain. She'd done as the Goddess bade her. It was finished. She was free.

"No sword," Grania said as she walked away, her back to him. As she rushed out, slamming the *grianan* door, she heard Niall's fist split the tabletop.

CHAPTER

6

"Stop that mewling cacophony!" The harper stretched his fingers taut over the instrument's brass strings and leaned the harp's spine into his legs. But there was no recovering the loosened song. It was Niall who'd bade him play the happy melody, but now the prince of Aileach looked ready to strangle him. Niall was in a royal, O'Neill mood.

All morning he'd barked and grumped like a blind old dog. Servants ceded the day to scurrying clear of him or holding their tongues and eyes in tight check. Even the best-mannered were unjustly reprimanded and had their parentage questioned.

Niall sent the musician scurrying out of the room with a rude swipe of his hand. Then he sank his tired weight onto the silk couch, its feather pillows sighing disconsolately on either side of him.

His bed had been all rocks the night through, and this morning no position seemed to suit him. His back ached

and cramps seized his calves. He skidded his palm, cal-
loused from sword practice, against the silk of the couch;
the irritating sound of it suited him.

Deirdre stared at her brother. Niall's blue eyes looked as
gray and rough as a storm sea. From the window she could
see their younger brother, Cael, testing the flex of his new
spear on the lawn below; even Cael had found excuses to
avoid Niall's bad mood these last few days. But Deirdre
was made of bolder stuff.

She smiled blithely, circling Niall like a slow-moving
eddy, her pacific features in stark contrast with Niall's granite mien. "It was you commanded the boy to play."

Niall snagged Deirdre's wrist as she glossed her hand
over a tabletop. He had the look of their father, Maelcova.

"You know nothing, Deirdre."

"I know this Druidess combs up the rage in you better
even than Fergus can." Deirdre pulled a pale strand of hair
across her pink lips.

Niall bolted up to his full warrior's height, his golden
girdle clanking as he rose. With a loud snap, he flung his
bratta over his back as he glowered at her. Then he broke
away, snatching up a leather bottle of mead and gulping
down a stiff draft without bothering to find a cup. He wiped
his dripping mouth on his sleeve and dragged a hand down
his face, spending another of the morning's many sighs.

"I could use some cheer, Deirdre. Instead you come here
to nettle me."

"I've come with a sister's love—and good advice. What
ails you is plain to see. Agree to the Druidess's offer and
you can take Connor the sword he bade you find."

Niall made a loud, rude snort. "I'll make the blade myself
before I'll consent to the witch's price!"

"All she wants is your bed." Deirdre stared up at him,
blinking ingenuously. "Would a wife be so steep a bargain?

Is there a man alive could not use one somehow? If she doesn't please you in bed, perhaps you could put her to use pounding the dirt from your clothes."

Under all her teasing, Deirdre was as sober as a new priest. This was hardly the first time she'd nagged Niall to marry. She'd flung her ladies at his head like fish to a pampered cat. And always with the same result: he was willing enough to bed them, but that was the end of it. He'd sworn to take no wife until Fergus was finished. Until Niall could finally be free of his shame.

His eyes raked up Deirdre's tall, athletic frame. At twenty-eight her milky skin, kissed with light freckles, had found a fine fit on the patrician bones of her face. Her hair swirled about her like a lush harvest of wheat. Her eyes, blue as robin's eggs, were a disarming mix of innocence and wisdom. Niall gave her as much of a smile as his sour mood could spare.

"I know you mean well. But I'll bed no *pitag*."

"Ahh, I see," said Deirdre, clucking as if she did. "This woman must be old and whiskered to inspire such distaste in you." She arched her brow coyly; a laugh curled, waiting, on her lips.

Niall plucked up the mead bottle again but changed his mind, hurling it sideways. He watched indifferently as its bottom split like an overripe melon, drenching the hide covering the table. Even liquor couldn't dull his thoughts of Grania, of her changeling beauty, so dark and divergent from the cool white doves that were the women of Aileach.

He remembered the turn of her mouth, how the moonlight had banked in the backs of her eyes, how the fire wind made her black hair dance to life. Bones and blood, the little *pitag* looked fluxed with magic. She'd managed to tempt him that night in the clearing at Uisneath. But he'd held off her sorcery—and he didn't mean to surrender now. He spun back to face Deirdre, his eyes newly resolute.

"She uses tricks to make herself beautiful."

"So do we all, brother," Deirdre purred, the color that stained her cheeks rising like pink coins.

"I'm not talking of girlish artifice. This woman works necromancy."

Deirdre caught Niall's chin with her slender hand. Her graceful features sobered. "Do you believe the sword was sweated with sorcery?"

"Perhaps," he said, his eyes drifting. "But it matters only that Connor does—and that he will not stand firm against Fergus without it. The high king's heart is too soft for the cur of Ulster."

"Then you'd best make your peace with Fergus," Deirdre purred. "For if you refuse the Druidess, there will be no sword. And no war with Fergus."

"Baiting me is dangerous business, Deirdre. You well know how Fergus rankles me. But Connor would never forgive me for taking a Druid wife."

"Who among us will tell him?" Deirdre asked, shrugging. She could sense Niall starting to weaken. "Dress her as O'Neill. If the Druidess wants you as badly as you say, she'll hold her tongue. And what if Connor were to hear the truth? He'd forgive any price for the sword—if it came of your love for him." She took her brother's hand. "I wish only to see you have that which you want. It is yours for the taking."

Niall pulled free of his sister with a sharp shake of his head. "The *pitag* asks too much of me. . . ."

Deirdre threw Niall a coy glance over her shoulder. "Surely you don't fear the Druidess can trophy your heart as well as your manhood?"

Niall flushed at the inference, sputtering protests. "But my vow not to marry until my honor—"

"You made the vow—break it." Deirdre's face was calm and determined.

Niall sank back against the wall planks, kneading his face as if the dilemma could be rubbed away. "Deirdre, you spend me faster than a champion's challenge. Leave me be. And send in Dermot. Perhaps a bard's tale will lift my misery."

"As you wish, but think on it, brother," Deirdre said as she turned toward the door. "Darker bargains have been made."

Niall flung a cushion from the sofa with a swift, wild backhand. A sword for a witch in his bed. It was an impossible trade.

A glorious disk of sun burned in the crisp blue sky. Autumn had bleached the meadow's grass from green to earth tones, but just for today, summer came back singing. Sunlight buttered the clearing, firing the oak trees at its far edge with unseasonable brilliance; the wind winnowed through the leaves. Murchad's coat, already thick for winter, shone with sweat from the ride.

Niall breathed in the verdant smell of sedge grass and lichen, shading his brow as he scanned a mottled mosaic of fields peppered with scraps of forest. The O'Neill lands stretched out before him like a warm, waiting woman. Grania, he imagined, wouldn't be so pliant.

He'd watched her from the *grianan* window as she stomped out of sight. He'd watched Connor's prize of a sword go with her. That nemesis of a sword. Deirdre, damn her, had spoken the truth; Niall had given up denying it. If he wanted Fergus's head, he'd have to take the little witch along with it. He'd marry her—if she'd still have him—and after a respectable wait arrange to divorce her. Deirdre was right: worse bargains had been made.

The fresh imprint of slender feet marked the road south. The impressions were light, like a small woman would make. Having resigned himself to marry Grania, Niall began to worry about her safety.

Fergus's cattle raids broached farther west every day; even if the Ulstermen didn't dare venture near Aileach, there were always wallet thieves seeking fresh prey. No doubt Grania imagined her magic would protect her. But then for all Niall knew, it would.

A crooked arm of a lake glimmered at the meadow's far fringe, its water blinking as it meandered seaward. Of all Niall's mensal land, this was where his heart was most home. This was where he'd come, as a boy of seven, to foster with Connor and been prisoner to Sweeney when Connor had abandoned him.

For five years Niall had been Sweeney's obeisant liegeman. But always he'd slept with a dagger in his bed; always he'd watched Sweeney with slivered eyes. Sweeney saw his hatred and repaid him well for it—insulting him publicly, making him sit close at the banquet table, dueling the boy on the practice lawn, knowing full well that a youngster Niall's age had no hope to win.

It was for Connor that Niall had endured it. Connor, still in thrall to his guilt for Fergus. But soon all that would end. Soon Niall's shame would be consigned to his past.

A red deer, its antlers still shedding velvet, exploded past Murchad, flushing two cygnets. The swans bleated, their muffled wings beating swiftly as they climbed toward the sky. The birds' orange bills lit to fire in the sunlight; a shudder snaked down Niall's spine. For a breath of a moment, the swans looked as if they were yoked together with ropes made of gold. Niall shook his head; no, this was no sign of magic, only a trick of the light.

When his eyes came back to earth he saw Grania. She stood stone still, starkly contrasted against the waving grass at the bell of the clearing. Even from a distance he could tell she was watching him. He couldn't make out the details of her face, but he imagined she was smiling. Why wouldn't she be? She knew he'd come begging, his contrite proposal of marriage in hand.

Niall reined up Murchad; horse and rider stood breathless as they loomed over Grania's small, silent frame. Eithne broke the tense stillness, yapping happily as she bounded up to Niall like an exuberant puppy. But Niall saw only Grania.

She blinked up ingenuously, the sun making her lamp-black lashes into spiders on the pale skin of her cheeks. Without her *bratta*, she looked even slighter than yesterday, as thin and lithe as a ravel tree. Her freshly plaited hair shone like polished jet, and half-dry tendrils rose in a dark helix around her face.

Niall's eyes clung to the swell of her small breasts. Slowly he realized the dress fit so well because her skin was damp. She'd bathed in the lake, a courtesy she hadn't bothered with when she'd come courting him yesterday. She gave off the sweet, cloying scent of magic. It frightened him— all the more because he found it pleasing. To his embarrassment, he shuddered visibly. Sweet Lord, had she begun to bewitch him already?

Niall slid off Murchad, his *bratta* coming down with a loud *whump* after him. "I'm here to agree," he sputtered, his hands making purposeless motions in the air. Grania stared up calmly. "Damn it, witch, I'm here to ask you to marry me!"

He felt strangely relieved as the proposal *whoosh*ed out of him. Grania's cat's eyes were wide, pulling him closer. He could still remember how slim and soft she'd felt as she'd shouldered him toward the spring at Uisneath, how her delicate hands wound gently around his injured rib cage. Damn it—was this magic or simple lust coursing through him?

"Well?" Niall wondered if she were going to make him ask again. She nodded in slow agreement. " 'Tis done, then." His voice was clipped and stern.

"Done," she said.

He reached out to her, knowing the bargain would be legal only if it were sealed properly, if he placed three kisses on her cheek. When Grania made no move toward him, he stepped close and seized her shoulders. He pulled her against him and pressed his unimpassioned lips against her.

And then, though he hadn't meant to, he held her—longer and tighter than was proper. Her skin was soft against his face, and her cool, damp hair smelled of lake flowers. Niall closed his eyes, forgetting his fears for an instant. Grania pushed him away.

"Done," she said again, her eyes riveted to the ground as she brushed out the folds he'd crinkled into her damp *leine*.

"Aye." Niall nodded a few times too many. Embarrassed, he turned to some useless business with Murchad's bridle as much to hide his blush as to clear his mind.

"We'll back to Aileach, then," he announced with a forced voice. "I'll take the sword to Connor. Then I'll summon the priest." He felt Grania stiffen behind him. When he turned back he could see his announcement displeased her. "Surely you expected nothing less than a Christian rite?"

Grania's shoulders froze midshrug. Her eyes were wide

with surprise. "Well enough," she said. "I'll agree. But after Aileach I want a wedding at Uisneath."

Those insidious Druid mists again. The very thought of them made his bones start to ache. But Grania's face was unequivocal: it was Uisneath or no sword.

"Uisneath, then." Niall wove his fingers together to give Grania a leg up onto Murchad.

She grabbed the horse's mane, but Niall overestimated her slight weight and pitched her with such force that she nearly fell off the other side. He grabbed the skirts of her *leine* to keep from losing her, then sprang up, settling awkwardly in front.

"The sword?"

Niall looked down. The Druid blade, still bundled in its woolen casing, lay propped against a nearby tree. He jumped off Murchad, strapped the weapon to his sheath, and shied his face away, hoping Grania hadn't seen his shame-flushed cheeks.

As they rode together Grania knew she had worked the heartspell as the Goddess had bade her—and it had succeeded. She hadn't wanted to conjure the charm. When Niall had refused her offer in the *grianan* at Aileach, for a brief, soaring moment, she had thought herself free. But the druidhect had seized her as she'd left the fortress—this time with demonic vengeance. Grania hadn't the strength to spend a lifetime fighting it. So she'd worked the magic for one last faithful try. And now she was to be Niall's wife.

She shivered, thinking of the bargain she'd made. She nursed no hope that he'd come to love her—that was the *last* thing she desired. But if Niall hated her, he could make her new life harder still.

Grania had few skills likely to please him. Her talents

were not for womanly things. She had no sly, canted eyes or shy, sweet smiles like the purring women in the apple orchard.

Whatever magic arced between them Niall was determined to deny. What matter if he held her gently or if his hands clung a little too long to her? It was the heartspell, nothing more. One glance at his pulled, tense face as he pushed away was enough to make clear he wished their bargain to be all business—and nothing more.

Murchad's sway pitched her chest against Niall's hard-hewn back, and in those spots where her *leine* was still moist from the lough, the heat of Niall's flesh warmed her pleasantly. Grania's belly and arms tingled where they touched him, as if Niall had the power to awaken parts of her that had lain sleeping. She wondered if this were part of the Mother's plan, too.

She had to clutch fistfuls of his *bratta* to keep from falling off the horse, but she was careful to hold her hands out so she wouldn't come in contact with his waist.

"Will you take the sword to Connor?"

"Aye."

"And then?"

Niall paused, obviously impatient. It wasn't hard to see Grania's questions displeased him. "Then we will bring the cur of Ulster to his knees," he said through gritted teeth.

"Why do you hate Fergus?"

"He is a hound in our herds."

"I should think him more deserving of your pity. His eye—"

"He sees well enough to raise his blade against us," he snapped.

"How was Fergus blinded?"

Niall gave a great sigh, like a parent fielding a child's nagging questions. "A wasp stung him when he was a boy."

"Were you there?"

Niall reined Murchad to a sharp stop and twisted to face Grania, his eyes pinpoints of fury. She'd meant only to fill up the awkward silence; now she wished she'd held her tongue.

"I've agreed to your bargain, witch. But I warn you. I'll have none of your prying. And I want this made clear: As long as you're to be my wife, I expect you to follow my Christian ways."

"Even Connor knows my father, Brian, once took a Druid wife. If you think to deceive the high king, to drape me in your lies, to expect my father to disclaim me—"

"If you mean to wed me, you'll hold your tongue about your Druid dam. And speak nothing to your father about our marriage. Do you understand me?"

Grania understood all too well. Niall didn't believe the marriage would last long past the ceremony; how else could he think to marry her and keep it secret from both Brian and the high king? She had no choice; she'd agree to Niall's shameful conditions and trust that the Goddess was guiding her.

"And I'll have no more of your dark necromancy. There'll be no spells conjured at Aileach. Do you hear?"

Grania nodded dumbly, her eyes heating with tears. Niall gave Murchad a quick kick and turned his face away.

Grania bit her lip so she wouldn't cry. What kind of miserable, anguished bargain had she made?

Without so much as a yap of warning, Eithne leveled her tail and cannoned off across the dusky meadow, ears flat to her head. Wolves were cursorial, built for running, and Eithne quickly reached the clearing's far end. Grania called out frantically, but the wolf was long past earshot. She gave

Murchad a swift kick and a loud cluck, hoping there was still time to catch her.

"Whoaa!" Niall pulled the horse up barely in time to check his spring. "I'm not chasing after her," he said sternly, his narrowed eyes confirming it.

"You *have* to."

"I do not," he said with slow emphasis. "Listen there." Grania stilled, hearing the call that had already caught Niall's ear, the chilling cry of a wolf pack at full bay. "There are five, maybe ten of them," he said, his head shaking.

"They'll kill her. Please . . ." Grania's hands clutched at Niall's cloak.

"The pack snags their victims from behind. Have you ever seen them disembowel their prey?" Grania's face went white as she imagined such a horrific attack on Eithne. "Don't think they'd spare us, either," Niall added sardonically.

Grania's dark eyes glazed with tears. "Please . . ." Her hands pressed like frantic compresses all over her face. "Eithne . . ."

"She didn't look so reluctant to join them."

"She's an underdog. The pack she was with when I found her had torn her near to death." Grania's voice was husky with fear. "She'll die."

"Then why did she go to them?"

Grania shook her head. "I don't know." Why had the wolf fled her? Why had she agreed to marry Niall? She knew nothing anymore. A sob lurched in her chest, and she clamped her hand over her mouth, trying not to lose what little control she still could manage.

More howls rent the air. "Oh . . ." She hunched forward, starting to cry in racking gasps.

"We'll wait for her at Aileach. Surely a wolf can track

our scent.'' Niall's voice was all false cheer; both of them knew it.

''You can't mean to leave her.'' Grania's fingers tore at his *bratta*.

Niall made a miserable, disbelieving face. ''God only knows if the pack's found prey—or if they're planning on us.''

Grania hiked her skirts over the horse's rump and dismounted. But before she could start off Niall slid down after her.

''If you're thinking to go after her, think about dying.''

Grania gathered her skirts in her hands, obviously planning to ignore him. Niall's arms imprisoned her shoulders. She writhed and twisted, desperation fueling her strength.

''Go home, O'Neill,'' she shouted, her voice cracking. ''I'm not leaving here without Eithne!'' She threw off his hands and raised her chin up defiantly.

''Good God, woman, she's just a wolf.''

Grania's eyes were strangely glazed. ''Eithne's my only friend. My only . . .'' The words trailed to nothing. Grania was prepared to stand her ground against him; she threaded her arms over her chest and plopped down in the billowing sedge grass.

Niall cocked his ear to place the new round of howls— they seemed to have receded a little—and studied the sky's dying light.

Aileach was a good stretch away, and there was no assurance that even if they hurried straight back, the pack wouldn't catch them. The wind, at least, had died down, so Murchad's scent would spread more slowly.

Grania stopped crying out loud, though her ribs still bucked and hitched silently. She looked pitiful but resolute, her spine rigid as an oak, her shaking lower lip pinned under a white clamp of teeth.

"Come here," Niall ordered impatiently. He held out his hand; if they were going to stay, they'd be better protected in the thicket than here in plain sight. His kindness undammed a new swell of tears in her.

"No more of that now," he said sternly, pulling her up to a stand in one smooth movement.

Grania was shaking badly, unable to quite catch her full breath. Her head was quivering and her nose stung from crying. She could feel her eyelids starting to swell.

Niall cupped her face in his hand and tilted it up to him. "We'll find her." He wiped the tears off her cheeks with his thumbs as Grania shook her head, disbelieving him. He pulled her to his chest, and Grania started to sob with hopeless abandon.

Finally she stilled, and for just an instant she believed it *would* be all right, not just Eithne, but everything, her marriage to Niall, her future in this strange, new place. For the first time she felt a sense of belonging. When Niall pulled back from her, his breath, like hers, was fast and ragged.

He cleared his throat and backed off, pretending to some business with Murchad's tether. "We'll wait." His stern voice was recovered, but his eyes still skittered nervously.

Grania nodded silently as she followed him into the woods.

CHAPTER

7

Grania surrendered like a drowning swimmer to the torpor of sleep. She was too tired to fight.

Enervating warmth oozed through her whole body—everywhere except the spot where something cold and bumpy dug into her cheek. Grania raised her hand to push the discomfort away, but her breath choked as her fingers traced the unsettling shape; she was sleeping on a cross, Niall's cross. On Niall's chest.

She was instantly, acutely awake, eyes dilated, half-formed protests damming her throat. She couldn't risk moving off him; she was afraid he would wake up before she figured out how to explain ending up like this. Explain it? She could barely remember it.

They'd been waiting for Eithne. Niall had kindled a fire, and Grania had obviously fallen asleep. But, sweet Mother, like this? She *didn't* recall that.

Moving only her eyes, Grania took stock of their melded

form. Niall's indigo *bratta* enfolded her body like a blue chrysalis, covering her up to her chin. The cloak outlined his thick, muscled arms, which wound around her in far too intimate places. One flattened her breasts. The other curled under her waist, then climbed up her shoulder like a libertine snake. Her belly pressed flat against his hip, and their four legs entangled like tree roots.

He had a cured, male smell that clung all over her. But there was a stranger, colder scent, too—the smell of metal. Grania pushed up just a tiny bit, stopping when Niall groaned. She craned her neck over his chest and caught sight of his sword, still sheathed, lying on the far side of him.

Niall's eyes were sealed peacefully. His mouth was loose, close to a smile, making for a sweet, almost pacific expression; Grania was sure he would be displeased if he could see himself.

They were both still clothed; that boded well, though skirts, Grania imagined, were easily lifted. But if she couldn't remember how she'd ended up like this, had she also forgotten other, deeper disgraces? She calmed her fears as best she could, her cheeks going crimson anyway. No, certainly she'd remember something that significant.

Before last night, she had never slept this close to anyone—each priestess had her own pallet at Uisneath. Grania had always thought it a luxury, but now she began to think it a hardship. The rush and swell of breath alongside her was profoundly comforting, and Niall was so warm. He made her feel safe and protected.

There was another, more unsettling feeling, too. The feel of Niall's massive bulk combed up a curling discomfort in her belly. It was a strangely delicious sensation—and it filled her with face-reddening shame. Niall, with his hot blood and belligerent ways, was antithetical to everything she believed in. He was O'Neill. She was Druid. More to the point, he'd made it clear that he loathed her.

She couldn't lie here next to him one moment more. Grania sat upright, then remembered Eithne. Her eyes raked the shadows of the clearing, but there was no sign of the wolf.

She started to cry, and Niall awoke, running his hands through his tangled hair. He tugged his *bratta* out self-consciously from under Grania's rump, then coughed and stood up, brushing a crackly web of leaves off his leggings.

"The wolf's not here?"

Grania's whole body lurched with a loud sob. She gave a sharp shake of her head.

"Maybe she's gone back to Aileach." Niall stared out at the grassy clearing. He untied Murchad, who was already grinding away loudly on a breakfast of sedge grass. Scooping up the saddle blanket he'd wadded for a pillow, he shook it clean with a loud, quick snap, then pitched it onto the gelding's back. He locked his hands, expecting Grania to place her foot in them. "Come on."

The prospect of leaving without Eithne spurred a fresh wave of misery in her. She crumpled forward as if she were deboned, her face buried in her arms over her knees. Niall's loud laugh turned her expression to stunned fury. Then Eithne punched her mistress's cheek with her black bulb of a nose.

The wolf whined, slathering her rough tongue down Grania's face. Grania hugged her, and the two of them tipped backward until Eithne lay belly up, paws flailing in the air. Grania managed to right them, and Eithne jumped, all wiggles and wags, onto her mistress.

Grania nuzzled the animal's soft gullet and cried for joy. She clutched Eithne tight, still assuring herself the wolf had really returned. Eithne smiled, looking none the worse for her expedition and oddly bemused by Grania's lack of faith in her.

"I knew she'd come back," Grania said, beaming.

"You knew no such thing. We could have been killed."

Grania's eyes were wide with gratitude. She ground her forehead into the wolf's rich coat and breathed in Eithne's cold, windy smell.

With a tart yap, Eithne jerked free, ears perked and tail raised. Grania lunged after her and cinched her arms tighter, determined not to lose her a second time.

"Here!" Niall cupped his hands around his mouth and yelled to the mounted party silhouetted on the horizon. The riders picked up to a run at the sound of his greeting.

There were five men; from their loud clanking, Grania guessed they were heavily weaponed. White breath shot out of their mounts' mouths, and Aileach's red silk standard lapped above them.

The men thundered in with a chorus of relieved shouts. They were led by a man wearing a wide gold champion's collar. The others were outfitted in leather vests painted with the red hand of O'Neill.

"We thought you'd met an untoward fate, lord," the champion answered, gasping for breath.

"Deirdre knew where I'd gone. I'm no unbreeched boy who needs nursemaids. It's a poor prince who cannot ride his own swordland," Niall barked.

The matter fell to silence as the war party's stares wound to Grania. She stiffened, tightening her hand on Eithne's collar and waited for Niall to offer some explanation. She doubted he'd tell his friends the full story—but she expected an introduction. Niall said nothing; he only winked and smiled at them. The men answered with an insulting grunt of laughter. Grania felt her ears heat as she realized Niall meant to make her out as his whore.

"I'm to be your lord's wife," she said.

The silence was deafening. The men turned back to Niall with expectant faces. But Niall said nothing; he only banged his hand on his sword sheath and stormed toward Grania.

His eyes seemed to grab and shake her. "Be still." He hissed the command through clenched teeth. His brows lifted in a fierce dare, defying her further impertinence. She decided to keep still.

Seemingly satisfied, Niall bounded onto Murchad with a single, furious spring. Grania's eyes popped wide up at him; had he decided to leave her here, to undo the bargain they'd made?

Niall reined Murchad sideways, his entourage falling in like ducks in his wake. Just when Grania thought he was going to leave, he turned toward her.

"Come on," he ordered tersely. "You'll walk home."

Grania fell disconsolately back upon the heavy silk bedspread, running her nails down Eithne's belly. For a day and a half she'd been hostaged in the gilded room Niall called the *grianan* with no one save the Briton slave Morgana to break her bleak isolation. Morgana's speech was broken and heavily accented; if she understood Grania's pleas for a loom or a harp—anything to occupy her time —she chose to ignore them.

Grania was bored to numbness; why else would her thoughts keep winding back to Niall? She remembered the pleasing low score of his breath as she half slept next to him; his scent, clinging to her skin even after she'd bathed. She remembered how he'd held her in his arms as she stood crying in the clearing, how the feel of him enfolding her had been both soothing and stirring. And how he'd turned away afterward, making clear it was the magic she'd worked, not the bent of his heart, that had gentled him toward her. For all she knew, Niall had changed his mind and decided not to wed her after all. He might even have left Aileach, for the little she'd seen of him these past two days.

Grania had only herself to blame; heartspells were unreliable things. Likely the magic had doubled back on her instead of working its powers on the O'Neill chieftain.

She rolled sideways, pressing her temple against the cool yew bed pillar. Never before had she slept in the luxury of a testered bed; its wool curtains and duck down mattress kept her so warm, she had to throw off the fur coverlet at night just to keep from suffocating.

Grania sat up, her shoulders sagging with a long sigh. She paced across the *grianan,* trying each of the room's furnishings repeatedly and finding them all lacking. Neither of the two couches, plumped with silk cushions, suited her. Nor did the view from the huge, brass-shuttered window. Its silk curtains rustled softly in the noon wind, teasing her with an expansive view of all her imprisonment denied.

More than once Grania had asked the door guard if she could leave for a walk—only to be told firmly that Niall wished her to wait here. She was beginning to wonder if she'd die of neglect.

The hearth fire was redolent with the crisp kiss of oak, but its warmth only reminded her how she missed the sun on her face. The fresh plantain rushes strewn on the floor smelled sweet as the fall fields, but they only made her remember how much she longed to stretch out in a meadow's fragrant matting. A tray full of wheaten bread and quickenberries laid untouched on a side table; Grania had no appetite.

A jail was a jail, even though nicely appointed. Grania

was exhausted with waiting. She'd reached a decision: If Niall didn't come to her by tonight, she was going to break their agreement and begin back to Uisneath.

"I thought you'd likely had enough of that small room."

Grania hiked up the new red *leine* Morgana had brought her and scurried down the *grianan* stairs after Niall's sister, Deirdre. She was so happy to be free, she didn't even wonder that it was Deirdre, not Niall, who'd come to fetch her.

Grania worked her short legs hard to keep pace with Deirdre's long, gamboling gait. The O'Neill princess was tall and blond and lithe as a summer doe. The two women wound their way out the inner raths onto the grassy lawn that stretched beyond them. Warriors stopped their business and stared as they passed. Grania knew they were comparing her dark features with Deirdre's smooth, golden mien—and finding her lacking.

She was breathless when Deirdre finally came to a halt. Niall's sister flounced her blue skirts as she plopped down at the gnarled base of an oak tree.

"Niall's left Aileach."

In her heart, Grania had suspected it all along; Niall found the prospect of marrying her so odious that he'd not only fled, he'd deeded the delivery of the miserable news to his sister. Deirdre's face was still and passionless. Grania imagined all the O'Neill blood ran cold as snow.

Grania shied her face down to hide her embarrassment. The Goddess had bade her to Niall, but he'd refused her. She was shamed—but relieved.

"Could Niall not have told me himself?"

Deirdre shrugged. "That is not my brother's way. You'll learn to understand him—in time."

What time? Niall was gone. It was finished. But Deirdre sat waiting and staring, her silence only deepening Grania's humiliation. What did these strange O'Neill want from her, anyway?

"I want to go back now," Grania said.

"You're angry with me. I knew I should have come to speak with you sooner."

" 'Tis your brother, not you, who makes a bargain and breaks it." Grania swallowed hard. She bit down on her lip, determined Niall's sister would not make her cry.

"Broken his bargain? Niall's gone to take your sword to Connor. What else did you think?"

Relief routed Grania's fear. *Connor. Niall had only gone to deliver the sword. He hadn't refused her after all.* She felt a blush work her face; she was sure that Deirdre must think her anxious and stupid.

"Whatever you believe my brother is, he keeps his promises. O'Neill honor our word."

"I'm sorry . . . I . . ."

"Shh . . ." Deirdre's mouth curved into a kind smile. She leaned toward Grania and pressed a finger to her open lips. Grania felt the dangerous, misplaced stirrings of trust. Deirdre seemed so nice, so friendly, but none of these O'-Neill had done anything to earn her faith.

"Niall is—" Deirdre spoke haltingly as if she were censoring her true inclinations. "Driven—in his own way. Like you, I think. My brother wants your sword for Connor. But I do not understand what it is you seek of him."

"The Goddess . . ." Grania knew the explanation was doomed before she began it. Things that needed explaining always seemed to defy it. She lifted her hands, shrugging.

Deirdre hooked her arm through Grania's and pulled her up to her feet, then steered her out toward the open fields that circled Aileach. As they walked, the wind rustled through the sedge grass; Grania was grateful to have any sound fill the awkward stillness roaring between them.

"I think you may be a good match for my brother after all."

"Niall made the match for the sword, not for me," Grania said.

"Perhaps."

Grania pulled her head back, angling to get a better look at Deirdre's face. "You're different than I expected."

Deirdre nodded, unsurprised. "You imagined I would be your enemy."

"Yes." Grania's eyes were wide with candor.

"I would see my brother wed. Happily."

"To a Druidess?"

"Until you, Niall swore to marry no one." Deirdre's light laugh faded quickly. "Druid or Christian. Are we not all of Inisfail?"

"Your priest Ossian would not agree."

"Ossian." Deirdre's calm features drew up in disgust. "There's a man to drive the most devoted to witchery." She blushed at her insult. "I'm sorry. I meant only to say there are many who follow our faith—decent, kind men— whose good hearts put the abbot's to shame. My brother Niall is such a man. It should please you to know he keeps no concubine."

"Concubine?" Grania hadn't even considered it.

"My husband, Baetan, keeps the bondswoman Cossa." Deirdre's mellifluous voice roughened. "Even Ossian with his priest's morals turns a blind eye." She read the shock on Grania's face. "What is, is," she continued in a flat voice. "I have no reason to grieve. My life is one of priv- ilege. I was allowed fosterage. And before Niall was born, many said my father valued me as much as a son. Even now I hold my own land and am wife to Aileach's champion. Baetan raises no hand to me. If he chooses to bed another, it is a small matter to me.'' Looking at Deirdre's fallen face, Grania could see it was no small matter indeed.

A false smile flickered on Deirdre's mouth. "Perhaps . . .'' Her voice became thin and wistful. "If I'd borne Baetan a child . . . but even Cossa has failed him there. Nine years and the both of us still are barren.'' Deirdre's face took on a strange, pulled look as she loosened her arm from Grania's. "Niall tells me you can work magic.''

"He fears so. If I sneeze, he chews his thumb to ward off demons.''

Deirdre's blue eyes froze on her. "But you do have powers?''

"Some.'' Grania shrugged, then sobered as she understood Deirdre's too keen interest. "What is it you seek of me?''

Deirdre drew her long, delicate fingers down the sides of her face, then pulled Grania under the dappled shade of an apple tree. She leaned in, whispering, "If Niall suspected I spoke to you—I know I've no right to beg your favors,'' she said, lowering her blue eyes, "but I'm desperate beyond all propriety. If there were potions or verse . . . if I could only bear Baetan a child . . .'' Her voice broke; tears glazed her wide eyes. "Druidess, can you give me a babe?''

Grania had never before worked a child charm. And Niall had forbidden her to conjure magic at Aileach. But looking at Deirdre, with her pained, wistful face, filled Grania with compassion. Surely Niall's sister would keep the secret— *if* Grania could manage it, which was doubtful. A child charm would take considerable skill. And yet all druidhect came much the same way, and the Mother, from whom it came, was capable of anything.

"Perhaps,'' Grania ventured cautiously. Deirdre's face

glowed with hope and her eyes danced brightly. "But I cannot conjure what's not meant to be."

"I'll pay you anything. Tell me what it is you want."

It was a rude affront. Did O'Neill think they could buy anything? Then Grania remembered Deirdre pled for a babe, for life—not like Niall, who had come to her for a sword to work death. "The magic flows from the Goddess, not from me."

Deirdre's mouth turned down sadly. "I don't blame you for refusing me."

"No, 'tis not that." Again Deirdre's face lit. "I make no promise, except to try. And I ask nothing of you, except your faith."

"Must I renounce the Christ to make the charm work?" Deirdre looked ready to do it.

"The Goddess will ask only that you open your heart to all possibilities. If the child comes, then it was meant to be. If not, you cannot blame the Mother for it."

Deirdre crushed Grania to her with an exuberant hug. Her body was like Niall's, only softer and lighter. When she pulled away, her face glowed with gratitude. "Thank you. Sister," she said, blinking back tears.

Grania felt a smile come up unbidden. The day, which had begun so badly, was improving.

Even with one eye, Fergus could see more than most men could with two. He could see things as they might have been. The Airghialla land that Connor had promised him finally folded back into the bosom of Ulster. His fosterling, Niall, who would claim the crown Fergus was denied, begging his mercy. And Connor, the man who had blinded him, dethroned in shame. With the eye still left to him, Fergus could see justice.

"Let it be, Fergus. Connor cannot return the Airghialla."
Brecc, chieftain of the Ulster tribe Dal Riata, gave his red
head a slow shake.

"Then we will seize it." Fergus wheeled his gaze over
the war maps littering his banquet table. Brecc was a huge
man, but his heart was decayed. Brecc's father had promised
Connor his tribe would not war against the O'Neill again,
and Brecc had suckled on his father's shame.

"Connor tosses us his leavings and you lick his hand.
Why do you think I took to exile with him? That I dared
to kill Sweeney? *For the Airghialla!* Yet still the land flies
the flag of the O'Neill."

"Connor would have kept his promise to you, but the
Airghialla refused us—what would you have had the king
do?" Brecc's eyes pled with Fergus's rage.

"Connor's sweet, winning lies mean only to keep Ulster
on its knees. Have you forgotten how he slaughtered our
warriors when we last met on the field?"

"It was you, Fergus, not Connor, who raised that battle.
And Ulster's dead will not come to life because we drum
our war shields. Nor will Connor spare our children if we
dare challenge him again. Even were we to best him, it
would not make you high king."

Fergus cut his thumbnail down the dye line on the map
that marked the boundaries of the Airghialla land. With his
other hand he traced the ridged contours of his withered
eye.

"Yes, I know it well, Brecc." His wide mouth poised
like a snake. "The kingmaking stone will not sing for my
flawed face. But an eye is a trifle to lose compared to pride."

"And if we make war against the O'Neill—and again
we fail?"

Maps flew up, then fluttered to the floor as Fergus's fist

struck the table. "Fail? What know you of failure, Brecc? Five years in exile, listening to Connor's lies, believing his promise to restore Ulster. It is I who failed. I trusted him."

"I cannot break my father's pact with the O'Neill."

Fergus snagged Brecc by the throat and jerked the man's huge face up to his own. "Swear your allegiance to me, Brecc—or else weapon your warriors to fight against me."

Brecc's hands were shaking, but his eyes were resolute. "How can you know we will win? That we all will not die?"

Fergus let Brecc go with a rough push, wiping his hand on his *leine* as though the Dal Riatan had soiled it. "I've been to the eastern kingdoms across the sea—to Pictland and Northumbria, even to Deira. Their warriors' fierceness lays your woman's heart to shame. The foreigners have promised to fight alongside me, against the O'Neill. Thousands upon thousands they will come. Until together we will surge like a tide over Connor's land."

"You think to beat the high king with bought men? Once your purse is drained, they'll break rank like sheep in a storm. I have seen it."

"You know nothing, Brecc. Injustice makes men drunk with courage. The foreigners will stand our cause."

Fergus's face wore a mad, sharp edge. "What say you? Will your Dal Riata stand beside me?" Brecc hesitated; Fergus drew his sword from its sheath. "Choose now!" He pressed the blade into Brecc's white cheek. "With me or no—live or die."

Brecc knew there was no winning. If he were doomed to fail, at least he would choose to go down fighting for Ulster.

"What say you, Brecc?"

"Aye, Fergus," Brecc answered with leaden eyes. "The Dal Riata will stand you well."

CHAPTER

8

Grania flattened her palms against her ears, but there was no escaping the bone-jarring din. Bells rang endlessly at the monastery of Derry, tolling the faithful to their ablutions of prayer. Seven times daily the monks fell to their knees in the church nave or the scriptorium on the far side of the compound, wherever they happened to be. Seven times daily the insistent ringing reminded Grania how far she'd drifted from Uisneath.

The matin bells had jolted her upright last night at midnight; she couldn't remember sleeping at all after that. Her bed was freezing except for the tiny valley where she lay, and its snarl of linens perfectly matched her fitful mind. Her shoulders ached, her eyes stung, and she had the beginnings of a bad headache. It was an inauspicious start to her wedding day—if that was what today would turn out to be. She hadn't seen Niall in over a month, and there'd been no word from him.

Grania had waited like a patient fool for him to return to Aileach. Niall's steward had mustered some excuse about a military expedition, but Grania doubted that. More likely Niall was off thinking of ways to keep the Druid sword without keeping her, too.

What mattered most was that he wasn't here. And it was Sunday, when both work and travel were strictly forbidden. Niall wouldn't be coming to Derry today, either.

Grania wanted him back if only to assure herself that her memories flattered him. In the little time they'd spent together Niall had nettled her in so many irksome ways. Yet he'd also tried to please her. He'd waited to help her find Eithne. And left orders with Aileach's backhouse to keep the fleshmeat she loathed off her meal tray. But most of all, it was his cocky, glorious face that haunted her.

Grania felt her mother's blood wane a little more in her with every day she spent at Aileach. As Niall had insisted, she'd adopted the trappings of his Christian faith. Deirdre had filled her head with psalm verses and saints' names, and she had memorized the dates of fasts and feasts until she could hardly tell one month from another. She was good at the charade; it was, after all, what she did best—pretending to fit where she really didn't.

But the two weeks she'd spent at Derry felt like an eternity. Grania guessed this was Niall's final test, to see if she could manage under Ossian's suspicious eye. She'd taken off the dragonstone, but she doubted the priest had forgotten it.

She did what she could to avoid him and was grateful for the compound's huge size. Each day Derry's eighty monks ground it to loud life with little thought for Grania and Deirdre, who, exhausted from the endless round of nighttime bells, were usually still sleeping. But dawn came mercilessly. Doors slammed, monks chanted, and milk pails banged like sour gongs.

The church had been founded by the Christian saint Columcille, himself an O'Neill prince who'd been deeded the land by Niall's grandfather. The monastery hovered at an ingress of northern sea, and the ocean's icy wind howled down the smoke hole of their beehive-shaped hut, turning Grania's hands stiff and blue. The pitiful scrap of a hearth failed predictably, and the rain-soaked walls made the air rank with mildew. The monastery's midden heap, perched all too close to their guest house, didn't help much.

Grania had taken to sleeping in her *bratta* to try to keep warm. She wound the cloak tighter as she walked to the room's sole window, hoping to find last night's rain had ended. She worked the shutters as quietly as she could—Deirdre was still sleeping—but the wood was swollen frozen and she had to give the locked hinges a loud, hard push to loosen them.

She leaned out, squinting into the watery dawn light. The sky was dark and burgeoning; even the weather augured badly. A phalanx of monks, eyes hooded, their hands buried in the bells of their sleeves, scurried past in tight twos and threes.

Graniá watched their stern-set mouths and kohl-blackened eyes; the look of them made for a grim good morning. Their shaved-head tonsure made even young men look old, and in a wry twist, their belted white robes gave them much the appearance of Druids.

They looked exhausted. Grania didn't doubt they were. Ossian worked them like cheap cattle, making them plow and milk and sing their ceaseless psalmodies from dawn to darkness. The priests' thin wool shifts and spare sandals were useless protection against the winter wind, and on the two days each week that the monks fasted, Grania wondered that they had the strength to rise at all. She pitied them, yet she wondered if Ossian's monks would judge Uisneath's lake-bound arrangement as hard as she did their lives at Derry. The body often paid for schooling the soul, and in an odd way, Grania felt a strange kinship with these lean, black-eyed men. They'd at least done what they could to make her comfortable. She and Deirdre were always served first at evening meal, and the rectory bench closest to the hearth was always left vacant for them.

The priests streamed by, most of them disappearing into the huge, rectangular church that was the monastery's centerpiece. Those too late to fit inside filled the seven smaller oratories that clustered nearby.

Grania heard the clanging of the morning mass bells. The prospect of several hours with Ossian made her sink back, disheartened. Deirdre rolled over, her blue eyes flickering to life as she stretched out like a waking cat, propping up on one elbow with expectant eyes. "Has my brother come yet?"

Grania shook her head. Deirdre sighed as she pushed up onto her feet and shuffled to the small window. She straightened the plaits of her long blond hair as she fixed her stare on the compound's front gate.

"He'll come. In the meantime, we'd do well not to make trouble with Ossian. He'll expect us for prayers."

Grania nodded as she smoothed her sleep-tangled hair. She'd go to mass, as Deirdre bade her. But she knew no amount of prayer could drag Niall to the altar with her. Not today—not ever.

Grania hiked up her *leine* over the muddy storm slop as she trudged past the church's tiny cemetery. The tombstones, many older than Derry itself, had been enclosed with a rectangular stone fence, an effort by the priests to disguise the earlier grave circle, which was a pagan arrangement.

The main oratory where services were held lay just beyond the graves. Its doorway was marked with an embedded cross limed white; Grania considered it a beacon of warning every time she passed under.

She crossed herself—in case anyone was watching—and ducked inside, struggling to adjust her eyes to the funereal light. The church's one window perched high up the wall directly over the altar. Candles, their tiny flames nearly snuffed by wind, jutted out from the wall on wooden planks but made no dent in the smoke-choked darkness. Grania ached for the open air of the Druid rites. Christians consigned their faith to black, dank places.

She breathed through her mouth to keep from gagging on the thick incense as she genuflected in the center aisle, nearly losing her balance on the uneven floor. Deirdre reached out a hand to help steady her.

Monks sat packed shoulder to shoulder on long wooden benches. Grania edged toward her seat, feeling the heft of their silent eyes. She slid in quietly next to Deirdre, grateful her diminutive size made her harder to see.

Ossian defended the slab of an altar like a wizened old warrior and shrank Grania with a look of rebuke. She'd been late again, and she'd have to confess it later. Maybe her penance would at least take her mind off Niall.

Ossian had shed his usual fleece *bratta* for a blue-and-white ceremonial robe that shimmered in the candlelight, making him look like a snake. He'd been black fasting for seven years—and bread and water had reduced the abbot to a loose draping of skin and linen on pointy bones.

The priest creaked open an ornate gold reliquary and pulled out what Deirdre had told Grania was St. Colum-

cille's own hand bell. Ossian rang it to signal the start of
the mass. Grania fanned the vellum of her prayer missal to
the proper place and began the litany. Her mind drifted
through the collect prayers, and she caught only scattered
pieces of the epistles, which Ossian read with more determination than inspiration.

When it came time for the Eucharist, Grania was half-
asleep and nearly faint from having gotten up too late to
bolt down even a quick bite of bread. She hoped the thin,
cross-stamped biscuit would improve her light head.

Ossian's assistant flushed the goblet and broke the bread,
then summoned the monks up for the wine. Each man pros-
trated himself thrice in the aisle before he knelt at the altar.

After the priests, Deirdre nudged Grania, and they too
went to their knees at the abbot's feet. Grania opened her
mouth and took a timid bite of the dry, yeasty bread. *"Peto
te, Pater, deprecor te, Fili obsecro te, Spiritus sancte."*
Grania closed her eyes as Ossian poured the wine, wishing
she were elsewhere as she gulped a quick drink. She recoiled, eyes wide, as Ossian's cold fingers brushed the bell
of her cheek. His mouth danced into a sly, slight smile,
making her shiver. Everything about him packed fear into
her.

There were more psalmodies, then the Gloria Patri. By
the time Ossian finished, Grania's rump was numb from
sitting so long. She stood up and stretched her stiffened
legs, then moved too eagerly toward the door. She ached
for fresh air; even the sound of the downpour outside didn't
discourage her.

Ossian scooted past, blocking her path. His mouth wound
into a smile as he dipped his head, leaning his slight weight
onto his staff. His face was all angles.

"Lady, do you need tutoring on the litany?"

Grania pulled herself up taller, fighting the inclination to run away. She gave her head a firm shake. "I was only a little slow today because I am tired, Father." That much was the truth, at least.

"Excitement for your wedding, no doubt."

Damn the priest. He knew as well as she did that Niall wasn't coming.

"Yes," she said quietly.

Ossian leaned closer still; Grania held her breath against his stale, old smell. He smiled and made the sign of the cross on her brow, then stepped back as Grania hurried out, preferring the pelting rain to another miserable moment in his presence.

Grania had never seen such a melted candle of a man. Niall's hair dripped down in lank, wet strings, and his *bratta* was splattered with road mire. A puddle swelled on the bullrushes under him, and rain shimmered on the ridge of his nose and his forehead.

"Brother." Deirdre nodded a quick, terse greeting and evacuated the hut with a speed that suggested it was about to catch fire.

Grania's hands went to her hips; she looked like a tiny rooster ruffling up for a fight. *This* was how he came to her on their wedding day? She'd have struck him if it wouldn't have dirtied her hand.

"I see you're ready for me." Niall's eyes ran a swift course down the length of her. Grania hated herself for agreeing to this wasted, foolish preening. *Just in case*, Deirdre had pleaded. *If he comes, you'll want to look like a bride*.

Trussed like a goose bound for the banquet table, that's what she was. Grania cursed every debasing, manicured detail: the white silk *leine*, its neckline and girdle peppered with Kerry diamonds; the new gold neck torque that hung over her chest and governed her galloping breath; the bells and river pearls woven into her clean, plaited hair.

When Deirdre had held the mirror up to her, for an instant Grania almost thought she looked close to pretty. Like a woman a man might want to marry. But as she stood staring at this insult that passed as Niall, she couldn't remember why she'd made the effort.

"You look like you didn't expect me." Niall's voice was maddeningly implacable. One side of his large mouth curved like a blade up his face. There wasn't a hint of apology in his eyes.

"I didn't expect you like this. With no warning."

"I'm not in the habit of announcing my plans—to anyone." He shrugged as if the matter were of no consequence, ignoring Grania's reference to his bedraggled appearance. "I didn't think you'd proceed without me."

"The altar wine's probably turned to water in this rain." Grania fiddled with her gold necklace, determined to conceal the extent of her rage. She wouldn't give him the satisfaction of detailing the morning's miseries; that she'd been waiting, exhausted, hoping he'd come, hoping he wouldn't, smiling when she felt like crying, feigning blithe humor with Deirdre, even as she was sure that Niall planned to leave her, humiliated and abandoned.

"I dance to no priest's tune. I've even broken custom to travel on Sunday—just to be here in time for our wedding." Niall stretched his arms out off his sides. "Ossian will pour the wine as I order it. I trust your stay here has gone well."

Grania's eyes narrowed. "I've frozen half to death in this sunless place, had my sleep churned to ruin by those maddening bells—all so you could test me. Wasn't it enough that you had my promise? Did you think I'd start charming and keening the minute you left me?" She felt a blush work up her face—she had, in fact, done just that.

He shrugged. "I only thought Derry might lessen the temptation."

"I've played your game well. Look here." Grania hiked up her skirt and pointed to her kneecaps, which were swollen and red from too much kneeling. She dropped the *leine*, realizing she sounded like a shrewish wife—and she wasn't even married yet. She hadn't planned this grim start to her wedding day. It was just that she felt so miserably bedecked and bewildered, all done up in plaits and silks, while Niall dripped indifferently all over her floor. She smelled of sweet herbs, he of horse sweat; Deirdre had strewn her black hair with river pearls; Niall's wild mop sported a netting of twigs.

"You've done well. Ossian had no tales to tell of you. But I must say, you look . . . different."

Color flooded Grania's face. "It was Deirdre's doing."

Niall appraised her dispassionately. He looked as if he were about to embark on something no more significant than buying a new mare. "Well, shall we to it?" He clapped his hands as if he were calling a pup.

Grania knew she'd been foolish to have expected more from him. She'd forced Niall to marry her; he was no saucer-eyed suitor. At least he hadn't laughed at her outright. And he was here; that alone was something. But she was through with this ridiculous ruse—there'd be no more of Deirdre's silly, embarrassing frippery.

The *clochan* door banged open on Ossian's drawn face. Startled, Grania scrambled behind Niall, catching her toe on the hem of her bridal *leine* and pitching down. She landed face first on the floor rushes.

She'd barely begun to get up before Niall dropped down next to her and winched Grania's body tight against his. He *whoosh*ed her up off the floor and shoved her veil sideways. Then he claimed her mouth with a bruising kiss.

Grania's eyes popped open, then fluttered closed. All the

blood seemed to drain out of her head as Niall twisted against her, wrenching her back as he clutched at the folds of her *leine*. When he finally let her mouth free, Grania stood stunned and breathless. Her pulse drummed in her temples and she could feel Niall's heart hammering against the skin of her breasts. His arms still held her; his chest still blocked her from Ossian's view.

"To the church, priest," Niall barked the order back over his shoulder, his eyes still boring down on Grania.

"Aye, lord," Ossian answered.

As Grania peeked around Niall, she saw for the first time that the priest's sallow cheeks had a hint of pink in them.

Ossian continued to nod as he closed the door. The minute its latch caught, Niall dropped Grania like a hot stone.

She stood, arms limp and mouth open, staring up at him like a dumb beast. Whatever she'd done to bring out his passion, she had the unsettling sense that she liked it.

"Cover that thing."

Niall's eyes dropped without flattery to her breasts. Grania glanced down, and the smile melted off her face. When she'd stumbled, her *leine* had slipped off its toggle, exposing the crescent tattoo on her chest.

She pressed her fingers to the moon sign, her eyes starting to sting with incipient tears. She righted her veil and flung open the door, bracing herself against a stiff blast of wind. She strode off, her new shoes, which she'd taken such care to keep clean, sinking into the oozing muck as she hurried toward the oratory. How she hated him. Niall had kissed her only to distract Ossian from the scar.

"I'm staying in the *grianan* with you. But only because I won't have my servants prattling." The matter of their sleeping arrangements at Aileach had nagged at Niall all the way from Derry. He stood with his back to Grania, seeming to announce his decision to the hearth wall, though he assumed she heard him. At any rate she made no protest, and he took that to be a good sign.

There'd been a thousand other ways to cover the marking, but he had kissed her, and now he couldn't stop thinking about it and wondering what had possessed him. He could only hope his careful, distant behavior since then had made one thing clear: that the kiss was to hide the crescent scar —and nothing more.

Connor had been pleased with the Druid sword, and he hadn't pressed Niall's lie that he'd traded the Druids a prize bull for the blade. Later—after Niall had divorced Grania—he'd confess the whole truth to the king. But more important matters loomed over him now. An O'Neill herald was already en route to Ulster with the blade. Connor hoped its magic would silence Fergus. Niall hoped it would only spur him.

Soon there would be war, and he would leave Aileach. By the time he came back he could divorce Grania honorably. But until then he'd just have to keep clear of her.

That's why he'd hurried back to Aileach. The Derry guest *clochan* was way too tiny, and he was sure Deirdre would have left him alone with his new wife. He could avoid Grania better here. He was master of Aileach; here, he had his bearings. And even if appearances drove him to the *grianan* every night, the room was big enough for the both of them.

Niall shrugged out of his wet *bratta*, which was twice its usual weight from the torrential rain. He flung it in a perfect arc sideways, landing the cloak on one of the wall pegs. The wet, muddy soles of his boots squeaked as he stepped close to the hearth. Water dripped off his sleeves as he lifted his palms to the fire's welcome sting.

Niall knew he was a muddied mess; he didn't begrudge

Grania her shock when she'd seen him. He was no soft belly, always whining for a comb and a hot tub, but he was fond of a bath and a fresh *leine*. Bad weather had slowed the trip back from Connor, and he had been forced to choose between filthy and present or clean and late. To look at Grania now, hovering in the shadows behind him, Niall wondered if he'd guessed wrong. He wondered if she would have preferred that he'd not come to wed her at all.

Grania was as far away from the fire as she could get. Niall knew she must be bone cold. She was so rain-soaked that she glistened. Her silk wedding veil was saturated to transparency, and the pearls in her hair shone like giant dewdrops. The white wedding dress and its wool *bratta* were soiled an uneven gray, and her skirts were splotched with mud half up to her waist.

Niall could hear her teeth chattering softly. "Come to the fire. It'll chase off your chill." He moved aside, making a space for her. When Grania did not budge, he turned— and saw her head shake firmly. "I don't want you to die of the rheum," he snapped irritably.

"Indeed?"

Her voice said it was fury, not fear, that froze her in place. Niall turned to face her, but the rage heating her green eyes was more than he'd expected. Though he could hardly blame her. The wheels of her chariot had locked twice in the mud, and the horses' hooves had flung glop back into the cart. From the look of her, Grania's face had caught a disproportionate share of it.

"I want you to know . . . that you're. . . ." Niall couldn't think of a sufficiently delicate word. "Safe. Here with me, I mean. I've no plans to—" Emotion flooded back into Grania's face; her huge eyes blinked at him, glazed with what looked like hope. Yet she wouldn't even stand next to him. Certainly she wasn't interested in sharing his bed. She was baiting him, anticipating the added pleasure of refusing his overture once she enticed him to make it.

"You sleep on the pallet. I'll take the couch."

She was still shivering. He wondered what he had done to be treated like a man who whipped horses and beat women.

"Good God, witch!"

Grania fell against the wall as he rushed up to her. Her hands rose up to his face, her nails, kenned red, poised for attack.

Niall wouldn't have it said he'd murdered his bride by letting her freeze on her wedding night. While Grania sputtered a protest, he dispatched her cloak brooches and pitched the soaked *bratta* over the back of a chair.

"There."

Grania let out a ragged sigh, looking as if she were relieved to discover that was all he wanted from her.

Black corkscrews of her hair, just starting to dry, danced up off her brow. Niall could smell the oil from her skin, set to full strength from the heat of the ride. She smelled thick and mysterious, and as he stared at her, he again felt the tuggings of desire. It began in him whenever they stood this close. She was breathtakingly beautiful. Her eyes went dark and silky, and her lips, still trembling, issued him a frightened invitation.

Niall wet his finger and cleaned off a small splotch of dirt from the crest of her cheek. His hand drifted to her chin, and Grania's eyes bade him closer. *She was his wife.* Niall remembered it like a warm, pleasant surprise. It was his right, maybe even his duty, to bed her. Maybe she wanted it as much as he did. He closed his eyes, wrapping his hands around her small head. Then he pulled her face to his chest and sank his head back, struggling with the maelstrom raging inside him.

Sorceress! The realization forked like lightning through him. Niall pushed her away. What he felt wasn't love, it wasn't even lust—it was nothing more than witch's alchemy.

He whirled back, marching toward the hearth, giving his temples a quick thump with the butt of his hand. He sank down on the couch and folded his arms over his chest. He had to keep his wits about him; he had to keep away from Grania.

CHAPTER
9

"Lady, I can accept no gift from you. The tale was my pleasure to tell." Dermot shook his head to refuse the bossed brooch Grania held out to him and shifted uncomfortably at the edge of the campfire.

"You've earned the wage, Dermot. Take the pin, please." Grania was in his debt. Niall had refused to let Deirdre accompany them to Uisneath, and but for Dermot's well-told bard's tales, the trip would have seemed interminable. Grania was glad not to have been left alone with Niall—her husband's beetle-browed mood hadn't improved a bit since the day he'd wed her.

Dermot leaned in toward her, his multicolored *bratta* lighting to brilliance in the firelight. He folded her fingers back over the brooch and shook his head again. " 'Tis yours."

"As you wish. But let me pay you in other kind. At least let me tell you a tale of my own."

Dermot's brown eyes lit and his gray beard spread like a bird's nest on his wide, grinning face. He stretched his legs toward the whirring fire, crossing his ankles and settling back on his elbows as he waited for Grania to begin.

All night Niall had paced behind her like a high-strung hound; but when Grania offered the tale to Dermot, she heard her husband's boots freeze. She waited for his reprimand—she had no bard's training, and it was audacious of her to offer to speak—but he said nothing. In a way it didn't surprise her; he'd barely said a word to her the full four days of their wedded life.

He'd assiduously avoided spending time in the *grianan*. Even at night, when appearances forced him to go there, he kept to his couch, making sure there was always a room's width between them. Grania even began to suspect that he was moving his makeshift bed. Tiny distances at first, then more obviously, until he was positioned a little farther away from her pallet each day.

She wondered how long her husband could endure their strange, strained charade. Or how long she could. Tomorrow—at Uisneath—she and Niall would be married again, this time with Druid rites. But that would change nothing. Niall was as distant and inaccessible as ever; and each sunset only put her a day closer to the time he would order her gone from him. But still she was committed to doing as the Goddess had bade her—even as she grew more sure she was failing.

"Know you the tale of Condle the Red?"

Dermot nodded, his eyes urging Grania on. She settled Eithne's head in the scoop of her lap and began.

"There was a golden-haired witch with silver eyes; it was said that men howled like wolves when they beheld her great beauty. The woman went to the fort of the warrior Conn, but only Conn's son Condle could see her. She was invisible to everyone else, though her sweet siren's voice could be heard by all.

"When Condle fell in love with her, his father's Druid banished the witch to the sea. Condle mourned her so deeply he fell ill, soon hovering near death. His cries raised up the witch and she returned to him, bidding Condle to join her in the land of the fairies.

"Condle could not refuse his love for her. He and the witch sailed off in a fairy boat made all of glass. It destroyed the king, but for all Conn's weeping, his son Condle was not heard from again."

Dermot clapped loudly, leaning close to Grania with a low, guarded voice. "You are Brian's daughter indeed." Grania's eyes went wide with surprise. Surely Niall hadn't confided her past to Dermot; he had explicitly forbidden her to discuss it with anyone.

"I too was at Tara for Connor's kingmaking," Dermot whispered. "I remember you—your eyes are the same shade as Emer's."

"You knew my mother?"

"A little."

"Tell me."

"It was long ago. But I recall how she moved among us, seeming larger than her small stature." Dermot smiled. "Like you. And it was said she loved your father, Brian."

"That," Grania said, "was a mistake that cost my mother her life."

Dermot shook his head slowly. "The mistake was the physician's who overbled her."

"There would have been no physician had my mother not chosen the wrong husband."

"You judge her harshly," Dermot said, clucking softly. "Since you are like her in many ways." He glanced toward Niall.

"I . . ." The match with Niall was hard to explain—
and Grania was tired, and it was late. "Niall has forbidden
me to speak of our marriage—even to my father. Please, I
would ask you—"

"Have no fear, lady. I'll keep your secret." Dermot
patted her hand. "Niall has no inkling. He lies even to me.
He's fashioned some excuse to send me south tomorrow."

"So you will not be at the ceremony at Uisneath. . . ."

"The task to better your husband's mood falls to you
alone, lady."

Better his mood? What magic could manage that? Dermot
cupped his hands around his mouth and called out to Niall.
"My lord, your wife has the sweet tongue of a bard."

Grania could sense Niall glowering behind her. "She
chooses a poor tale to tell."

" 'Tis only a story, lord, no more," Grania said. In fact,
she'd picked the tale most carefully. If her husband would
bear her like a silent burden, he deserved to be baited. But
when she raised her eyes off the fire, Niall loomed over
her, his hands clenched to fists level with her eyes. The
firelight contoured the planes of his face into a dour mask.

He snatched her up onto her feet and dragged her into
the darkness, out of Dermot's earshot. "I'll hear no more
talk of witchery!" he whispered through clenched teeth.

Grania knew his bad mood was not for the tale, but for
what would happen at Uisneath. Tomorrow, in a midnight
forest, he would be bound to her in the most ancient of
ways. And each time she mentioned it, the color drained
from his face.

Grania pulled up boldly. "You'd best make your peace
with the druidhect. Even an O'Neill cannot forbid it at
Uisneath."

"I said no more!" Niall's body stiffened as the words
flew out of him.

"Is it your custom to silence that which frightens you?"

"I've no fear of your alchemy, *pitag*."

Grania knew his bravado was all a lie. She'd seen the terror on his face the night he'd come seeking the sword at the quicken rite.

She shook his hand off her arm and sauntered away from him, then turned, smiling slyly back over her shoulder. "Good. If you've nothing to fear, then you'll not resist me."

"Woman, you press me overfar. I may yet break our bargain."

"Do it, then." Grania's clear eyes defied him. "Better than this abuse of me. I'm no thrall you bought at auction, O'Neill."

For all his impressive size and station, Niall looked helpless with rage. "Damn it, woman, what is it you want of me?"

Exactly this was what she wanted—some kind of reaction. Grania had imagined her fate at Aileach a hundred different miserable ways. But she'd never planned on Niall's calm indifference. If he had no love for her, then she'd beg his hate.

Niall charged after her, clamping his hands down on her small shoulders. She stared up wide-eyed as he yanked her onto her toes, glowering. His look was fierce and cold, and just for a moment he frightened her. If he killed her—right now—he wouldn't even have to divorce her.

"It's all a game for you, isn't it, little witch? You share secrets with my sister, tell tales with my bard, all the while brewing your dark spells. Filthy changeling."

"Changeling?" Grania swallowed the end of the word, tears shimmering in her blinking eyes. She threw off Niall's arms and spun away from him. With a loud sniff, she grabbed Eithne's collar and pulled the wolf away. When they were out of Niall's sight, she slumped down to the sod, swearing she wouldn't cry. But, sweet Mother, how she wanted to, for her curse was always the same: There was no place she could call home.

"Where is your husband?" Maeve rested her hands on the loom's wooden frame and craned her face down to get a better fix on Grania.

"Shaking dice . . . or finding some other diversion to take his mind off tonight. My husband does not share his plans with me." The loom's brass wires pinged as Grania jammed the bone sword into them. The silk was badly snagged from her swift, missed passes, but it made no difference to her.

"You should work it more slowly." Grania knew Maeve was not speaking just of the loom. "Niall fears you."

Grania's head jerked up. It was a preposterous premise. It was her sullen husband, not she, who called the tune of their days. "Is that why he's done naught but punish me?" She jammed the sword through the wires even harder this time.

Maeve drew up a stool and drifted a cool, loving hand down Grania's flushed face. "He has not taken you to his bed yet?"

Grania's unfocused eyes wheeled past her aunt. "He sleeps on his couch with a room's width between us. Though it makes no matter to me. I've wed him, as the Goddess bade me. Bedding the O'Neill is the last thing I'd long for."

Maeve's loud sigh announced her disbelief.

Grania gave up on the fabric and placed her hands into her lap. "Still I do not understand my purpose with him. Look about us; Uisneath is safe. Why does the Mother make me feel I must stay with him? The marriage is worse than a hasty match made at a fair. Tonight I'll be twice wed and still spinstered.''

"It makes my heart ache to see you unhappy." Maeve's softly lined face filled with grief. But she would not say what Grania longed to hear. They both knew the futility of questioning fate.

"Are you sure Niall doesn't want you?"

"I'm nothing like the silk doves he's used to at Aileach." Grania's voice was cold and contained. "If he could show me even a touch of kindness . . . But his distaste for me is plain to see."

"Niall too fights his fate."

The heddle slipped to the floor as Grania bolted upright. "It is not fate he fights, but *me*. He treats me as if I'm some foul, evil thing. He buries his hands in his *bratta* when he stands alongside me, fearing his flesh will burn if we touch accidentally. He avoids my eyes when we speak, as if even my glance could thieve his soul from him. He rails against my magic more often than I could summon it were I the witch of witches."

"And yet the druidhect still passes between you. And, I think, a finer sort of magic, too."

"If Niall desired me, he would never admit it."

"He might—if we lessened his fear a little. . . ."

Grania knew instantly what Maeve was speaking of. And she'd have none of it. "I'll conjure no more heartspells. This war of a marriage is tainted already. What passion stirs in Niall is for murdering Fergus, not husbanding me. I won't brew some potion to seduce him."

"A charm cannot urge a man to things he would not do."

Grania wasn't so sure of it. A charm had bade Niall to wed her—and that magic had soured quickly. It made her laugh now to think she'd feared Niall would bed her, when obviously that was the last thing he intended.

Yet all too often Grania imagined him coming to her in the dark of the night, imagined his mouth on hers, his hands caressing her face. But to drive him to her with some priestess's charm would be to admit she could have him no other way.

"The magic will only kindle the desire he already holds for you." Maeve's voice curled persuasively. "Let me work the potion."

Grania had no strength left to argue. She looked up at her aunt and nodded slowly. Once again, she would try.

The brilliant, gibbous moon shone like a bright stone in the night sky. Stars streamed like water around it, worsening Niall's spinning focus; closing his eyes only distilled the vertigo. His feet felt like sand, his body lifeless. He smelled the humid must of sod and realized he had ended up on the ground, though he could not remember how.

Jagged stone megaliths jutted up like mammoth teeth all around him. He lay in the hub of a great wheel of white-robed women. Their breath marshaled into a soft, sweet keening, and a bronze trumpet sang out its long, lonely wail.

The women's heads were shrouded in hoods, their faces lit only by quick kisses of firelight. Their white *leines* glowed like bleached bones, and their slender hands stretched out from under their sleeves in unfathomable signs.

Niall could feel the weight of their eyeless stares pressing him deeper into the warm, soft earth. This was all the nameless things he'd feared; his heart beat weak and fast. How had he come to this eerie, purple place?

An old man approached him. His hair was sage white; a speckled cloak made of colored birds' wings trailed off his frail frame. He tinkled an apple branch in Niall's face, and the women, still watching, joined their voices in a low thrumming. The wheel kept on turning, and Niall's head spun as his stomach twisted. He was sure he was going to be sick.

He saw everything with a dreamer's distortion. He was being asked to surrender something—and, though he didn't know just what, he knew he would not resist. His vision shrank until all he could see were two woad-stained wrists, marked with crescents, reaching toward him.

It was Grania. Niall's blurred eyes made out only the gross contours of her small form: white robe, dark hair, huge, silent green eyes. She smelled of plantain and herb oil. The indigo moon sign seemed to glow on her pale breast. Why couldn't he focus his eyes?

The air filled with a sound that was not quite song, but more like a wordless hymn. Niall tried to remember where he was, why he'd come to this ungodly place. His thoughts escaped him, like leaves floating away on a swift stream.

His flesh sank and his soul levered out of him. He had the disturbing, oddly peaceful sensation that his chest was opening, that some weighty thing inside him was drifting up, leaving a shining, silver heap of skin and bones.

His head lolled backward as he felt a subtle sting, not wholly unpleasant, on the beam of his chest. When he finally raised his eyes, Grania's face glimmered like a dark jewel in front of him. He could smell the sweet scent of magic all over her. He wanted to pull back, but he couldn't move; he was hopelessly, wonderfully ensorcelled.

A wild shudder tingled down his spine. Niall sensed he was being drained, dragged to the far edge of danger. His breath thinned as he watched Grania lean toward him, her glistening eyes closing in soft, slow beats. She parted the folds of her *leine*, fully exposing the moonscar. Niall's hand wound unthinkingly to the stinging spot on his own chest, and as he looked down he saw that his flesh bore the same sign.

When he looked back up, Grania's guileless eyes were bright and moon huge. Her hair flew like black silk in the fire wind, and her head was crowned by a slender pearl-strewn plait. Niall longed to press her down under him in the most primal of claimings, but the women were watching . . . or were they? His head swam; his drunken perceptions bulged and waved.

The quicken fire exploded with a loud crack, and Niall realized this was no dream, however it seemed. He trembled, for this was the most ancient of baptisms, the great remembering.

He swept his mouth down on Grania's, their lips twisting and exchanging heat. Niall's fingers winnowed through her hair, then inched down her neck and shoulders until they brushed her breasts lightly. When he could bear no more distance between them, his arms encircled her, wrenching her tight against him; she molded in perfect surrender. Feeling her shiver spread to his own spine, he knew he would pay any price on heaven or earth, as long as he could have her.

Maeve had made her drink the same magic they'd used to drug Niall, but Grania didn't care. The druidhect coursed through her stronger than ever before, and she wanted Niall as much as he wanted her.

She pulled back, staring at Niall's eyes, which shimmered, deep and clear as crystals. Starlight dusted his naked shoulders as Grania knelt, not quite touching him, feeling the soft thump of his heart as it pushed air between them. She raised her palms and Niall mirrored hers, their seamed hands joined in the midnight air.

The moon was gone and an alder canopy spread out over the sky. The Druid rite and the quicken fire faded to distant memory. There were only Niall's cool, languid eyes claiming her. Grania canted her face sideways, and Niall moved in opposition.

Grania wondered that she'd ever thought him so different from her. The mistrust between them was all healed now, their former schisms all illusions.

Niall's lips brushed her forehead and eyes, then drifted down to her parted mouth. Where his kiss had gone, his hands followed. Grania took each of his fingers in her mouth as Niall trailed them over her. He tasted of sod and the woad dye where he'd touched the moonscar.

Niall traced her face as if he were blind, his hands hungry for every swell and hollow of her. He caught Grania's chin and tipped it toward him, and as he spoke her name soundlessly, Grania felt the sure hand of the Goddess guiding her.

Tides of blood surged through her and a red wind drummed the breath from her chest. This was the true alchemy, in the sublime touch of Niall's hands, in the dark, dreamy glass of his eyes. This was the raising of the great wind, the final washing clean. Grania sank against him, wanting and fitting.

Niall kissed her moonscar, then splayed Grania's fingers over the mark on his own chest. He was all warmth and sinew, and she could feel his heart drum, feel the spurt of his pulse as it moved under his skin. Niall lifted her arms to circle his shoulders and pulled Grania so tight against him that she could barely breathe. His mouth drifted to hers with a soft entreaty, and she thawed like spring snow against the heat of him.

Niall tilted her head at reckless angles to deepen his kiss as his fingers made tangled circles in her hair. Together they sank to the ground, Grania's head *flesc* thumping softly back onto the sod.

Niall pushed himself up, kneeling over her, and at the sight of him, Grania felt her skin prickle like gooseflesh. Niall cupped her skull in his hands and she twisted deliriously, drunk on the magic.

With his knees straddling her hips, Niall peeled Grania's *leine* free and threw off the remnants of his own loose *bratta*. His eyes drifted over her naked body, and Grania felt herself open like a flower beneath him. When his hands settled on her waist, she clutched them, shivering under his sure, tight grip.

He arced over her, sliding his mouth in a wet trail down her neck. His hands moved across Grania's ribs, then circled her breasts with a touch soft as spindrift. One hand wound back to the flat of her belly, and Grania pitched her body against him.

Needing no further permission, Niall parted her thighs with his knees and pressed his full weight onto her. He glided in easily, then burrowed deeper. Grania struggled to catch her breath as he began a slow, aching pace.

Starlight danced off the soft nubs of Niall's spine, and Grania set her chin on the ridge of his shoulder while her hands combed his back. She felt his muscles stretch and shift as he moved inside her. The world turned like a lathe around them. Soon it took all Grania's concentration just to hold on tight.

As Niall drove them forward, hurtling into the sweet, dark night, Grania's core twisted and begged as she enfolded him. Her eyes lolled back in her head until finally, fingers tensed to the sky, she felt there was no trace of herself left. She'd been extinguished, joined to him in the deepest, most ancient way.

Niall seized her one final time, then collapsed, his sweat-soaked cheek pressed to her ear, his breath doubled and hard. Grania kissed him everywhere her lips could reach— his shoulder, his neck, his cheek. He lifted his head up, and just as she sought his mouth, Niall's quizzical stare froze her.

The magic was waning. Grania could feel it draining out of her. She knew Niall sensed it, too. The wind was silenced and the quicken fire, which had been blazing wildly only moments before, began to die. The two of them lay, still entwined, brushing the cobwebs of magic off their minds. The shining prize of a moment was fading away.

Spells worked in odd ways, out of proportion to time, not even according to the potion's strength. Magic stayed only as long as there was need; and Niall's need for her was well spent.

He rolled free and sat up, rubbing his brow as if he'd taken a stiff fall off Murchad. His blue eyes calcified as he stared at the moonscar marked on his chest.

"You cut me. You . . ." Niall rubbed the wound, then jerked his head up, gawking at Grania as if she were some kind of monster. "Did you drug me with magic?"

Grania snatched up her *leine* from where he'd flung it and covered herself, scooting away as she rolled into a tight, sad ball.

"Did you work a charm?" he demanded furiously.

"Is not love magic however it appears?" Whatever she said, Niall would make their sharing a shame.

"Merciful God."

Heat singed Grania's cheeks. "I too was drugged." She could see that made no difference to him.

"Who cast the spell on me? It doesn't matter," he said, giving Grania no chance to answer. "You've had what you wanted."

"Yes," Grania drawled, all the love and joy that filled her moments ago routed by rage and pain. She stood up, never feeling more sure that she and Niall were fated, and knowing he had never been more determined to deny it.

CHAPTER

10

Grania tightened the tuning key on the last of the harp's twenty-eight strings, then gave one brass wire a plaintive pluck. It was said each song had only one note as its true mate. This string's mournful burr begged a lament; so, too, did Grania's miserable mood.

It had been a fortnight since she and Niall had been wedded in the Druid rite, and Niall had not come to her bed since. Each night he slept on the couch in the *grianan*. Or at least he pretended to. Grania was sure his eyes were open, just as hers were. But while she lay wishing that he'd come to her, she knew Niall's mind ran a different course; likely he was only thinking of ways to escape their marriage without losing face.

Her days with him were not much improvement over her nights. Niall avoided her religiously, marshaling flimsy excuses to keep to the sword field or closeting himself away in the hound hut or the smithy. On those occasions when they met unavoidably, he was pointedly civil, according Grania the respect he would a man with whom he had business—and no more.

Maeve had said a heartspell could not bid a man to do things to which he was not inclined. And yet Niall had come to Grania once but refused her thereafter. Perhaps the magic had been too weak. Or perhaps Niall had overcome whatever inclination he had for her with sheer volition. Whatever had gone wrong, Grania's husband's distaste for her was plain to see.

She'd done the Mother's bidding, made every effort to be a wife to Niall. And failed. Now she sensed even the Goddess would not fault her for leaving him. Yet it was something beyond duty that bound her to Aileach. For Grania had reached a cold and unsettling conclusion: She loved Niall.

Day after day she stood in the *grianan* window, listening to Niall's laugh drift up from the game plain. She felt her heart quicken as she watched him tease Deirdre at dinner while she sat in silence, wishing that he'd care enough to tease her, too. She admired him as he sat in the banquet hall, settling a villager's land dispute with fairness and justice. But Grania was no more than a voyeur to his life— outside, looking in, always longing to recover the shining moment they'd shared in the clearing at Uisneath. It was a moment she knew would not come again.

Lately, Deirdre had been her only comfort. Niall's sister came to see her often, either to gossip or pitch dice, and she'd been in high spirits ever since Grania had promised to work the child charm. But that breath of happiness would soon die, too, for despite Grania's best efforts, her magic to make the babe had gone awry.

Grania had performed the motions repeatedly, standing on one foot, making the hand signs, speaking the proper verse. But not once, for all her determination, had the Mother's power filled her. Perhaps magic was impossible in this cross-cursed place. Whatever the reason, Grania was sure there would be no babe. And she would not torture Deirdre with false hope. Today, when Niall's sister came, she would tell her the child could not be.

Grania settled her harp in her skirts and plucked a short, sad strain, but she was too tired to finish it. Sleep eluded her, leaving her exhausted and irritable. When she did sleep, she woke often—and the sight of Niall, tossing and turning a room's width away, would only bring back her insomnia. Grania sank her head down over the harp's glossy spine and leaned her cheek into its hard, cold wires. She barely lifted her eyes as she heard the soft knock on the door.

Deirdre burst in like a windstorm, pulling the harp out of Grania's lap and lifting her up into a bone-crushing hug.

"How can I thank you?" She pressed an explosion of kisses on Grania's head.

"What is it?"

"I am with child!" Deirdre flung her arms around Grania again. Grania pushed away and stared at Deirdre's belly with blinking, incredulous eyes. Deirdre caught her chin with her cool hand and lifted her face. "Surely you are not surprised?"

"Are you sure of this? How can you know that you carry a babe?"

Deirdre spun in a joyous circle, the skirt of her *leine* belling with air. She stopped, cupping her hands over her belly. "I know as all women know. I have all the signs. But even before they came, I knew. I was right to trust you. I knew that, too."

Grania plopped back, dumbfounded, onto the creepie stool. She was sure the charm had failed; there had been no mistaking it. Yet if the child Deirdre spoke of had come to be . . . Grania shrugged and smiled. Well, most children came without aid of magic. Perhaps Deirdre only needed to believe it was possible to make it so. What mattered was that she was pregnant. Grania would not darken her happiness by confessing she'd failed.

"I am pleased for you," she said, beaming. "Does Baetan know?"

Deirdre gave her blond head a shake. "I thought you should be the first."

Grania laughed softly. "Unless you wish to earn me your husband's wrath, I think you should tell him quickly. And the sooner he knows, the sooner he'll order Cossa away."

"Yes, oh, yes!" Deirdre squealed, drawing her hands to her face as she skipped and giggled across the room. She rushed Grania, planting another loud smack of a kiss on her cheek before she bolted back toward the cracked door.

"Thank you, sister," she called. "For the charm that made my babe." As Deirdre spun around, the smile left her face. She stood toe to toe with Niall, who towered over her, looking all fury and stone.

Niall quickly strong-armed Deirdre down the stairs and past wide-eyed onlookers, pushing her inside her quarters in heated, silent rage. The door latch barely clicked into its fitting before he stormed toward her, his huge fists clenched at his sides. She sat back indignantly on the bed, trying to catch her breath and her wits.

"Tell me what I heard was a lie."

Deirdre stood up slowly and straightened the mussed folds of her *leine*. She knew there was no point in lying. "It's true—I am with child."

Niall drew a long, stiff breath before he spoke again. "How came the babe to be?"

''What matter?'' Her blue eyes flashed like sky at him. ''You of all people should know how I've ached for this.''

''How came the babe to be?'' Niall's voice was as solemn as a church bell. Deirdre said nothing; her silence was answer enough. ''Then that *pitag* wife of mine worked a spell on you.''

''Your wife . . . gave me the one joy I have longed for. Can you not share my happiness and forget how the child was made?''

Niall's eyes softened a little, as if only now had he begun to consider that his sister would finally have her fondest wish—to mother a babe. But his face resculpted to furious planes. ''I forbade her to practice her dark arts here.''

''And I begged her to. Grania would have refused me if I hadn't pled without shame. Nine years I have waited, Niall. Waited and watched while Cossa stole my husband's nights. Men have their wars and weapons to divert them; but what of me? A husband I must share. And a babe, the one thing that might be mine alone, denied me.''

''You are O'Neill. Is that not enough for you?''

''No, the loneliness you bed is not enough for me. Your wife has given me hope to fill my days—and befriended me. Here.'' Deirdre pressed Niall's hand against her belly. ''This is what her magic has wrought for me. Could such a wondrous thing be a crime?'' Tears trickled down her cheeks. ''If you think to send Grania away, I shall lose the babe. You must not make her leave. Please, Niall. Please . . .'' Deirdre's voice trailed to a whisper as she sank her head against Niall's chest. Her hands hung limp at her sides.

''I forbade her . . .'' Niall mumbled.

Deirdre drew back, looking up at him. Her desperate eyes glistened. ''She helped me out of love, not disobedience to you. Can you not see the great goodness her heart holds?''

"I see nothing but evil in her witchery," he said, pinching Deirdre's arms to make the point.

Deirdre threw his hands off her. "Pffft! What is magic but dreams which come to be? Here," she said, stretching her fingers over her stomach. "This, inside me—if it be magic, it makes no matter to me. Bringing life should not offend any God, pagan or Christian. And if you can find no love for your wife, Niall, then find some, at least, for me. Say you will not send Grania away. For if she leaves, I go with her."

Niall turned from Deirdre, raising his hand to his brow. He stood still for a long moment, then with a heavy sigh turned back, his eyes newly calm, his shoulders schooled down. "I won't make Grania leave . . . until after the babe comes."

Deirdre wept for joy as she pressed a kiss on Niall's cheek. "You won't be sorry, brother. This I promise you."

Niall mustered a thin smile, knowing Deirdre was very wrong. He was sorry already.

Grania waited in the *grianan* until it grew dark. At any moment the door would open on Niall's furious face. There was no point in running from him—that was exactly what he wanted. He'd probably track her down anyway, if only to have the pleasure of banishing her. Who could blame him? She'd broken her promise and worked her necromancy. Or so her husband believed.

It was the cruelest of ironies: that Grania was about to be condemned for magic she was too inept to make. Still, she had *tried* the charm. And Deirdre, at least, believed she'd succeeded. That would be all Niall needed to know.

Grania didn't doubt Deirdre would try some skillful lie. But she'd fail. Niall had been in the doorway when Deirdre had spoken; he'd heard the mention of magic. It would be all the indictment Niall would need.

Grania gathered up the few things she'd brought with her from Uisneath. There wasn't much—a few pieces of jewelry, the blanket in which she'd wrapped the Druid sword, and several simple linen *leines*. The dresses were modest compared with the gowns she'd become used to. The embroidered silks and satins Deirdre had pressed on her were the most elegant garments she'd ever owned. Grania realized her change in appearance would be only one of countless adjustments she'd have to make in returning to Uisneath. The changes inside her would be more difficult.

But there was no sense bemoaning her fate. She could endure no more abuse at Niall's hands. Even the Goddess could not ask that of her.

Grania yanked off her gold cuffs and jeweled neck torque and laid them on the night stand. Then she drew the simple white *leine* she'd worn when she first came to Aileach out of the bottom of the box at the end of her bed.

She eased off this morning's blue silk and stood in her underdress, staring at the priestess garb as if it were new and strange. She'd lost weight since she'd come here—mostly from worrying—but the *leine* was loosely cut and would likely still fit her. But what of Uisneath? Would its mists and magic fit better than before? Would the Mother finally find a niche for her, now that she had passed the test of her faith?

"You'll have no need of that." Grania clutched the *leine* to her breasts as she stared up wide-eyed at Niall. He stepped in slowly, kicking the door closed behind him.

"I'll be gone on the morrow," she answered calmly. "If you can loan me a horse, I'll go even sooner."

"You're going nowhere. I mean you to stay."

Grania shut her open mouth self-consciously. Was it possible, after all, that Deirdre had made him believe her lies?

"I know of the babe," he said. "That you worked a charm to make my sister pregnant. Deirdre will not lie to me. Unlike you."

Grania was red-faced with confusion; how could Niall know she'd worked magic and still mean to keep her?

"If you think to make sport with me . . ."

"Damn it, I want you to stay. For Deirdre," he added softly.

Grania understood. It was his sister that Niall was thinking of. Grania would have none of it. "Deirdre doesn't need me. The babe—" She stopped, sure Niall would disbelieve her. But she would not leave him with a lie. "It was not my magic that conjured the babe."

"If you think I'm fool enough—"

"It was Baetan, not I, who made Deirdre's babe."

"Deirdre says otherwise."

"She believes the child came from magic. And I confess I tried—but the charm failed. The druidhect was too weak in me. That should please you."

"How can you know your necromancy didn't make the babe?"

Grania knew only a Christian would ask such a thing, for there was no mistaking the Goddess's power when it came. But Niall wouldn't understand any explanation she could make. "How could it serve me to lie to you? You forbade my magic, and yet I confess to it. If I were lying, would I not plead you're mistaken?"

"Then why let Deirdre believe?"

"Would you take from her that faith which helped make the babe? What matter if it means keeping a lie?"

"You defied me."

"Aye. Because Deirdre needed me." *And you didn't,*

Grania thought painfully. "Though I doubt you could understand such a need."

"The Druids stand as enemies to the O'Neill. And yet you use your magic to help my sister?"

"The druidhect makes no choice as to Druid or Christian."

Niall had the look of a man who'd swallowed something bitter. "If you are to stay at Aileach—"

"You wish me to stay only for Deirdre. And when the child comes, then you will send me away." Grania shook her head. "I've had enough of your misery, O'Neill. You were right; this foolish match of ours was a mistake."

"But Deirdre's babe . . ."

"The babe will be fine with or without me. I will make sure Deirdre knows before I leave."

Grania stood waiting, but he didn't move. Whatever had made the babe, Deirdre believed she'd lose it if Grania left her. So he had to make her stay—and apparently had to make her believe it was he, not just his sister, who needed her.

"I want you to stay at Aileach. Not for Deirdre. For me. Please."

Grania's eyes flinched with distrust. Niall stepped close, and when he saw Grania shiver he wrapped his arms around her. He tried to detach himself, to think only of his promise to Deirdre, but his eyes slid involuntarily to Grania's gel linen chemise. The nightdress was gauze thin, and the outlines of her dark nipples were too easy to see; Grania saw him watching and lifted up the *leine* to shield herself, her eyes swimming with a strange mix of emotion.

"I know it's been difficult for you, that I've been—"

"Please . . ." She tried to pull back, but Niall wouldn't release her. He tilted her face up; it was like a pearl under her dark helix of hair.

"Stay with me. Please."

Grania gasped softly as Niall lifted her off the floor and laid her on the pallet. She knew she should resist him, at least make some token, prideful effort to keep him at bay; yet her hands let him pull loose the *leine* from her breasts.

Niall tossed the dress aside and unhooked his sword's sheath, then let the weapon clatter to the floor. His eyes riveted on Grania, he peeled off his own *leine* and leggings. And all the while Grania waited, stretched out on the pallet that for months had been cold and lonely—and hers alone.

Niall pulled her underdress over her head and pitched it sideways. Grania's breath shuddered as he slid toward her.

Niall watched her, hypnotized. She was so blindingly beautiful. He had the sense he hadn't looked at her—really looked at her—before this.

His hands came to rest on the crest of her hips, then circled over her, pressing her flesh from hipbone to hipbone, slowing on each pass over her womb as if that were where her magic hid.

As his fingers crept higher, Grania gasped softly. Niall traced the base of her breasts, and she let out a soft moan as he took each nipple in his mouth, sucking gently until she arched her head back.

Her fingers wound through his hair; her spine tingled with delight. Their lovemaking in the Druid clearing had seized them like a wild, fitful thing. But this coupling was slow and lush, like a taste of aged wine.

Grania lifted Niall's head off her breast; she wanted to see his golden face. The firelight gilded his brown skin and lit his blue eyes like stars; they mirrored her own desire for him.

His belly was warm and hard as he lay next to her. He slid his hand down her stomach, and with maddening slowness, his fingers made slow circles around Grania's core.

She lifted her hips up, but still he denied her; his hand poised on her soft thatch of hair, teasing her to an exquisite ache.

"Have you bewitched me?" He pressed a kiss to her earlobe.

She writhed against him as his finger brushed over her, teasing and making her wetter. "I made no charm." Her voice was ragged.

"Liar." He slipped a finger inside her as his mouth covered hers with a hard, grinding kiss. Grania arched up to meet him. Again his hand and mouth withdrew.

"Please," she gasped. She'd make any promise, deed him anything. He was a fool to fear her; it was she who was his slave.

His eyes clouded with languor as Grania moaned, spreading her legs beneath him. Niall straddled her knees and squared her head. Then he took her lower lip gently between his teeth, drawing Grania's mouth into a soft, then a hard kiss. She let his tongue explore her, mimicking him shamelessly. When Niall bore down so hard she couldn't breathe, Grania literally took her breath from him.

Making love in the fire circle had been a smooth, edgeless blur. Now each jagged, brilliant detail was wonderfully new. As the magic lived and breathed, it filled them both every time Niall entered her. Each time he withdrew, it pulled him back inside her, melding their flesh until Grania couldn't tell Niall's hands or legs or mouth from her own. This was the finest witchery, him driving into her, lifting her up until they were weightless, until they flew.

Then, like a flawless note falling to silence, they lay still and warm, wrapped together under the sound of their breathing. Whatever came tomorrow, Grania could bear it. Niall would stay with her tonight.

CHAPTER
11

Grania woke a thousand times throughout the night. And each time she was wonderfully aware of Niall's warm nakedness lying next to her. Even in the darkness she struggled to open her eyes to see his strong, beautiful face, to listen for the sound of his breath swelling under her. She wanted to memorize the musky smell of his tanned, muscled arms and the feel of his hair curling softly across his chest.

She wanted to remember every exquisite detail so the glorious moment would never escape her because she feared, when morning came, nothing would have changed between them. Niall had made love to her once before, yet she recalled all too well how that passion had cooled. What hope could she have that this time would be different? It was nearly dawn; soon he would wake up—and leave.

Shafts of sunlight filtered in from the window, lighting Niall's brown hair to a golden hue. Grania's ear lay over his thudding heart and her fingers splayed across the soft matting of hair on his chest. The dye markings of the moon-scar from the Druid ceremony had long since been scrubbed to extinction, but the subtle tracings of the knife still remained. Grania's fingers followed the contours. She was pleased to know this part of her, at least, would stay with him.

He shifted underneath her with a satisfied sigh, and Grania lifted her hand, sure he would open his eyes and push her away. Niall caught her hand midair; he pressed it back to his chest.

Grania twisted to look at him, still waiting to hear him clear his throat nervously as he bolted out of the bed with some awkward explanation. But instead he tilted his head back and raised her face up to him. Then he smiled at her —smiled! Grania's heart filled with joy.

"We have been enemies long enough, I think." It wasn't exactly what Niall had meant to say—the words sounded so calculated, like a offer extended to an adversary in war —but he was new at making amends, and it was the best he could manage.

Their joining last night had stormed him like a sweet, furious dream. He'd gone to the *grianan* meaning only to fulfill his promise to Deirdre and make Grania stay; but she had stayed for him, not his sister, and oddly, that pleased him. This morning was a surprise, too—he'd expected to feel more regret for this twisted arrangement of limbs and torsos.

Grania could fire his passion—he had known that for a long time. What he hadn't known, until today, was that she could stir his heart, too. How could he find the strength to hate her when she was willing to risk so much to help Deirdre?

Remembering how badly he'd treated Grania shamed him. He hadn't meant to be cruel; it was only that he hadn't wanted a wife, much less a Druidess. And yet he had both. At least until Deirdre's babe came.

He cradled Grania's small head against his chest and listened to her soft, whispering breath. He smelled her dark, cool hair, and for the first time, he chose not to fight against what he felt for her. Instead he surrendered, wondering if keeping Grania while they waited for Deirdre's babe would not be so arduous after all.

Grania lay still for a time, making no answer to Niall's offer of peace.

"Are you sorry . . . about last night?" he asked.

She scrunched the bed covers over her breasts as she sat up, facing him with large, disbelieving eyes. Niall still might send her back to Uisneath after the baby came. But she didn't care. If this were all her husband could give her, it would be enough. And maybe, by the time the babe was birthed, it would be enough for Niall, too.

"No, I'm not sorry," she said, shaking her head. "And you?"

Niall invited her back down under the covers with an open hand. Their past joining had been a furtive midnight coupling, as if their lovemaking would not withstand the scrutiny of the light. But this request for her was made boldly, in sunlight. Grania snuggled down against Niall's chest, sighing as she felt him kiss her head. She turned to him and he lowered his mouth to hers. He kissed her gently at first, almost kindly, then with kindling passion. Sun streamed like golden ribbons all around them, and as Niall pulled her body close against his, as Grania listened to his breath quicken as he touched her, she began to hope, for the first time in months, that her fate was improving.

Grania tipped her face up to the bright autumn sky. She felt as light-headed as the clouds that drifted itinerately above her. She could still hardly believe last night and this morning hadn't been a delicious dream. But it was true; Niall had forgiven her. He'd made love to her. And if her husband's passion for her was driven by duty to Deirdre, not love for her, at least this time it wasn't driven by magic.

Things were stilted between them, but Grania hardly expected their uneasiness with each other to disappear instantly. Only last night had they become truly wedded. The day-to-day business of marriage would become easier in time.

Niall had promised her she could watch sword practice on the lawn this afternoon. This morning he had business with Baetan. Grania was glad of it; she wanted to sort through all that had happened, to learn to believe in it. She shifted the cache of apples she'd salted into the skirt of her *leine* and imagined what the coming months might bring. When the weather warmed, she and Niall would share fruit and wine in the fields. They would walk, hand in hand, lie down in the sedge grass and let its softness wash over them as they made love.

Eithne's growl jolted her out of her reverie. She shushed the wolf and spun around into Ossian's cheesy white face. He looked even more skeletal than the last time she'd seen him. "My lady." Ossian scraped a rigid kiss down her cheek. "Your wolf thinks me her foe."

"She is a dumb beast," Grania said, thinking she'd trust any animal over him. "I thought you were still at Derry."

"Business bids me back to Aileach." His face slid into a greasy smile. "Have you word from your family? I had hoped to meet them—since they were unable to attend your wedding."

"My father is old and the journey from Raphoe too vigorous for his frail health." Raphoe. A father who worked as a brazier. Grania tried to remember all the lies she'd told.

"Raphoe." Ossian drew out the word. "Only last week I attended to a tithe there."

Grania's pulse quickened. As if he knew it, Ossian smiled at her.

"Let's put an end to this foolish game." His face steeled as his eyes dropped to her breast. He had seen the moonscar. He *knew*. All the color slid from Grania's cheeks.

"Lady," he purred, "you lie."

"What is it you accuse me of?"

Ossian's upper lip twitched. "We both know the meaning of the mark on your breast."

"My husband would be displeased to hear you speak so impertinently to me. Shall we call him? Then you can take up whatever grievance you have properly." Grania began back toward Aileach, but Ossian grabbed her wrist and spun her to face him.

"We both know." His voice was flat and cold. "You don't belong here."

"I do," Grania proclaimed boldly, only today, for the first time, believing it.

"A Druidess . . . married to Connor's heir? The high king would be most displeased."

There was no point in trying to marshal a lie. All Grania could do was tell the truth and hope Ossian had some shred of mercy in him. She doubted it. "I mean you no harm, priest. What blood runs through me is none of my doing. Is it not enough that I follow your God, that I abide by your O'Neill ways?"

"You twist Niall's ear with your lies. You work your witchery on him. And his sister."

"What has Deirdre to do with this?" She tried to stay calm.

"Indeed? There is word she is with child."

"If that is true, then I am pleased for her."

"As you should be—since your dark arts made the babe."

The priest had to be bluffing; Grania tried to believe it. "Whatever my past, I have forsworn all witchery here. You have no reason to think otherwise."

"I have well-placed eyes and ears that shame your lies. You cannot disclaim your hand in making Deirdre's babe. And when Connor learns of it, your marriage will be finished."

"Why do you persecute me?"

"My fight is not with you, *pitag*, but with your faith. My church and I are still young in Inisfail. I can allow no challenge to our future here."

"I steal nothing from you."

"Your presence is thief enough. If you value your life . . . and your father's, you'll pack to leave."

Grania realized there would be no clemency. She'd have to meet Ossian's threats in kind.

"If you value your life, priest, you'll not question the honor of your prince's wife. Niall could claim your wild tales to be greed-driven lies. And Connor would not be pleased to have you impugn Niall's honesty." Grania stormed back toward Aileach as Ossian stood openmouthed at her audacity. But her bold words belied the fear that was making her shake from head to toe.

"The babe quickens." Deirdre clutched her hand over her belly, which was just beginning to swell. It was no less than a miracle; after nine barren years with Baetan, suddenly a winter child danced within her.

The tiny flutterings had stirred her womb for almost a full moon; the baby kicked and spun like a top against the press of her palm, stilling Deirdre's incredulity with every insistent movement.

"Quickly." Deirdre's eyes deepened to sea blue as she pried Grania's fingers off the distaff and hurriedly unfurled them over her abdomen.

The trickster babe stilled and the women waited. Then the whisper of a movement stirred again, as gentle as the beat of a butterfly's wing. Grania's smile mirrored Deirdre's.

"How can I thank you?" Deirdre's eyes shimmered with gratitude.

Grania gave a soft shake of her head, deciding yet again not to protest the belief Deirdre clung to. She stretched out the filaments of the bone-colored fleece and with speeding, dexterous passes wound the threads around her spindle's thickening waist.

"Has the magic made me Druid?" Deirdre clutched her hand to her chest, pretending distress.

"No more than I am Christian." Grania's muted laugh faded. She'd become expert at mimicking the O'Neill ways. She was careful to invoke the name of the Lord at any mention of magic and crossed herself whenever a cold wind blew. She even wore a tiny crucifix that Deirdre had given her.

In some ways the pretense had gotten simpler, and Grania might even have let herself breathe easier had it not been for Ossian. He'd been gone a full month to Derry, but his threats still haunted her. She had to believe that he wouldn't expose her, that she'd managed to silence him.

But she was more than uneasy. Now, for the first time, she had something of value to lose. Niall had opened to her, finally made her part of his life. Nothing could be allowed to jeopardize her happiness—even if it meant she must keep Ossian's accusations secret. What passed between her and Niall was so new, so fragile; she wasn't sure it could bear any strain. For now she would keep her peace—and pray that Ossian would do the same.

"Do you miss it?"

"Hmmm?" Grania raised her drifting eyes to Deirdre.

"Uisneath. Is it very different from Aileach?"

Grania had to think hard to explain it. Uisneath *was* very different, but not in the way a crannog hut differed from a stone fort. "There is no talk of swords or wars there. It is faith, not the promise of battle, that sustains us. Faith that conjures the mists that protect us." Grania did miss Uisneath. For all her newfound happiness here, the tides of the old blood ran through her still.

"And yet you feared the mists were not strong enough —wasn't it fear that sent you to Niall?"

"It was . . . duty. Though it seems odd to me now that I thought Niall would shelter us. Perhaps it was *I* who was meant to help *him*. When he sleeps, dreams crease his brow. His eyes tighten as if he is gauging an opponent's strength, and he mouths the O'Neill battle cry. The fight with Fergus torments him. Perhaps we are fated so I can bring him peace."

Grania realized the notion sounded bold and ridiculous. Who was she to change the O'Neill's warring ways? But what other purpose could she have here?

"Niall will not change, Grania, even for you."

Grania pictured him, sword in his hand, begging a death fight. Deirdre saw the fear in her vacant eyes.

"If you loved him a little less—it would not be so painful . . . were he to die."

"Deirdre—Niall is your brother. And Baetan his champion. Your husband too must stand in any O'Neill fight."

"Yes, and the fear wears all the rougher if you make no peace with it. Niall and Baetan carry on, as their fathers

did, as their sons will." Deirdre laid her hand on her womb.
"It is our task to wave and smile as our hearts break watching our men leave the rath gate. And to succor them when they crawl home from the battlefield. You cannot ask Niall to be less than he is," Deirdre said.

Grania sighed. "I stare out the window, wondering when Connor will bid Niall to carry his war banner. I see my husband cudgeling on the green with his cattle lords, and the scene decays to a bleeding dream—Niall, crushed under horses' hooves, a meal for carrion in some nameless field. How can I bear to lose him?"

Both women's eyes glistened with tears. Deirdre pushed up, looking determined to muster a happier mood. She plucked a mirror from the side stand and plumped a sagging plait of hair with well-practiced stoicism. "We should talk of life," she said, patting her belly, "not death. How will this one grow, I wonder . . . herald or chieftain? Perhaps he'll choose the cloister. There's a sweet, safe fate—mother to a priest."

"Mother to a dog," Grania mumbled, quickly sorry she hadn't censored herself. "I didn't mean to offend you. I know your faith gives you peace."

"You shouldn't let Ossian frighten you. He's only a sour old man."

Grania couldn't tell Deirdre the truth, not without risking that she'd confide it to Niall. "Ossian is . . . different from other men I have met here. But what matter of him? He's gone now." She tried to be cheerful. "Back to Derry."

"Derry?" Deirdre shook her head as she reset the gold *flesc* that encircled her brow. "Ossian passed through Aileach yesterday. He's gone to see Connor at Fort of the Shields."

Grania's distaff slipped out of her hand and rolled across the uneven floor. All her morning's work unwound.

* * *

· Grania paused on the *grianan* stairs as she stared up at Niall. He gazed out over Aileach's battlement, squinting in the crisp winter wind. He looked like a bolt of sun with his golden brown hair and his bright red *bratta*. He stared out at the Great Wood that was a green blotch near the blue lake to the west. Grania had never felt more hopeful of his feelings for her; but she had come to tell him she was leaving. Ossian had gone to tell Connor she was a witch— and that meant she couldn't stay.

Niall turned to face her. The wind drew Grania's black hair up in swirling ribbons and her face looked calm in the midst of the confusion. She needed no magic to bewitch him; her flesh and bone could do it easily.

He'd broken his bargain to keep Grania only for Deirdre. For it was not his sister but himself he had been thinking of. The dark little Druidess had filled his bed and his heart and brought him to a notion that would have seemed impossible only a short month past: he wanted to keep her as his wife.

He reached out to her, and Grania took his hand, stepping up to stand next to him. They stared out silently over the parapet. The high view took in marsh and forest land, mountains and farm plains. Grania could see the ocean from here, and the monks' compound at Derry.

She shivered. Niall tried to draw her under the folds of his cloak, but Grania refused him. "You've a strange mood today," he said. He tipped Grania's chin up, but she looked away, sure she could not speak while she was facing him.

"I'm going back to Uisneath." Tears began in her chest and welled upward.

Niall stared at her silently, his eyes flinching in confusion. "If you miss Maeve, I'll have her brought here."

Grania waved her hand to dismiss the notion. When she

looked up she could see Niall knew she'd come to speak of something more serious.

"Ossian's gone to tell Connor about me."

Niall took Grania by the shoulders and pulled her close. "You've been talking to Deirdre," he said, clucking.

Grania pulled back, wide-eyed. "Then you knew he'd gone?"

Niall shrugged. "There's no need to fear him. We'll go to Connor and explain. It's time your father knew, too. I've had the chariot readied—we'll leave on the morrow."

"No," Grania blurted, starting to cry. "The priest knows I'm a Druidess. He knows I worked the charm for Deirdre." She clutched at Niall's arms, her head sinking as she squeezed her eyes closed.

"But the charm failed. Deirdre's child came from Baetan."

"Even if Ossian believed it, do you think it would matter? He'll condemn me for trying. I cannot stay," she said. "I don't belong here." Grania whirled away from him.

Niall pulled her back gently, pressing a slow, soft kiss on the top of her head. "Shhh . . . it's nothing, love. Nothing. Connor will forgive me."

He didn't understand, she thought. Even if Connor believed she'd worked no magic, she would have to commit to a lifetime of pretending, a life of grueling scrutiny under priests' watchful eyes. Then there was Brian. Whatever Grania felt for him, he didn't deserve to be dragged into her deceit.

"Connor will forgive me," Niall repeated as if that settled it.

Grania's eyes were brimming with tears. "Forgive you —*for me.*" There it was, the unspoken thing that lay cold and insistent between them: the fact that Niall could not accept her as she came to him. He would love her if she were O'Neill, if she pretended to his Christian ways. She was forbidden to be herself; and if she were to belong, it would ultimately be only because she played a charade.

Niall tried again to assure her. "You've done well . . . if you forswear any more druidhect . . ." Grania stared up at him with desperate, glistening eyes. "I am heir to the O'Neill kingship," he said, his head slowly shaking. "You know I cannot keep you if you claim the Druid ways."

Grania had struggled to deny their deep differences, to ignore Niall's intolerance for the blood she could not change. But Ossian had exposed her self-deceit. "I am what I am." She'd stopped crying; her eyes were hard and clear.

"As I am," Niall said.

"So I must go."

Niall looked as if she'd struck him hard. "Is this the limits of your . . . feelings for me?"

"It is because I care," she said, careful to avoid speaking of love, "that I must leave. If I stay, my past will ruin the both of us."

"Ossian's only a priest! I'll take his head if you want it."

"If Ossian falls, another will only rise up in his place. I am not one of you. I never will be," she said slowly.

Niall stared down at her. What Grania saw in his eyes was love—shining, pained love. Her heart felt as though it were being twisted and torn a thousand miserable ways. But still she knew what Niall felt for her was a delusion. Her husband loved a woman she could not be. Grania parted the folds of her *leine* to expose her moonscar.

"I had thought . . . you would stay with me," he offered softly, as if it were his last defense.

Grania recoiled from his outstretched hand.

"I want you with me."

"I don't belong here," she said, turning her eyes away.

Niall's face waxed darker, edging toward anger. Had he come to trust her only to have her betray him? If she would not stay for him, she would at least stay for Deirdre.

"I forbid you to go."

"You speak like a jailer, not as my husband."

"If you will not let me husband you, then it's jailer I'll be. I mean to keep you at Aileach."

"Do you plan to chain me?"

A pall limned the stark planes of Niall's face. "Yes," he answered deliberately. "If that's how you'll have it." Before she could speak, he snatched up her wrist and dragged her toward the *grianan* at a punishing pace. He pushed her inside and slammed the door. Grania heard the lock click into place.

She sat down, holding her head, stunned. Then, as the reality of the nightmare set in, she began to cry. Everything had gone miserably wrong. But whatever it took, she swore she'd find a way out of Aileach.

CHAPTER
12

For three days Niall held Grania prisoner in Aileach's *grianan*. And for three nights he slept elsewhere while she lay alone on her pallet, miserable and terrified. Even Deirdre hadn't been in to see her; Grania could only believe Niall had forbidden her to come. There was only Morgana; lacking any other companion, Grania was grateful even for the broken, accented sound of her shrill voice.

Reaching the decision to leave Aileach had been agonizing. But Niall's decision to imprison her had pushed her anguish to panic. Who could say what Connor would do once Ossian bent his ear? Druids were outlawed in Connor's court; the king would be furious to find a sorceress filling his heir's bed. Grania didn't share Niall's notion of Connor's charity. Every breath she took at Aileach endangered her, her husband, her father.

But Niall was adamantly ignoring the danger. Whatever misguided thinking made him determined to hold her—

O'Neill pride or fear for Deirdre or even his affection for her—Grania knew her husband nursed no thoughts of setting her free.

Their differences, which had seemed so insurmountable when she'd first come to Aileach, had now all but dissolved in Niall's mind, even as they rose, renewed, in her own. But Grania realized no pretense would make them vanish.

She was past tears. Her misery vented in a constant, dull headache. She'd eaten only enough to sustain a bird, and with no hope of relief from the claustrophobic *grianan*, whose walls seemed slowly to engulf her, Grania soon surrendered all interest in her appearance. Her gold jewelry lay discarded on the couch cushions, and she wore the same *leine* day after day, ignoring the freshly laundered dresses Morgana brought in for her. Even her hair was uncombed and dirty; she didn't care.

From the *grianan* window she could see Niall, practicing swordplay on the lawn below, his eyes always holding fast to his blade, careful never to stray toward her. His broadsword sliced the air with battle force, and Grania didn't doubt she was the cause of it.

He wouldn't come to her. What point would there be? He knew her heart wouldn't change. Even if she chose to plead it had, he was past believing her. He'd think it was a trick, only a ploy to make him let down his guard so she could get away—and he'd be right.

Grania wet her fingers and plastered back a loose strand of hair as she slumped bonelessly onto her pallet. The light was waning; dinner would come soon. Ever since Niall had locked her here she'd not eaten elsewhere; how she longed for the loud company of the mead hall, for the fresh snap of winter wind on her face. Niall must know how desperately she longed to escape him, to refuse to allow her even a brief moment outside.

"Shhh . . ." Grania jumped up as the door opened; she smiled when she saw Deirdre, who slipped in, finger to her lips. Deirdre eased the latch closed and rushed toward Grania, half picking her up off the bed in a tight, frantic embrace.

"You shouldn't have come. Niall will be furious."

"He's too distracted to know. Are you well?" Grania could see from the slow, worried pass of Deirdre's eyes that her sister-in-law didn't think so. She didn't wonder; she'd never been so disheveled.

"I would be better if I could leave."

"I know." Deirdre gave a slow, sad nod and closed her eyes. She drew Grania to the edge of the pallet. "Is there no way you can stay? If Ossian promised—"

"It's too late. The priest has already gone to Connor. And even if he recanted his claims, it would not alter the Druid blood in me. I can't be the wife your brother needs. You of all people, Deirdre, should know that I've tried."

"You've done well," Deirdre said hopefully.

"I don't belong here."

"Niall loves you." Grania stared back blankly; Deirdre's pronouncement changed nothing. Deirdre reached out, pulling Grania's head close against her. "Are you sure you want to leave?"

"It makes no difference what I want," Grania said, her expression drifting. "I am prisoner."

Deirdre whispered in Grania's ear, "I've a chariot and the brothers Mescan and Matha to drive it. You can leave tonight."

Grania bolted back, her eyes wide, her lips parted in surprise. Sweet, sweet Deirdre. Her heart jumped, longing to agree to the generous offer. But she couldn't risk subjecting Deirdre to Niall's rage.

"Your brother's fury would know no limits."

"He is wrong."

"Right or wrong will not matter to him."

"Niall trusts me too much to accuse me. The men are mine—they won't be missed—and Niall won't think to look for my chariot; I told him the wheel was broken. Mescan and Matha can drive you tonight." She caught Grania's protesting hand. "You'll fly my O'Neill standard. The chariot will be thought Niall's. No one will dare to stop you."

"But if Niall learns that it was you who—"

Deirdre puckered her face. "He'll lock me in my room for a day, and eventually the whole business will fade to memory. If you must go, I mean to help you."

Grania's throat blocked with tears as she clutched Deirdre to her. "How can I thank you?"

Deirdre battled down a swell of emotion, her eyes glistening with tears. "You could stay. I know," she whispered quickly, sure it was a wish that could never be. "Your heart's beleaguered enough already. I won't add to it by begging you. I'll only say, could I have chosen a sister, I'd have chosen you. Will you think me selfish if I say that without you, I worry for my babe?"

Grania pressed her hand to Deirdre's belly. "The babe is safe. I promise you."

Deirdre gave a stiff, stoic nod and pulled a small package from the folds of her *bratta*. "Here. Some jewelry to barter."

"I need no wealth at Uisneath. Nor any finery."

Even as Deirdre smiled, a heartrending cry escaped her. She pressed her head tight to Grania's face.

"Godspeed. Sister."

Grania kissed Deirdre's brow. Aileach held so very much she'd come to love.

* * *

Fergus shuttered his hand over his brow, shading his good eye against the bright dawn. He hadn't moved since sundown yesterday; like all the men of Ulster, he respected the ancient prohibition that forbade him to march at night. But now the sun crept over the hills' gravel spines, and he could move on his fate. It would be a crisp, clear day. A fine day to seize Niall—and trade him to Connor for the Airghialla land.

A goshawk dipped and squawked; the sound made Fergus's ribs swell against the yew slabs he'd packed under his corselet to protect his chest. The bird cry was an auspicious omen. In a single bound, he sprang onto his stallion, Saran. Ten men behind him followed in quick suit.

The warriors were no hired soldiers. They were the *feinnid*—the finest fighting men of Ulster, stouthearted men who drew their breath from the sweet ring of iron on iron, men who would choose a well-delivered sword blow over the soft thighs of a willing woman. These men gambled life for the sublime pleasure of cheating death. They were Fergus's deliverers.

Today's victory would be a sweet answer to Connor's insulting sword. The high king must have been mad to have thought he could frighten Ulster with some magical Druid blade. Fergus had thousands of weapons—all fluxed with Ulster's rage. He had sent Connor's messenger home with the sword and a promise of war. And now, as Fergus had expected, Niall was en route to Fort of the Shields to make war plans with Connor.

The beacon fire announcing Niall's sighting had been lit late last night. It was good news. Swords clattered and poisoned spear tips clicked and *ding*ed. The air choked with lime from the *feinnid*'s shields. Fergus meant to challenge

Niall man to man, but he was ready for whatever treachery might come.

Drumming his shield for his brother was a time-honored challenge. Niall wouldn't refuse him; to do so would be an answer of shame. The O'Neill prince would fight, and when Fergus won he would drag his brother, chained, back to Ulster's capital at Rath Mor. Then he would send word to Connor of his proposed trade.

Although Fergus was ready for full-scale war, kidnapping Niall was a better revenge, for Connor would loose the Airghialla without having even the satisfaction of raising his blade.

Fergus's veins were full of the old power today. He was costumed for a fight but knew he needed no wood vest or leg casings to shield him; the magic of destiny was protection enough.

He drew his sword, Hard Blade, out of its plated sheath. It had been his mistress in Pictland while he suffered in exile, and he had used it to trophy Sweeney's head—to make Connor high king. Today Hard Blade would work its best justice.

"They come, lord!" The herald was breathless with excitement as he called back to Fergus. Leather squeaked and horses neighed. Fergus squinted at the broad stretch of valley below him.

The red-handed banner snaked between two light-splotched hills. Incredibly there was only one chariot. Fergus laughed; it was a strange, careless choice, for Niall to travel such a dangerous road without a party of guards.

He tilted Hard Blade up to the sky. "All for Ulster!" The cry echoed from man to man behind him as Fergus spurred his horse down the hill, bearing down hard on the red banner. Aye, it would be a sweet, bloody day.

* * *

"Down, lady. *Now!*" Mescan wasted no manners on Grania. He yanked her off her chariot seat and shoved her roughly onto the cart's wicker floor. The woolen blanket she'd wrapped her legs with snapped down like a lid on top of her. But before she could catch Eithne, the wolf bounded down from the chariot, her teeth bared and her hackles bristling. Grania huddled silently, a useless, shaking lump of luggage.

Matha heeled his horse to front of the team and felt his heart pump wildly at the breath-stealing sight; it was the banner of Ulster flying toward him, its yellow lion licking the orange sky. Even from a distance he knew the standard. He knew too that the three of them were dangerously outnumbered.

The raiding party swept down with demonic speed, swords drawn and glinting sunlight. Matha set his hand on his sword hilt; he was no seasoned man of war, but he'd promised Deirdre to protect Grania.

The Ulster horses pulled up nearly on top of the chariot, their hooves churning up a cloud of dust. Matha had been an unshaven boy four years ago when Ulster had last fought the O'Neill, but he too had heard of Fergus's grisled eye. Incredibly, here stood Fergus now, the lion of Ulster looking as though he would ride his blade straight through the three of them.

"I am Fergus of Ulster. Where is your lord Niall?" Neither Matha nor Mescan spoke; they both knew anything they said would surely betray Grania. "Well? Has Niall taken to cowering in the trees?" Fergus pitched his eyes to one side of the road, then the other.

"Our lord Niall is not with us." Matha could feel his hand start to shake on the sword hilt.

"I'm no fool, boy." Fergus's good eye tightened. "I see the O'Neill banner. It doesn't fly for raw recruits like the two of you." The brothers stiffened with the insult, but neither moved. "Where's your lord?" Fergus shouted with thinning patience.

"My lord Niall bids my brother, Mescan, and me to the Fort of the Shields. The O'Neill banner flies to give us safe passage." Matha doubted Fergus would believe it, but he could think of nothing else to say.

"We have no cattle," Mescan blurted, hoping foolishly that was what Fergus came seeking.

Fergus hawked and spat, his spittle landing just shy of the chariot's wheel. Eithne growled, lowering her head and sighting her yellow eyes on Fergus, who smiled blithely.

"It's another bull I come seeking. I come to challenge Niall," he called out, again scanning the clearing as if he expected his daring words to bring forth his brother. Fergus whumped his blade against his shield. Lime flew up and drifted in the air.

Matha took a deep breath. "I accept the challenge—on my lord's behalf." He jumped down off his horse and drew his blade from its sheath, squaring its tip on Fergus's face.

A loose, madman's laugh ripped from Fergus. "I don't waste my swing on insolent puppies." He hauled back, his sword edge knocking Matha's weapon loose with shocking ease. The O'Neill fell to the sod with the blow, scuttling backward like a frantic crab.

"Perhaps"—Fergus's voice deepened and darkened—"watching your head fly would bring Niall out of his burrow. Say your prayers, boy."

Matha squeezed his eyes closed, bracing for the slice of bronze on his neck.

"No!" Grania sprang up out of the chariot, her panic overmatching Mescan's efforts to push her back down. She flung the blanket off her shoulders and jumped down, her hair flying, her eyes wide. Eithne bounded alongside her, fur stiff and tail raised. Fergus's mouth curved into a slow, malignant smile.

"Well, what's this cargo?" he drawled.

"Fergus," she said, the memory of him from Tara's plain still too much with her. "Do you ply your trade murdering helpless boys?"

Fergus jumped down and jammed his sword into the ground with such force its blade *ping*ed. He appraised Grania with languid eyes. To her horror, Grania could see that she pleased him. A smile creased his features, then froze when it reached his twisted eye.

His mouth opened, suddenly agape. *"You."* Grania could see the memory dawning on him as his greedy stare scoured her. "I know *you.*"

"And I know your kind," she snapped. His beautiful, damaged face, sculpted with hate, was as haunting as it had been that very first day.

"Tara." Grania's stomach pitched as he spoke the name. "You're the harper's whelp."

"Let us pass." Grania lowered her voice, she hoped authoritatively.

"Where are you traveling under Niall's flag?"

Fergus stepped closer; Grania took a step back. He came close again, and again she retreated, the two of them partners in a dance of aggression and fear. "Are you my brother's mistress?" It was an obvious assumption. She couldn't be his wife—Fergus knew Niall had vowed not to take one. Yet she flew Niall's flag.

"I'm no man's whore!" Grania blurted, stiffening.

Fergus's eye widened on the gold cuff Niall had given Grania to seal their marriage. He took another step closer; this time Grania refused to retreat. She could smell the horse sweat on him. And the more she tried not to look at the maimed eye, the more it drew her. Fergus snatched her wrist up to his face and squeezed her skin until it stung.

"I knew Niall's mother. This was hers." He flashed Grania a smear of large white teeth. "Sweet Jesus, you're my brother's wife!" He tested the words as he spoke them; Grania's eyes confirmed what he'd only been guessing.

Mescan popped out of the cart and lurched toward Fergus, his dagger drawn on the Ulsterman's blind side. A burly trio of *feinnid* warriors subdued him with rough speed.

"Pffft." Fergus threw down Grania's wrist. "Two grim weeks in Niall's swordland. No sleep and cold food—all for a dark little woman."

For just an instant, Grania hoped Fergus might leave her. Then his face brightened, as if a thunderhead of thought were gathering inside him. Either he was going to rape her or abduct her, she wasn't sure which would be worse. Her lungs hitched and shivered, and she couldn't seem catch her breath. She swore she wouldn't faint.

Fergus let his shield drop to the sod as he reached for Grania's face. She shuddered at his cold, slick touch. He glared at her green eyes, wide and frightened as a colt's just before breaking. "Yes," he breathed, "I'd hoped for Niall . . . but you'll do. A woman for the Airghialla. It's a fair trade—one faithless thing for another."

Grania jerked her face loose of him. "Connor will not trade for me." Fergus's questioning eyes bore down on her. She had to make him believe she was useless; it was her only hope Fergus would release her. "I'm not to the king's liking."

"I'll bargain with Niall, then. I imagine he likes you well enough."

Grania's ingenuity had only worsened her predicament; she scrambled, trying to think of another way.

"Niall's cast me out. From his bed," she added for emphasis. "Why else would I be traveling like this—" She pitched her head back toward the chariot. "What man would send his wife out protected by only two callow boys?"

Her argument looked to be gaining ground. Fergus's eyes raked down her, adding to the weighty stare of his men, whom she sensed were silently undressing her.

Fergus laughed loudly. "Two boys and half a woman flying the O'Neill heir's flag. Strange indeed. . . . But *this* much I know: However you left my brother—in love or anger—he'll want you back when he learns you're at Rath Mor."

Rath Mor. Grania remembered the name; Niall had spoken of it, this place that was Fergus's fortress in Ulster. Her mouth went dry.

"I won't go." Whatever Fergus had in mind for her could only be worse there.

Fergus's brows rose in surprise. "What a plucky little thing. Do you think you have a choice?"

"I'm not going." Grania threaded her arms over her chest and glared at him. Better to take his blade here, before Fergus and his men had a chance to . . . She shuddered again.

"It would be a small matter to dispatch you," he said, shrugging, "but the O'Neill boys . . ." He turned toward Matha and Mescan. "I shouldn't think you'd wish *them* dead, too."

"Lady, have no worry for us. We are sworn to Deirdre." Matha's whisper trailed off as he realized he'd betrayed them.

"Deirdre?" Fergus's tense face loosened as his white eye drew into an uneven seam. "Can it be you've fled my brother's bed?" Fergus trailed his fingernail down Grania's pale cheek. She drew her shoulder up to her ear and shivered. "Was Niall's hand too rough for you, little one?"

If she'd thought about it at all, Grania never would have had the nerve. But her hand flew up of its own accord, clenching into a tight, furious fist. She struck Fergus squarely and hard right in the mouth. He barely even flinched—only rubbed his jaw and stared back at her as if he were well used to being hit. Grania braced herself; surely he'd return the blow. But Fergus lowered his hand to his side.

"So you love Niall after all. Well, little raven, you needn't fear me. I've no inkling to taste my brother's spoils. Not tonight, anyway." He let out a smug laugh. "You can tell me the rest of your sad tale later. For now, we're back to Rath Mor."

Grania would rather die than go with him. But Matha and Mescan had risked their lives for her. She couldn't repay their selflessness with Fergus's blade.

With a snap of his *bratta*, Fergus sprang onto Saran. He reached a hand down to Grania, but she refused him, glancing back at the chariot. "Oh, no, pet. *That* stays here. I shouldn't like to have your husband following that snail of a cart."

Grania pulled Eithne, who had kept up a low growl, close to her. "I'll go. But I'm walking."

"As you wish," Fergus said, smirking. "But it's four days to Rath Mor. And from the look of the sky, it's going to rain."

From the smell of the air, Grania could tell he was right. As if things weren't bad enough already, she'd have to negotiate the long road in mud. She was already tired; she and the O'Neill brothers had ridden all night to get clear of Aileach. Fergus's offer of a ride was tempting; but he couldn't be trusted. Grania shook her head and set her eyes on the road stretching in front of them.

His sword tip caught her quivering chin. "Don't look so frightened, little thing. I too have my honor. Besides, if I'd wanted you, I would have taken you by now." Fergus clucked to Saran as his *feinnid*, swords clattering, dragged Matha and Mescan up behind. "Perhaps you'll learn to like Rath Mor," he said lowly.

"Never."

"Well then, think of this. By taking Niall's place there, you may well save his worthless life."

CHAPTER
13

Grania could endure worse than this before she'd sweeten Fergus's galling smile with a complaint. She tried not to think how much her feet swelled from the sod's rocky attack on her thin goatskin slippers. Or how viciously the wind cut across her neck and cheeks. Or that her calves burned from Fergus's pounding pace. She set her mind on one thing only: she wouldn't give him the pleasure of protesting.

For three days he'd pushed them, dawn to darkness with no respite except for cold, gobbled meals and short snatches of sleep. If Fergus hadn't been forbidden to travel at night, Grania imagined he would have driven them constantly.

Each morning's spare ritual was always the same: no fire, for fear it would call attention, just stale barley bread and a quick flitch of bacon. Rowan berries lined the road, but Fergus wouldn't allow Grania time to stop and pick them. She snagged what she could on the run, but her bloodied fingers got more thorns than fruit.

For the first two days, Grania refused the briny pork the Ulstermen were unimaginably fond of. But the stiff pace of the march soon gnawed at her strength. Fearing if she faltered Fergus would force her to ride behind him, she made an effort on the third day to eat some of the brackish meat.

She managed two swallows before she spit out the last bite and wiped her drooling mouth on the dirty sleeve of her *leine*. If Fergus saw her, he had the surprising decency to hold his peace. If she had to eat this bile, she resolved she'd do better with smaller portions.

She trudged along behind Saran, watching the back of Fergus's *bratta* sway with the horse's swagger. The cloak looked like a miniature of his *feinnid*'s banner—all shining yellow and sea green silk, its edges thick with gold fringe. Fergus's rich dress surprised her; Grania expected his garb to match his dark, brooding face.

The road east to Rath Mor wound past farms and smoking villages full of field workers and barking dogs. As prince, Fergus would have been entitled to a rich hosting at any cottage, and the thought of a hot meal and a real bed nearly made Grania's brain ache. But there was no hope of stopping.

Not that where she slept mattered, anyway. When the war party finally pulled to a halt each night, she barely had the strength to find a flat place for her head before she collapsed and nodded off. And it seemed that no sooner did she tumble into deep, dreamless sleep than she was routed by the rude sounds of morning: the jangling of horses' halters and the scrape of gold girdles against the *feinnid*'s bronze sword sheaths.

Pain shot up Grania's calf from the foot of her left leg. She doubled over, twisting her sole up as she plucked out a small, sharp pebble. She pitched the stone with all the anger she'd pent up for Fergus and limped on, dreaming of Deirdre's chariot like a beggar would fresh bread.

When Fergus had insisted on leaving the cart, Grania had assumed it was only because it was too slow. But now, looking at the narrow trail, she realized the chariot wouldn't have made the journey at any speed. There was no real road to speak of between Aileach and Rath Mor—only a rucked cattle path that was so narrow even a mule laden with wicker creels would have scraped its sides on the trail's hedge walls. A chariot would have been hopelessly wide. The thorny path bore witness to what Grania already knew: that Aileach and Rath Mor needed no roads between them. Whatever business they had was settled with swords, not commerce.

Another stone bit into Grania's heel. She scuffed it free, thinking she was at least getting more inured to the pain. Her toes were nearly numb from the constant marching, and she was tired to tears. She wiped her cheeks with the backs of her hands, then smeared the dusty paste onto the skirt of her *leine*.

Eithne trotted alongside her. Grania imagined the wolf's poor paws stung like her own feet. But, like her mistress, Eithne refused to whine.

Grania could make out only scraps of the *feinnid*'s strange dialect, but understanding their meaning was miserably easy. Every time she looked backward there were rude gibes, followed by a low chorus of hoots and laughter. Grania braced herself for another blast of comments as she turned, trying, as she had before that day, to catch a glimpse of Matha or Mescan. But all she could see were marching *feinnid*, all leering, all grinning.

Each night when they stopped, Fergus sequestered Grania away from the others. That he'd specifically forbidden her to talk with the O'Neill brothers was a particular hardship; Grania was much in their debt, and she was sure Matha and

Mescan were as tired and dejected as she was. The hapless, loyal boys; they too had gotten more than they'd bargained for. She prayed Fergus would let them go, even if he kept her.

The path disgorged into a wide belt of open land more barren than yesterday's rough terrain. The noon sun shined its black basalt, and as Grania had once missed Uisneath, now she was homesick for the smooth elegance of Aileach. She missed its green ribbons of fields, the tangy scent of its forest stands. Ulster, with its naked horizon, smelled only of wind and sea salt.

Fergus pulled up Saran as he waited for Grania. She slowed, hoping that he'd leave her be. But he slowed to match her. She could hardly imagine that he wished to speak; since the day he'd hostaged her, Fergus had been as still as a stone.

Grania glanced up furtively, as she did whenever she thought Fergus was distracted enough not to notice her looking—whenever he studied the sky or rifled his wallet for morning rations. She thought maybe, if she observed him carefully, he might drop his guard, might inadvertently clue her on how to escape him. But he offered up nothing but his haunting, silent, unsettling face.

Niall had said Fergus was only twenty-two. But years of soldiering on the harsh eastern coast had weathered his dusky skin to ruddy splotches, and his eyes, one ghostly white, the other black as a night storm, looked as icy as the winter sea.

His hair was blue black; loose, jet curls fringed his low brow and high cheeks. His features were haphazard, though handsomely arranged, if she could manage to overlook the withered eye. His face proclaimed his heritage, that of the famous Red Branch knights of Ulster, of his famous ancestor, the great warrior Cuchulain. But bitterness had over-sharpened his heroic look, and his mouth was set in perpetual challenge, shaking what small faith Grania nourished that he might still show her some mercy.

Dermot had told her tales of Ulster. He'd spoken of halls filled with severed heads, where victims stared out shriveleyed, their flesh rotting as the Ulstermen raised cups in celebration. Even the *feinnid*'s weapons were thought to be fearsome. Their spears were said to writhe and twist, their tips so hot that their owners kept cold water nearby to cool their frenzy.

"Tomorrow we reach Rath Mor."

Grania continued to stare at the road ahead. "Niall won't trade for me," she announced, marching forward resolutely.

"We'll see." Fergus laughed loudly. "If you were *my* wife, I'd want you back. And quickly." His filthy stare made her feel naked. Every piece of her skin itched and flushed. "However he lost you, Niall's a fool."

Grania's feet froze as her eyes tightened on him. "You're not fit to speak his name." She blushed. Her anger had been an instinctive—and, for Fergus, an instructive—mistake. She struck a faster pace, wanting only to escape him. Fergus clucked Saran up to match her.

"You talk in your sleep."

Grania wheeled her head back, her mouth agape.

"Only Niall's name. Though I'd have liked to hear more."

"You were with me—while I was sleeping. . . ." Grania grabbed her *leine* so tight, her knuckles blanched. The thought of Fergus standing there, leering at her while she slept, made her furious.

"Easy, little raven," he said. "I only brought you a blanket to keep you from shivering." He smiled as Grania straightened her *bratta* and cleared her throat indignantly.

"The warrior who doesn't study his enemy is a fool—or dead. But then you know that, don't you?"

Heat climbed up Grania's face until her ears tingled. Fergus knew she'd been watching him. She swore not to underestimate him again.

"If Connor gives you the Airghialla, will you let Niall be?" Fergus's invidious grin spiked cold terror down her spine. She could see letting her husband go was his last inclination. "Murder is all you know, isn't it?" she said, her mouth tightening.

"I want the Airghialla," he answered calmly. "But if Niall's head rolls with it, I'd not be displeased."

"His head won't bring back your eye."

"This," he said, gouging his finger into the grisled eye, "is a warrior's face. This is Ulster. And as long as I've one good eye left to sight on the O'Neill, I will not stop fighting."

"Then trade me for the land if you can. But let Matha and Mescan go. Please."

"A man's honor is counted by how many hostages he keeps. Matha will be put to work at Rath Mor. Mescan's gone."

"Did you kill him?" Grania braced for Fergus's horrible answer. He only blinked at her, barely suppressing a laugh.

"Kill him? I set him free."

Grania didn't believe that for an instant. She stood on tiptoe, craning her neck over the bobbing heads of the *feinnid*. For the first time that day she could see Matha. Only Matha.

"He'll tell your precious husband what's become of you. Though perhaps the boy will be too ashamed to admit he's lost you. Who can say he won't fashion a lie? Say that you came with me willingly—"

Grania's throat went dry, first with anger, then fear. She knew Niall would be furious to find she'd escaped him. If, on top of that, he thought—No, she dismissed the unsettling notion. Mescan would tell the truth. A lie would not serve him.

"My husband will refuse to trade if he thinks I've betrayed him. I doubt you sent Mescan back without counsel."

"Well," Fergus said, winking his good eye at her, "at least you've a brain in that pretty head."

Grania could only hope whatever attraction Fergus had for her might be massaged into a favor. "Please, let Matha go, too." If she could persuade Fergus to free him, she could be mistress of her own fate; and there'd be no mistaking the choice she would make. She was ready to die—if it meant keeping Niall clear of Fergus. "He's no better than a frightened boy. . . ."

Fergus's hand shot up, his fingers twisting into *ogham*, the Druid hand language. The gesture meant no; Grania startled visibly.

"I thought so. You've the look of the druidhect clinging all over you."

"Druidhe . . . I don't know the word."

Fergus clucked his tongue. "Shall we waste time playing this foolish game?"

"You can't believe Niall would wed a *pitag*."

"I believe my brother is full of surprises. And I understand why Connor would be displeased with you."

"Then tell him. If it's Niall's dishonor you seek, tattle your tales to the high king. Let that be the justice you seek."

"I've no mind for that—yet," Fergus drawled, smiling. "I'd see Niall ride to your rescue first. After that, we'll watch him plead to Connor that you mean nothing to him."

"If you think me Druid, then you must know I have powers." It was a bluff: Grania's last defense. She tried to look threatening. "I could raise boils on your face or madden your mind with a fluttering wisp."

Fergus stretched out his arms, taunting her with a feigned surrender.

Grania's fists shook with impotent fury. Fergus was confident she couldn't harm him; and he was right. Sorcerers could charm a man to madness or death, but not Grania. She spun away, sputtering as she heard him laugh.

"I don't doubt for a moment you've great magic within you. But not yet, little raven. And until you find it, you're all mine."

"Stay where you are, *pitag*!" The guard shoved the food tray through the souterrain's pursed opening, then hopped quickly out of the underground cave. Even in the gloaming light Grania could see him rubbing his hands on his trouser legs, looking as scared as a flushed hare. He thought her witchery could injure him; she wished it could.

She plucked the honey cake off the oak tray and stored it in her pocket for later. She certainly had no appetite now and didn't imagine she'd find one as long as she was prisoner in this dank subterranean cave.

She pushed the small bowl of milky stirabout up to Eithne's nose, watching the wolf take in the porridge with loud, grateful laps. At least the bleak meal wasn't completely wasted.

Grania plunked herself down on the clammy sod, hugging her knees in an attempt to warm herself. She'd only been here half a day, but already her breath choked inside the cloying earthen cell. The air was stale and it was getting dark, making the cave feel as though it were shrinking in the waning light. There was only one tallow candle sticking out wistfully from a spike on the wall. It only added to the souterrain's strange, twisting shadows.

Rath Mor, what little Grania had seen of it, was a palace compared with the abyss of this place. If it wouldn't have shamed her, she'd have begged Fergus; she'd always been frightened of tiny, dark spaces. But despite her efforts to stay calm, there must have been fear in her eyes. For an instant, before Fergus pushed her inside, she'd seen a glimmer of pity cross his face. But her hope was quickly extinguished. Fergus mumbled something about her magic and gave her a rough shove inside.

Grania was sure the souterrain had an opening in back to match the front door; and she was sure too that Fergus had blocked it. She couldn't see all the way to the rear, but she could tell enough to know the back of the cave channeled into a narrow black crawl space. If she'd been braver, she would have explored it. But to go belly down, guided only by faith into that tight, rocky sheath terrified her. Likely it was a pointless prospect. There was only one way out, and the guard wasn't about to let her slip through it.

The cave wound under a hillock south of Rath Mor. It had obviously been used for both storage and siege. Empty wine puncheons and rusted meat hooks lay abandoned against the wall, and a huge wooden plug of a door, cut to fit the arched opening, lay propped free of its hinges. Grania cheered herself with small assurances: at least at the front, the souterrain was tall enough for her to stand without hunching. And the walls were buttressed with huge slabs of basalt, so her jail probably wouldn't collapse on top of her.

But the light was waning, as was the cave's meager heat. The guard, instructing Grania to stand back and lock her hands behind her, apparently so she couldn't seize him with what he assumed to be her potent magic, had built a pitiful one-log fire in the cavern's center. Grania scooted closer to the flames, doubling her skirts under her rump to insulate against the cold clay floor. Eithne sidled up next to her; Grania hoped their two bodies together could create some heat.

The light in the cave dimmed suddenly. Grania jerked in panic toward the opening, thinking the guard planned to drag closed the door. But it was only his fat head, blocking the light from his own fire, which flickered outside. He peeked in, then bolted back out as she looked up at him. The fool was scared. It was all too ludicrous. Even Fergus was scared of her. Scared of a helpless witch.

Grania started to wonder . . . No, she had no herbs, no quicken wood, nothing to work a proper charm. There'd be no drugging this nervous sentinel. If she were going to get out of here, she'd have to . . . She shook her head; it was impossible. Maeve or the Regaine might marshal such druidhect, but her skills were fledgling and at best uneven. The summoning of great magic took strong blood and years of practice. It was a chancy thing; the druidhect could even turn back on the conjurer if it were worked unsurely.

Eithne licked Grania's cheek, her brown eyes urging her on. And slowly, against all reason, Grania felt belief start to grow in her.

She combed over every chant and charm she'd seen or heard; yet she could retrieve only scraps of what she'd need. The ancient rhymes sang in her memory, then drifted away, like a half-forgotten child's refrain. If the spell could be summoned, it was her blood, not her mind, that would have to do the remembering.

Grania rose, shifting her weight to one foot. She cupped her hand over one eye, assuming the proper position for conjuring. Her shoulders rose and fell with deep drafts of breath, pulled up from some place farther down than her lungs, somewhere deep in the earth itself. Almost instantly she felt dizzy. She was making herself sick, that's all.

Grania opened her eyes and sighed. This wasn't going to work. Eithne whined again.

She reconciled herself to one more try. But she couldn't make the charm; her only hope was to let it happen. She breathed . . . and breathed again, until air flowed in and out of her, becoming one great continuous breath. Time trickled around her like a slow winter stream. Grania began the small part of the chant she knew, and to her amazement, the rest bubbled out of her as if it had only been waiting for her silence to find voice.

The tiny fire popped and danced, increasing itself. Its smoke smelled unearthly, like burning stars might. Sparks shot off, then froze like diamonds in the cave's dark air. Wind keened off the flames, whistling as it gusted through her skirts, then swirling like an eddy around the cave's curved walls. It spiraled back to her, doubled in strength, teasing her with fingers that made serpents of her mussed hair.

She stretched out her palms and felt herself sink under the press of magic. Her flesh prickled and itched, and tides roared through her veins. The cavern was reeling, gleaming, pregnant with light. The druidhect filled her.

Grania lifted her hand to rotate it in front of her eyes. Her fingers had no flesh or bone. She reached down and, where Eithne had been, ran her hand through the wolf's thick hair. She felt her—but Eithne, like her mistress, was no more to be seen.

Together they moved toward the cavern door. The guard made almost no note of their passing. Only a slight flinch of his eyes marked that Grania stood next to him. That and a loud sniff, as if he were smelling something he had not noticed before.

He sighed, then resettled his fat frame in the warder's seat. The magic coursing through her made Grania bold;

she bent over, staring. His eyes, straight on her, saw nothing; they were dazed and languid with sleep.

Grania walked through the fort's outer gate, into the sweet, dark freedom of the night. The moon was full, but neither she nor Eithne threw any shadow. She had called up the greatest of magic; she was invisible.

If she'd hadn't been worried about Niall, Grania would have been halfway to Uisneath by now. But Mescan had probably reached Aileach, and knowing her husband as she'd come to in those last weeks, Grania was sure he'd hurry to free her from Rath Mor. She prayed she'd be able to intercept him.

It would be a full day at least before Niall reached Rath Mor. Grania had chosen a hiding place far enough from Fergus's fort to keep safe while close enough to make sure Niall didn't slip past her unnoticed. She hoped.

So far, in her two days squirreled in the oak stand, nothing had gone as she had planned. With no *bratta* to protect her, the north wind drove like a knife through her thin *leine*. And the druidhect had bled every ounce of strength from her. She could barely stand, much less run if she needed to. And at this moment she needed her legs more than anything—because something was stalking her.

The footsteps sounded again, dashing Grania's hopes that she'd only imagined them. The underbrush crackled behind her, vaulting her heart to plug her dry throat. She knew instantly the fire had been a stupid indulgence. It had taken her hours to scrounge for flint and kindling, and now her few moments of warmth had earned her a midnight predator.

Grania listened so hard her ears ached. She shook violently, half-afraid her ribs would rattle out loud. She stood up, plucking a burning log from the fire, unsure she had the muscle to wield it.

More footsteps came. It couldn't be Niall—it was too soon. And Fergus wouldn't stalk her at night. It had to be a cougar. Grania remembered the deep, ripping gouges that had marked Niall's thigh, and she shuddered, imagining the same on her face.

The log's flaming tip began to wither; Grania huffed on it and the embers flared briefly, though finally failing. She said a prayer that the cat would kill her quickly.

Eithne trilled a low growl, her tail standing vertically. Grania shushed her, realizing that the cougar would take on Eithne before it turned to her. Her blood thinned to water as she struggled against the incomprehensible urge to lie down and let herself sleep.

But she hadn't come this far to surrender to anything— human or bestial. The crunch came again. Grania spun on her heels, her eyes huge and useless in the moonless night. She couldn't even tell where the sound came from now. Was there more than one cat tracking her?

She crouched down, her legs quivering as she waited to dodge the animal's spring. Nothing came. She needed thicker cover than this lean group of trees. Grania and Eithne backed into the night. She held the barely glowing log in one hand and clutched the skirt of her *leine* with the other, inching backward on her toes and trying to keep the leaves from crackling under her.

She glanced behind and gasped at a squat shadow before she realized it was only a blackthorn bush. She dragged Eithne with her as she hunkered behind it.

The air smelled of horses. Sweet Mother, she'd misjudged; with a bittersweet mix of terror and relief, she realized it wasn't a cougar after all. Fergus wanted her back badly enough to track her in the dark.

Grania plumbed for the magic she'd marshaled in the souterrain, but her concentration was hopelessly scattered.

The footsteps stopped, replaced by a roaring silence. She closed her eyes and braced herself, mouthing one final, hopeless prayer.

Eithne's low growl swelled to a sharp bark. Grania's eyes bolted open on a huge, hulking form that was rushing her. She squinted and blinked, breath squeezing out of her chest as the huge shadow of a sword rose over her head.

"Show yourself." Eithne exploded from the blackthorn bush, her tail wagging furiously. Relief gushed out of Grania as she stood up, her knees wobbling, her eyes hot and unblinking as she stared at Niall.

His sword clanged to the sod as she crumpled forward, her hands covering her face. Grania burst into relieved tears.

The impact of his huge body nearly toppled her. Niall crushed her quaking form to him, peppering her hairline with a spate of kisses.

Instinct blocked memory. Grania forgot why she'd ever thought to leave him. She only remembered how she'd missed his touch, how she'd worried that her decision to flee Aileach would cost him his life.

"Thank God you're safe." Niall's huge arms shook, all the strength that he'd thought to spend on some wild opponent now embracing her. He pushed back for a better look, as if he needed actually to see her to believe she was safe.

Grania could still hardly believe her own eyes. He must have ridden like a windstorm to reach her this quickly. "You shouldn't have come. Fergus meant to trap you." *But he did come*, her heart breathed. Surely there was some way, some place, they could be together. If not Aileach, then Uisneath. She traced Niall's mouth with her fingertips.

"Did Fergus harm you?" His voice caught on the words. Worry stitched his brow tight; Grania knew he feared that Fergus had raped her.

She stroked her hand over the skin of his cheek and smiled up at him. "No. I was kept prisoner in the souterrain."

Niall closed his eyes with a weighty sigh; he knew the place. "Bastard. He's bought himself a slow death for abusing you."

Grania plied her hands softly against his chest. "No— I'm not hurt. And I would have no sword bloodied in my name." She unfurled his fingers on her cheek.

"How is it you're free?"

Grania's smile faded. Her tale of magic would not sit well with him—even if she managed to make him believe it.

She stepped back, shying her face out of the cast of firelight. "I conjured a Druid's charm. The guard didn't see me." She squinted back tentatively, bracing for his inevitable questions.

"You drugged him?"

"I was . . . invisible." The words spilled out of her like a lump of oatmeal. She waited for Niall to scold her or even to laugh, but he did neither; he only stared back, his face frozen in accusation.

"You tempt our fate by working more of your necromancy? If Connor learned how you managed to escape—" The reproach boomed out of him. In the heat of their reunion, she had forgotten their rifts. But Niall's anger resurrected them. Clearly he expected her to go back with him to Aileach—and on his terms.

Fergus had been ready to trophy her husband's head. And might well have, too, if Grania hadn't raised the druidhect to escape. If she hadn't waited, at great risk, to warn her husband. But Niall had no gratitude, only an angry indictment for her disobedience.

"So then . . . nothing has changed between us."

"You are still my wife, if that's what you mean."

Grania felt tears start to rise in her. "You and I have no need of Ossian or Connor to create a breach between us. We are finished before we start, you and I. I won't be someone I'm not meant to be," she said, her voice eerily calm.

Niall's hands balled to fists. "Any other woman would be proud to be wife to a prince of the O'Neill."

"Then find another. Go to Rath Mor. Bang your shield for your brother. I belong at Uisneath."

Niall's shoulders sank down, and Grania could see that her husband would argue no more with her. He stood silent for a long time before he spoke again. "As you wish. But it's too dangerous for you to travel alone. I'll at least see you safely back to Uisneath."

Grania couldn't bear being so close to Niall knowing she'd have to leave him. "I don't want you to."

"It would be a dishonor to me for send you unescorted."

It wasn't Niall's love but his pride that drove him. Always his great O'Neill pride. Grania had no strength left to disagree. She smeared the tears off her cheeks and nodded in resignation. "To Uisneath, then."

Before Grania mounted she turned back, her eyes riveted on him. "Fergus isn't the hellhound you think," she said, remembering his withered eye, thinking if Niall could only forget his own misery, he might see some of what Fergus had suffered, too.

"You dare defend that cur to me? Perhaps your tale of magic is a lie. Did you bribe my brother to release you?"

His expression branded her. He thought she'd whored her way free. Grania wheeled a loud slap across his face. "I too, husband, have my honor."

Niall rubbed his cheek, then set Grania on Murchad. Without so much as a word, he jumped up behind. The gelding trotted off down the darkened road; it was several miles before Niall spoke again. "With fair weather, we'll make Uisneath in two days."

"Press Murchad as you can. The sooner there, the better," she said coldly.

The realization came on Niall slowly, like an ache that becomes a chill, then escalates to a raging fever. But once the notion seized him, it held fast and would not leave. He knew he loved Grania.

He'd tried to believe it was only her sorcery that bound him to her—or maybe merely his duty to Deirdre. He'd even tried to believe it was only lust. But in his heart, he knew better. He loved her—and it was too late.

"We're here." Grania stared at him quizzically. Niall realized why; he'd allowed Murchad to plod on way past where the mists began, past where he might have left Grania safely. Thick fog swirled all around them. He should have known; that damned familiar chill was seizing his spine.

Grania's green eyes were huge, and when Niall said nothing she hesitated before she slid off the horse. Niall wondered if she might not want to stay with him after all. But her behavior the two days past on the road murdered his slim hopes. Grania had slept on the opposite side of the fire from him and spoke to him only when it was unavoidable. Yet he too had been sullen. And still he loved her.

He thumped down after her, reaching out his hand. When Grania ignored it, he stepped closer and tipped her chin up to him.

"Please . . . come to Aileach with me."

Grania's blank eyes refused him. He squinted past her face at the swirling, cloying mists that dripped like batter off the trees. If he would stay—here at Uisneath, if he could manage to make this cold place his home, Grania might still have him. But his heart belonged to Connor, too. And to

Aileach. There were things to be settled there, matters of honor that would not wait. There was no future with Grania as long as he was bound by the shame of his past.

"So . . . we part," he said lowly.

"Aye." Huge tears pooled in Grania's eyes, but they refused to fall. "The wind with you."

Niall nodded silently as he closed his eyes. He loved her. Finally, after all the months of resisting, he knew it. He would not let her leave him unless she knew. He opened his eyes; Grania was gone. Not so much as a dimple in the mist marked the place where she'd stood. For the first time, he had been willing to deed his heart. And Grania had thieved it.

CHAPTER
14

"Again, Father, you let me win." Niall snatched the jeweled chessman off the inlaid board with a quick flick of his wrist. Rocking back on his stool, he rolled the king piece in his palms, making its gold go warm from friction.

Connor had been drawn and disinterested all morning, missing obvious plays. Niall hoped the king was preoccupied with Fergus's war call, but he suspected the cause of his bad mood was worse: that it was Grania.

Niall had been scouting the north for the past month, and he didn't doubt that by now Ossian had bent Connor's ear with tales of his Druid wife. At least ten times today Niall had started to explain the whole twisted mess. And always the words stopped like a fist in his throat.

He'd have to swear that Grania meant nothing to him, for only then would Connor forgive his lie about what he'd bargained to get the blade and forgive his breach of Christian faith in marrying a Druidess.

Niall had denied his feelings for so long; now, in perfect antithesis, he could not escape them. Still he slept on only half of his pallet, as if he expected Grania to lie down next to him. Even in the midst of the boisterous cups hall, as his men drank and cheered, he heard silence, for Grania was not there. And Aileach's parapet had become a place of pain for him; he kept no more vigil there. He could not bear the memories of that last day, of Grania's determined good-bye.

He loved her; now, when she was finally lost to him, he could admit it. But he wouldn't consign his fate to some mist-choked lake. His place was beside Connor, among the O'Neill. To safekeep that legacy, he would lie again, claiming to Connor that marrying Grania was no more than business. In time, with work, he would make truth of his deceit.

Connor heaved himself off the deerskin couch and stared absentmindedly around the *grianan*. His stern mouth coaxed into a terse smile—as much of a smile as Niall hoped to see today.

The sounds of dinner, its midmorning preparations already clanging away in the backhouse, filled the silence. Spencers' knives clicked, bubbling cauldrons splashed and hissed, kitchen maids argued loudly over burned meat and cream accidentally churned to butter.

A cold plate of mutton and dry eggs lay untouched on the side table. Neither Connor nor Niall, each man for his own reasons, had appetite today.

Connor unhooked a leather bottle from its wall peg and poured wine into a tall blue glass. He offered the vessel to Niall without comment. Niall took it, drinking deeply, thinking there was not enough wine in all Inisfail to numb the pain in his heart.

Connor's *grianan*, built for his wife, Lendabair, had been modeled after the one at Tara. With its sunlit, limed walls, it might have offered some cheer; but the king had ordered its brass shutters closed today. Despite that, sun winnowed in through cracks and crevices, and this, too, seemed to irritate Connor.

The king's bolelike legs bought the small room's width in three strides. Connor turned, flattening his hands on the table behind him and leaning his weight back as he closed his eyes with a fatigued sigh. He dragged his huge hand down his black bolt of beard and stared at Niall.

"You secrete your heart from me."

Niall pushed back from the game table and leaned over his thighs. "Ossian has been to see you."

"Is this your love for me, that I should hear more from some priest than my own son?"

"You are right to be angry with me." Niall dropped his chin nearly to his gold neck plate. Any other man could expect harsh, swift justice for lying to the king. But Niall knew Connor would be lenient and that the look on his fosterer's face punished him better than any whip lash.

Connor clamped his hand on Niall's shoulder. "Had I chosen either of my blood sons, Oengus or Lucan, as heir to my kingship, I could not have been more sure of them than I was of you. You, Niall, among all O'Neill, have the fire in your heart. And honor. Even as a smooth-faced boy you raised your sword fairly. I watched your mind's mettle grow to match your body, and I smiled, thinking, *Good. Already the boy has the pith of a king*. But now you sadden me. You have learned to lie."

Niall stood up, meeting Connor's indictment with calm, honest eyes. "I made the match for the sword. Nothing more."

"Could you not have told me?"

"I knew the pairing would displease you. I see now I was wrong, that my waiting displeases you more."

Connor ran his thick fingers through his black thatch of hair. "Then Ossian tells the truth: the woman is indeed a witch."

Niall didn't doubt Ossian had embroidered the tale as it served him. "She carries Druid blood, but she is converted to our ways. Grania worked no magic once she came to Aileach," he said, hoping Ossian had not left Connor with proof to the contrary.

"The priest says Deirdre is finally with child. And that the babe is the doing of your wife's necromancy."

"Ossian lies. Did he tell you too that Grania is the bard Brian's child?" Connor nodded. "Then you must know she is also half O'Neill. That she could not mean to injure her own kind."

"Her ties to Brian mean nothing if she clings to the old ways. Ossian fears she has poisoned you, that she turns you against me."

"I wed her to gain your sword," Niall stated with slow emphasis, his anger heating. How dared Connor distrust him? "Is this all the faith I've earned from you, Father?"

"It is not you, Niall, but the *pitag* who worries me."

"Grania has returned to the Druids at Uisneath. The marriage is no more." Niall hoped the truth would lay the matter to rest; but Connor still pressed him.

"You are divorced, then?"

"Yes," Niall said, resolving to call the brehon when he returned to Aileach and legalize his separation from Grania.

"And she agreed?"

Niall cringed as he thickened his lies. "She wanted cattle. And gold. I paid her handsomely. In exchange, she promised to leave me be. It was a well-made trade, Father. Did I not earn the sword in the bargain?"

"You are truly free of her, then?" Connor cocked a black brow, as if he still could not quite believe.

"Aye, well free." Niall turned away, mustering some business with the wine bag, hoping Connor would not see the deceit that blazed in his eyes. "The priest has a loose tongue," he mumbled angrily.

"Ossian came to me honestly. You come with lies. Who is truly traitor here?" Connor's thick brows fell over his narrowed eyes; Niall knew there would be no more arguing with him.

"I know you meant well," Connor said, his voice finally softening. "You were—misguided." He paused. "There, then." Connor clapped his hands as if the matter were finished and gave Niall a rough *whump* on the back. "There'll be time enough later to find you a wife like my Lendabair—after . . ."

His voice drifted off, but Niall knew what he'd started to say. After *Fergus*. All morning Connor had dodged the dark question of him.

"The Druid sword did not stop Fergus's rage."

"No." Connor's voice was sad and his face was sodden.

"Well? Will we to war, then?" Niall saw what he'd feared in him: that Connor still pined for his lost son.

"Father, I've traveled to Ulster. Rumors of Fergus's insurrection gather like flies on bad meat. He took my wife . . . the Druidess Grania," Niall corrected, trying to sound more impersonal. "He meant to trade her for me. And me for the Airghialla. But she escaped, and now Fergus can do no less than raise his war flags against you. He boasts of Picts and Northumbrians come to stand alongside him. Will we sit helpless, waiting for Fergus's blade in our teeth?"

Connor's head sagged, a storm of emotions buffeting his face. His eyes, smaller and darker for the bright gold blade on his brow, clouded, then flinched. He looked as if all spirit had suddenly oozed out of him.

"You hesitate," Niall said. "Surely you did not think that in sparing Fergus's life you had put an end to his greed? If you'd taken his head—" He stopped, thinking he'd over-stepped his rights.

"You think I am weak."

He did. So too did the great army of the Fena, the soldiers who still wondered why Connor had refused to do what any other king would not have spared a thought on. "I think you love a dangerous man too dearly."

Connor poured a stiff draft of wine and gulped it down, then sank onto the couch. He canted his face up, staring at the *grianan* ceiling. "You're young, Niall. You remember the high kingship being only O'Neill. But the crown has belonged to each province in turn. Who can say, but for Fergus's eye, that the throne might not have been his and not mine—" He drew a deep, ragged breath. "He was blinded for my fate, don't you see?"

Niall saw this—that this misguided lie was what drove his fosterer. "You speak of his eye. But what of his heart? How came that to be traitored?"

"Fergus is a man denied."

Niall thought only of his own denial; how, for Connor, he had refused to go with Grania. "You defend Fergus as if he were some honored champion. I respect the bent of your heart, Father. But do not ask me to love Fergus, too."

"Niall, this is not your fight."

But indeed it was. Ever since Connor had taken Fergus with him to exile.

"Father, I cannot watch you play Ulster's fool."

Connor's dark eyes were large and unblinking. "Must I build my king's fort on my children's bones?" When he spoke again his face looked long and his eyes were exhausted. "Even if I chose to move against Fergus, winter is on us. It would be a hard time for a fight."

Niall had lost all patience. "Do you think Fergus will wait until we're fat to take us to slaughter? You must move on him *now*!" His face grew red.

Connor bolted to his feet, his huge gold neck plate swinging out and knocking the wineglass loose of his hand. The vessel shattered on the floor, leaving tiny shards of glass glistening on the birch branches.

"And your hot head will push us into the abyss. You love this sod no better than I do. And, mark me, if I must bury Fergus to fly our flags, so will I do it. But a wild beast at bay will fight to the death; Fergus is nothing if not that. If we press him before he is ready, we stand to lose."

Connor plucked the chess king from where it lay tipped on the board and shook it hard in Niall's face. "However you wish to disbelieve it, even O'Neill are not invincible."

Niall was finally relieved; at last Connor had been moved to agree to the fight. But if he waited, as he intended to, it might cost them their lives. "Do you deny the saint Columcille's prophecy that you are Inisfail's rightful king?"

"Your father too was king." Connor's implication was obvious. "Temper yourself, Niall, or you'll not last the first day on the battlefield. If we must war against Fergus, then we will crush him. But for now, let him think we cower. Let him bring his Picts and Britons and any other traitors he can pay. He will not outmatch or surprise us; even Fergus holds to the honor of a fair fight. Go home to Aileach. Lime your shields. And when the snow melts, be ready for him."

"What then?" Still he needed to hear Connor say it.

The king closed his eyes as he spoke. "When Fergus comes . . . we will take his head."

Finally, blessedly, Connor had rallied. Come spring, there'd be justice. Niall had only to wait—and find a way to keep his mind off Grania. "We will make Inisfail whole again," he said confidently.

"Aye." Connor looked up to his shield, Red Backed, which hung on the wall above him. "Inisfail will be one. If I have to cleave it in two to make it so."

Grania tipped her face up to the crisp, cloud-scalloped sky. The sun was high and pale, and the wind smelled newborn; winter was coming. Her nostrils tingled with the cool air and gooseflesh sparked down her legs. She collapsed into a loose heap in the soft sedge grass and let its waving fringe shelter her against the sharp cut of the breeze. She drew her knees to her chest and bound her *bratta* like a sheath around them.

She watched the wind-pocked lake. Winter had faded the blue water to dull gray. Even the sedge grass and marshmallows on the lake's edge had taken a chill, dimming from bright green to a flat brown shade. Everything around her seemed to draw into itself, darkening and dying—and so too did everything inside her.

She'd expected to find solace at Uisneath; but what she found was a home that fit worse than before. She hadn't thought anything held her to Aileach. But every hut, every tree, every knoll and meadow of Uisneath that she'd hoped would comfort her looked strange, as if she'd never really known them. More than anything, though, with her every breath she missed Niall.

His blue eyes haunted her days and his face rushed her when she tried to sleep. Her pillow felt cold and empty compared to the memory of Niall lying thick and warm next to her. Mornings were a little more bearable, until she remembered. Then her memories of him dragged down her days.

It would have been easier if Niall had refused her, if he'd

been the one to order her away. But the choice had been hers: she could have stayed at Aileach—if she were willing to change.

It was no longer a question of appeasing Connor—even if Niall's uncle approved her, Grania could not approve of living a lie.

She stretched out her legs on the cold earth and knuckled her sleepy eyes. A full month here and she could hardly count one good night's sleep. Even Eithne was exhausted, struggling to find comfort against Grania as she spun the night through like a gamester's top.

Grania lolled her head to her shoulder and listened to the soft sough of the wind moving through the sedge. She opened her arms, hoping to absorb some of Uisneath's peace; but, as always, her unsettled thoughts undid her. She gave up and hiked to her feet, shading her brow as she scanned the shoreline for Eithne.

A flash of silver fur sped toward her. Eithne's paws flung clumps of spume, and her long, powerful legs brought her up fast. The wolf crashed into Grania, jumping up, paws on her mistress's shoulders. Both of them toppled backward. Eithne slathered her pink tongue down Grania's face, wetting her from chin to brow.

"You have cloistered yourself from me."

Grania turned to face Maeve. She hadn't heard her aunt coming, but she was too tired to be startled. She eased Eithne off her and managed a weak smile. She stood up and her feet drifted forward, without destination. Maeve followed her.

"I've been unfit company." That much was true; but it was not why she had been avoiding Maeve these weeks. Often she'd wanted to go to her aunt; she ached to sink into her warm, consoling embrace. But there would be questions.

What point was there in talking of things that couldn't be changed?

They walked in silence. Finally Maeve stepped in front of Grania, catching her eyes. "Why have you come back to us?"

Grania shied her face down; she couldn't look at Maeve while she lied. "As I told you, because of the priest." It was a half-truth, but better than telling a whole lie.

"Yes. I know. You believe that he went to the high king." Grania nodded. "Then where is your joy? If you had no choice but to leave, have you not done the Mother's bidding? Is not returning here what you'd hoped for?"

The wind blew Grania's hair across her eyes. Maeve reached up, brushing it back into place. The gesture of kindness undammed Grania's tears.

"Mother." Grania crumpled forward and started to weep as Maeve's arms enfolded her.

Maeve cradled her head, wiping the warm tears off Grania's cold cheeks. "Did Niall harm you?"

Grania pulled herself up a little, trying to suppress a building sob. She smoothed her mussed hair and cleaned off her rest of her tears.

"No," she chirped bravely. "It would have been easier had he abused me. His failing was only that he could not love me unless I would change for him. I would have had to renounce all our ways."

Maeve's face cocked in surprise. "Did you think to do less when the Mother bade you to him?"

Grania hadn't really thought it through at all. When she'd first gone to Niall, the idea that he'd even accept a Druid wife seemed so incredible, so unlikely, that she had marshaled all her energies toward only that end—and nothing more. Then she'd agreed to pretend to the charade, sure at any moment Niall would order her back to Uisneath. The realization that she would have to relinquish her past came to her too late—by that time she longed to stay.

"The O'Neill would never have let me be."

"Did Connor forbid your marriage?"

"Ossian went to him, that's all I know. But I can well imagine the high king's rage." As she spoke, Grania realized her decision to leave Niall sounded hasty.

"Were the O'Neill so terrible?"

Grania tried to remember what she'd found objectionable. But all she could think of was what a good, dear friend Deidre had been. And how much Grania had come to love her brother. "They fear us."

"As we do them."

Maeve was making it sound so maddeningly simple. Grania could see her plan, the argument her aunt meant to make.

"Niall forbade my magic. He wished me to pretend to his Christian ways," she said, stiffening defensively.

"Perhaps he only meant to protect you."

"My mother tried to fit in their world, too. And she failed."

"But she tried. You share her blood—perhaps you share too what drove her there."

Grania's eyes flashed sharp as flint. "I've done fate's bidding. Uisneath is safe. And the O'Neill will never do other than harm us. My duty is finished."

Maeve shook her head softly. Her eyes were firm and unblinking. "I think not."

A new fear gripped Grania: that she would not be allowed to stay at Uisneath. It was true that the lake didn't feel like her home now, but where else could she go? "Am I unwelcome here? The Regaine said—"

"Shhh." Maeve pressed a finger to Grania's open lips. "You may do as you choose. As your conscience bids you. But I beg you to choose wisely."

"I'm a healer. Perhaps I could earn my keep in the southern provinces, away from this warring. . . ."

"There's no road that will lead you past your heart."

Grania began to feel faint. The edges of her sight started to blacken and she leaned over, trying to still her spinning head; but she only got dizzier. She slumped down in a heap on the sedge as she collapsed over her knees. When that didn't help, she lay down, pressing the back of her hand to her clammy brow.

"I should have eaten," she said, breathing in short, shallow gulps.

Maeve stroked her hand down Grania's soft hair. "It's not hunger that makes you ill, my love. You're carrying Niall's child."

Fergus squinted against the stale, smoky air of the Royal House and clutched his hand to his mouth. The rank smell of bed linens gone too long without changing hung everywhere. The corbeled sky hole begrudged almost all of the morning's light, and at first he couldn't tell if the queue of pallets lining the long side wall held patients or corpses. As his eyes adjusted to the darkness, he realized that the difference between the two was slight.

He shuffled down the long center aisle, still unsure of his footing in the dusky light. Ghostly, vacant eyes tracked him. Pillowless heads lay propped like melons against the wall. The men's uncombed hair stuck up wildly, making them look like gray, maverick bushes.

Fergus couldn't tell if the old warriors' faces were so pasty and translucent from lack of light or bad food or both.

Their sagging skin looked as if it would fall off the bones of their faces, and even covered by blankets, their wraithlike bodies looked skeletal.

Fergus shuddered. It was considered an honor to be retired here as one of the champions of Ulster. But looking at this dank, silent tomb, he knew he'd rather take a blade in the teeth. Faded standards drooped off the wall, marking each old soldier's tribe. All the fabled warriors of Ulster held court here.

Fergus felt his way down the long, dark rows, using wooden clothing chests perched at the pallets' ends to guide him. The house steward had said his uncle Dunchad was near the back. Fergus hoped he was wrong—he would wish none of his blood kin a fate among these shells of men.

"The lion rises." The voice was distant and frail, but Fergus knew it instantly. He lifted his candle higher, expanding its ring of light.

"Uncle." Fergus smiled, easing down carefully onto the bed, mindful not to jostle his uncle's old war injuries. He shifted abruptly as Dunchad's sword creased his thigh. The old man was still a warrior, even in his infirmity; no Ulsterman worth the lion's banner ever slept unprotected.

Dunchad's weathered face softened into a sad, grateful smile. For an instant Fergus saw an echo of his father's own eyes. Dunchad's, like Scannlann's, had seen Ulster denied. But today Fergus would make them dance again.

It had been two years since he had seen his father's brother, and Dunchad had aged fast; the muscle had wilted off his once wide chest, and his eyes, which Fergus remembered as fire hewn, sank like dull pebbles into a puffed, sagging face.

With a groan Dunchad pushed onto his elbows and reached out a spindly arm. With surprising strength, he pulled Fergus into a tight embrace.

Fergus felt the old man's chest hitch with a sob. "Is it you, Fergus?" Dunchad whispered, holding Fergus's head tight against his ear. "Or your father, Scannlann, come back from the grave? How we cudgeled and fought on the game plain at Rath Mor. Other men would have dropped in exhaustion, but your father . . . *there* was a warrior of Ulster. You have the look of him." Dunchad stopped, his confused eyes flitting.

Fergus finished the sentence for him. "Except for the eye."

Even in the dimness, Fergus could see Dunchad's face flush with embarrassment. Dunchad always forgot, always discovered the injury anew each time Fergus came to him. Fergus gave his uncle a heartening thump on the arm. "I see well enough to know this is no place for you. Today you come with me—out of here."

Dunchad had spent all his strength just to get upright, and he couldn't maintain the position; he thumped back onto the feather mattress, hacking. More coughs echoed down the pallet rows.

Dunchad reached up his huge, mottled hand and patted Fergus's cheek as he shook his head. "These men," he said, scanning the room, "they're my friends. The nurses bring me mead and light a fire in winter. I am kept here by the grace of those I've fought for. What more could a soldier need? I won't be squirreled away in some soft *grianan*. Why, I'd start to sprout breasts!"

Fergus clucked and smiled. Scannlann would have answered the same. "Come with me for a short while, then —long enough to watch Ulster lay the O'Neill on their knees."

"Don't tell me you're still taking all comers?"

Fergus remembered Dunchad always behind him, watching as he fought the other boys at Rath Mor. Even with one eye he'd refused to be bested. He'd fought any challenger with their choice of weapon. And always he had won.

"I drum my shield for Connor, O'Neill. I've sailed to Pictland and Briton. I've gathered a phalanx of cold, steely gifts to deliver to the high king."

"Ehh . . ." Dunchad sucked in his lips and cleared his throat, then hawked and spat, then just missing a jar on the floor. "I've heard tales of your *tains*. Pfft! How many cattle does a man need?"

"Enough to cover the Airghialla," Fergus said, his mouth curling in a sly tease.

Dunchad's eyes widened, glistening and expectant. Then the old man sank back, dismissing the wild hope. "You tried before. I'm old, but not daft. I remember the last time you warred on Connor."

"I was a boy then. It is a man who stands before you today. Even the chieftain Brecc joins me; he's cracked his promise of peace to Connor like a war lance over his knee. The kings of Pictland and Northumbria and Deira promise to come, too. With whole battalions of men to join me. Strong men, bearing writhing, hungry blades."

Dunchad doused Fergus's growing fire with a cold look. "You're a spinster dreaming of a wedding night. The O'-Neill hold the Airghialla land like a kitten in their fist. You cannot think to best Connor there."

"Magh Rath. You know it, Uncle—the plain on Ulster's southern border. It is there that I mean to take Connor. Say the name 'Magh Rath' softly now, for soon it will be shouted through all of Inisfail as the place where Ulster finally claimed its glory."

Dunchad swiped his hand through the air and spat sideways, dismissing Fergus's budding dream.

"Uncle, are you not with me?"

Dunchad's eyes flew back to him. "Did Scannlann teach you nothing? A soldier bought is as easily sold. There'll be no *leines* long enough to hide your foreigners' fetters—and make no mistake, you *will* have to fetter them, for when the battle roars and a man sees his life come up like a ghost before him, it's what's in his blood, not his purse, that makes him stand the fight.

"Connor will seed your bought troops' terror like a ripe field. He'll catapult heads to your campfires. He'll shred your war banners while you sleep unaware. The men will run. I have seen it."

Fergus's good mood stung with his uncle's dour prediction. He'd come to Dunchad for support, not this grim admonition. "I need your blessing, Uncle, not your augury of doom."

Dunchad studied him, his eyes softening a little as he saw that Fergus would not be moved off his wild notion. "Then you will fight the O'Neill—no matter my advice?"

"I will do what I must to break their yoke on Ulster." Fergus spoke with slow, deadly intent.

"Even to slay your brother Niall?"

"Niall is my fosterling—I have no brother."

Dunchad groaned as he pushed up to a sit, his arms shaking. He plunked his head back against the wall and drew a long, ragged breath. "Can I not dissuade you?" Fergus shook his head emphatically. "Then you must win. Or die."

"I am unafraid."

"Brecc and his Dal Riata are not enough for you. Have you all Ulster's other tribes, too?"

"Aye, all. There is not a man does not hunger to end our servitude. Connor has no men to match us. He was so desperate he hoped to frighten me with a Druid blade."

Dunchad's eyes narrowed in question. "It was nothing," Fergus said with a swipe of his hand. "A sword. Nothing more."

Dunchad seized Fergus's collar and yanked him down until Fergus could feel the old man's sour breath heating his face. "If you would do this—"

"I will," Fergus droned intently.

"Listen to me. Ulster—and what other men you can buy—cannot carry the battle for you. But there is another ally—"

"Uncle, I've promises from all the tribes—"

Dunchad clamped his hand on Fergus's jabbering mouth. "Have you been beyond the mists . . . have you seen the Druids?"

Fergus pushed free of him, squinting in disbelief. "Druids!" He could only think Dunchad had gone senile, to offer him such strange, crazed advice.

"If you mean to win the day, you must have the force of the old blood, too." The edges of Dunchad's mouth tightened as he whispered.

"My men need no druidhect to protect them. We will craft our fate from strong will and hard blades," Fergus snapped defiantly.

"Yet you failed against Connor before. . . ."

"I have more men now," Fergus protested. "Better, braver, seasoned men."

"Connor will match you head for head, heart for heart."

Disregarding all respect for his uncle's age, Fergus took Dunchad by the shoulders and shook him as he stared into the old man's calm face. "This business of the moon and the Mother is for witches and old men."

"You're too young, Fergus. But I remember . . ." Dunchad's eyes drifted. "The druidhect is beyond anything your sword can dream of. In the time of the Red Branch knights, Ulster's warriors would not have gone to battle lacking it.''

"The old ways are dead.''

"So it seems. But the Christians have only dusted their faith on more ancient beliefs. There is blood aplenty that still runs hot for the Beltane fires. What man does not shiver and stand guard at a sidh wind? Whose ears do not cock for the raven's croak? There is a great wave in the land still, waiting to break.''

Every fiber of Fergus refused Dunchad's mad notion. It would be an incredible, impossible alliance. Even if Fergus wanted it, the Druids had committed to back Connor with their sun-sweated blade. Even if he were to go seeking their help, surely they'd refuse him, surely they'd remember how he'd treated Grania.

But Fergus hadn't forgotten how she'd slipped free of him. If no more than a fledgling priestess could wield such great druidhect, what wild feats could seasoned sorcerers make? His mind spun thinking of it.

No. He would beat the O'Neill with swords, not sorcery. It was enough that he had the Picts and the Britons. Dunchad was wrong.

"What say you?'' Dunchad's hand shook as he held tight to Fergus's *leine*.

"I say I'll do what I must to bring Connor to his knees. Even if that means seeking the druidhect.'' Fergus saw no point in upsetting the tired old warrior. Dunchad's eyes lit bright as a young man's as he smiled.

"Good, then. The lion of Ulster will triumph once more.'' The warrior's fire drained out of Dunchad as he slumped back on the pallet, spent.

"Rest, Uncle,'' Fergus whispered, stroking his brow before he rose to leave. "I'll bring you news of our victories.''

Fergus stepped out of the Royal House, shielding his eyes with his hand against the bright sunlight. The winter sky was clean and perfectly unclouded. Dunchad was mistaken. Fergus would have no need of the druidhect; his blade was charmed enough already.

CHAPTER
15

Fergus assured himself it had to be a rodent or a foraging night bird crunching the brush behind him. But his eyes jerked to the sound and his nostrils flared at the scent of danger. In his heart he knew this was no forest thing. Something unearthly stalked him.

He shifted the reins to one hand and reached with the other to make sure he still had the pouch of feat apples tied to his belt. His fingers froze on the bag as he realized his naiveté; no missile, however well flung, would rout magic. Again the sound called to him. Again it died in the mists.

He'd ridden all day, seeking the Druids and their cold, powerful magic. There was no need to fear what he'd come to embrace. He tried to believe that as he and Saran plodded on through the fog-choked woods.

Deciding to seek the Druids' help had come hard to him;

but Fergus had finally realized that Dunchad was right. If Connor had commissioned a magical blade, he would be a fool not to marshal the same.

But it was more than some sun-soaked weapon he came here seeking, however, he wanted no less than all the druid-hect that could be raised to defeat Connor.

Fergus reached back, checking the gold reliquary tied to his saddle blanket. The box was still there. Inside it lay the serpent-shaped necklace he'd had made for the Regaine. He had promises, too, pledges of power and prestige. Fergus had come ready to outbid whatever Connor had offered the priest. But his bribe would be worthless if he couldn't find Uisneath.

The air was palpable. It pulsed around him, breathing like a great behemoth. It settled on and into him, running his bones through like a vaporous sword.

Saran plodded like a sleepwalker, going forward but with no destination. Fergus couldn't guide him—he didn't know where they were going, either. Uisneath couldn't be found by map or trail mark; when the time came the wind would rise and the Druids would find him. He wondered if even now he stood in their midst, stared at unawares by a corps of silent eyes.

The gelding clopped to a halt, as if to announce they'd arrived. Fergus wheeled his gaze around the green womb of a clearing, combing the right half of the circle twice; it was his blind side and he feared attack most there. There was only blackthorn and quicken, though their arms, pleached in a snarl of shadows, could have taken strange, eerie shapes in a nervous man's mind.

It was dark now, but Fergus ignored the prohibition against night riding; this quest was one that could not wait. A hunter's moon blazed in the sky. It was a good night for being found. The winter light was lean and blue, and thunderhead chariots glided over the heavens, impaling on star clusters. Rocks and scrub glistened on the ground as if they'd been dusted with snow.

Even Fergus's thickest wool *bratta* couldn't keep him from shivering. It was the chill of magic; he'd felt it all the way from Rath Mor.

Fergus doubted the Druid mists would part for his full retinue, so he'd come alone. Right now he rued the choice.

He wondered how many other Druid enclaves he'd passed on the way. Hills of magic were said still to bloom near the villages of Westmeath and Clogher. Fergus didn't doubt there were a thousand other points where the old blood still lived in between. This was what Dunchad spoke of—the great hidden wave.

Moonlight glinted off a rock at the fringe of the clearing. Fergus urged Saran on tentatively. Soon he saw Uisneath's fabled five-sided stone, cut with the ancient signs of *ogham* to mark the meeting spot of Inisfail's five provinces.

The marker was taller than the monoliths and stone circles that had littered the road south. Every cattle path and royal road bore witness to the island's magical past. With faith and a squint, it was easy to conjure the ghosts of the ancients. It was said they lived on, in the touch of the mist and the call of the wind, even squirreled under the earth in glittering fairy palaces.

Fergus knew this much: the magic was fresh here. It pulled hard on his chest as he caught a sharp, rancid smell. Here, in the cool shroud of the fog, the alchemy crackled and burned.

The air began to thin and flutter, moving past him like a fast current of stream. Soon he couldn't remember how long he'd been in this midnight clearing. The world seemed to halt all around him.

A sudden sidh wind stirred the folds of his *bratta*. Fergus squinted in amazement as the breeze took on colors: first purple, then blue, suddenly white as a gull's wing, then red as blood. It went speckled, gusting stronger until the trees trembled. Fergus bent down over Saran's withers and sheltered his face. There was no mistaking it; magic was making.

Silence fell around him. Mist soaked the air, dense and choking as green wood smoke. It dripped like lace off the boughs of the trees and the moonlight, sieved through it, peppered the air with what looked like diamonds. He felt a woman's small fingers raise gooseflesh as they trailed down his face; he turned to the touch, again and again. No one was there.

Saran pealed off a high, frightened whinny, his ears flat to his head. The mist closed in tighter, bleaching the sky white except for a small disk of night. Inside it the moon dipped and plummeted.

Fergus's eyes dropped to the earth and his breath froze in his gullet; a man stood in front of him. It could only be the Regaine. He was swathed in a thick, bone-white *leine*, and he smelled of tamarisk. He wore a shining gold skullcap over plaits of white hair that were woven with tiny gold apples.

His fingers were as gnarled as tree roots and jointed with bright rings; in his hand, wielded as scepter—or, perhaps, a weapon—was a staff made of yew. The old man's earlobes were stretched thin with heavy ear clasps, and a huge gold breastplate blazed on his chest like a torch on snow. A dragonstone lay in its center.

"Fergus of Ulster." The voice was bell clear and carefully measured.

"I am." Fergus felt the marrow in him go to water. "I seek the Regaine."

"You seek Connor's head," the Regaine answered, cocking a knowing brow.

"You know then what I want of you," Fergus said, squinting. The Regaine's mouth eased into a placid smile, but his eyes struck a hard vigil. Fergus wondered how long the old sorcerer had been watching him.

He was not what Fergus expected. This Druid was no young buck, but neither was he the frail relic Fergus had thought to find. The priest wore a full white beard, like a man of nobility; its fringes curled up his cheeks, nearly meeting the downturn of his small, dark eyes.

"Tell me, prince of Ulster, what you come asking of me."

"It is as you said, priest. Connor's head."

"You came weaponed," the Regaine answered, his cool eyes sliding from Fergus's bag of sling stones to the sword half-sheathed at his side. "Did you think to threaten me?"

Before Fergus had time to fashion a lie, the old man turned and, as if their business were abruptly finished, began to walk away. The mist, thick as sea foam, parted, then swallowed him. Fergus grabbed the reliquary and sprinted in his wake, frantically breaking hedge branches to mark his path back.

"I came bearing a gift," he blurted as he caught up, shoving the ornate coffer rudely in front of the Druid's face.

The Regaine stopped, using the crook of his staff to push the reliquary aside. Again he began forward, this time at a young man's pace. His eyes, dark pits shaded by tufts of white brow, fixed front. "I need nothing from you, prince of Ulster," he said serenely.

"Not your rightful place on the dais alongside the high king? If we meld my men and your magic, who can say that your Goddess may not reign again as she did before? Would you not walk in the light—instead of some moon-dark clearing?''

"You are bold. You come begging alliance with us when you have no respect for our ways.''

"But I do.''

"Be still.'' The old man raised his palm to Fergus's face. "You think to make me a partner in your blood thirsting. Yet you steal one of the Goddess's daughters.'' Fergus started to protest; again the priest raised his palm preemptively. "I know you took Grania.''

"I was wrong.''

"You're a fool. No army, however great, could drive Connor's priests away.''

"I have seas of men waiting to move with me. The Picts and all the tribes of Ulster drum their shields to join us.''

"Do you think wars are won or lost by men?''

"Men fight. Weak men lose,'' Fergus said as if it were a simple, obvious thing.

"Yet you lost when you fought Connor before.''

Fergus set his jaw hard to keep from speaking impru-dently. That shameful day always haunted him. "I am stronger now,'' he said with a bite in his voice.

"I have no powers to make you high king.'' The priest stared at Fergus's grisled eye.

"Yet it was your power that took the crown from me. It was your judges who made the law barring an imperfect ruler. This,'' Fergus said, gouging his finger into the white, "may well be the debt you owe me.''

"We are judges no more. Though I see you are still a warrior, blood and bone. You think well under attack. When one pass is blocked, you seek another. If your blade breaks, you reach for your sling. First you come wooing me with promises of grandeur. Now you seek to bind me to you with shame. Which is it, Fergus, prince of Ulster?"

Fergus's expression darkened. "I demand your magic by the same right that you deed it to Connor. Will you send him a sword sweated with druidhect, yet deny me?"

"Connor's sword is made of metal, like all blades."

Fergus shook his head, eyes asquint, his expression branding the priest a liar. The old man shrugged. "Men believe what they will of things."

"If Connor is not your chosen, all the better to conjure your magic for Ulster." Fergus clamped his hands around the old man's arms and pulled him up to his face. The Regaine was maddeningly imperturbable, his face calm and enigmatic. At first Fergus could make nothing of his odd expression; and then he knew. "You play a foul game with me, priest. You refuse me because you believe I will lose."

The Regaine chuckled softly. "See there, for all your brave words, you'd fail with or without me. It's your doubts, Fergus, not your allies, that will undo you."

"And a loose tongue will undo you." Fergus snatched the old man half off his feet by his gold neck torque, then, embarrassed by his loss of control, set him free.

"I'll have no more of your sport with me." He strode angrily back toward Saran.

"Fergus!" the Druid called, hands cupped to his mouth.

Fergus turned; the Regaine stared back coolly. "In a thousand lifetimes I would not choose to follow you. But the choice is made for me." Hope rose like a high tide in Fergus's eyes. "The Mother has bound our fates. Why else do you think she would part the mists for you?"

The reliquary banged to the ground; Fergus was dumb with relief. "But you sport with me."

"I would know your mettle." The Regaine extended his

open hand. "The druidhect, as I can wield it, is yours for the taking. Muster your men, prince of Ulster. Lime your shields. When you are ready, the magic will find you."

Fergus nodded, struck silent by this turn of good fortune. It didn't matter if the old priest was crazy. He'd promised his magic to Ulster. Fergus picked up the reliquary and smiled smugly. When he looked back the priest was gone, and Fergus was alone in the mists.

"Apostate. You cast our lot with a snake."

The Regaine crouched down, studying a diving wheel that spun on the hut's floor. He looked up at Grania, regarding her with a deliberate mix of shock and displeasure. The glimmering disk's tiny river pearls made a white blur as it whirred. The Regaine, hands on his knees, stood up with a low groan. The wheel ground to a halt, tipping off its fulcrum with a harsh clang.

Grania's breath caught in her throat. Even Maeve, with her high standing in the Druid community, wouldn't dare such a bold affront to the priest who led them. But outrage forced the words out of her. If no one else would speak the truth to the great Druid, she would.

"You interrupt the Mother's business."

"The devil's business." The wind gushed in through the hut's door like a frigid tide. She gave the door a rough shove; it slammed close, making the wall's stakes shiver. Grania's eyes were flinty and full of fire. One hand braced behind her; the other stilled her babe, who shifted in her belly with each hitch of her heaving chest.

The Regaine stepped close and reached a gnarled hand out from his speckled *bratta*. Grania shook her head indignantly, brushing away his offer of peace.

She still remembered that first sunlit day when she'd seen

him, when Maeve had brought her as a babe to Uisneath. Priestesses whispered of the tall, black-haired priest—that he conjured the greatest, most potent druidhect. It was said he made deadly battle charms, the he could maledict an enemy to death. It was said the Regaine could even raise sidh winds powerful enough to cleave the sea. But with Fergus the priest had heaped shame on his brilliance. This was not the man Grania had worshiped as a little girl; this was a disloyal snake. Her eyes damned him. He read her fury and settled into himself, obviously meaning to ignore her challenge.

"You come to speak of Fergus."

"Tell me the alliance is a lie." Grania had laughed when she'd first heard rumors of the incredible pact. She prayed it was a terrible jest.

"Our fate is tied to the prince of Ulster." The priest's eyes made no apology.

A turf of peat thumped off the top of the hearth pile; the Regaine poked the smoking clump with the butt of his staff. Again the peat caught flame.

"What could the one-eyed cur have promised you?" She could hardly believe the Regaine could be bought—but why else, what else, on heaven or earth, could have driven him? "If it's gold, I swear the O'Neill will double his offer. If Fergus promises to restore the Mother's greatness, I say he lies."

The Regaine set his staff against the wall and lifted his hands, petitioning Grania to reason. "I speak, but you do not hear me. The match with Fergus is fated. By the earth and the moon, this decision is not mine to make. If it were I who worked our destiny, don't you think I'd choose otherwise?"

His eyes held a feral glint, and for the first time Grania

could see that the old priest, too, hated Fergus. Yet he'd thrown their fate to him. "How can you do this—when you know?"

"I owe you no explanation. There is more to understand than the little our eyes see. There is no promise that our pact with Ulster will serve us. But we must make it all the same. The Sight has revealed this to me."

The damned Sight again. Grania's hands fluttered and flew around her face. Words couldn't express her rage. When finally she found her voice, it was slick and cold.

"We shall pay—more than you know—for your misplaced trust. I know Fergus as you cannot. He wets his blade for reasons no better than lust and greed. Already he has slaughtered Sweeney. Now he hungers for Connor's head. And Niall's, too. Your promise of aid only encourages him. Can you think he'll spare us his treachery?"

"I trust in fate, not in men."

Grania's eyes twitched as she paced the floor. "Fate." She spat out the word. "I've had enough of it. What guiding hand sent me to Niall only to wrench me back here? Will you now tell me the Mother means to deliver us to a butcher?"

"Is Fergus that much worse than your husband?" It was a cruel question. And a fair one. Niall too lusted for war. "If is not your place to indict me." The Regaine's eyes were still and glassy. She could see she'd pushed him too far.

Then she remembered the babe. She still had strength to fight for it. "It is not your place to decide that my child will die." Her hands poised on her womb in poignant accusation.

"The babe is Niall's." The priest spoke matter-of-factly. "The child will be spared."

This lie, at least, she ached to believe. But how could

she trust anything he said when the Regaine had already betrayed her? Grania's fear turned to misery. Soundless tears washed down her cheeks. After a long time, she calmed a little. She swallowed hard and glared up at the priest, wiping her wet face dry with the edge of her *bratta*. If she couldn't appeal to his conscience, maybe she could appeal to his fear.

"Do you think Connor will spare even one of us when he learns of your alliance?" Her voice was calm and logical. "No druidhect will stop the O'Neill's vengeance for us. Connor's weapons will rain down on Uisneath until our blue sky turns gray with them."

"And if Fergus wins?"

The thought punched the breath out of her. She'd always thought of O'Neill as invincible. And yet Ulster hadn't always served as their handmaiden. Once it was the name Cuchulain, not Connor, that formed on men's lips. And Fergus had the druidhect. Grania's eyes stung with peat smoke and fresh tears. If Niall won, the Druids would die. But if Fergus carried the day, she would be safe. But not Niall. She would lose either way.

"Father," she begged, her fury routed by desperation, "however I turn, I am betrayed. Every faith I hold dear deserts me." She began to sob loudly.

The Regaine pulled her close and stroked her shaking head. His dark eyes softened on her. "No one betrays you. But we must do as the Mother bids us. Though I won't force you to stay here."

He let her go and poured out a horn of hind's milk. The priest drank it down and wedged himself, groaning, into a hen's niche in the warm wall next to the fire.

For the first time since she had stormed into his tiny crannog hut, Grania realized the old man was not his usual regal self. Bone combs hung half out of his snowy hair, and the gold breastplate pinning his *leine* to his chest sagged down dejectedly. The priest's flesh was pale; he looked ill. This decision to go with Fergus had taken its toll on him.

He watched the fire with glazed eyes as he spoke to her. "I hope you can find some peace with my choice, Grania. But however you choose, my decision will not change. I have promised Fergus what magic I can make."

"Do you know how the battle will end?" The Regaine shifted his eyes without moving his head. "I've the right to know." Grania's nervous hands wadded up fistfuls of her *leine*.

"No fate changes for the knowing of it," he answered quietly.

"Please," she gulped, her voice thin and unsteady. "Will Niall live or die?"

The Regaine paused for a long time, then sighed before he answered her. "Niall will fight. I can tell you no more than this."

CHAPTER
16

A fresh jolt of pain sent Deirdre arcing into as much of a ball as her swollen belly would allow. It was months too soon for the contractions—and yet they were getting worse.

She began to keen as she rolled rhythmically from one side to the other of the sweat-blotched pallet. Her knuckles went white as she gripped her knees; she was an eerie, pain-racked imitation of the child curled inside her.

The frightening twinges had begun yesterday. From the start, Deirdre had struggled to deny them, biting her lip until her teeth drew blood, finding some pretense to turn her face to the wall so Morgana wouldn't see her grimace in pain. But the needling misery hung on, and now, when it came, it was more insistent, more frightening, than before.

"Try not to move, lady." Morgana bent over the pallet's end, tucking the blanket tighter under Deirdre's toes, which were pointed in pain. She didn't want her mistress to read the fear in her eyes, to know that the babe was lost already. Morgana had midwifed a great number of Aileach's women. She'd seen many chart this rugged course, the pains coming too soon, bringing the fever. Few finished it without losing the babe or their life or both.

Morgana wasn't surprised that Deirdre was having difficulty. From the moment the child began to grow in her, Deirdre had been gaunt as a sylph, too thin everywhere except for her burgeoning breasts and belly, which looked all the larger for the contrast with the rest of her.

In the beginning, Morgana had thought Deirdre suffered from child sickness; women often paled when they first learned to carry. She'd urged her lady to take one more bite at each meal, to walk in the fresh air when the weather allowed it, and to sleep whenever she felt tired, night or day.

But Morgana's relentless ministrations made no difference. Deirdre's statuesque frame continued to shrink; now, two months from the babe's time to arrive, Deirdre had less strength than a sapling and the burden of the baby's growing weight made her more drained every day. Even her fine freckled skin had gone flat and translucent, as if the child leached the life straight out of her. Morgana blinked back a tear as she looked down at Deirdre; to be sure, it was the devil that had her lady by the throat.

Morgana peeled the linen compress, now warm with fever, off Deirdre's brow. She swished it through a bowl of cool water by the bedside and pressed the back of her hand to Deirdre's tacky cheek; still the fever raged. Morgana wrung out the cloth and arranged its folds carefully so it would cover Deirdre's forehead.

Sweaty tails of hair fringed Deirdre's face. She smelled of sickbed and poultices, not the sweet harebells she was so fond of peppering throughout her blond hair. She was too weak even to open her eyes, and Morgana was glad for that; she couldn't bear one more moment of her mistress's glazed, vacant stare. She wondered if Deirdre would last the night.

She gently unfurled Deirdre's shoulders and knees, trying with only slight success to soften her body, gone rigid with repeated passes of pain. Deirdre groaned as Morgana tried to straighten her and blinked up, her eyes watering, her breath short and ragged.

Morgana mustered a false, hopeful smile. "If the babe is to stay inside you, you must not move. Even when the cramping comes."

Deirdre nodded and swallowed with a loud gulp. Panic rucked her beautiful face as the demon fear screamed again in her mind: *The baby will die.* She'd feared it every day since she'd learned she was pregnant. And been sure of it from the day Grania had left Aileach.

Every tiny, meaningless thing became a cause for alarm. If her legs felt moist, Deirdre rushed back to her quarters, frantic to assure herself she wasn't bleeding. If the babe slept, unmoving, she pushed and nudged her belly with a gentle hand, desperate for assurance that the child hadn't died. If she vomited from too strong a seasoning on her meat, she worried the child would fade for lack of nourishment.

Grania's magic had planted the babe in her womb, but Deirdre could find no faith to believe she could keep it. She didn't deserve to. She'd failed at the one thing Grania asked in exchange for the child charm: that she believe.

Deirdre drew a deep, croupy breath. Her lips were so dry—she would have asked for water, but she knew she couldn't hold her head up to drink it. Her brow was on fire and her feet were freezing. She wondered if this was what dying felt like. She made another of the countless silent bargains she'd struck with God that day: *Take me, but let the babe live*.

She was vaguely aware of Morgana talking, but Deirdre's world had shrunk to tactile sensations: Morgana's cool hand stroking her open palm, the scrunched bed linens riding uncomfortably against the aching small of her back, the pillow puffing around her head, sticking to her sweaty temples.

She sank into her own dark center, plumbing for the will to continue. Maybe, if she could relax, just a bit, she could will the agony away.

Eyes closed, she imagined Aileach in springtime, its walls brilliant with sun, its forest thick and green and wet with new life. Then she flinched, her knees jerking up to her belly as she writhed and twisted, caught by another searing wave of pain. She might as well try to sleep while drowning.

The pain crested and Deirdre sank flat again, mumbling weakly. Morgana pressed her ear to her mistress's lips, which were barely moving. "The baby. It's coming," Deirdre breathed.

Morgana shook her head in slow despair, blowing on Deirdre's brow to cool her. "Have faith, lady. Hold fast."

Morgana planted a kiss on Deirdre's sticky cheek and eased herself off the pallet, then hurried to the hut's door. Her voice betrayed her panic as she popped her head out and screamed.

"Fiall!" A scraggly-haired girl bounded out of nowhere. She was small and ill kempt, and except for her skirts, she might well have been mistaken for a dirty boy. She followed the crook of Morgana's finger, leaning her owl-eyed face just inside the door, then recoiling abruptly at the stench of sickness.

"Mistress?" she asked, still standing in the darkness, her jaw slack with fear.

Morgana grabbed her brooch and pulled the girl's face close. "Fetch the physician," she ordered. "Tell him his medicine is too weak." The girl froze under Morgana's wild face. "Make your heels fly!" With a rough shove Morgana pushed her free, then gave her a stiff smack on her backside as the girl turned. Fiall's feet tapped off into the dark courtyard as Morgana eased the door closed.

Deirdre's face was calmer now, frighteningly so—serene with exhaustion, rather than peace. Morgana scooted a stool next to the pallet and rearranged the woolen blanket tight like a shroud around her, snugly tucking its ends under Deirdre's hips. "Is that better, lady?"

"Better." Deirdre mouthed the word soundlessly. She squinted up at Morgana through eyes swollen from crying and managed a wan smile, though she could not hold it.

She hadn't wanted to give voice to her fear; a thing said was more likely to come to pass. *But it comes anyway,* she thought miserably. She stared up with pleading, watery eyes. "The physician cannot help me."

Morgana knew what little control could still be had over the too eager babe's fate hung on Deirdre's state of mind; and from the dispirited look of her, that was all too fragile. Until the doctor came, all she could do was try to buoy her mistress's sagging mood. "There are medicines we have not tried. . . ."

Deirdre's fingertips climbed over her belly and began a slow, loving dance there, as she'd done so often in the last months of her pregnancy. The hollow that was once between her hips was plump with life—it seemed too incredible, too horrible, that now, so close to holding the miraculous child in her arms, it could all be wrenched away from her.

"No medicine," Deirdre murmured, drifting farther away. "Only magic can help me."

Morgana covered her face with her hands and began to cry. The fever was climbing; Deirdre had gone delirious. She was going to die, and soon, from the look of her.

Deirdre had expressly instructed her not to call Niall. But Baetan had gone last week to the Airghialla, and Morgana wouldn't let Deirdre die without kin beside her. Before she could finish working the latch, the door flung inward, thumping her forehead with a loud, painful crack.

"What's this?" Niall moved like a gale toward the pallet. He screeched to a stop, his mouth open and his huge hands loose in shock.

"Lord." Morgana scurried up behind him, still massaging her throbbing brow.

Niall didn't even look back as he caught hold of Morgana's *bratta* and yanked her up next to him. He squeezed the Briton's chin, but his eyes clung to Deirdre. "Why was I not told of this?" He was too impatient to wait for any answer. He let Morgana go and eased down onto the pallet next to his sister.

"My lady did not wish to alarm you," Morgana sputtered, thinking Niall looked so distracted, it was unlikely he even heard her.

"The babe?" Finally Niall's eyes wrenched off Deirdre and pinned Morgana.

"Yes, 'tis the child." She nodded.

"How long has she been like this?"

"Since breakfast yesterday." Morgana took a step backward, worrying that Niall's rage would find vent in a fist seeking her face. "Though I think your sister has been ill much longer—and kept silent on it."

Niall peeled the old compress off Deirdre's hot brow and rang out a fresh one, cursing the distractions that had kept him from seeing that his sister had been so sick. She hadn't looked herself for some time, but he had ascribed it to the normal drain of pregnancy. He'd been too busy with Fergus—and struggling with his own demons over losing Grania. That Deirdre had never looked quite this wretched before barely consoled his cringing conscience.

Her soft, pink cheeks had gone ashen and her eyes looked too large now, sinking like dark wells into her white face. Niall knew nothing of childbed, but he'd seen death before, and this cold mask that covered his beautiful sister's face was it.

"Will she die?" he whispered in an aside so Deirdre wouldn't hear him. Morgana recognized the fear in his voice, and it made her own blood tremble.

"She is gravely ill. But I worry the most for the babe."

Niall was precariously close to tears as he stared down at her. He laid his hand to Deirdre's belly; the child twisted inside her, as if it too were fighting to survive. He had never felt so useless, so impotent. He'd decided the fate of whole armies, ended a man's life by the simple turn of his blade —but he could do nothing to keep his sister's wish child safe in her womb.

It had been a generation since the king's quarters at Aileach had been home to a babe. For a brief time he had hoped that Grania . . . He shook his head; this was no time for such self-indulgence. If any child would grow at his hearth, it would be Deirdre's. He meant to do what was needed to keep the baby—and his sister—alive.

"Where's the physician?" he bellowed, startling Deirdre awake. She blinked up at him through slitted, glassy eyes, then slipped back to her netherworld, barely conscious. Niall turned to Morgana, a shout not far behind his whisper. "If he's leeched her too often, I swear I'll spike his head—"

Morgana caught Niall's clenched fist as it railed in the

air. "It's not the potions. Even a healer has no power over matters such as this," she said, her voice dropping soddenly. "Some things are not meant to be."

"Where's Baetan? Why is he not here?" Niall's face convulsed with rage. "Any decent husband would be with his wife."

"Gone to the Airghialla, sire. Have you forgotten you sent him?"

Niall had; he was so panicked with worry he could barely think. "Call for him—now!"

Morgana snapped a quick curtsy before she scurried outside.

Niall raked his fingers down his face. This disaster was Grania's doing, the fruit of her dark witchery. Even if she hadn't made the babe, she'd dared give his sister the hope that had allowed the child to come to be.

"Niall?" Deirdre's voice startled him. He pushed his *bratta* sideways, leaning closer. He pressed a tender kiss on her cheek, and the hot feel of her skin horrified him.

"Rabbit." It was the pet name he'd teased his sister with since childhood; he hoped invoking it now might cheer her. "What's all this lying about? You won't be able to chase my nephew from bed."

"Your nephew—or niece—may well meet the world without me."

Niall schooled his face into a calm facade, determined that Deirdre would catch no glimpse of his fear. "As I breathe, Deirdre, I won't let you or your baby die."

"Please . . . I want you to send for Grania."

Deirdre's words were mere wisps of sound. Niall leaned closer, hoping he'd misheard her, doubting he had.

"Who is it you want?"

"Grania . . . she made the child. Only she can save it."

Morgana, who had come back in, heard Deirdre's plea.

She leaned toward Niall with a whisper. "Her brain's sick with fever, lord. She's been mumbling like this since this morning."

Grania was the last misery Niall wanted here. If she would even agree to come for Deirdre, certainly she wouldn't stay; and it would only mean one more agonizing parting. But he would do anything if it would buttress Deirdre's faith.

"Yes. Shhh." Niall kissed his fingertips, then pressed them to Deirdre's brow. "Yes, rabbit. If you think it will help, I'll fetch Grania."

For the first time since he had come into the room, the gray pall lifted off Deirdre's face. Her blue eyes glistened and opened wide; then, just for an instant, Niall thought he saw a pinch of color flush his sister's cheeks.

"Morgana, have the groom saddle Murchad. Quickly!"

Morgana flew out of the room—she'd given up bothering with closing the door—and after a commotion outside, she gusted back in, announcing the horse was ready.

Niall cupped Deirdre's pale face and pulled her up like a large, limp doll. "I'll be back with Grania. I need you to promise me you won't surrender." He watched her eyes try to focus on him, then slide off his face.

"I promise," she repeated.

"Hold fast. You're O'Neill."

Deirdre nodded as she managed a brief, feeble smile. Then, even before he could lay her back down on the pallet, she went mercifully unconscious.

Niall spilled the wooden water bowl as he rushed toward the door, nearly toppling Morgana as he spun around with a final dictum. "Get that cursed physician to do what he can." Morgana bobbed a quick curtsy, then went to work drawing a fresh basin of water.

Niall was so fire-filled, he vaulted onto Murchad with one quick leap, landing with such a thump that the startled

horse danced sideways, whinnying. "Damn her magic."
He jammed his heels hard in Murchad's sides as they bolted
out the main gate. "Damn *her*," he mouthed as they thundered into the night.

Grania checked the mallow roots she'd bagged in her belt
pouch; finally she had enough to plaster Maeve's twisted
ankle. It wasn't the walking but the bending that tired her.
Lately even short outings exhausted her. She felt as sleepy
and clumsy as a winter bear.

For six months Niall's child had turned inside her. Yet
she never quite got used to the wonder of it; every morning
she struggled up through the balmy currents of sleep, blinking and stretching, and then, with a surge of joy, she remembered she was pregnant.

The realization made her heart soar. Finally, after all the
endless, lonely years, she would wholly belong to someone,
just as the babe would wholly belong to her. It didn't matter
that the child would have Niall's blood, too; in her mind it
mattered only that it was the fruit of her womb. If everything
around her thundered to pieces, she didn't care. She had
the babe.

She trudged back toward the cluster of crannog huts, her
slow gait making loud crunches on the hoary, frostbitten
sod. A lapwing cried out with its nasal *peeweet*; Grania
stared up at the bird's jerky flight, then watched it settle on
an oak bough, the green sheen of its wings the only splotch
of color on the stark, leafless tree.

Winter had cleansed the land of its foliage. It was a
purification, a proper readying for the birth of spring. Yet
even now, in the chill and frost, Uisneath was a wondrous
place. It was a white package all wrapped up with spring
inside. Grania knew she would miss it terribly.

She stopped to catch her breath, rueing that she'd let

herself wander so far from the lake. She was tired and cold, and the child was so huge and heavy inside her.

She could never have imagined she could have been so filled up with life. Her belly was stretched taut as a drumhead from her breasts to her hips and little toes—or so she guessed—snagged on her bottom ribs at the most inopportune times.

The small mound of a child spun and shifted inside her, as if the baby couldn't quite find a comfortable place. To Grania's amusement—and her misery—the child was most lively when she tried to sleep. And always, like a tiny trickster, it danced away at the press of her delighted hand.

A pregnant woman was a rarity at Uisneath. In their youth, many of the older priestesses had taken part in the field rites of Beltane, but none had ever conceived a child. Maeve said conception was an act of wanting, that it did not come unbidden.

Grania had shaken her head at her aunt's pronouncement, for she'd made a charm against becoming pregnant; she didn't want Niall's child when she lacked his love. But her druidhect had had not worked. Grania would never understand how she could summon the great magic required to escape Fergus's cave, yet fail at a much simpler task.

Some force greater than her own will had clearly guided the babe into being. And, though she hadn't wished for it, she couldn't have been happier.

She and the babe were coddled shamelessly. Grania's priestess sisters thought her a wondrous anomaly, and in the first months of her carrying, when a few fall berries still could be found, they were sent to Grania even before being offered to the Regaine. In winter most hearth fires were stoked with peat, but Grania was sent precious bundles of oak because of its sweet-smelling flames. And, against her protests, she'd even been excused from her usual household duties for fear any burden would endanger the babe. Maeve would have consigned her to sickbed if Grania hadn't protested. She'd never been further from sick; she was wondrously alive.

It had been two moons since the Regaine had thrown the Druids into league with Fergus. Fortunately Ulster's fight with the O'Neill had not yet bloomed into war, and the druidhect the priest had promised still lay sleeping. But Uisneath rumbled with gossip and inchoate fears. The other priestesses knew how the Regaine had dismissed Grania; not one of them dared to question his decision. Instead they waited for word that Fergus had struck Connor's shield in challenge, even as they prayed it would not come.

Like her sisters, Grania too had given up trying to change the Regaine's mind; instead she focused on holding tight to the babe. She'd had disturbing dreams. She remembered only sketchy details of them: a rank bed alongside physician's *gipnes*, a room dark and blurry, and cloying air that made her work to breathe.

Always, when she woke, she sensed something had been wrenched from her. Always the dreams made her fear for the babe. Deep, elegiac moods seized her in the dark dawns that followed the nightmares, moods that leached the color from her face and drained courage from her heart.

Now, just before she closed her eyes each night, Grania tried to put faith in the Regaine's augury: that whatever happened, no harm would come to her babe.

This much she knew: the hybrid child inside her had filled her to the brim with druidhect. When she breathed the whole universe suffused her, and when the baby moved, she felt capable of anything. Except forgetting Niall.

He was still a ghost in her dreams. Grania tried desperately to hate him; she tried to picture him bedding other women. She'd been gone from Aileach for months now.

Surely her husband didn't still mourn her like some widower would a lost wife.

For all she knew he'd divorced and forgotten her. But however she struggled she saw Niall only one way: lying dead, facedown in the cold sod. And each time the vision came to her, another small piece of her heart withered away.

Not a day passed but that she wondered if she were wrong to have kept silent, if she should have gone to Aileach and told Niall of the Regaine's alliance with Fergus. But then Niall would know about her babe. The news that he would soon have a child might make him back off from Fergus's fight. Or drive him to commit himself more deeply to it— and to thieving her unborn babe.

It was beyond her means to mete out fate. She'd tinkered with destiny once before—and failed miserably. She would stay at Uisneath and hold her peace.

She pulled at her *leine*, stuck in the cleft between her breasts and belly, and wound her *bratta* tight around her shoulders as she glanced up at the sky. It had been clear and cold for days, but now clouds rolled in and a stiff wind was churning. It smelled like snow.

She quickened her pace, cupping a cold hand to her mouth and giving a long call for Eithne. The wolf, flush in her winter coat, had sprinted off a few minutes earlier after something—a badger or titmouse—that rustled through the brush.

Grania was too tired to wait; Eithne knew her way home. She plodded on, walking slowly to keep from snagging her slippers on the frozen twigs of the scraw. She called again for the wolf, and this time a familiar yelp rent the air. Grania turned, her mouth gaping in shock; Eithne bounded toward her, smiling—alongside Niall.

It was too late to think of subterfuge; Grania's belly filled her *bratta*, and the child inside her was in bold, full view.

Niall's eyes quickly narrowed. His face mirrored her own dismay.

He looked even finer than in her dreams. His hair had gone uncut since she'd last seen him, and he hadn't bothered to plait it; instead it fell in soft shanks on his shoulders. Even in winter he was golden with sun, except for the tiny white wrinkles fanning out from his eyes. Those blue accusations were just as she remembered, as brilliant and mercurial as storms in spring. Niall's brow glistened with sweat from the ride; Murchad too was slick and shining, breathing in loud, explosive blasts. Whatever had driven him to Uisneath had driven him hard.

Grania gave a him slow, cautious nod. Niall took it as tacit permission for him to approach her. Murchad clopped through the marsh grass, bowing his head as Niall pulled him up, hoof to toe with Grania. Niall's boots landed with a thump in a battle stance. He stared again at Grania's middle, his face red as coals.

"Did you plan to keep this from me?"

"I . . . you were at Aileach," she said flatly as if that explained it. She wanted to scream out that she'd ached to share her secret with him, thought of it a hundred times every day, but always she'd forced her longings to silence. She would not use the baby to fetter him to her. And neither would the child change what had driven her from Aileach in the first place.

Niall's blue eyes were raw with indignation—it was the same look Grania had seen the day he'd locked her in the *grianan*. She knew, in keeping her pregnancy secret, she'd offended his honor. It was always honor, exalted over everything, even over love.

"You would have had my child—and kept me ignorant?" The question thundered out of him, flushing a nearby wisp of snipes. Grania felt her stomach pitch and her legs, already wobbly from the long walk back, started to tremble. She was frightened but resolute.

"The child is mine."

"The child is O'Neill!" Niall bellowed.

Grania wove her arms over her chest in unmistakable defiance as she lifted her chin to him. "What would you do with a baby? Pack it in a chariot off to the war plain? Sing it battle dirges as lullabies? This," she said, snapping her head rudely at him, "how you are now—is why I sent no word to you. No child of mine will take first food from a sword tip. O'Neill." She spoke his tribal name like an accusation. Niall just stared at her.

When she'd first caught sight of him, Grania had thought he had somehow gotten news of her pregnancy, that he'd come to stake his claim to the babe. Or, though it was too much to dream, that maybe he'd changed his mind and decided to ask to join her at Uisneath. But his face spoke of darker things. The babe had clearly surprised him. And he was no apologetic, besotted suitor coming to woo back her heart. Some other matter had sent him into the mists.

"What is it you want of me?" Grania knew the answer before the question died. She and Niall spoke the name simultaneously. "Deirdre."

Of course. This was the stuff of Grania's nightmares, the disquieting hint of a Sending. Grania had feared for her own fragile babe, but it was Deirdre's child that was in jeopardy.

Niall's eyes were banked with fear. "The baby comes too early. Deirdre is weak and feverish. Morgana fears . . . the both of them may die." He turned his face into the stiff wind.

Grania counted back the months. Deirdre had two moons'

wait before the babe could come safely. Children could be
born small and survive, but not this early.

This was why Niall had risked the mists to come begging
her. Why his eyes were so crisp, why they crackled with
fear. He'd come to plead for his sister, not for his wife.

Grania doubted she could help him. The druidhect was
strong in her, but the magic was tight and contained, like
the eye of a storm. It would be hard to loosen. "I doubt
I've the power to keep her from death. . . ."

"You let her believe. As sure as if your charm had
worked, you made the babe. Deirdre is convinced only
you can save it." Niall's eyes were febrile. "You owe her
this."

He was right to accuse her; but not even a surfeit of the
druidhect could buck death's tide. Tears of helplessness
stung her eyes. "If I had the magic within me, do you not
think I would?"

Niall charged her, pinching her arms. "Damn you, *pitag*!
Do you think to thieve all the children from Aileach—first
Deirdre's, now mine!" When he realized Grania was trem-
bling, he let her go, a flush of shame coloring his face.

"Please," he breathed softly, his eyes entreating her,
"please." For a strange, pained moment he looked helpless
and vulnerable. Then he pulled himself back, targeting her
conscience in lieu of her heart. "Deirdre is desperate for
you. Surely that means something."

Even as she hoped differently, Grania knew Deirdre's
babe couldn't be saved. But maybe Deirdre could be.

Grania's magic waxed and waned, but if she could loosen
the power she drew off her own babe . . . And how good
it would be to see Aileach again. Though going back would
only mean the added pain of another leaving.

She'd find a way to bear it; how else could she repay

Deirdre's unselfish love? "If I come with you, I make no promises I can save the babe. . . ." Grania's heart shivered at the implicit lie. The baby was as good as buried already.

The worry left Niall's face, then returned as he stared at Grania's belly. "Can you ride?"

She nodded. Niall laced his fingers. When she didn't move, he realized that with the added weight she had no hope of springing upward. He'd have to lift her. His hands jerked uncertainly as he tried to decide just how to take hold of her.

Finally he lightly gripped what used to be her waist. And as he touched her, the baby rolled sideways and kicked him. His face lit with a strange radiance—if he hadn't been O'Neill, Grania would have said it was the druidhect.

"He moves." Niall smiled in wonderment.

"She," Grania answered unthinkingly. She knew their child was a girl; and luckily so. Boys were valued higher among O'Neill, for the tribe groomed them for war from the cradle onward. Niall would be less likely to steal a girl child from her. "After I tend to Deirdre . . . you will let us come back to Uisneath?"

"I don't take prisoners. I am not Fergus," Niall answered coldly.

"I was your prisoner once," she said.

"If you help Deirdre, you may go as you wish."

Niall hoisted her up and then sprang up behind her. He adjusted his arms awkwardly around Grania's wide belly.

"Ossian," she hissed fearfully, wrenching her eyes back to meet Niall's.

"Connor's returned him to Aileach. My fosterer sees the priest's presence there as a mark of my good faith. A promise that there's no bond left between you and me."

Grania nodded, then turned her eyes front. She didn't want Niall to see how close she was to crying.

"You needn't worry," he said. "I'll see that the abbot doesn't threaten you."

"Take me to Deirdre as fast as you can."

CHAPTER
17

Grania shuddered as she stared up at the carbon sky. Dark clouds cleaved the moon in half; it was a bad shape, one that presaged disaster for the days ahead. The moonlight was unearthly thin, turning Aileach's stone rath to pearly white and limning the bones of Niall's face in eerie, silver shadow.

He lifted her off Murchad without so much as a word. Grania followed the silent bid of his eyes, winding behind him as he led her to Deirdre's quarters. Grania listened to his worry-notched breath, the squeak of his leather vest. She smelled him, all horse and sweat and metal.

She could still feel his arms as they encircled her, his chest a firm, warm wall as he rode behind her. The journey had sped by too fast for all the pieces she meant to thieve of him—those final, fading details she meant to safekeep forever.

They reached Deirdre's door and Niall turned to face her.

His eyes were as dispassionate as diamonds in the moonlight. He seemed to look through her, as if he were sighting beyond her face.

Niall had spoken no more of their child, though Grania often caught his eyes clinging to the swell of her belly when he thought she didn't see. But if he doubted her tale of escaping Fergus with magic, Niall said nothing. There were no more suggestions that she'd betrayed him.

Yet she had. Not with her body, but with her silence. Every moment that passed that she said nothing of the Druid alliance with Fergus, she knew she traitored Niall all over again.

The Regaine had snagged her as she was gathering her things to leave Uisneath and told her Fergus meant to war on Connor come spring. The Picts and the Briton tribes would be marshaled by that time. So, too, Fergus expected, would the druidhect.

Grania planned to be safely south with her child by then. And she hoped, too, with less optimism, that the bloodbath of Magh Rath might yet be stayed. But more likely the battle would come. And Niall, if he knew about Fergus's pact with the Druids, would rush to the fight. And lose. How could he not in the face of the druidhect?

Grania had to keep the lie; whatever the love between her and Niall had decayed to, she would not see her child orphaned before it saw light.

"Promise you won't let Deirdre die." Niall's face was a cold burn. A vein in his neck swelled and pulsed; he looked like a storm ready to break. Fear drove the faith from his eyes.

"I'll do all I can," Grania answered softly. She prayed that between her magic and her herbs, she had some chance of succeeding.

Niall gave her a stiff nod as he cracked open the *clochan*

hut's door. Grania leaned her head in. The room was as dim as a dying fire. Baetan sat hunched on a small creepie stool, his back broken forward, his head sloped against the folds of the bed drapes.

He looked too tired even to be startled. He stood up slowly and turned to face Grania; she tried to conceal her shock at the sad sight of him. Fear and fatigue had drained all strength from his sturdy face. His eyes were dull as mud and his red beard, usually well groomed, squirreled out wildly. He stared at her, then dropped his eyes back to Deirdre. He sighed as he folded Deirdre's pale hand like a flower for keeping, laying it gently on her belly.

His feet struck a slow dirge as he moved toward Grania. His *bratta* sagged like wet bunting off his shoulders, and his pants were splotched with sweat and blood. He smelled sour.

It had been months since Grania had seen him. Last time, in the cups hall, he'd laughed at Dermot and hoisted toast after toast of too much mead. But there was no mirth, only hopelessness, in Baetan's pulled face tonight.

"Please." The whites of his eyes were yellow and spidered. He made no bother with Niall; he trained his smoky stare on Grania, knowing she was his wife's only hope. Grania nodded wordlessly, too shamed to confess the numbing fear that she'd likely fail.

"If you must choose, Deirdre matters more than the babe." It was a poignant instruction; Grania knew how desperate Baetan was for a child to carry his name. She pressed a respectful kiss on his cheek and hurried to the pallet, while Niall drew Baetan into the icy night.

The room was rank with the smell of sickness. Cups of filmy potions littered the bedside. Wooden tubes and used physician's *gipnes* bestrewed a side table as if they'd been thrown there in haste. Copper-stained linens and a small blood-caked bowl sat on the floor. *The fools had bled her*. The same way Emer had died.

Grania stripped back the curtains of the canopy for a better view. The sight of Deirdre made her breath gel; she knew little of childbed, but she'd seen death. And it now glazed Deirdre's pale face.

Deirdre's flesh sagged off her fragile bones; her smooth complexion had gone rough and wan. Blue half-circles smudged the scoops of skin under her eyes, and her lips were cracked into tiny planes from hours of labored breathing. Already her skin had the glow Grania had seen on those who'd crossed over. Grania shuddered; for an instant she thought she saw a shadow inside Deirdre, writhing to get free.

Grania pressed her hand to Deirdre's brow, then recoiled from the tacky, feverish feel of her. Grania would need all the druidhect she could gather tonight; whatever cursed the child poisoned Deirdre, too.

She peeled back the otter coverlet. A seeping red butterfly soaked either side of Deirdre's hips. Linen had been wadded in a large clump between Deirdre's legs, but from the wet, red look of it, the fabric had done nothing to check her bleeding.

Grania shaped her hands around the contours of Deirdre's womb. The swell of flesh was a fuller imitation of her own, though frighteningly different—Deirdre's stomach was still and hard, even under the insistent press of Grania's hand. What she'd feared all the way from Uisneath was true: the baby was dead already.

But Deirdre still breathed, and Grania drew faith from that. She unknotted the drawstrings on her leather herb pouch and dumped its contents in a jumble on the bed. Her frantic fingers sorted out like-shaped piles. She tried to stay calm; Deirdre needed her clear thinking.

"Baetan?" Deirdre's voice was little more than vapor.

Grania scooted up the pallet. "Deirdre . . ." She cupped her hands around Deirdre's face and tried to catch her fluttering eyes. "It's Grania. I've come to help you."

"Grania." Deirdre's lids flickered, then sighed closed. She mouthed Grania's name again, soundlessly, her head barely lifting. Overcome by the effort, Deirdre sank back, groaning, onto the sweat-stained pillow.

Grania plucked yarns of wet hair off Deirdre's brow, mustering what she hoped was a cheering smile. "It's all right. I'm here."

"It's too late."

"No." Grania trailed her cool fingertips over Deirdre's sticky cheeks.

"It's too late for the babe. I know that—" Deirdre's brows flinched with pain. Her eyes were closed and her pale hands groped in the air until they caught Grania's cloak brooches, tugging weakly. Grania leaned down until she could smell her dry, stale breath.

" 'Tis not true about the babe." Grania bristled with the lie; but she was willing to say anything to shore up Deirdre.

"Promise me you'll stay." Deirdre smiled wanly. "Even if I can't be with you, you mustn't leave—"

"Save your breath for the child. . . ." Grania pressed her fingers to Deirdre's mouth, but Deirdre pushed them off, insistent on speaking.

"Niall . . . has missed you. He'd never admit to it. . . ." Deirdre lurched from word to word as if she were hopping stones in a roaring stream. Grania pressed her cheek to Deirdre's hot face and cradled her head with her hands, trying to shush her; but Deirdre would have none of it. "It's your name he whispers at the night."

Deirdre's eyes rolled back in delirium. She panted, her breath shallow and rasping. After a while she managed to open her eyes again; they brightened as she caught the shape of Grania's full belly. "Oh . . ." She smiled, laying her palm to Grania's stomach. Tears trickled down her cheeks.

Grania flushed with shame at her good fortune. Fate was a blind craftsman.

"I am pleased for you." Deirdre made a soft smacking sound when she spoke.

Grania started to drag a cup through the bucket by the bedside, but Deirdre reached down, snagging her wrist with surprising strength. "I must talk to you."

Grania shook her head, protesting. "You must let me heal you. I've brought medicine."

Deirdre managed a soft, elegiac laugh before a new swell of misery seized her. She gasped, arcing up a little off the bed, then sank back, silent and not breathing. Grania let out a terrified cry, then heard Deirdre draw a long, restorative breath. Grania was near faint with relief.

"I cannot fly from death," Deirdre whispered, her eyes calm and resigned.

"Don't speak of such things."

"Already I am on the path from here. Maybe to Magh Mell, your Druid plain of pleasures, where the sick are healed." Her eyes fluttered open and closed as she spoke, as if words and sight were too much for her to manage together. "They say one apple lasts a hundred years. That it tastes of every flavor on earth. They say birds sing—" Deirdre's eyes squeezed shut. Again her breath froze.

"I can stop the bleeding. But you *must* rest," Grania pleaded. Deirdre lacked strength to argue; she nodded weakly and gave a soft moan as she turned her cheek into the pillow's heap.

Her hands shaking with fear, Grania plucked her mortar from the bed and scooped into it what plantain she could find. She pulverized the leaves so hard and fast, the pestle pocked her palm painfully. She raced to the fire and poured a draft of boiling water on top of the plantain. The paste was sloppier than she would have liked, but it was the best she had time for.

Deirdre was slipping off fast; her ragged breath, which had been painful to hear, now calmed Grania—it was a sign, at least, that Deirdre still breathed. Grania fumbled the mortar bowl, half dropping it, just catching enough dollops of the poultice to treat Deirdre's womb.

Grania washed her hands in the basin, then rubbed them dry on the skirts of her *leine*. Silent tears streamed down her cheeks as she stared at Deirdre. Niall's sister would have to birth the child, dead or alive, but if she kept on bleeding, she'd be too weak and would die.

Grania started a nettle tea to numb Deirdre's pain. It would cramp her womb and speed the delivery; if Grania could get enough of the tea down her, it would help Deirdre sleep between the contractions. Grania stirred furiously, relieved when the nettles dissolved. She lifted Deirdre's head and poured small sips of the tea down her.

"Again," Grania commanded softly as Deirdre took a third, then a fourth drink. Finally, blessedly, Deirdre's eyes cleared, softening with relief.

"I've missed you." Deirdre's voice was firmer and cooler now. "Promise me you'll stay at Aileach." Her brows went up in a plea.

Grania nodded, but Deirdre could see the lie in her eyes. "You mean to leave. If only you knew how much Niall . . ." Deirdre arced upward as another sharp pain bit at her womb. If it hadn't been for the sense-numbing tea, Grania was sure Deirdre would have screamed. She spooned another sip into her.

"He won't ask you to stay. . . ."

"We can talk of this later." Grania patted Deirdre's hand

and scooted down to check the fresh linen she'd wadded between her legs. At last Deirdre had stopped bleeding. Grania was heartened—until she saw Deirdre's face. There was a strange, vacant peace in her eyes; Grania could tell she'd surrendered. Her hand was limp and cold as Grania lifted it. "Shall I call the priest for you?" Grania asked, dropping all pretense that Deirdre might still recover.

"No, no priest!" Deirdre pleaded desperately, her eyes frantic and wild. She clamped her hand on Grania's wrist and spoke through clenched teeth. "Ossian." Her dry, pale lips twisted in distaste. "Niall still allows him here, even though it was his hate that drove you off. It was Ossian who killed my babe. . . ."

Grania was desperate to still Deirdre's agitation. What little strength the O'Neill princess had left should not be wasted on anger. "Your child is fine," she lied. "I chose to leave. It had nothing to do with the priest." She hoped Deirdre was delirious enough to believe her.

Deirdre squeezed her eyes closed tight. "The baby—" Her hands wound over her belly. "I know now. . . . what it is to have the whole world within me. With all my heart—thank you. Grania . . . my sister."

The medicine had done all it could; the druidhect was all Grania had left. She closed her eyes and trussed her hands around Deirdre's frail shoulders. She plumbed for the magic—if she could kindle its heat, she might still leach life back into her.

Grania felt it begin. As it had in the cave at Rath Mor, her blood began to ache and pound. If she could only sustain it . . . Deirdre's chest spasmed suddenly, arcing upward. Then she collapsed, limp and still.

"*No.*" Grania wrenched Deirdre up again like a spineless doll. She could feel her body thinning to nothing as she held her in her arms. *Please*, she prayed, knowing the entreaty was hopeless. *Let the next breath come. Let her breathe.* Grania laid Deirdre back down, and when she looked at her, she knew, inexorably, that neither potion nor charm could have stayed Deirdre's fate.

Deirdre's eyes, blue and peaceful as summer sky, were still open, as if she saw something exquisite, something far beyond the *clochan*'s dark confines. Her hand curled on the crest of her womb, and her mouth, no longer twisted in pain, curved into a tranquil smile. She was dead.

Grania's chest lurched with loud, racking sobs; cool tears streamed down her flushed cheeks. Her whole body began to shiver violently. She winnowed under the coverlet, snuggling close next to Deirdre.

She looped her arms like a frightened child around Deirdre's neck and pressed her cheek to her face. Already the warmth of life began to leach out of her. Grania slid her head down to Deirdre's breast, then bolted upright as she felt something break free of her still body.

The wall sconces danced with wind as the door flew open. Grania startled but was too miserable to rise. Silhouetted against the night, Niall loomed in the frame like a stoic sentinel. Ossian's raven eyes peered over his shoulder. From the look on their faces, Grania could tell they both knew.

"Deirdre is dead," she said, her voice shaking, her arms still locked around Deirdre. If Niall had given her even the tiniest encouragement, a bidding look or an outstretched hand, Grania would have fled from the bed and rushed to embrace him.

But he froze in place, his face frosty and still. Grania heard him swallow hard and saw his chest lurch. For a fraction of an instant, she thought he might cry. Then his features settled into icy order. He nodded slowly as his gaze dropped to the *clochan* floor.

"Murderess," hissed Ossian. "The Druidess has killed your sister."

It was a desperate day. The sun slept, and the wind, which had rioted every second since Deirdre had died, threw off a rancid smell, as if it had been siphoned off the bowels of the earth. Even the land held to black, though it was hours past dawn. Today, the day of Deirdre's burial, a dark pall seized all of Aileach.

Grania was forbidden to witness Deirdre's entombment. She wondered if ever again she'd be allowed to see anything beyond the confines of this bleak room that had become her jail. For ten days Niall had imprisoned her in the hostage hut. For ten days she'd waited, disbelieving that Ossian had swayed Niall to his outrageous lie that she'd murdered Deirdre. Grania had come to Aileach at Niall's bidding, risking her own life to save his sister's. How could Niall think otherwise?

She could explain the misunderstanding—if only Niall would come to her. But it was her husband's steward who'd been sent to arrest her. And only Morgana after that, bringing food and firewood. Even Echu, the guard Niall posted at the hostage house door, had been instructed to keep still around her.

Grania wondered if Niall had gone mad with grief; since Deirdre had died, there'd been times she had felt near possessed by her spirit. Waking or sleeping, Deirdre's face floated past her like a diaphanous dream. Perhaps Niall suffered the same malaise; maybe his great loss unbalanced his mind.

Or maybe—this was the most painful thought to Grania—Niall was right to judge her. She had, after all, agreed to conjure the babe; she'd given Deirdre the faith that let the child come to be. Then she had been too weak to summon the druidhect when Deirdre needed it. Grania wondered if she was guilty and if her punishment for her crime was to lose not only Deirdre, but Niall, too.

She pushed a stool up to the hostage hut's small window and peeled back the sheepskin drape. She leaned out as far as her belly allowed. Pricks of icy mist needled her eyes as she squinted up at the *grianan* perched on Aileach's wall, its silhouette roaring against the dark dawn. Deirdre had been moved there from her *clochan* when she'd died; king's candles, burning since that fateful night, doubled the size of the shadows of the women attending her corpse.

Ten days and nights all of Aileach had waked Deirdre, the women's shrill keening broken only by the drone of priests chanting in the courtyard below. Grania could not shake the painful, imagined picture from her mind: Deirdre's silky hair, washed and scented, arranged into long blond fillets. And the white winding sheet they'd cocoon around her body, swelling in the middle where she bulged with the babe. Grania wanted to cry, but her tears had been bled dry.

On mornings when the mist thinned enough to allow it, Grania could see the burial hillock up the knoll to the fortress's back side. She'd heard Niall's men felling saplings for Deirdre's bier. She'd smelled the birch branches that the women of Aileach passed by carrying, the greens that would make the death broom to cover Deirdre's beautiful, wan face.

Today they would bury her, then burn the litter so fairies wouldn't spirit Deirdre back out of her grave. It was an old custom, Druid in origin; Grania didn't doubt Ossian would wince at the pagan smell of it. Even as Connor ruled with his priests, the Druids still had their pockets of sway. But a Christian cross would also claim Deirdre's resting place; in death, too, the church staked its claim.

Grania slumped back from the window. She pressed her hand against the aching saddle of her back as she waddled to the tiny hearth carved into the hut's far wall. This hostage house was one of five stone structures, each shaped like a beehive, that clustered on a mound beyond Aileach's outer rath. The cottages were not meant to be prisons; hostages stayed willingly as tokens of their tribes' good faith. They could come and go as they pleased—except for Grania.

The loose stone walls were no match for the winter wind. Cold air muscled easily through the hut's loose seams, choking the struggling fire near to extinction. Grania lifted her palms, but the pitiful heat from the turves only made her flesh sting.

The wicker windbreak shuddered as the door slammed closed. Grania eased down onto the creepie stool and brushed the dust off her tiny table, readying for another cold, lonely breakfast. Only when Brian cleared his throat did she realize it was not Morgana who'd entered. She spun to face her father with huge white eyes.

"Daughter, will you not stand to greet me?" His voice was as thick and mellifluous as Grania remembered it. She stood up, wondering if Brian had come to free her—or condemn her.

She shifted her *bratta* to cover her belly, but from the displeased look of her father's stern face, Brian had already seen.

"It's no bastard. I'm married," she stated matter-of-factly.

"I was told of your match with Niall—but not of this." Brian's eyes clung to her stomach. "What have I done that you keep such secrets from me?"

Grania's imprisonment had made her strangely free, for now she could speak her mind and they could do no worse to her. "You can leave if you've only come to accuse me."

Brian's eyes remained unflinching, and Grania remained undaunted; she met his stare with fiery insolence. Yet, unwillingly, she softened a little, for she could see the years had worked Brian hard. The bones of his face had thickened, and the fillets of his hair, pinned to his skull by his gold head blade, were shanked with gray. Brian's eyes, once as blue as a shallow lake, had turned to the color of cold sea. Her father seemed shorter and heavier; he looked tired. What right had he coming here, looking so sorry?

It had been four years since he'd bothered to come see her at Uisneath. He'd delegated his visits to one of his messengers, who came in his stead to beg Maeve to send Grania back to him. At least Brian had known better than to force his daughter's return. Though now it seemed he'd won her after all; however bleak her present situation, she'd finally been pried free of the mists her father hated.

"I've come with the king to bury Deirdre."

So this was the clatter that woke her last night: Connor's funeral party, come to eulogize Deirdre. Grania wasn't surprised. Niall had told her Connor always favored his sister, particularly since he'd sired no daughter of his own.

"So you come for the O'Neill, but not for me." Her voice was flat and bitter.

"Why should I come for you, when you refuse even to let me know you are among us? It was not I who crafted our rift."

Brian stepped closer and Grania recoiled, raising her palms against him. "Have you come to chide me for foiling your fate? Is Connor displeased to find his bard's child has defiled the bed of his heir?"

Brian lifted his hands impotently. "I never meant to cause you this pain. I watched your mother struggle in my O'Neill world. I thought only to spare you—" The corners of his eyes sagged down dolefully.

"You sent me away."

"To a kinder fate. That was what I hoped you'd find at Uisneath. I didn't know then how much I'd miss you—" Brian's eyes wandered the hostage hut as he let out a heavy sigh. "Why, when you refused to stay with me, would you come to Aileach?"

There was no point in explaining to him; Brian was no believer in fate. He'd only laugh at her.

"It makes no matter now. I don't belong here. And unless you've come to help me leave, neither do you."

"I *have* come to help you."

Grania blinked at him, her eyes full of distrust, her hands flexing and releasing nervously. "Have you brought me a horse? Or did you think to bear witness at my trial?"

"Surely you do not hope to be tried? You'd surely be condemned for such a terrible crime."

Hot tears filled Grania's eyes. Even her father believed her a murderess. Likely he'd come here today in secret, to beg her to disclaim any link to him for fear her Druid blood would shame his bard's name.

"Get out." She levied her finger at the door and shook it hard when Brian made no move.

"There is still time to refute the pact with Fergus. Still time to save yourself."

Grania's eyes grew enormous with question. "Fergus? How would you know of that—have you talked to my sisters at Uisneath?"

"All of Aileach sings with your treachery. They say Niall will belt your head for allying the Druids with the cur of Ulster."

Grania plopped down on the pallet, dumbfounded. Niall didn't think she'd killed Deirdre; he thought she'd enlisted Fergus to try to kill *him*.

* * *

Niall had decided Grania was to die. She was sure of it. Why else had Echu taken her from the hostage hut, gagged her, and brought her to these midnight woods? Niall didn't blame her for Deirdre's death; it was worse than that. He believed she had crafted Fergus's alliance with the Druids and kept it secret from him. He was half-right.

Grania tried to keep her tongue off the wool gag, but it cut too deep through her mouth. She salivated at the dry, nubby taste of it; if she could have, she would have vomited.

Her wrists were tied so tight she could barely catch a fistful of the horse's mane. She had to scrunch forward, pressing her cheek to the gelding's withers just to keep her balance. The odd angle stole her breath and jammed the baby into a hard lump under her. The baby that would die along with her. A sob rose up, clotting her throat.

She'd waited for days to hear news of her trial. But her hope waned with each sunset, and soon she'd realized Niall had no intention of calling his judges for her. So she'd taken the only recourse left—she had fasted against him. It was a time-honored way to resolve disputes. The aggrieved fasted to demand a public judgment. And always it came, for even the most callous lord would not let a man starve in his keeping.

In fact Grania had eaten enough to keep the babe safe, arranging the leavings to look untouched on the plate. But her cunning had worked too well; Niall, outraged, had not called for the judges. Instead he'd called for Grania's head.

The thumbnail of a moon lit the swinging sheath of Echu's blade. The door keep was old and palsied; if the blow was sloppy, Grania knew she'd survive it to suffer a second one. A violent shudder racked her, pitching her farther forward on the horse's withers. The gelding, sensing her fear, danced and neighed.

This was all a huge, tragic mistake. Even if she'd kept news of Fergus's alliance from Niall, her sympathies had been with her husband, always. She'd risked her own life to warn him about Fergus's trap at Rath Mor. Pleaded desperately against the Regaine's decision to support Ulster. And once the terrible alliance had been made, she had kept still only to keep Niall from rushing toward the deadly fight. She'd even come back to Aileach to try to save Deirdre. Yet Niall would repay her fidelity with death.

If it weren't for the babe, she would have been happy to have it finished. The only peace she'd known was the brief snatch of time she'd had with Niall; now that was only a tattered memory. Tears plopped off her chin onto the horse's red mane.

Sounds swelled in the dark. The dirge of hoofbeats, the distant lisp of a stream. Trees enfolded them, but Grania was so frantic she couldn't recognize where they were.

She wrenched upright as the gelding clopped to a sudden stop. Moments ago she was ready to surrender; now her every instinct told her to rally and fight. But her hands and mouth were bound, and she was alone in the woods with a man meaning to murder her.

She tried to twist off the saddle blanket, but Echu's large hands caught her halfway down. When he loosened the gag from her aching mouth, it struck new terror in her; they must be very far from Aileach if he didn't even care if she screamed.

"Please . . ." she gasped, closing her eyes as she leaned back against the horse's side, knowing her skirts would hinder her if she tried to outrun him. She could only hope the old man's blade would be sure and swift—and succeed on the first pass. Silence roared up around her; when she opened her eyes and looked up, she was alone.

She spun in a frantic circle. Did Niall mean to leave her as carrion for the wolves? Footsteps crunched the brush behind her. The horse pitched his head, his nostrils wide. Was this some perverse O'Neill game?

Her hands still tied, Grania grabbed fistfuls of the animal's mane and tried to spring back onto him. But with each jump her face slammed into the gelding's slick, sweaty withers and her handfuls of his hair couldn't hold her. The horse was way too high and she was too heavy. She'd have to outrace whatever was tracking her.

She hiked up as much of her skirt as her tied hands could manage and bolted off wildly. Even with the drag of the baby Grania ran as if she'd caught fire. Sod hurled off her heels as she gasped for air, eyes wide. The night was blacker than black, and it swallowed the path back. Not that it mattered; Aileach was the last safe place she could be.

Grania didn't see Niall until she rammed straight into him. She froze, stunned, at the chilling realization: he'd come to exact his own dark justice.

She lurched backward; he lunged after her. She hopped back again, this time losing her balance and falling with a loud thump onto her backside. Niall dropped to his knees and scuttled up next to her. Grania gulped as his hand went out, then was struck silent as Niall lifted her gently to her feet. She wondered how cruel he could be.

"The baby—are you hurt?" His voice was strangely soft as he held her hands.

"Don't touch me," she hissed, sure he must loathe her to torture her so. She thrust up her fists, shaking his hold off her.

"I didn't mean—"

"Get on with it," she blurted furiously. "If you're going to kill me, then do it now." Even as she tried to look bold and courageous, a whimper escaped her. She swallowed, closing her eyes, waiting to hear Niall's sword scrape as it left its sheath. But there was only silence. She blinked up at him.

Niall's eyes pulsed at her, then narrowed as if he'd reached a conclusion. "I came to speak with you," he said slowly. "I could not come to see you in public at Aileach. Connor would not have allowed it."

Of course—likely Connor would rather see her starve than see Niall come to her. "Speak with me?" Slowly, Niall's words sank into her. *She wasn't going to die. He wasn't going to kill her.* She was jubilant with relief. But her happy reprieve died under the furious set of Niall's eyes.

"I won't have my wife starving herself. You're to end this fast—now."

"But I only did it because—"

He snatched her chin up with his hand as his eyes pinned hers. "I won't have you hurting yourself—" His voice fell off the end of the word. "I won't have you endangering the babe."

That he cared for the child at all resurrected hopes Grania had buried. Was there a chance he believed her innocent? For a brief instant she considered lying. She could plead she knew nothing of Fergus's pact with the Regaine. But in her heart she knew Niall wouldn't believe it. The best she could do was be honest with him.

"Please, let me explain. I begged the Regaine against the alliance with Ulster. I warned him about Fergus. I would never have done anything meaning to hurt you—"

"Be still." Niall raised his palm to her face. His eyes

indicted her. "You should have told me. I heard from Fergus."

Grania slim hopes were dying. She knew she'd committed the gravest transgression: she'd cuckolded the almighty O'-Neill pride. "I meant to tell you," she gushed. "It was only that I feared . . . that you would die."

She thought Niall would take her confession as evidence she still loved him. But his head snapped back as if she'd struck him and his dark eyes swam with disgust. "You think Fergus can best me." His voice damned her.

"You cannot fight the druidhect," she said, amazed as she understood he meant to try.

"Your druidhect will die with Fergus. Like your lies. You plead it was me that you feared for, but it was only Uisneath. Did you think I was so monstrous I'd war on your lake? Did you think I cared so little for you—" His voice broke as he stared at her, his eyes glistening in the moonlight.

Grania raised her hand to her brow. Uisneath? No, that wasn't it, she'd hardly thought of that at all. Perhaps she should have, but she'd kept silent only to help Niall, only to keep him from speeding toward what would be a deadly fight. When she looked back up, all the pain and charity were gone from his face. "I should by all rights have had your head," he said.

Grania wished he'd taken it. She'd pleaded her cause as best she could, and still Niall believed she'd traitored him. What more proof did she need that his love had died?

Grania's mind considered the grim possibilities of her captivity. Niall didn't mean to kill her; he could have done that tonight had that been his intention. But neither did he plan to let her go back to Uisneath.

Then, she knew. It was what she'd feared when he'd

come begging her to return to Aileach for Deirdre: Niall had lied. He meant to keep her here so he could steal her babe.

"If you think me in league with Fergus, there's something else you should know." She paused, taking a deep breath to force out the chilling words. "The child is his."

Niall's eyes looked like cold stars as he glared at her. Grania wished there'd been another way. But he had forced her to this cruel deceit—and she would play his suspicions as best they served her.

"You lie."

"How is it you think I got free of Rath Mor?"

"You swore it was the druidhect." This was an unlikely turn, she claiming her magic had failed while he argued it hadn't. "Why then have you not used it to escape your hostage house?"

She would have, had she been able. But the disaster with Deirdre had drained all the faith from her. She would have no more magic until the babe was birthed. "Deirdre's death has left me ill."

He tilted his head back, squinting first at her face, then her belly. It was as if, if he looked closely, he thought he could know the babe's true parentage. "When the child is born . . . I will have my answer. Until then, you will stay as my prisoner."

"Then your promise to set me free was a lie."

"There are lies aplenty between us, it seems."

She was right; he did want the babe. "Even when the child comes you'll see nothing. Is my hair not dark as Fergus's? Are my eyes not as clouded with deceit? How can your heart be sure?" It was a question even Niall couldn't answer. "Let me go," she said icily.

Niall glared at her, then pulled a small knife from his belt. Grania stepped back, thinking she'd overpressed him, that he would kill her before he'd set her free. He raised the blade and sliced the ties off her wrist.

"Get on the horse," he snapped.

Her heart sank. She'd seeded doubt in his mind—but even that wasn't enough to make him free her.

"No," she announced defiantly, courage rising up from some place inside her even she hadn't known existed. She wouldn't go back to her cold jail only to wait for Niall to seize her babe. "I won't be prisonered without a trial. If you mean to make Fergus the excuse for jailing me, I have the right to be tried. I'll starve myself until all of Aileach sees. Even Connor will not dare deny my fast."

Niall pitched his head back with a furious laugh. "Do you expect me to call a brehon to judge you?"

"I do."

He squinted at her incredulously. Grania could see the thought sinking in with him—and how much it angered him. She was within her rights, and he knew it. Her fasting had only gone on for two days. But if she continued, the whole of the dun would learn of it, and Niall would worry even more about the safety of the babe.

"The judge is on circuit," he clipped. "It will be months before he returns to Aileach."

Niall might be lying; or maybe not. There *were* too few courts for the many claims, and the judges were often out on the road. But the babe would come before his judge did—and she could not afford to wait.

"Get on the horse." From the tone of his voice, Grania could tell Niall's patience was waning.

She leaned back on the gelding's flanks and took a hard, wide stance. "If there'll be no brehon, I demand to prove my innocence in the time-honored way. I demand the cauldron of truth. I demand my right to an ordeal."

CHAPTER
18

"Lady, please." Morgana's knuckles blanched as she wove her hands into a tight knot. "Let me say the child has made you too ill for the ordeal. Your husband will not force you to face the cauldron. You cannot risk this. Think of your babe."

"It *is* the babe I think of," Grania answered, her face schooled to calm even as her voice shook. She stared out the hostage hut window at Aileach's limed walls. Today, more than before, the dun loomed over her like an angry challenge.

She feathered her fingertips over the swell of the babe. "No child of mine will take first breath in this angry place." Her eyes drifted, then filled with determination. "And if I stay, Niall will take the baby from me."

This was her greatest fear, not the boiling water that would test her innocence. She could bear pain—but not to lose her babe. The ordeal was her last hope; if she survived it unscathed, by law Niall would have no choice but to let her go free.

"Here, then." Morgana pulled a tiny gold box out of the pocket of her *leine*. She twisted its top off and pushed it at Grania. Inside was a clear, viscous salve. "The honey will protect you against the water's burn."

Morgana's chest jerked with stopped sobs. She and Grania both knew the cauldron's sting would be the least of it; if Grania's hand burned, it would be taken as a sign she was guilty of treason. And the sentence for that was death.

Grania drew the Briton into a tight, desperate hug. In the past weeks Morgana had become her only link with the world outside her hostage house—and, with Deirdre gone, her best friend at Aileach.

"Shhh," Grania whispered, pulling Morgana against her as she stroked her mass of thick blond hair. "I'll have no tears for me. Let Niall accuse me of siding with Fergus. My conscience is clean." She tipped Morgana's teary face up. "I need no ointment. The water will not harm me."

"Please, lady." Morgana pressed the box into her hand.

Grania smiled but shook her head and set the honey aside. "I'm innocent."

She hoped virtue would be sufficient to save her. No matter what Niall thought, it was love that had driven her silence. She prayed the cauldron would give testimony to the truth.

Brehon law said the skin of an honest claimant would not even redden as it passed through the boiling kettle. But to be sure, Grania had keened the night long, her hands winding into the serpentine signs of magic to conjure the druid-hect. She'd gathered all the will and determination that could be had by her. If that failed, then she was ready to die. Better that than see her babe suckled on the O'Neill's warring ways.

"Let me coat your hand." Morgana's eyes were glazed with tears as she made one last, desperate plea.

Grania shook her head softly. "Niall would only take it to mean I doubted my innocence."

Morgana threw her eyes to the floor and drew a long, tired breath. "It is time, then. I was sent to fetch you."

"Then we go," Grania said with a brave, resolved smile. She wrapped a stiff arm around Morgana's shoulder.

The day was crystal cold, and the bright winter light nearly blinded Grania. Glistening hoarfrost scrunched under her slippers as her lungs breathed in a deep draft of the crisp, clean air. With a curt nod to Echu, whose own eyes were also tinged with fright, Grania wound her way through the outer raths toward Aileach's main gate.

As she entered the compound she realized it was Dermot who'd been harping the dirge she'd heard all morning. His fingers froze on the harp strings as she passed him, and he smiled at her with sad, helpless eyes. Knowing that he pitied her hardly buoyed her fragile mood.

A weight of stares came to rest on her. The peal of a bronze war trumpet pierced the cold, glassy air. Voices stilled and birds swallowed their calls. The stiff morning wind died. Grania pressed a quick kiss on Morgana's cheek and left her at the gate. She walked forward, unaware of her feet, moving like a ghost into the dun's shadowed circle.

Her eyes took in the thick crowd; she'd been confined in the hostage house for nearly a full month now. Faces from memory stared at her. Baetan and the physician who'd bled poor Deirdre. Serving boys she remembered from the cups hall. And Ossian, his black eyes just shy of delight as he watched her approaching her treacherous fate.

Witnessing an ordeal was considered a great honor; all of Aileach had come dressed in its finery for the spectacle. Wide gold neck plates caught flashes of the dawning sun, hair bells tinkled as heads shook in dismay, and the soft fringe on chieftains' *brattas* fluttered in the morning breeze.

Only the crackle of quicken fractured the silence. Grania looked past the expansive courtyard to a huge steaming cauldron that had been dragged to the dun's hub. Alone in her hostage hut, she'd envisioned it as little more than a large meat pot; but this was no kitchen kettle. It was hammered gold, its plate flashing with sunlight. The bright garnet rivets studding the pot's rim glistened. Fire flames licked at its shining belly, turning its metal bottom almost white.

Niall stood behind the cauldron, silent and impassive. His hair was pinned down by a golden skullcap, and he wore a huge prince's breastplate under his pied satin *bratta*. He made no greeting, but his wide eyes begged Grania to change her mind. She walked to the kettle's thick lip and set her jaw tight.

Hot steam twisted and curled off the water's surface, condensing to beads on her cheeks and her chin as she stared at the popping bubbles. Grania closed her eyes against the liquid's wild heat, struggling with the fear that gripped her.

"State your claim." Niall's voice was as solemn as she had ever heard it.

Grania lifted her chin to him. "I demand the right to prove I am innocent of treason. I sought no pact with Fergus. Nor did I keep silent to bring you injury. I have not betrayed you, Niall, lord of Aileach. I demand the right, once proven innocent, to be set free." She made no assertion that she had not betrayed him with Fergus's bed, too; how could she when she'd claimed otherwise? But if Niall suspected

Fergus as the babe's sire, he would not accuse her. Even speaking the claim would shame him unthinkably.

Niall's face was a battlefield. His eyes were languid at first, then raged to hard, angry points. His mouth was soft, then tightened to a thin, mean seam. His hands flexed, then balled to fists as if he were trying to grab some amorphous thing. It was a long moment before he answered her. "Your demand is granted. If God and truth be with you, the water will not harm you."

Grania put no stock in the O'Neill God. It was justice that earned her faith. She prayed the truth would prevail— and if not, that the druidhect would rise to save her.

She stepped closer, pushing her *bratta* clear of the flames. Morgana let out a muffled whimper somewhere behind her. Grania rolled up her sleeve and bared her forearm. In one sharp movement, she thrust out her hand, palm up and fingers splayed. With a deep, steadying breath, she mined for the feel of the magic. She was as ready as she'd ever be. The crowd hushed.

In a deep, wide arc, Grania plunged her hand in. Pain instantly prickled every nerve ending. She jerked her arm back, but it felt as though the water held her prisoner. She pulled free with such force that her shoulder popped audibly. Beads of scalding water flung back, burning her neck and her face. Grania let out an involuntary, ragged cry.

She sagged back, her head slumping down as she held up her throbbing hand in the cold air. The pain was so intense, she could barely breathe. A thousand needles riddled her skin, and even without looking she knew that the cauldron's water had burned her badly. She could feel blisters starting to form. She'd failed the test—and Niall would judge her guilty.

When she opened her eyes they were glazed with tears. It was just as she knew: both her arm and hand were terribly burned. Even Morgana's salve would have been useless. Grania looked up to Niall and saw his eyes, too, were brimming with tears. But it would make no difference that he pitied her. She had begged this fate, and now she would take his verdict honorably. She cleared her throat and held herself upright.

Niall lifted his hand, rubbing his downturned face. When he raised his face back up, his eyes were closed. Grania knew what had once been no more than suspicion was now confirmed to him: her burned hand meant she'd plotted with Fergus to defeat him. And to worsen it all, her guilt supported her lie that the child was not Niall's.

"What say you, lord?" Grania gasped with pain as the brehon spoke, unfolding her bloody fingers for Niall's scrutiny. But Niall said nothing; all of Aileach held its breath, but her husband did not speak. Grania was impatient to be done with it. She'd hear his condemnation—and bow her neck for the swing of his blade.

"What say you?" she cried out in a half sob. "Say it. Judge me."

"I say you are innocent."

Grania knew Niall had seen her injury. Yet he denied it. His grieved eyes bore down on her. What she'd thought was betrayal on his face softened to something kinder. Could it be that he would refuse the ordeal's judgment and let her go free?

The brehon released Grania's shaking wrist. Tears streaked down her cheeks as the terror drained out of her. The whole circle of Aileach seemed to sigh in relief.

"What say you, brehon?" Niall's voice was low and surly. The brehon, like Niall, didn't look at Grania's hand. He too lied. "I say innocent, lord."

"And you, Dermot?" Niall called up the harper from the circle's rear. Dermot too pronounced Grania innocent.

By the time Niall's brehon had marched Grania around the courtyard, everyone, from chief to plowman, had pronounced her free. Everyone except Ossian.

"Priest." Niall gestured for Ossian to stand beside him. Grania extended her blistered arm, waiting to hear the priest's condemnation. Unlike the others, he would not lie for her. Ossian's eyes clung to the red pustules peppering her burned skin. All the while Niall's stare bore down on him with an unmistakable directive.

"What say you, priest? Will you pronounce her innocence, as the rest have?" Niall leaned toward Ossian, speaking through gritted teeth. "A mistaken pronouncement might cost a man—or a priest—his head."

Ossian glared back at Niall with dark, furious eyes. "Pronouncing judgment is a task of great import. The high king would not wish a mistake."

"Connor would hear nothing from the lips of a dead man." Niall's hand curled around his sword hilt as he watched the priest. Grania could hardly believe it; he was willing to kill Ossian, to risk Connor's wrath, to ensure she went free. There was a long, pregnant pause as Aileach waited.

Ossian jerked his kohl eyes up to Grania's then, with a slow shake of his head, cast them back down. "I say innocent."

Every man and woman had lied for her. Grania would live. She could leave Aileach. She began to sob with uncontrollable relief.

It was the same sweet, haunting dream. Niall's fingers made soft, lacy swirls on the taut drum of her belly. Grania flattened her hands on his fingers, pressing his palm against the bulges that were tiny elbows and knees, watching Niall's face light as he felt the child inside her, the child that was hewn of both Christian and Druid blood. She raised her eyes to his and felt trust flower inside her.

Niall's hands caressed her rib cage, reaching the slim ridges of her shoulders. His fingers crept up her neck, cupping her face as his thumbs traced the soft contours of her cheeks.

He twined his fingers through her thick fall of long hair, lifting it up until its ends hung in soft, ragged wisps; Grania felt cool air filter down her neck and shivered as Niall placed a warm kiss on her nape.

His mouth lingered on the shell of her ear; he said her name in a whisper. Grania's world shrank to a fine point of pleasure as she lolled her head back, arching her breasts against him. And then, as each time before when she'd dreamed Niall came to her, she woke—alone. Always it was the same. Grania rolled over and began to cry.

The sounds of dusk shook off her grogginess. A cow lowed as his milkmaid tethered him in for the night, and iron pans in the field hands' backhouse clattered. Dogs, finally loosed for the night, yelped with glee.

She imagined everything on earth was freer than she was. Niall had pronounced her innocent; then, knowing she was too pregnant to walk to Uisneath, he'd forbidden anyone to lend her a horse or a chariot. He'd left for Fort of the Shields, abandoning her here, furious and helpless. Grania had survived the cauldron, but she was still prisoner of Aileach.

She could have walked home as little as a month past. But now the child was too close to coming; its weight drugged her with a deep, draining fatigue. She couldn't even manage the width of the practice field without feeling her breath thicken. Escaping would have to remain a distant, painful dream.

Her imprisonment was bad enough, but the added misery of her pregnancy made it particularly unbearable. Grania barely slept for the babe's constant turning. When she did, stabbing leg cramps seized her the night through. Her lungs couldn't draw proper air for the size of the babe, and anything she ate, even bland porridge, made her throat burn as if she'd swallowed fire. She wondered if she'd ever be right again.

She did her best not to lose hope. If Niall were detained with Connor, if he didn't return to Aileach until after the baby came, she could still flee. If, by then, she had the strength left.

At least the conditions of her jail had improved, Grania guessed because Niall felt guilty keeping her. Her hard pallet had been replaced with a testered bed that looked eerily like Deirdre's, and a downy mattress had supplanted the straw cushion she'd slept on when she first came. Lately her dinner trays arrived with fresh-baked wheaten, and she was even encouraged to take a daily stroll, though her profound fatigue sorely governed her sojourns.

She was happy when she did manage to get out; even in winter, Aileach's game plain was a busy place. Women, their heads bundled against the stiff north wind, nodded as they passed her, smiling and staring at her huge belly. Those few soldiers still left to protect the fort stilled their practice spears as she waddled by, wishing not to frighten her. Morgana had told her that it was Niall, not she, who now earned Aileach's enmity.

If this were true, one friendly face might well help her. There was not a day Grania didn't think of begging a midnight cart to see her home. But Niall had made a clear injunction against any assistance. Whoever disobeyed him would be punished severely. Grania would not ask; her conscience could bear no more misery. She held her peace—and waited.

Even Echu had grown solicitous. When she left for her

daily walk, he bade her to watch her step on the uneven ground. Often, late at night, Grania heard him tiptoe inside to stoke her fire back up. In the oddest of ironies, Aileach, now her jail, began finally to feel like home.

Grania wiped off her wet cheeks and rolled over, careful to shift off her back quickly since her stomach couldn't bear the baby's great weight. She curled up like a sow bug and waited for dinner.

She drifted a little, almost sleeping, until another wild cramp seized the calf of her right leg. She jerked down, trying to knead out the pain, but the bulge of the babe kept her from reaching it. She tried to be stoic, but the calf hurt so badly and she was so very tired. She ground her head into the pillow and began to cry. She didn't hear the door latch until it clicked closed.

She bolted up. It was Ossian. She hadn't seen him since the day he'd been forced to pronounce her innocent. He looked much grimmer than she remembered. They both knew only Niall's threat had made him spare her. Grania wondered if the priest had come to collect on his charity.

"Lady." He made a shallow bow, lowering his oily eyes.

"What is it you want of me? Have you come to fling another false accusation?"

The priest gave a nod, acknowledging her score on him. "You've good reason to hate me. But I've always been honest with you. So I trust when I tell you that I've come here to help, you'll have the sense to believe me."

Grania pitched her head back, laughing loudly. "What? Have you suddenly styled yourself my protector?"

"I could be that indeed." Ossian arched a black brow at her.

Grania was too tired to have any patience left for him. "Get out." She plopped back onto the bed and turned her face away.

"I come with news of Niall."

Grania rose up, staring at him. "It's said Fergus gathers his forces on a plain south of Ulster," he continued. "That Connor means to meet him there."

"What interest would I have in the O'Neill blood thirsting?" Grania was interested indeed. She needed to know Niall would be kept away until well after the child came. And she ached to know, too, that he was still alive.

"There is talk of a great battle."

"Have you come to bring me widow's weeds?"

"I've come to tell you Niall is too occupied with Fergus to keep watch on you."

"Why would he need to when he has you here?"

Ossian went on, undaunted. "I come to tell you that your husband is too busy to seek your whereabouts—should you leave."

"You know Niall's ruling. It is forbidden to help me. And, as you can well see, I can't walk to Uisneath. Niall wishes me prisoner, and that is what I will be. The prince of Aileach speaks and all Aileach obeys."

"Not all." Ossian drew a spindly finger across his pursed lips. It was a strange expression, one Grania could not quite read. "I've a chariot and a man to drive it for you."

She was shocked. "You bow to Niall's threats and pronounce me innocent, yet now you expect me to believe you'd disobey him? Why would you, of all men, risk so much to help me?" She expected Ossian to lie, but still she would hear it.

"Let us say . . ." Ossian glanced sideways for an instant, then stared at her. "Perhaps your return to Uisneath would serve the both of us." Incredibly, he looked earnest. Grania studied him, sure there was some telling detail she'd missed, some catch that would explain this sudden charity.

Then she understood. If she stayed at Aileach, Niall would take the babe. No matter what became of her, a half-Druid child would be the O'Neill heir. And Ossian would not allow it.

But she knew the priest too well to trust him. He'd rather watch an animal suffer than take pity and kill it. "Shall I say yes and send you run tattling to Niall? Or do you wish to track me yourself—which pleasure, priest, is it you seek?"

"If you leave and I tell your husband you've fled, he would surely know it was I who aided you. Such a choice, for me, would be most—unwise. Whatever I am, lady, I am no fool. My offer is genuine."

For once the priest's greed served him; it gave him credibility. Grania indulged the wild possibility Ossian preached. *Freedom.* The word rang like a sweet, distant bell. If she left Aileach, she could keep the baby. She could return to Uisneath until the child came, then make a new life in the south of the island. Lately she hadn't allowed herself to think of such sweet temptations.

"You see, for once our purposes are not in opposition." His thin mouth curved into a smile.

"When would you propose this act of defiance?"

"Tonight." Ossian leaned forward, looking ready to move on it. "There is no cause—or time—to wait."

The priest's eyes shone with uncommon brightness, and Grania could see his ambition feeding on her hope. "You've only to open the door. Echu is off to the smithy. And I've food and a driver bought to take you."

Grania's heart rose briefly, then sank. "The baby—I don't know if the ride would be bearable . . . even in a chariot. . . ."

Ossian stayed on her like a lean-ribbed dog digging for a fresh bone. "Would you stay here, then, and lose your babe?'' He plumbed her fears too well. ''You can take the Briton Morgana with you. The cart is large.''

Grania had failed the last time she'd tried to leave. But if she stayed Niall's prisoner, gambling he'd keep away until the babe came, the stakes were intolerably high. Perhaps, she began to think, if Morgana would agree . . . Grania's head filled with indecision.

''My choice may cost you your life, priest.'' She could hardly believe she'd said it. She should have thought Ossian, of all men, expendable. Yet even as much as she hated him, she wished no blood spilled for her plight.

''Niall will spare me. *If* he returns. Many who set out for the battlefield do not come home again.''

Grania wanted the snake of a priest out of her house, out of her sight. This was the thieving opportunist she knew Ossian to be. If Niall died, the priest wanted no one left to challenge his power at Aileach. That's why he was determined to help her. It was not unheard of for abbots to raise their own kin to kingship. Ossian was a man who would succor such hopes.

Well, she decided, if the priest was willing to risk his scrap of a life for her, it wasn't her task to refuse him. This fate, like all else that had befallen her, was beyond her making. If Morgana would come, she would agree.

She stood up, her eyes glinting bright and hard. ''Harness the team.''

Ossian's lips curled into a strange smile as he left the hostage house. A shudder, not cold, or even fear, racked Grania. The world had surely waxed mad; her husband had become her captor, and tonight her worst enemy had befriended her.

For once, the bloody hand of the O'Neill, raised so often in attack, might have prevented death. But Grania had trav-

eled under Niall's banner before—and paid dearly for it.
This time her chariot would fly no flags.

Ossian, too, was determined her flight would succeed.
He'd outfitted the chariot well, including two Welsh horses
less likely to be missed than the stouter but more valuable
plow stock. The Briton team was faster anyway and better
matched to the sleek, four-wheeled cart.

Dill was to be her charioteer; he'd been deemed too old
to battle and left at Aileach. Grania was glad of it. He had
a quick, seasoned hand and the horses trusted him. What's
more, he was kind to her. She guessed he might have helped
her even without Ossian's bribe, but that the old man didn't
want to miss the pleasure of bleeding the priest's coffers.

The leather panniers strapped to the cart's wicker sides
were well stocked with cold eggs and salt beef and a currant
cake thieved from Aileach's backhouse. Ossian had even
purloined two skin cushions to be used as chariot seats.
Grania assumed these were less for her comfort than to
lessen the likelihood of a complicating miscarriage.

The unlikely trio had left late last night. Dill had avoided
the main road, thinking it was too obvious. Instead he'd
opted for a path that detoured through the western Connaughta land. The province had strong O'Neill blood ties,
and Grania hoped that if they could not pass through unnoticed, the Connaughta would be at least be amicable. Yet
she was ever mindful of the dangers of war. No rider was
without suspicion, no chariot safe from attack. They could
easily be condemned as spies or have their horses seized
by hungry men roaming the roadway. Grania breathed easier
with each mile they covered—and feared for the many yet
to come.

She shifted on her cushion, leaning at odd angles as she
tried to find the least jostling position. Dill held the team
in check, shy of their full pace, mindful of her pregnant

misery. But the ride was one sharp punch after another. Every now and then Grania could not help but moan.

"Take my pillow, lady." Morgana had been watching her.

Grania shook her head and managed a small smile. "It would make no difference. It's the babe, not the ride. Uisneath is all that'll ease my discomfort. With luck we'll make it in two days. After that, I'll worry for you and your trip back to Aileach. I stand to miss you." She noticed Morgana was oddly quiet. "Do you not wish to go home?" She had never considered the Briton would want otherwise.

Morgana's eyes were guarded, as was often the case with slaves. In her years of laboring in Inisfail she'd learned telling the truth rarely served her. "I would go back to Briton. Where I could be free again. I was not born a slave, but sold when one of your southern tribes took me in a raid."

Grania nodded. Morgana too once had family and home—and still had longings of her own. "Ossian pressed some gold on me before I left Aileach. It will help you buy your way." She fumbled through her leather satchel, but Morgana stopped her.

"All of Inisfail drums with war. A boat and a pilot would be hard to come by. But there is a place I should like to see . . . I have been thinking about your Uisneath. . . ."

Morgana wanted to come with her. Before now, Grania had never considered it. It was a comforting prospect. She trusted Morgana, and she could certainly use a friend. But Morgana knew nothing of the old-blooded ways. She, even more than Grania, would never find peace behind the veil of the mists.

"It's difficult . . . when a place is not meant to be home to you." Grania was thinking of her own fate, both at Aileach and Uisneath.

"So I know, lady," Morgana answered softly.

Grania's cheeks flushed. Of course Morgana knew; she'd been kidnapped from her family and dragged an ocean away. "See there?" Grania pointed toward a distant blue hill, wishing to change the topic. "Already the rocks of Aileach give way to a gentler land."

The chariot clattered over a boggy causeway. Grania listened to the crisp snap as the cart's iron wheels bore down on the branches laid to stiffen the road mire. The noise was head-splitting. It was said that the higher the rank of the rider, the louder a chariot creaked. Grania wished their wheels silent before they drew robbers—or worse things.

But there was no one to hear. The few villages they'd passed en route had become ghost towns of war, filled with women and children, their men gone off to die alongside Niall. There was no clatter of spears on their practice fields, no smell of meat over their fires. Spits turned only with what could be hunted by women and dogs.

The air hung with the eerie silence that was the harbinger of war. Grania closed her eyes and listened to the chariot's leather awning catch the wind.

The coach edged off the causeway, and the team began to neigh, their call full of fear. Grania snapped her head forward as Dill slowed the team with a warrior's vigilance, his eyes narrowing as he scanned the cluster of hills surrounding them. He cinched one hand tight on the reins; the other wound instinctively to his sword.

Grania pushed up to a stand with the help of the side bar. Then she saw what had drawn Dill's blade: three men on two horses stood in silhouette, unmoving, at the crest of the next hill. In less than a breath, they swept down on the chariot with the speed of a field fire.

Dill swiveled his head, scouting cover. There wasn't much, only a lean stand of oak shooting off to their right.

It was too sparse to couch the chariot but might work to hide Morgana and Grania. Dill hustled the women down with brusque efficiency, all but dragging them into the woods. Neither Grania nor Morgana had time to protest.

"Stay here." Dill pushed Grania down into a crouch. A thick bush of furze fronted her.

"Let me stay with you." Grania's voice was adamant, though shrill with fear. "They've seen us. If they mean you harm—"

"All the more reason to keep covered. You too." He nodded at Morgana, who stonewalled his instruction with an indignant stare.

"You cannot stand them alone," she said tonelessly.

"And I suppose *you* can thrust a spear?" Dill's face ended the argument. Morgana sank back, sighing. "I saw no banner," he said hopefully. "They may yet prove friendly. But if not, I want the both of you here. Stay down." Morgana crouched alongside Grania as Dill sprang from the thicket with a younger man's speed.

Grania fought back tears while visions of a similar scene—when Fergus had seized her—flooded her mind. Dill's team neighed nervously as the three riders thundered closer. Grania could just make out the insignias on their shields.

"See there," she whispered to Morgana, pointing. "Airghialla. They are O'Neill allies."

Dill jumped back into the chariot cart and tried to straighten his old man's back. "I am O'Neill," he called out, hands cupped to carry his voice. Grania knew his fear: if he couldn't prove his tribe, the Airghialla might well deem him enemy.

Grania scrambled to her left for a better view. She glanced back, meaning to motion to Morgana, but the Briton was gone. Grania spotted her darting from tree to tree; she was following Dill.

"I am O'Neill," Dill repeated, raising his hand in salutation. The horses' mouths belched steam as their riders pulled them up in front of the O'Neill team. The men stared at Dill like predators assessing prey.

"What's your business on the road, charioteer?" The man who spoke looked of bad ilk; he was fierce-featured, and his half beard was poorly shaven. He was obviously no chieftain.

"I travel to see Connor, high king."

Grania's heart plugged her throat. Matha had tried this argument, too—and failed. Her eyes darted from Dill to Morgana, who was still dashing from tree to bush.

"It's a fine team, driver." Greed lit the Airghialla man's dark eyes.

"The high king would have no less."

"You fly no banner."

"Our flags have all gone to fight Ulster. Why waste one on an old charioteer?" Dill loosened the team's reins from where he'd tied them at the front of the cart. "Connor waits for me. Godspeed to you, Airghialla." *Let him pass*, Grania prayed silently.

Before Dill had time to turn the team, the man who had spoken broke into a stained, broken-tooth smile, then surged forward, snagging one of the Welsh horses by its halter. "We lost my friend's gelding at camp last night," he said, nodding toward two other men who were doubled up on a sag-backed mare.

Dill's hand eased downward onto his spear. They were too far away for the swing of his sword, and likely he couldn't wield the weapon with much strength anyway. The man dismounted with a thump, and before Dill could lift the javelin, the stranger grabbed his collar and yanked him roughly out of the cart. With a sickening smack, his shield struck Dill's face. The blow was a double insult; the Airghialla man didn't even deem him worthy of his blade.

"Out of my way. Old man," he added, sneering.

His javelin still in the cart, Dill pulled his dagger out of its belt sheath. A second knock of the Airghialla's shield sent him flying. Dill landed on his back, grabbing his shield off the chariot's side as he fell. His arm, threaded under the crossbar, shattered like kindling as the Airghialla man slammed his boot down. Dill rolled his eyes toward his limp, useless hand. He didn't see the death blow come to impale him.

Grania's tooth bit through her lower lip as she watched in horror. She made no noise, yet someone screamed. It was Morgana's wild, furious wail. The Briton lunged forward, cursing, her arms flying as the Airghialla man began to unharness the chariot team. Morgana's tiny knife was a pitiful threat against his huge, bloody blade but she raised it like a champion wielding a broadsword. Grania prayed they would at least kill Morgana quickly. It wasn't to be.

One of the double-mounted men jumped off, seizing the chariot team. The other galloped toward Morgana, hooking his arm under her waist and hiking her crosswise over his horse's shoulders. He carried her off like a screaming, kicking sack of mill flour.

The men parted the team from the cart quick as lightning. Grania barely had time to struggle to a stand as she watched Morgana being hauled off by the horrible Airghialla men, her shrill voice hurling British epithets that soon fell to echo.

Grania's mind was a jumble; she could barely even focus on the raiding party as it shrank out of sight. She was so deeply ashamed. She should have stayed with Dill, fought for Morgana, done anything but crouch in dumb, shameful silence. Yet she had made the disgraceful choice not for herself, but for her babe. Nothing an unweaponed woman could have done would have altered anyone's fate. She said it over and over again, trying to believe it.

Strength drained out of her. Grania collapsed on the sod, leaning her face into its cool compress as she began to cry. Dill was dead, Morgana was gone, and she was alone with no horse, a useless chariot, and no hope of rescue. Only Ossian knew where she'd gone and he wouldn't be sending out any search party. Her voice climbed skyward in a scraping, torn wail.

She wept her way to a blinding headache. When her tears were spent, she lifted her face and stared down the empty road. The sight of Dill's sad, shattered body made her cry again, though this time soundlessly. The horseless chariot, so full of hope just moments ago, lay upended next to him, broken and empty.

Grania tried to think. It was a full day back to Aileach mounted, two days on foot. But, heavy with the babe, she would never make it. She'd be safer among the strangers of the Connaughta. And closer to Uisneath, though even that destination was still leagues away.

She pulled up to her knees and wiped her face. Clearly she couldn't stay here; already the wind was stiffening and the shadows of the trees were starting to lengthen. The babe kicked inside her, reminding her that she must keep fighting.

She should start walking now—but it wasn't strength, it was will she was lacking. Grania thought of Niall, of the O'Neill blood that drove him on unreasonably even against all odds. She stood up and began forward.

She averted her eyes as she walked past Dill. She was too big from the baby even to think of burying him, but leaving him here . . . Her cheeks went red with shame. Still, she had to keep moving.

Grania rifled the chariot's upended panniers. She'd never be able to carry the whole basket but could manage some of the lighter stores. The meat could stay; she'd pluck out the eggs and the wheaten.

She cinched her hands under her belly and snatched up a bread loaf. She stood up and looked down the road. The raiders were gone. There was no more reason to wait.

But the moment she began, a furious fist hurled through her belly. Grania dropped the wheaten and doubled over, breathless with pain. *It was a kick*, she assured herself. *Only a strong kick*. Yet it was so different from anything she'd felt before. Grania beat down her fears. The movement was a good sign: the child, like her spirit, rallied.

When she moved again she felt a cold, damp sensation oozing between her legs. She looked down and saw that a huge wet spot soaked the front of her *leine*. Her water had broken.

Even with the best of midwives, a woman could die birthing. Grania nearly went blind with panic, thinking what perils would befall her, suffering the horrors of childbirth alone on this darkening, desolate plain.

She racked her memory, trying to recall if they'd passed any of the crude hospitals called public houses. They were little more than places to lie down and be bled, but anything was better than this. She painstakingly retraced every vacant mile. It was useless; there'd been nothing but a few scattered villages, and even those were far beyond the means of her strength.

Daylight edged toward gloaming, honing her senses to instinct. She tried to think calmly. How would she fend off animals? Keep warm? How in the Mother's name could she hope to give birth here and still stay alive?

The chariot offered some meager shelter, but it lay upended in an open clearing and Grania feared that the riders who'd killed Dill—or other thieves of like mind—might return to claim it. With a gangling discomfort already working her womb, she limped back to the oak stand where she'd hidden during the attack and lay down.

The soft earth went crunchy and cold with the oncoming night, but Grania had no energy to worry about such small miseries. Already she was sweating with fear. And she was terribly thirsty. She scanned the thicket with weak, languid eyes, but there looked to be little hope of a stream. She shimmied her back against the oak bole and rested her head on its rough bark. Another spasm pressed her womb through her spine.

She washed like driftwood on great, rolling waves of pain. She was desperate for water; how sweet even one small sip would be. Finally she plucked up leaves that had fallen to the ground and licked off the night dew that had started to bead on them. But she was still aching with thirst. She began to cry, and finally, exhausted, she slept.

Grania dreamed it was she, not Dill, who'd taken the marauder's blade. When she woke, she was sure of it— except the sword seemed to be cutting its way out of her, not coming in. For all her healing, Grania had never witnessed a birth, and it took more jolts of pain before she realized it was this grinding agony that would force the child out of her.

She'd heard the birthing could last for days. Already the sharp spasms stole her breath. She ground her skull back against the oak tree. If this was how her labor would begin, she knew she'd never live to see the end of it.

Water leaked out of her continuously, wetting her skirt and making her back shiver and her teeth chatter. Chills racked her; fever drove them away.

There were only brief gaps between the seizures shaking

her womb. It felt as if the child were trying to break free of her. The pain leached out from her core into her arms and legs. She ached all over, blood and marrow. Her strength, already badly sapped, waned.

At first she held her breath through the pains. But as the knife strokes lengthened, she found she grew faint when she didn't breathe. She began to pant, air whipsawing in and out of her chest. She stared up at the half-mooned sky, her eyes lolling to white. The night mirrored her own black, hungry pain.

Grania was grateful when a ragged wind rose up, cooling the sweat off her brow and soothing her itching skin. She snatched sleep where she could, even in the brief seconds between one slap of pain and the next.

She'd never been so thirsty in all her life. She looked up and her heart sank on the dry, cloudless sky. Everything she had done up till this moment had been for the child. Now, in her delirium, she began to think only of herself, and when she did, she wanted to die.

The next pain put the others to shame. Grania clutched and clawed at the sod, screaming. The contractions bled straight from one to the other, with no rest in between. It was all a blur of wrenching, seamless agony. Even in the strong grip of the druidhect, she had never been conduit for such shuddering power. This couldn't be the Goddess in her; surely it was Morrigan, the raven of death. Grania sensed something was terribly, irrevocably wrong. She was sure she and the baby were both going to die.

The pain ceased abruptly, only to be supplanted by a leaden swell that pressed her whole body down into the earth. She longed to expel her very insides; resisting was beyond her means. With a groaning, wild scream, she bore down repeatedly.

She bellowed and pushed, her breath rasping, her palms

bloodied from the cut of her nails into them. She could feel the pall of death come over her as the baby shifted downward. The child levered her hips apart with exquisite agony; Grania was sure she would split like soft fruit under a sharp knife. She closed her eyes, unable to watch her flesh rent from her bones.

When she thought the pressure could get no worse, it did. She was hysterical, sure that the child would never leave her alive. She struggled to sit up and reached downward, gripping at her twisting center. Her hand recoiled in terror and amazement: she could feel the baby's head coming out of her.

She pushed again, and this time, she thought her stretched flesh had caught fire. She felt herself slipping into a dark, deep abyss. Only instinct drove her, telling her to push one more time.

Her body gave one final, racking shudder. With a relieved heave the baby's head, then its shoulders, slipped out of her. Grania could feel the child, squirming and warm and wet on the cold night earth. Strength ebbed back into her as she stared down, crying with relief and joy. Strung to her with a thick, pulsing cord, still part of her, yet now separate, lay her baby daughter.

CHAPTER
19

Flawless, tiny features nuzzled against Grania's breast. She had clutched the child—her precious, tiny newborn child—in the cradle of her arms the freezing night long.

Grania had lain in the same rigid position ever since she'd used a sharp rock to cut the cord that bound them. She'd been too afraid to gamble the pitiful heat they'd managed to capture.

By all rights, she should have felt miserable. She was cold and weak from losing blood. But she felt euphoric. She felt she'd always known the warm, pliant contours of the baby's tiny arms and legs, the undulant cheeks that puffed in and out, nursing even as they both slept. She knew how her daughter gurgled and sighed. And the sweet bloody smell of her small head, its wispy hair so fine it tickled her lips as she kissed her.

Now, as the sun crept over the distant hills, Grania caught

her first real glimpse of her daughter's face. The child was Deirdre come again. She had the same robin's-egg eyes, swimming with trust, the same pink, seeking kiss of a mouth, the same hair, the color of sunlit wheat. Despite her lie that Fergus had fathered the babe, she knew once Niall saw her he'd know the truth: the baby was all O'Neill, completely his. Tears welled up in her. She adored her daughter beyond anything she'd felt before. This was flesh cleaved from her own, the best of what she and Niall both might be. The babe was Inisfail's past and future incarnate; Grania prayed their angry world would make a place for her.

How Niall would smile when he saw her. Grania froze, realizing she had to stop the indulgent wishing. If Niall saw the babe, he would surely seize her.

She had lost Niall twice now, once as husband and again as father. She would not lose this flesh born of her own, too. But unlike her own father, neither would she deny her daughter's heritage; she would call the child Isolde, in honor of Niall's mother. This, at least, she could offer him.

There was some slim chance Grania and the baby could vanish into the tattered fabric of Connaught. But even the smallest hamlets would soon shudder with war. No mortal place would be safe; only Uisneath could shield them. Grania guessed that the trip, lacking horse or chariot and with the burden of a suckling babe, would take her nearly two weeks. No matter; she had to try.

Clutching Isolde, she staggered to a stand and discovered she'd overreckoned her strength. Her vision ebbed; black pinpoints pocked her sight, and her knees wobbled as if her joints had been shaken loose of their fittings. Bracing herself on a tree, she bent her head down, trying hard not to faint.

She ached as if she'd been beaten. Vague memories of

clutching and pulling at the sedge grass washed back to her. Grania could recall few specifics, but she imagined she must have acted crazed to hurt so exquisitely today.

She took a tentative step forward. With the shift in weight, Isolde's neck, still too new to support her oversize baby's head, flopped backward. Grania gasped, righting the baby quickly and readjusting her hold on her.

She watched the blue spiderings of veins pulse on Isolde's eyelids, as translucent as vellum. When the stiff wind that had buffeted them all last night began to rally again, Grania cocooned her *bratta* tight around Isolde and wished she had something softer to swaddle her in than the scratchy wool cloak.

She longed to sit and rest, just a minute more. But she knew she was like a horse that, once down, wouldn't rise again. So she pressed on toward the chariot, every step a wearing, bone-creaking agony.

Her hips, wildly levered by the child's riotous descent, felt as if they could slip out from beneath her. Her breasts were red and sore from Isolde's near constant nursing, and to make it all worse, she could tell she was still bleeding. But these problems would have to wait. She needed food.

She trudged on determinedly, squinting at the purple hills, which were just beginning to shake off the dark blanket of night. There were so many lakes and miles yet to go, so many hazards she couldn't even foresee. But she couldn't let fear be her taskmaster; she couldn't make Morgana's and Dill's sacrifice meaningless.

Dill lay in the same gruesome tableau as when Grania had left him yesterday. The broken arm was horribly bent, and the other hand was frozen, rigid and white, clutching his dagger. His eyes were open. He deserved a full burial, but Grania had no hope of managing it. She was so weak she felt transparent. She'd have to trust Dill's soul to the Goddess—and his flesh to the carrion.

There were apparently those aplenty. The panniers and the supply bags had been clawed open during the night, and food lay strewn all around the chariot's base. Much had been carried off or half eaten, but Grania managed to find two dirt-caked eggs and a torn loaf of wheaten. If she rationed it carefully—and if she were lucky enough to find edible roots and water—she might make it to Uisneath without starving.

She stashed one cold egg in her pocket and wiped the dirt off the other with the only clean patch she could find on her *leine*. She gulped down the pitiful breakfast in three loud bites. Her strength and her spirits began to rise.

Balancing Isolde in the crook of her arm, Grania plunked her cache of plantain and another half loaf of wheaten into the doubled-up loop of her skirt. She hooked the hem over her belt and turned back to Dill.

He smelled ripe. Grania breathed through her mouth as she knelt down and held Isolde out to him. He had the right to know why—and for whom—he'd died. Grania held her breath and pried his stiff fingers off his dagger. The cold, rigid feel of him nearly brought the egg back up her, but she swallowed hard, refusing to be sick. She needed both the egg and the knife.

Grania staggered to her feet, gave Dill a respectful goodbye, and combed the clearing for some hope of water. She'd guessed right; a slender brook gurgled at the far side of the oak stand. She staggered toward it and dropped to her knees, cupping clear, wonderful handfuls of water to her mouth. She scooped and drank until her whole face was slick with the stream's wet, cool glory.

Grania guessed Isolde would wake soon, wanting milk.

She needed to earn some road before then. She reached through her legs and cinched up the back of her *leine* to stay the bleeding. With a stiff breath, she began.

Grania tried to focus her thoughts on getting to Uisneath. But each bend of the road brought up Niall's face. He would come for her. He'd come for the babe.

She'd birthed a girl. That fact gave her hope. Even if he found them, Niall might leave the child be. Girls were considered useless things, good for little beyond bedding and bride price. But Isolde bore Niall's sister's face. And her husband, Grania knew well, didn't think like other men. She should fear him, avoid him at all costs. And she would, even though she ached to show him the sweet, precious child they had made.

Grania pressed a kiss to the soft spot on Isolde's head and shuffled on. For now, at least, the baby was hers alone. But tomorrow . . . or a thousand days from this day . . . who could say? This much she knew: Niall would come for them eventually—providing he was still alive.

The mists were gone and the lake was burning. From the acrid smell and the smudged sky, Grania guessed the fire was fresh. And huge. The stench leached out miles from Uisneath, like a dark, deathly greeting.

Grania clutched Isolde tight to keep from jostling her as she bolted down the path to the lake. Her lungs screamed for clean air, and her feet, already mushy from two weeks' worth of stones, began to sting so badly that she limped as she ran. Thick smoke choked everything; the spell that guarded Uisneath was broken.

Grania blinked in slow horror as she stared pool-eyed at the marsh fire that had once been her home. She covered Isolde's eyes, shielding her from the macabre sight and the intense heat of the still raging blaze.

Maeve. Eithne. Grania longed to believe they were safe, but she knew better. The horrific scene defied all her hope. Crannog huts flared like giant tapers. Columns of fire raged skyward where roofs had once stood. Pulley ropes arced and snapped like burning snakes.

The shoals' reflection doubled the flames. It took Grania a moment to realize the shore burned, too. Firestorms shot through the stone *clochans*' windows, and tongues of flame licked out of their wall seams.

How had the fire ever jumped the lake? With slow horror, Grania slid a hand to her mouth as she understood—Uisneath had been set to flame. She spoke the accusation out loud: O'Neill. She dropped her head to her shoulder like a wounded bird and let out a low, lost moan. Niall, who'd damned her for failing to believe he would protect her, had burned Uisneath.

The air roared and hummed all around her. It smelled of charred fleshmeat and singed woodbine. Except for a few bleating, confused goats, Uisneath's livestock too had fallen prey to the flames.

Stacks of combed flax burned like torches in what was left of the storage shed. Churns and looms that had not yet caught flame lay spilled and upended, as if they too had tried to flee.

Cool tears made tracks down Grania's hot cheeks. Flecks of soot stuck like grit to her face. Slowly she edged backward, her eyes glazing as she tried to think.

For Isolde's sake, she needed to find a safe place. They certainly couldn't stay here; the O'Neill might well come back again. And she still lacked the strength to travel all the way south, clear of the fighting.

She wondered . . . was there some chance the Regaine and her sisters had sought shelter at Rath Mor? Whether they had or hadn't, Fergus's fort was the safest place in the midst of this madness. She too had no choice but to seek protection with the Ulstermen.

She turned, ready to bolt, but her head jerked up on the muzzle of a huge black destrier. The horse's hooves danced just in front of her toes, and as Grania's wide eyes climbed, the rider appraised her with a steely, dark stare. He wore a strict leather helmet, and he was weaponed for war. Grania's eyes froze on the horse blanket—it bore the red hand of the O'Neill.

"Praise our Lord Jesus. I thought I was lost here." Grania's heart bucked at the lie, but she'd pretend to be Christ himself if it would safekeep Isolde.

"What's your business, woman? Don't ye know this is a cursed place?" Red hair shanked with gray squirreled out from his skullcap, and bronze bands straked down from the man's headpiece, nearly obscuring his beady eyes. A filleted beard sheathed the lower half of the warrior's face. From the set of his mouth, Grania could tell he nursed no thoughts of befriending her. "What's yer business?" he repeated, his voice growing agitated.

"I am lost. Sir," she added with a respectful tone.

"Indeed. There's nothin' to seek here."

"I was searching for a hostel. As you can see, my babe is newborn." Grania's eyes beseeched him.

"This grave was a Druid place," he answered, ignoring Isolde as his nose twitched at the smell of the fire. "Ye'll find no hostel here." The man's mouth twisted as he assessed Grania. "Have ye no man—or horse?"

"My horse," Grania answered slowly, forming the explanation as she spoke it, "loosed his tether and slipped away. And 'tis a man I am seeking. My husband. He is soldier to Connor. I'd thought he was camped near here, but—" She raised her hand to her throat as if the very thought of Uisneath made her go faint. "I am sorely misguided. My husband, like you, sir, is O'Neill. I only wish to show him his newly birthed babe. Before he dies.'' Her voice broke perfectly; her ease with the lie surprised her.

''He would surely beat me if he knew I came after him. But I was left with his mother, and after the child came—'' Grania leaned onto the horse and vaulted up onto her tiptoes as she whispered, ''The woman was a shrew, and I could bear no more of her.'' She settled back as if telling the secret had relieved her. ''I know my husband would shelter me elsewhere—if I could find him.''

The O'Neill rider stared down indifferently. Then he rolled back his head and exploded in laughter. A sloppy smile buttered his ugly face. ''All Inisfail is hosting for war and ye set out to track your wayward mate. Plucky thing, ye are. If ye think to find your husband among Connor's countless battalions, your chances are better with his shrew of a dam.''

For a spate of reasons, not the least of which was that she thought her barely controlled panic might serve her, Grania started to cry. The O'Neill froze for a moment, then clucked, waving his hand frantically as if he would do anything to make her stop.

''I can't bear women weeping. Here now,'' he said, nodding in disgust at the roadway. ''I'll walk ye to the village. Then yer on yer own. I'd advise ye to hurry home. There's danger about.''

Grania nodded and made a point of sniffling loudly. The O'Neill let out an exasperated sigh. ''What is it, sir?'' she asked ingenuously, wiping her teary cheeks with the back of her hand.

''This husband of yers—''

''Mannu,'' Grania chirped brightly, her lie growing neater by the moment.

''Are ye sure he's on host with the O'Neill king?''

"Aye, Connor," Grania said, punctuating her answer with quick little nods.

"Then he's likely at Magh Rath. I'd have been there too by now had I not been assigned to scout this graveyard."

"Then you were not here to see the fire?" Against all odds, hope rose in Grania. Perhaps Maeve and Eithne had not been here, either, perhaps they'd escaped in time. She braced herself, unsure if she could bear to hear the details the O'Neill might know.

"Nay . . . I did not see it. But ye have only to look to see what became of the pagans."

The stranger knew nothing Grania's fears hadn't told her. "Aye," she answered softly. "Does Connor plan to meet Fergus soon then?"

"Soon," he said, smiling boyishly as if he could barely wait. " 'Tis said it's a fine fight, fast aborning. I should be at Magh Rath, too. On to home with ye," he said, shooing her off with his hand.

Magh Rath. The name of the place where Niall would die.

"Please, sir, if there's any way at all— *any* way—you could help me . . ."

The soldier shook his head preemptively. "Pffft. I can't waste my warrior's time nursemaiding some bale-faced wife."

"I'd be no trouble, I promise you," she gushed, lowering her eyes. "But I can see you have important business. I won't press your kindness," she said, her chest hitching poignantly. "If you could only tell me which road . . . perhaps the child and I might be able to—" Her tremulous voice broke.

Fury and exasperation dueled in the O'Neill's flat face. Grania could see she was making headway. "By our Lord, yer a pitiful thing. Your husband has never even seen the child?'' Grania shook her head, still sniffling. The warrior snorted, then reached down a huge dirty hand. ''The high king will belt my head if he hears of this,'' he mumbled, making a face.

''I'll praise your name in silence, then.'' Grania's eyes lit brightly. The soldier pulled her up onto the huge black destrier. Grania wedged Isolde safely between them.

''The Lord protect you, O'Neill.''

The stranger gave his mare a swift kick as they began north toward Magh Rath. Everything else had gone wrong for Grania, but not this. She felt a smile warm her face. If Connor knew what baggage this O'Neill carried, he would indeed have the hapless warrior's head.

Rath Mor was different from the last time Grania had seen it. When she'd been prisoner here before, everything about the dun had been filtered through a dark fog of terror. This time, life seemed to blossom here.

Women strolled on the game plain, the early spring breeze making their linen skirts billow like foam at their ankles. They laughed as they wove bone combs through their long, shining hair and smiled at Grania as she passed them cautiously. Inside the compound walls, sword boys wearing vests marked with leonine insignias clustered in twos and threes as they limed shields. Chained dogs barked. Cows mooed, and somewhere a child laughed. Life seemed strangely bright, oddly normal. There was no sign of the Druids.

The only oddity was the chariots. Four hundred easily, maybe more, stood stationed at the edge of Rath Mor's outer gate; their wheels were newly tired with iron and their leather sides freshly painted with the rampant lion of Ulster. Fergus's warriors used the carts in warfare—unlike the O'-Neill and Connaughta, who preferred horses or foot fighting.

But the chariots stood silent today, waiting for drivers and battle cries. Soon they would thunder across Magh Rath's plain—aiming on Niall.

Grania didn't doubt Connor would be ready. When the O'Neill soldier had dumped her at the edge of O'Neill hosting, she had hardly believed what she'd seen: miles' worth of troops, sprawling everywhere, moving and shifting like a great weaponed beast.

The land was white with O'Neill tents, and the blue sky turned gray with the smoke from their cook fires. Wherever Grania turned, she heard the deafening clatter of spears and swords and the unnerving scrape as men practiced unsheathing their blades. She had wanted to stay, to find Niall, to plead with him one more time. But there was no point— he wouldn't listen. And she had Isolde now. Rath Mor was the only safe place they could be.

The gate warder admitted her easily. He'd smiled when she'd asked to see Fergus, ushering her up the inside stairs without a blink or a question. Grania realized how better plans might have served her; a smuggled knife could have ended Fergus's scheme. But she'd lost the dagger in her panic at Uisneath, and likely she wouldn't have had the strength for it anyway.

She was shown into the *grianan*; like Aileach's, it rode over the fort's front gate. The lean spring sun streamed in, buttering the satin wood that planed the walls. Beaten-bronze bowl lamps, suspended by thongs, swayed lackadaisically from the *grianan*'s ceiling, adding to the surfeit of light.

The door lintel shimmered with pounded gold. Fresh floor rushes were fragrant and soft under her feet. . . . This was not at all what she had imagined; the thought of Fergus sitting here, smug and warm while she'd shivered in that cold souterrain, made her wish she had brought a knife after all.

She snuggled Isolde closer and sat down on the edge of a red couch. A wood-and-bone chessboard lay on the table beside her, its pieces half-played. Grania glanced at it and looked up to see a small woman, red of hair and white of face, standing in the doorway's brilliant light.

She stepped inside and cocked her head at Grania. Her hair was strewn with mussel pearls and piled high in elaborate plaits. She was gowned simply in white, and a huge black-stoned gorget collared her small neck. She stared at Grania with wide, questioning eyes.

"I was told to wait here for Fergus." Grania nodded respectfully.

"The child—a boy or a girl?"

"I have a daughter," Grania answered uneasily, clutching Isolde tighter.

"Luck is with you." The woman's eyes fanned into a smile. "They make no warriors of our kind."

Grania realized who the woman must be. This was Fergus's *grianan*—and the woman was dressed too finely to be his serving maid. Likely she was Fergus's mistress. Or his wife.

"May I hold the babe? For a moment—please?" The woman stretched out her short arms.

She clutched Isolde tighter. Since the day the baby was birthed she'd been held by no one except Grania. But something elegiac in the woman's eyes drew her. "I don't think . . ."

"Please. For a moment. I'll ask no more of you."

Ruled by instinct, not logic, Grania loosened her grip and let the woman take Isolde. She slid her palms under the baby's head and legs ever so gently, molding her arms to

Isolde's small contours. The transition was so smooth that the child didn't wake. The woman looked down adoringly, making the same nonsensical clucking sound Grania knew she often made. The *grianan* light dimmed as Fergus blocked the doorway.

"Brona." Fergus's face went rigid and his maimed eye slivered tight. "Give back the child." Grania watched tears glaze the woman's eyes. "Return her, Brona. *Now*."

The woman blanched with anger. Grania could see Fergus's rude tone was familiar to her. Grania started to explain that she'd given her permission, but the woman handed Isolde back before she could speak. In a blink, Fergus's wife was gone from the room.

He slammed the door closed. "This," he said, nodding at Isolde. "Is it Niall's?"

Grania gave a slow nod. She would have pleaded a lie had she not been sure Fergus would catch her—and end up all the angrier for it.

"A son?"

"A daughter." Grania's tense face loosened in relief. Fergus was less likely to kill his rival's daughter than his son. "The woman you called Brona—I allowed her to hold the babe."

"Only I decide what is allowed for my wife."

"She only wished—"

"She wishes a child," Fergus snapped coldly, turning his face away. "Yet Brona cannot abide the touch of me." He whirled back, staring at Grania as if she were greening meat.

Grania met his stare with bold, wide eyes. Like Rath Mor, Fergus too had improved from her memory of him. This time he was not caked with dirt and sweat from the road; his sable skin was smooth and clean, and his black hair glistened. He was robed royally and jeweled with gold rings that burned bright against the dark skin of his fingers. A huge wheel brooch, carved with a lion's head, pinned his pied *bratta*. Even the maimed eye seem less grotesque than before. Grania realized, to her shock, that she might almost have thought him handsome—had she not known the dark set of his heart.

"Can it be you now prefer my company to Niall's?" Fergus quirked a brow at Grania and smiled as he saw her anger rise.

"I've come seeking your asylum. Well you owe it to me. It's your pact with the Druids that set Uisneath to flame. Are my sisters here?"

"Have you lost them?"

"Tell me—are the Regaine and the priestesses here?" Fury hiked up her voice as Grania saw he would only tease, not answer her.

Fergus smiled. "Ahh, so the rumors of Uisneath's burning are true. That's what sends you knocking at Rath Mor's gate."

"It is desperation. I would protect my babe."

Fergus stepped close; he smelled of spring herbs and lavand. He caught Grania's chin and canted her mouth up to him, his eyes roaming her face. "Perhaps, little raven, there is a pact we can still make."

Grania pushed him away. As she did, Fergus's stare froze on her burn-scarred hand. He drew it up to his good eye. "Is this the love your husband shows you? A love you must prove with a painful ordeal?"

"The cauldron was my choice."

"Your choice makes us kin." Fergus pressed Grania's scarred fingers against his grisled eye. She recoiled in horror at the pleated touch of him.

"I share nothing with you!" she said coldly, taking a step back. "I was kin to Uisneath. Now that too is stolen from me. . . . I shouldn't have come," she said, shaking her head.

"But you are welcome here," he answered calmly. "I'll have Brona ready a pallet for you. Unless you'd prefer to share mine."

Instinct exploded in her. Grania knew nothing could drive her to trust this animal that passed for a man. She'd chance her fate to the forest beasts before she'd consent to a night at Rath Mor.

"You have nothing I seek."

"Indeed? Come here, little raven. Then decide." Fergus tossed her a sly look, and Grania followed him to the *grianan* window.

She peeked out, ready for some awful sight. But on the Rath's far side, beyond a stand of trees, sat Eithne. Alongside her was her aunt and the Regaine.

CHAPTER
20

"Cur of Ulster, show your face!" Niall hurled the challenge louder this time. His angry summons volleyed up the hillock that was Rath Mor's base, then died, unanswered, against the dun's limed walls. Clouds drifted over the pale sun; the spring air was still and cold. Niall had been awake since well before dawn, readying to challenge Fergus. Now he began to wonder if the day would deny him.

Milkmaids tending their herds in the fields below had hushed as he passed them. Dogs were curtly heeled in by their masters, and the warriors already gathering on Rath Mor's practice field set their sword tips into the hoary sod and watched him ride by silently. He moved like an ally, not an enemy, among them. It was as if Fergus expected him, but he was nowhere in sight.

Niall's eyes fixed on Rath Mor's main gate. Its door lintel was stained crimson, said to have been colored with the blood of battle-fallen Ulstermen. Niall smiled; after Magh

Rath, the O'Neill would wash Rath Mor's every wall brightest red.

The banner of Ulster snapped like a saffron whip off the *grianan*'s parapet. Standards from the province's other tribes flew beneath it obeisantly. Soon the O'Neill hand would rule over them all.

"Cur of Ulster!" Niall cupped his hands to his mouth as he shouted.

"Our lord wouldn't cower from the likes o' you, O'-Neill!"

Niall's eyes bounced up to the top of the wall. A plump fishwife leaned out precariously, breasts dangling and her fists and face clenched. She wound back and hurled a small stone that landed with a soft thud at his feet. The woman disappeared abruptly, as if she'd been yanked back. Gradually a phalanx of wide eyes rose over the fort's wall, and soon the entire catwalk was choked with peering, curious faces. But not one of them was Fergus's.

"Tell your skirted king he cannot hide!" A chorus of incensed shouts rained down to answer Niall's insult.

"I would only hide from that which frightens me. That's hardly you, O'Neill."

Niall turned toward the voice, toward Fergus's beautiless face. Niall's gleaming blade poised in the crisp air.

Fergus too was dressed for war. Leather casings fronted his shins, and his sword swung from an etched scabbard cinched so tight it grooved the top of his shoulder. Fergus wore no helmet; it pleased Niall to see how the years had dulled the intensity of his jet black hair. Fergus's brow, once smooth, was now scored with lines, but the eyes, one fire, one ice, were the same. It had been four years since they'd last met in the battlefield. But the heat of the fight had not left either man's face. Or their veins.

"Here I am, brother. Tell me what it is you come

seeking.'' Fergus raised his arms in wry question, smiling gamely.

Niall paused before he spoke. "My lord Connor bids me sue you for peace.'' The words caught like bones in his throat. How he longed to throw Fergus a challenge instead of Connor's softhearted entreaty. But he had promised his fosterer to make one more try.

Incredulity washed over Fergus's dark face. Slowly at first, then like water starting to boil, a laugh grew out of him. Soon it boomed over the fields below Rath Mor. Fergus smacked his fist with obvious relish against his hide shield.

"Peace! So the great O'Neill king fears a one-eyed Ulsterman.'' He sighted on Niall, suddenly sobering. "Or does Connor still love me better than you?''

The charge was like salt in Niall's wounds. He ached to send his brother's black head flying with one swift, cracking blow. Then Fergus would see what his rash laughter would buy. But he had promised Connor.

The watching crowd hushed. "Apparently our father loves the Airghialla more than you—or else you would have had the land in your fist by now. Connor's offer of peace is only pity for you, no more.'' Niall said smoothly, his lips spreading over his clenched teeth.

Fergus glared back, unblinking. "Connor asks my surrender, but offers me nothing in exchange?''

"The Airghialla will never fly your flag, cur. What Connor offers is to spare your life.''

"I'll take Connor's head first.'' Fergus's face steeled and his cheek ticced. His fingers curled around the hilt of his blade.

Niall couldn't have been more pleased. Fergus had refused the offer of peace; now justice would come. He rushed forward with a blood-chilling war scream, levying his sword over Fergus's head. Fergus struggled with his blade but couldn't unsheathe it in time for Niall's blow. He flung up his shield, and Niall's weapon creased it with a hard, hollow *thwack*. Fergus staggered backward under the strike, falling to the ground. He lay on his back, his seething eyes fixed on Niall. The challenge for battle had been formally issued.

"Man to man we will fight, then. The winner will take all rights to the Airghialla." Niall longed to take Fergus's head right here, right now. But the brehon law had strict rules for combat challenges: there must be witnesses, both parties must agree to abide by the outcome, and five days must elapse between the challenge and the fight. "Well? Do you agree?"

Fergus stood up, brushing the frost off his *leine*. He was still breathing hard as his eyes rose to meet Niall's. "My blade hungers for justice like yours, brother. But I refuse your challenge."

Niall's blade dropped as his face flinched with disbelief. "What's this?" he asked with a snide laugh. "Is your spine as yellow as Ulster's flag?"

Fergus's face was a study in barely schooled rage. "I can't abide by the terms the law requires of me."

This was better than Niall had imagined. Fergus was so eager for the fight that he couldn't wait. Niall sighted his sword on his fosterling's face and struck a battle stance. When Fergus refused to move, Niall shook his sword angrily. "Come on."

Fergus laid down his shield, threading his thick arms over his chest. "We'll fight, brother. But not today. I'll agree to no challenge that binds me to a dog's terms."

"The terms are fair. You forfeit the Airghialla only if you lose. Do you lack such faith in your *feinnid* that you cannot believe they might lead you to victory?"

Fergus's head shook in wide swipes. "I'll win, O'Neill.

But the Airghialla land no longer satisfies me. There's something more I hunger for. . . ."

"Name it. We'll fight."

"I want Connor's eye."

Even Niall hadn't thought Fergus's heart could hold such rancor. Connor had sent him to Fergus with a bid for peace, a chance to spare his life; and Fergus answered with this twisted malice.

Niall's nostrils flared as he drew in a cold bolt of air. "Then sharpen your blade, brother. For it will have to wheeze through my neck before it touches the high king."

"So be it."

Fear shot down Niall's spine. He wasn't frightened for himself. He'd courted this fight, and he had fought swifter, angrier opponents than Fergus. But he worried for Connor.

The high king stood strong, even at two score years. But even a fine warrior couldn't hold rough combat against a man half his age. Connor would be safe, but only as long as Niall stood close to defend him. And there the rub lay. Battle was an unplanned, chaotic thing. Men were easily split off their ranks, guards parted from their troop chiefs. If Fergus were to find Connor alone, without Niall there to protect him, then nothing would be assured.

"Yours is a boy's vengeance, brother, not that of a man."

"It is all the more fitting, then. Was I not a child when I lost the eye? Connor has lived his manhood with a whole, handsome face. What could I take from him that he values as much as what *I* lost . . . except the high throne? A throne that will refuse an imperfect king."

"You loathed him as you swore your love to him. All those years in Pictland—they were only lies." Niall had hated Fergus, but until now he had not understood the depths of his fosterling's evil. Fergus's mouth wound into a chilling smile. "You cannot think to replace him," Niall droned bitterly. "The law will also refuse your devil's face. . . ."

"Perhaps it will even turn from you, Niall. If Connor falls, you will be heir no more."

Niall's hands were slick with sweat as he reset his grip on his sword hilt. "Your spite will doom you."

"And Magh Rath you," Fergus said. "How many men stand the high king?"

Niall longed to lie, if only to make Fergus cower against his promise of ten thousand warriors. But there was no honor in a victory bought with unevenly matched troops. "Six thousand. And Ulster?"

"Nigh the same."

"Picts and Britons, too?"

Fergus's mouth snaked into a smile. "So you have heard of my alliances?"

"I have heard bought men will run from a fight. Take what faith you can in your hirelings. When the battle comes, they will lead you to shame on the plain."

"And will you find no shame when your O'Neill are snared by the druidhect?"

Niall's face ruddied with rage. Even if Connor didn't believe it, Niall knew the Druids might well give Fergus the advantage. The king had been foolish to dismiss the old magic, just as he'd been rash with Uisneath, intent on burning it despite Niall's pleas.

"It's sharpened steel, brother, not some wispy sorcery, that will fashion your fate." Niall spoke boldly, forcing his voice not to betray him.

A shrill yelp rent the air. Niall spun backward; he recognized the familiar call instantly. Eithne rushed him from the fort's front gate. She wove in and out of his legs, shrinking and whimpering, slapping his calves with her wagging tail. Niall's throat went dry with a hard, choking knot. Could Grania be here, at Rath Mor?

He whirled back, his eyes focusing on Fergus. His blood boiled at the sound of his fosterling's laughter.

"You see, brother, I've more than the druidhect on my side. I've your wife."

Niall ached to believe that Fergus was lying. Grania was at Aileach; he had left her there. Surely Eithne had only come with the Druids from Uisneath. Yet Fergus's face held no lie. He must have kidnapped Grania. What else could drive her here? If Niall had been ready to fight Fergus before, now he was mad for it. "You'll pay for this, brother."

Fergus pitched him a cheeky grin. Then he hooked his hand under Eithne's hemp collar and dragged the wolf, whining, back inside. He yelled over his shoulder, "Don't worry, your wife may yet live. Providing, of course, that the O'Neill die."

A huge salty hand clamped Grania's mouth from behind. She jumped up like a netted fish, the half-stitched bedclothes she was sewing for Isolde falling in a clump at her feet. She snapped her teeth like a furious turtle but couldn't catch any flesh; the hand was too wide and flat and strong. She raked her nails down her attacker's forearms, driven by one chilling fear: Fergus had finally come to take what he wanted from her.

She'd die fighting before she'd submit to him. With a buck and a grunt, Grania whacked her heel hard against his shinbone; she was heartened to hear him moan in pain. She twisted furiously until the two of them lost their balance, flopping backward with a thud onto her bed.

"Be still." She quieted instantly, her eyes opening wide. The hand loosened on her mouth as she turned, and her whole body went slack with relief. It was Niall, not Fergus, who had come up behind her. He rubbed the bloody wakes her nails had left and stared at her belly.

"The child—" His eyes were impatient and tinged with fright. Grania had seen this pinched expression before— the night Deirdre and her unborn babe had died. Niall feared that the same disaster had befallen their own child. "Does the babe live?" he asked softly.

She could end his threat to her with the simple cruel lie that Isolde had died. The baby was outside with Maeve; clearly Niall hadn't seen them. But even her fear that he would take Isolde couldn't drive her to such a pitiless lie.

"She lives."

Relief gushed out of him with a great, loud breath. "She . . . a daughter?"

Grania nodded. "She's well," she said.

Niall nodded, his mouth verging on a smile. Grania could see he'd never subscribed to her lie—that he knew it was not Fergus who had fathered Isolde. He claimed the baby, even without seeing her. Grania ached for her husband to claim her, too.

All the memories she'd exiled since Aileach pounded back at her. Niall's blue eyes—hard, then gentle, so incongruous in his stern, warrior's face. The cured, crisp smell of him and the soft, tousled look of his hair.

But this was her past, not her present. Too much lay shattered between them. Painful choices, lost days. Even if their weighty pain could be vanquished, Niall would have to take her as she was, not who he wanted her to be. Nothing about his face nourished that hope in her.

"Fetch the child and we'll make free of here."

Grania blinked up, her eyes widening with hope and doubt. Could his heart have changed for her? It seemed too sweet to believe. "Where would you take me?"

"To Connor's tent."

Grania's head dropped down disconsolately. "Then you still ask me to be what I am not."

"You are my wife."

"I am a Druidess."

"You are Fergus's prisoner," he barked back angrily.

She realized he thought she'd been forced here. "I came to Rath Mor of my own choosing."

"It is a lie."

"It is the truth."

Niall was silent for a long, awkward moment. Grania could see he was struggling, trying not to believe her. He jerked his head up, his eyes taking hers hostage. "If he's threatened to injure the babe—"

"I am here because I wish to be." Her words were slow and deliberate. "I sought protection—for me and my child."

"*Our* child."

"She is mine. And safe here. As am I."

"No one is safe near Fergus's madness. He is the foulest of beasts."

"He's no different than you with your warring ways. Except that he allows me to be as I am." Grania would not say what Niall already knew: had his love for her been great enough to accept her, she would gladly have gone with him. Silence fell between them like a light, sorrowful rain.

Niall tilted her face up to him, paralyzing her with the soft touch of his hand. Grania wanted to flee but could not break free of him. He asked again.

"Please, come with me. I won't keep you at Aileach if you wish to leave. But if you stay here at Rath Mor, you'll surely die. The child will die," he said, his voice softening.

Grania jerked her face out of his hands and shook her head. "You march toward death like the O'Neill you are.

Full of yourself, oversure. Do you think even Connor's Fena could defeat the druidhect?''

"You still have no faith in me," he said.

"You are still blind. Fergus has magic; he will win."

Niall acted as though he hadn't heard her. "There will be no safe place for you when Ulster falls. Uisneath is no more."

"Yes," she said, her green eyes narrowing. "You've seen to that."

"I . . ." Niall stopped. "It was not my doing. But what happened there should make clear that your magic is weak."

"The O'Neill cruelty has made us stronger against you."

"Uisneath will pale compared to the vengeance Connor means to exact on the battle plain. Against Ulster—and your sisters, if they stand with Fergus."

"Go. I pray the Goddess to spare you from the fight." Grania turned away from him, unable to bear one more moment of Niall's tortured face.

"Don't waste your prayers. It's the battle I seek," he answered coldly.

Niall stopped as he stepped toward the door. "Connor's sword—is it cursed?"

Grania knew he must loathe begging the question of her. But his fear for Connor overshadowed his pride. Fear for the father who still would not claim him.

"The sword is made of steel. Not magic."

"But the druidhect . . ." His eyes questioned her.

"Connor's blade will stand him well. I know nothing else of his fate."

"Then I follow mine." He turned to go.

"Wait." Hope banked in Niall's eyes as he swiveled back to face her. "The child—would you see her before you go?" The rash offer poured out of Grania before she could censor it. She only knew she couldn't let Niall die without seeing their babe.

Gratitude softened the hard planes of his face. "Yes. I promise not to harm her. Or take her from you," he added quietly.

For some reason, Grania believed it. She'd never seen such a look of debt in Niall's eyes. She peeled back the window skin and called to Maeve. In an instant Isolde's squirming mass came inside. The babe quieted, staring up wide-eyed as if she knew the huge arms in which Grania had laid her. Niall's face melted with awe at her blue eyes. Deirdre's eyes.

"She is called Isolde," Grania said.

"Isolde." Niall repeated the name with reverent disbelief. "My mother's name." He held the baby silently for a long time, then pressed a soft kiss to his daughter's brow before he handed her back to Grania.

"Safekeep her." She heard him swallow hard.

"And you."

Niall was gone too soon. Grania nuzzled the top of Isolde's head and began to cry softly, her tears soaking the baby's fine, fuzzy hair.

Maeve stood in the dark for a long time, watching the Regaine's serving maid ferry buckets of bath water in and out the door of his small *clochan*. Behind the hut's roof Rath Mor's parapets flared with war torches. It was the battle eve. But Maeve's fight would come tonight.

She followed the Pict slave inside and dispatched her with a quick, stern wave of her hand. The Regaine stood with his back to the door. He made no acknowledgment of Maeve but continued to arrange the gold bells and combs in his long white hair. Yet he knew she was with him.

He looked calm and dispassionate as he turned to check his appearance in the metal wall mirror. The priest ran his knobby fingers over the curved grooves of the breastplate that was the emblem of his Druid leadership. The end pieces angled upright off his shoulders and rose behind his ears like huge gold saucers.

He wore a fresh white *leine* belted with fistwide, glistening white gold. A single flawless crystal lay like ice in the center. His hair was still wet from the bath; damp, white-tipped curls licked at his weathered brow. The priest adjusted his gold Druid's crown over his filleted hair and wheeled slowly to face Maeve.

"Say what you've come for."

Maeve's fury balled up inside her—and found vent in her strained voice. "What you've done cannot pass unaccused."

"Accuse me, then." His eyes were peaceful and half-closed.

"You commit us to Magh Rath. Knowing we will lose."

Maeve waited, expecting the priest to deny her—at the very least to question how she'd come to her accusation.

The Regaine lowered himself onto a chair next to the fire and jangled the chain ring on his little finger. He studied its gold links, glinting with firelight. "The Goddess bids us stand by Fergus. What more need we know?"

Maeve rushed up, kneeling next to him, her frantic eyes seeking the priest's. "You *know* Fergus will die—and we along with him!"

He rotated back to her, still unwilling to meet her anger in kind. "We are fated. However Ulster fares."

Maeve had never expected this calm, cool reprisal. The horrific Sending, the vision of Fergus lying headless and bleeding, had seized her last night—and with it, the knowledge that the priest knew, too. Since then Maeve had struggled a hundred different ways to understand why the old man had chosen this course for them. Had Fergus bought him? Or perhaps the Regaine had gone mad. Maeve never considered that he could condemn them to death knowingly. She levied a furious finger at him. "Will you deny that Fergus is fated to fail?"

The Regaine smoothed out a long wet fillet of mussed hair, sighing as he closed his eyes. When he finally looked back up, Maeve expected to find some artifice, some deceit, in his face; there was none. "Fergus will die," he answered as if it were a matter of small consequence.

"If you know this, then we must break with him," she said, her voice rising. "Surely you will not choose to lead us to our graves!"

"It is the Mother, not I, who leads us."

Maeve's whole body quivered with rage. "She would not bid us die!"

The priest's faded eyes softened on her as he reached out a veiny hand. Maeve refused it. "I make no pretense with you, sister. There are things beyond even my ken. But this I know: The day of the druidhect, the rule of the great magic, is all well past us. We no longer crown kings or augur great wars. The flame of our faith wanes. Whatever passes at Magh Rath, whether Connor, the O'Neill, wins—even if Fergus should carry the day—our time is done here."

"No." Maeve still nursed hopes he could be persuaded. "If we renounce Fergus now, the O'Neill king might show us his charity. . . ."

Anger filled the hollows of the Regaine's ancient face. "You cannot think fate is made by men? If we win Connor's heart today, then tomorrow he will turn it against us. Or perhaps another—an O'Neill or a different tribe—will deliver our fate. The Goddess works us in her own ways. It is not her task to champion our needs."

"Who else serves her? I won't believe she'd reward our loyalty with such pain."

"We choose no destination, only the path."

Maeve bolted to her feet and started to pace. It was hopeless. The priest was resolute; he would not be swayed. But she could not silence her accusations. "You have no right to choose death for us. For me."

"It is a great honor to die for faith."

"We will die for an infidel." Tears trickled down Maeve's face.

"There is more magic in Fergus than you can see. More even than he knows. Can you not accept that with Magh Rath, our task in Inisfail is complete?"

"If so, then let us go elsewhere. If Uisneath is lost to us, we will take boats to Pictland or Briton. There are a thousand seas, a thousand hills, to hide us."

"Would you scuttle like a roach from the light? Would you have the bards write songs of our shame?"

"Let them. I won't sacrifice Grania and her babe for your pride." Maeve had stood dry-eyed as she'd watched the flames take Uisneath. But now she mourned, sobbing loudly, for all she'd lost, for all she would yet lose.

The Regaine stared back calmly. The cold message in his face made Maeve shiver. Resignation crept into her, slowly but surely. As much as she wanted to deny it, she knew it, too. The priest was right; their fate was bound to Fergus.

The Regaine saw her eyes agree. He drew Maeve close, holding her shaking shoulders and shushing her as if she were a frightened child. "Grania and the baby won't be harmed," he assured her. "This knowledge too came with the Sending." When Maeve looked up there was a strange peace suffusing the old man's face. "It is not our task to mold fate. No one must know that Fergus will die."

They sensed Grania's presence in the *clochan* doorway. She stood silent, her eyes enormous and nearly white with surprise. "Fergus will die." She repeated the pronouncement monotonously. Guilt flushed Maeve's face. She rushed toward Grania, but it was the priest her niece wanted.

"You should not listen at doorways," he said.

A flush of color drove the pallor from Grania's face. "Tell me what I heard was a lie."

The cores of the Regaine's eyes shrank to dark coals. "You must not tell Fergus what you have learned here."

Grania stared at the floor, her eyes glazed and purposeless. "Then it is true."

Maeve felt so helpless, as if she were watching a drowning swimmer and could not get free of the shore.

"You and the babe will be safe. And if Fergus dies, Niall might well live," Maeve offered in a choked voice.

"Is this true? That Niall will survive?" Grania stormed the priest with desperate eyes. Even now she cared more for her husband than for her own fate.

"I cannot say as to the O'Neill," he answered tonelessly.

Grania's head fell forward into her hands. Her eyes fluttered and twitched as she began to mumble, "If Fergus knows, he will not fight . . . then Niall will be safe." She spun back to the Regaine, pain rucking her face. "Can you hate Niall this much? To keep silent so he will die? Do we blood thirst like the O'Neill you claim to loathe?"

"It is evil, not men, that earn my hate," the Regaine said.

"Yet it is evil you choose for."

"The task of meting out justice is not mine. Nor yours, Grania. I must have your promise. Fergus cannot know what you've heard."

"Mother . . ." Grania dashed to Maeve, clutching at her. "If I go alone, Fergus will never believe me. But if you came to tell him the fate of his doomed fight . . . Please, I beg you . . .''

Maeve shook her head softly. "I cannot. The Regaine is right; we are fated. If you choose to go, I will not stop you. But I cannot help you.''

"You're both mad!" Grania's eyes shifted furiously between the priest and Maeve. "I'll make Fergus listen," she swore, railing at the air with her fists. She rushed the door, but her feet froze as the Regaine spoke again to her.

"Do you think, even if Fergus believes you, that he will not fight? In his heart, he knows already how it will end. And still he will fight.''

The priest's eyes were bold as Grania stared back at him. How she wished he were lying. But she knew he wasn't.

CHAPTER
21

Grania rested her head against the outer wall of the banquet hall. She held her breath, waiting for a glimpse of the boy. The scout had been sent to reconnoiter Connor; now, in the deserted cups hall behind her, he filled Fergus's ears with what he'd seen. And if Grania could catch him, he'd do her bidding, too.

The soft sounds of death coming drifted over the courtyard. Bards' voices wove ribbons of faith in the dark night. Cheers swelled up in waves from the warriors' ranks, boys and men alike banking courage for tomorrow's battle with tonight's hope and mead.

More familiar sounds beckoned from beyond the outer wall—the sound of Druid voices keening in the making of magic. The night washed over Grania like a sweet, deadly dream.

She cocked her head around the corner of the hall, looking

for the boy. He'd been inside too long. She hoped she hadn't missed him.

She hoped too that Fergus wouldn't discover her lurking here. He'd ordered her out of his sight once he'd heard her prediction of doom. Grania had begged him, sworn over and over that the outcome of his fight was predestined, but Fergus had refused to believe her. He'd accused Grania of lying and trickery. Yet even as he railed, Grania thought she'd seen doubt cross his face. But if she'd combed up fear in him, it made no difference. Magh Rath would come on the morrow. And Fergus would fight.

Grania heard footsteps and saw what she'd hoped for. The boy bounded out of the cups hall, walking light with eager feet.

She cupped her hands to her mouth. "Here, in the dark."

He hooded his brow, squinting straight at her, but he saw nothing; his eyes were still too fresh from the light. Grania didn't doubt he was heading toward the *tendal* fire, to listen to the bards' tales for Fergus's warriors. From the look of him, though, she could hardly imagine this sapling among such men.

The boy was all angles and bones, tall enough to be a man, but lacking proper meat. One cleave of a seasoned warrior's blade could easily quarter him. Yet above all other men, this boy had been chosen to reconnoiter Connor because of his great running speed. Tomorrow that skill would serve Grania.

"Here," she called again.

"Who goes?"

Grania pitched out of the shadows, grabbing his arm and yanking him violently back into the dark. The boy's feet skidded out from under him as she dragged him farther away from the light. He stumbled, then fell in a gangly heap at her feet.

"Lady?" He squinted up, shamed to have been snagged by a woman—and a small one at that. Grania couldn't quite tell if he knew who she was.

"Shhh . . ." Grania seized his collar with both hands and jerked him to his feet. They weren't safe, even in this dim light; she hauled him into deeper shadow. With a quick, rough shove, she slammed his back against the wooden wall, then gated her arms on either side of him.

She couldn't conceal her surprise as she stared at him. As she'd watched him enter the cups hall earlier, she'd thought him more of a man; but he was no better than a milk-faced boy. Single, sparse hairs peppered his face where a warrior's beard should have been, and his eyes were lit like those of a child. Well, Grania thought, the easier to frighten him into doing her bidding.

"Do you fight with the army tomorrow at Magh Rath?" The boy brushed off her hands and straightened his skewed tunic, nodding proudly. "Good," she breathed. "Then you'll help me." He pulled up taller, his chest belling out as he smiled; Grania knew his face would change soon enough when he understood what she wanted of him.

"How can I serve you, lady?" Grania pinched his chin painfully, training his eyes on her. "This." She pried his fist open and ground her dragonstone into his palm. "I want it delivered to Niall."

"Niall, the O'Neill?" The boy's voice was incredulous, as if he were sure he'd misunderstood her. Her eyes imprisoned him; the boy didn't even spare a glance to the serpent's egg.

"The same."

He raised the egg into the lean light, then let it go like a hot stone. "Lady, 'tis a serpent's egg. Whatever evil you work, I'll have none of it."

Grania plucked up the necklace and ground it into his

cheek, fully meaning to hurt him. "He must have this."
She felt her face flush with shame at her rough handling of
him. But there was no other way. The dragonstone was all
the magic she could muster.

The boy shivered his head, eyes wide as he tried to slither
free of her grip. "Lord Fergus!"

A timely cheer rose up from the campfire, swallowing
his panicked call. Grania pulled the dagger she'd hidden
from her bodice and pressed its cool blade against the stem
of the boy's neck; the knife would persuade him to keep
still.

"Shhh!" She raised a finger to her lips.

The boy's features tangled. Even in the shadows, Grania
could see he was sweating. Tomorrow this poor frightened
thing would be Fergus's war fodder. More the shame to
Ulster.

"Kill me here if you will. I'd rather that than turn traitor
to the prince Fergus."

"Traitor? I betray no one." Grania smiled, she hoped
convincingly.

The boy squeezed his eyes closed. He was shaking visibly
as he braced his hands on the wall behind him. "I'll make
no pact with a *pitag*."

The boy was built of stern stuff for his age. But he was
no match for Grania. "The Druids stand alongside your
prince. . . . My magic is meant to help him, not harm you."

He blinked at her, looking relieved as she eased the knife
off his thin neck. "What is it you conjure?" His contralto
voice cracked as he spoke.

"The egg . . . will kill the O'Neill prince."

The boy's face constricted with disbelief. "Then you
should take this cause to the lord Fergus, not to me. . . ."

"Fergus longs to belt Niall's head in the fight. But your
prince may be wounded—or worse—before he succeeds.

Fergus is a great warrior of Ulster. But the O'Neill will be on him like flies. I give you the chance to turn the tide Ulster's way—before any injury comes to the lord of Rath Mor.''

Grania could see her reasoning starting to work on him. ''Would I be among you if my heart were elsewhere?'' she pressed, smelling victory. She let the knife drop and gave up a sweet, winning smile.

''Why would the O'Neill accept this from me?''

''Tell him the gift is from Grania. He thinks I befriend him. Niall will take the stone.''

''Why of all warriors have you chosen me?''

Grania had no time for the boy's questions. ''Who among us does not know you? Your feet fly like the wind. Once already you have served the prince Fergus. I offer you a second, even sweeter victory than that you already own.''

She leaned her mouth in so close that she could feel her breath bounce back off his face. ''Tomorrow, while Fergus's men gather with the Regaine, leave your battle gear and go to Niall. You have enough of the look of a boy that you will pass unchallenged. Though all here know you as a fearless man,'' she added carefully. ''Do this for me— for Ulster—and you will be the stuff of the tales, mark me.''

The boy's gap-toothed grin widened to a broad, beaming smile. ''Yes,'' he answered, tentatively at first, then with more conviction as he repeated himself. ''Yes, Druidess, I'll help you.'' He snatched the dragonstone out of Grania's hand and spun to go. Grania snagged his sleeve.

''Fergus will forbid you to risk yourself if he knows of our plan. Let this be our secret, our triumph.''

''Aye.'' The boy nodded as he wound the thong tight around the egg's glassy ball. He tucked it inside his girdle and shot off into the night like a spark seeking fire.

Grania leaned back and let the tension pour out of her. If there were any magic left in her, the boy would take it to Niall on the morn.

Her husband had chosen the O'Neill blood-lust over her. But she still loved him. She doubted ever to see Niall again—but with luck and the boy, the dragonstone would keep her husband alive.

Niall closed his eyes as he plumbed for the familiar war rage. He was ready, only waiting to be seized by the hot feel of too much blood in his veins, to have his senses heightened and sharpened. To have the hilt of his sword ache in the palm of hand, to have its blade cry out to swing. But he was cold and empty and nothing came.

He opened his hand and stared at the glistening red egg. Had Grania's magic thieved his fury? The boy had sworn it was a gift of well-wishing. Niall longed to believe, even after everything, that she would not harm him. But so many rifts had cracked the trust once solid between them.

Hoofbeats thundered around the battalion's flank. Murchad whinnied, shifting nervously. Niall snapped his hand closed on the dragonstone and looked up to see his brother Cael.

"O'Neill." Cael pulled up his mount, raising his hand in salute. Niall echoed the greeting.

"There has been no sign of the Druids today. Perhaps their magic fails Ulster even before the fight." Cael's light laugh died under Niall's stern glare.

"Their magic travels farther than any war spear. Keep your eyes to the battle, Cael. Don't doubt the forces Fergus marshals today." Niall was secretly relieved; Grania, at least, was not here, not in jeopardy. He could only pray she was someplace safe.

His eyes roamed out over the vast emerald plain. Mist drifted restlessly over its face, allowing only fleeting glimpses of Fergus's ranks. The warriors of Ulster were darkly helmeted, and their saffron vests glowed in the haze like distant candles. Since dawn he had listened to the snap of their standards, to the clank of their heavy swords and their clacking spears.

"Has Fergus's herald come to say they stand ready?" Niall was eager for battle. Maybe the blow of an enemy blade would finally comb up the rage in him.

"Connor waits for word. There." Cael nodded toward the small knoll where the high king addressed his thousands of men.

Connor looked glorious. O'Neill preened for war like it was a virgin awaiting them. His shield, Red Backed, had been polished to rival the sun. And his black hair, freshly washed and filleted, was bound by a slender gold head *flesc*; its crimson ribbons danced in the slight morning breeze. The king spoke of Saint Columcille's prophecy that the O'Neill would see a great victory today. Kings often spun lies to inspire their men, but this augury, Niall knew, had been foretold. He hoped it was true. Connor drew his blade and shook it skyward, pulling a riotous cheer.

The king deeded the reins of his horse to Cuanna. Even Niall's half-witted fosterling had claimed his right to fight today, though Connor had placed him well in the back of the battalion where he would be kept safe. Cael bolted off to his assigned position as Connor strode toward Niall, who dismounted to meet him. Both men would fight on foot, for this was where true valor was made.

Still holding the serpent's egg, Niall wedged his hand under the bar of his shield. He sighted his eyes on Connor and unsheathed his blade.

His fosterer's face doused what war fire Niall had managed to muster. His father's eyes were vacant and glazed; his features hung heavy on his face.

"The hour of glory is upon us," Niall said with a loud, hale voice.

Connor sighed wearily. "I take no pleasure in lifting my sword against Fergus."

Niall bit down his indignity. If Connor loved Fergus better, there was no winning him now. All Niall could do was mine enough anger to keep the high king alive. "My fosterling betrays you like a pup biting its master. You saw it well in your dream."

"Aye, I saw it. As I saw Inisfail, whole in peace. Must it come like this, Niall, with such a slaughtering of heads?"

"It comes as it can." Niall's bones were cold with fear for Connor. He should have been swearing and waving, brandishing his sword. Each man fought on the field alone. Without the rage, Connor would surely die. And so too, Niall thought, would he.

Connor smiled wistfully. "Your eyes say you fear for me."

"I have seen you better stood," Niall answered tactfully.

"I have faith in my fate. However my heart leans, the O'Neill will champion this day." Connor glanced back at the six thousand Fena that stood ready behind him; it pleased Niall to see the king look a little more robust for the massed sight of them.

The Airghialla were positioned in the front ranks to taunt Fergus. Behind them were the foot soldiers, their limed wicker shields making a bumpy white sea. Thousands of sword points rose to prickle the sky. Horses whinnied as the mounted men tightened their reins, gathering in their animals' fear for the fight.

Men of uncertain heart had been fettered to braver ones,

then carefully skirted so Fergus wouldn't see. A captain's banner fronted each hundred men, and in front of every three captains another standard marked their tribe. The red, raging hand of O'Neill railed from the front lines. Niall focused on its snapping tail and again sought the battle will.

"Have you the battler, Niall?"

Niall nodded as he reached back. He felt the saint's bone gouging out the sides of his leather wallet. Connor had ordered the relic blessed by the priest, then carried thrice sunwise around the whole of the army. The high king staked great faith in it, believing the battler would hasten his victory; Niall wondered which was stronger, a piece of leg bone or a Druid's egg.

Fergus's champion galloped toward them, his station declared by his huge gold collar. He pulled up his horse, trailing a cloud of mist and dust, and slid down, raising his sword over Connor's head. Then, as O'Neill and Ulstermen held their breath, the herald struck Red Backed. Connor stood unflinching as his shield took the blow.

"To the fight, then," Connor said.

The champion nodded. "My lord Fergus waits."

"Find your place, dog of Ulster. Tell your lord the O'-Neill run to meet him."

The herald sprang back onto his horse, disappearing as fast as he came. O'Neill war cries taunted him home.

"Death to the weak!"

"Hard to the fight!"

"Blade to the teeth!"

The men of Connaught and the Airghialla called their epigraphs in turn. Connor waited silently, allowing the momentum to swell. The din grew, crying out for release.

Niall closed his eyes, plumbing one last time. Still he could not catch the scent of the fight. It must be the egg, leaching life out of him. What else could have such power to weaken him? Desperate, Niall opened his hand and let the charm slip to the dirt.

"Red Hand to victory!" Connor's war call was quickly echoed by thousands of voices behind him. The roar of men on the march filled the crisp spring air. Magh Rath had begun.

The wind haunted Rath Mor, bringing the rasp of metal on metal and the wail of war cries up from the battle plain. Grania couldn't drive the shrieking din out of her mind, even at night when both Fergus's men and the O'Neill troops rested. She was glad Fergus didn't return to Rath Mor, that he camped on the edge of the plain; she couldn't bear to see his warriors' reddened swords, to wonder if it was Niall's blood that had wet them. She had done what she could. Now she prayed.

News from Magh Rath was infrequent and lean. Fergus's warriors either stuck to the fight or died trying. Those few who staggered back for fresh blades had seen only the faces of the men they had slain. There was no word of Niall.

The priestesses had to depend on the Regaine, who saw the melee in visionary fits and starts. His glimpses were of the men who made the grist of the war, not their chieftains. Their collective misery boiled through the old man's brain, and almost from the start it bled him like an overeager physician.

By the close of the fight's first day, the priest's brow was blanched with fever. Now when the visions came they cracked like lightning through his frail frame, arcing him up off the pallet and palsying his hands. His eyes would go white, then flutter closed like the wings of a dying bird. On the third day the Regaine lost consciousness, and the priestesses knew that Fergus too was failing. It was then they retreated to Rath Mor's souterrain.

The cave's cold, loamy smell was worse than Grania remembered, and the close-packed walls seemed to have shrunk since the last time. Twenty priestesses and the old man filled every pocket of free space. The women scrunched three abreast on the narrow wine puncheons and warmed themselves at the tiny fire they'd kindled in the center of the cave.

Grania's feet and hands were perennially cold, though her sisters often forfeited their turns at the fire for Isolde's sake. But it was a chill deeper than the underground stone that seized Grania; she knew this frigid cave would likely be the last place she and her sisters would ever see.

The priestesses had made a bed for the Regaine with their *brattas* on the floor. Grania knelt next to him, tending the sickness brought on by the druidhect until her knees went numb, plying him with warm tea and soothing his brow with a cool cloth. She pressed her ear to the Regaine's mouth for every word, every moan, praying he would speak something of Niall. There was nothing.

On the fourth day of the fight, the Regaine no longer even moaned in his sleep, and Grania and her sisters knew he was dying. No compress or charm would stay his fate. If Grania were to have any vision of Niall, the Sight would have to come through her.

But when she plumbed for the druidhect, she was always denied. This was the bitter harvest of betraying her faith. Grania had failed the Mother, who now failed her. Always the circle turned.

Except for Maeve, who had sat silent, rocking and hugging her knees ever since the battle began, the priestesses did not admit their despair. But their faces were pulled with fear and fatigue, and when the Regaine finally died, Grania decided to break her silence.

"Ulster will fail and Fergus will die." She'd expected

the other priestesses to question her, but they answered only with knowing eyes. "The Regaine—" She would have detailed his betrayal of the Druidesses, but Maeve's shaking head stilled her. Her aunt was right; it made no matter now who was to blame. What mattered was living.

"If we go back to Uisneath, there's a chance we can reweave the mists with our faith."

Some of the priestesses mumbled about marshaling boats to sail to the eastern isle. But such plans soon died, and after a pause, the women nodded, one at a time, agreeing with Grania.

"Sweet Mother, guide us."

The invocation came from a young priestess standing in the back of the cave. Each woman repeated it softly. They gathered their meager belongings to set their feet on the road and their hearts on Uisneath. It was their last, dimming hope.

The plain below shrieked and clanged on as the women dug a deep grave and buried the Regaine with a simple ceremony on the hill over the fortress. Rummaging the dun's backhouse for fruit and oatcakes, the women packed what they could carry without protest from the kitchen staff. Fergus's people too sensed the dark, dawning end of the fight. Wallets full, *brattas* wound tight, the ragged group of priestesses marched south on the road.

Isolde slept in Grania's arms as they passed through the outer gate. The clamor of death railed from the nearby battle plain; the air smelled of blood. Grania averted her eyes as the war field came into sight. But a paralyzing jolt of pain seized her lungs and she knew what she'd feared had indeed came to pass: before Magh Rath was finished, Niall would be wounded by an enemy's blade.

* * *

Niall leaned, gasping, against the oak bole. His lungs stung from the cold, morning air, and the muscle he'd pulled in his upper back twinged and tingled. Hooking his nose guard, he ripped off his leather helmet and ran his fingers through his wet hair, which was sweated to his skull from the heat of the fight.

He squinted out at Magh Rath, its golden field still milky with morning fog. The battle ebbed and flowed like a bloody tide, bearing the strong back into the broil, leaving the dead beached where they fell. The familiar war rage had not come yet to drive him. It was determination and skill that had kept Niall alive for the five days of the fight. And Niall, clinging to Connor's side, had saved the life of the high king.

He shaded his eyes, scanning the plain for Fergus, but again, as for the past five days, his fosterling was nowhere to be seen. Behind him Connor was being tended by a physician for a shallow cut he'd taken in his leg. Connor called out to Niall and they again took up swords, starting back toward the fight.

Bodies lay in their path, twitching eerily, and for a moment Niall thought the dead still breathed. He levied his sword down, swiveling wildly. Then Connor gave a nod to the sky. "See there." The heavens jettisoned a driving hailstorm. Niall shuddered; it was the worst of all possible omens.

A boy of Ulster, no man from the look of him, came to engage Connor. Niall wished he could take on the fight, but to do so would be to insult the high king. The best he could do, as he'd done the past days, was stand close by.

Niall roared out a challenge, but no one charged him. In the thick of the chaos he stood alone and peaceful, a calm in the eye of a deathstorm.

"Niall!"

Niall spun, his blade poised. It was Fergus; finally the war rage rose in Niall. Blood roared in his ears, and his sword felt right in his hand for the first time. He sighted its tip on Fergus's foul face.

Fergus slivered his good eye to match the venomous one. One side of his mouth scythed into a vicious smile. "You'll make a fine feast for the wolves."

Fergus's blade wheezed past Niall's waist, missing him by less than a hand's width. Niall swung to match him with a guttural roar. Fergus jumped sideways, barely shy of Niall's blade. The men's gleaming swords swung and hissed in deadly turn, as their backs bending and twisting at wild groaning angles. The sod heated to mire under their lunging feet. All the while the sky raged on, hurling waves of icy misery.

Fergus let out a crazed yell as his blade whipped toward Niall. He missed, but the wild pitch unbalanced him. Fergus staggered sideways, catching his ankle in a sod hole and buckling backward. His sword banged loose of his hand as Niall stood, his blade tip pinning him. Niall smiled, waiting to savor the fear he expected to find in Fergus's eyes. But Fergus's calm face denied him.

Niall hefted his sword overhead. "Beg." Fergus said nothing. "Don't you know I could kill you?"

Fergus's mouth eased into a strange, distant smile. "Don't you know I'm ready to die?"

Niall hiked his blade higher, eyeing the proper angle to deliver the blow. But his arms would not move. The blade hung suspended, quivering. The rage had drained out of him; Niall could not swing.

Quietly, miserably, he knew: he couldn't kill Fergus, not now or ever. It wasn't his fosterling who had been his nemesis. Niall had been opponent enough to himself. He had chosen to suffer, allowed himself to bear a mantle of shame that was not rightfully his, begged after a father who'd refused him like a nagging child. And what for? To lose Grania . . . and his babe. Fergus lay helpless on the ground beneath him; Niall had waited a lifetime for this shining retribution, but now, when he had it, he could make no claim. His sword sloped down, thudding to earth.

"Get up." Niall raised his fists. Even if he couldn't kill Fergus, he wouldn't turn spine from him. Fergus staggered to his feet, but before Niall could deliver a blow, a burning brand pierced his side.

Niall clutched at his ribs, twisting his head back. He expected a chieftain, or at least some foot soldier, but the blade was held by a smooth-faced boy. Grania's boy, who'd brought him the serpent's egg. The youth stood wide-eyed, his sword drooping and bloodied, his mouth open in shock at his bold success. Niall's vest was blood-soaked; he slumped down with a moan, vaguely aware that the sedge grass was reddening around him.

He was losing consciousness. *He had to get up.* If the boy didn't finish him, Fergus would. Niall pushed, but he couldn't rise. He could barely lift his eyes in time to see Fergus sight his spear on the high king.

Fergus thrust the javelin with a wild, gut-sprung yell. Three O'Neill rushed in, raising their shields to protect Connor. Fergus's spear pierced them, before its point connected with Red Backed. Niall heard Connor's shield moan—then collapsed in relief as he saw Connor, unharmed, still standing behind it.

Niall lay helpless and bleeding, sure Fergus would retrench his assault on the king. But instead Fergus ran, his heels tearing sod, out onto the battlefield. Niall blinked incredulously. A strange, calm figure emerged from the mist, walking toward Fergus. It was Cuanna, the half-wit.

Niall shouted a warning, but his voice was too weak. Fergus would carve up the poor, dumb O'Neill like a bull at a banquet, then return to his assault on the high king.

Fergus sped toward Cuanna, but his sword was not raised. When he reached him, Fergus held out only his open hand. Cuanna's face went vacant, then took on deadly purpose. With one cold scream he drove in his blade, twisting and pushing until the tip slid out Fergus's back, dripping red.

Niall's mind blurred into a great, blood-washed dream. His side burned; his brain felt thick and slow. It took much effort even to think. He knew he was going to die. And the last thing he thought of, before he lost consciousness, was Grania.

CHAPTER
22

"Will he die?"

Niall's mind swam through a dark, foul miasma. He could hear Connor, but he couldn't see him. Blackness pressed down on him, muting his senses, thickening his mind.

"The blade went deep. His brow burns with fever. I cannot say—"

"Damn you, physician, I asked you if my son will die!"

"Aye." The voice was heavy and distant. "Niall will die."

Niall felt like a wave ebbing back to sea. Huge arms hooked and lifted him. His head lolled lifelessly to one side, and his limbs were numb. A rank, curdled smell hovered over him.

His body was a limp shell. Inside it he was in thrall to a swift, dangerous current. He couldn't breathe or speak, couldn't open his eyes. He was being pulled down and under, free of his flesh and bones. Like a warrior lifting his blade for one final, hopeful blow, he struggled to find strength.

"Niall."

His cheek was wet. Somehow Niall knew it was Connor holding him, Connor weeping. He slogged on toward consciousness; the wound in his side started to throb acutely. Soon every pulse of his heart pumped pain harder through him. His thigh stung, too, and now his arms.

The memory of Magh Rath and Fergus fingered through his fogged mind. With a great, convulsive effort, he opened his eyes on Connor's dark, drawn face. "Father."

The physician rushed the pallet, eager to claim credit for Niall's miraculous recovery. Connor waved him off irritably with a quick swoosh of his hand, then leaned down over Niall, easing him upward gently. He plumped the deerskin cushions, cradling Niall's head.

Connor poured a cup of water. Niall gulped it down gratefully, then trailed his fingers through what was left and smeared its coolness over his face. His vision cleared a little, but he was so stiff, head to toe. He felt as if he'd been beaten with the trunk of a tree. He pushed up onto his elbows, wincing as his wrapped ribs shifted. They felt like crushed kindling.

He blinked, trying to focus on the blurring room. It was a tent, Connor's battle tent. The king was clean and well groomed. His soldier's helmet was gone, replaced by a gold head *flesc*. Connor's beard was filleted, smelling of bath herbs. He wore the full ceremonial dress of high king.

"Ulster has surrendered," Connor said with a tired smile.

"Father . . ." Niall sank back on the pallet. Even speaking drained him. Something magnetic pulled his eyes to the far flap of the tent. He focused on it, and his mouth went slack with horror.

Fergus's severed head lay tilted in a shallow basket. The

maimed eye was poised, as always, half-closed; the other was frozen open, cocked in wry, morbid question.

"It is done."

Niall waited, expecting Connor to show the anguish of a father grieving. But Connor's eyes were passionless and indifferent. For so long it had been Niall's fondest hope to see his father disclaim Fergus; but now, his wish fulfilled, the victory was worthless. Was this the cold accounting of Connor's love?

"Cuanna?" Niall rubbed his head, remembering. The details floated back in bits and pieces. Fergus, lying flat-backed on the sod. Fergus, rushing toward their half-witted fosterling, his sword at his side, Fergus's arms open and trusting. Cuanna's swift blade, killing Fergus with the blow Niall could not make.

Niall couldn't wrench his eyes off the basket's grisly sight. He was a seasoned warrior; he'd seen men's heads taken before, but never—the words choked in his mind—*never his brother*. He felt disgusted, sick with sorrow.

"You fought well," Connor assured him, mistaking the pain in Niall's eyes for shame. The king was too quick to forgive him. This was the same blind love he'd reserved for Fergus. And now that Fergus was dead, it belonged to Niall.

Niall wanted to shout out that he needed no assurances of his valor, that he was glad he'd held back his blade. That he didn't want a father's love that was this fickle, this untrustworthy. He knew now what he'd hungered for had been miserably misguided. A thick knot choked his throat as he stared, silent and pained, at Fergus.

"Connor, O'Neill?" The low voice issued from outside the tent.

"Who goes?" Connor stood up, no more Niall's nurse-maid, but again the high king.

"Brecc. Of the Dal Riata."

"Enter."

Brecc's face was unwashed; he still wore the sweat and blood of the battlefield. The insignia of the Dal Riata blazed on his chest, and his leg shields were caked with filth from the fight. He came to the tent as a challenger vanquished, to offer Connor his formal surrender. The Dal Riatan lowered his eyes obeisantly. The floor rushes crunched softly as he dropped to his knees.

"High king." It was the second time he'd addressed Connor formally, and it acknowledged the O'Neill's full sovereignty over him. The battle was truly finished. No more blood would run today. None except Brecc's.

The Dal Riatan nailed his eyes to the floor. "I come to beg mercy for Ulster. Connor, O'Neill."

"How stand your tribes? With me?"

"All in your vassalage, lord."

"And the Picts and the Britons?"

Brecc's face was a sodden mask. "Killed. Or else surrendered."

Niall waited for Brecc to disclaim Fergus, to plead that he'd been forced to the war pact against his will. It was well rumored—and his only chance to save his life. Brecc continued to kneel and said nothing.

Connor seized a thatch of Brecc's fiery hair. The king's sword made a rough scrape as he unsheathed it. Connor's blade creased the dried dirt ringing Brecc's neck. The Dal Riatan closed his eyes, bracing for the blow.

Connor held him for a long time, then gave his head a rough shove back. His blade tip sank to the floor.

"Go, Brecc of the Dal Riata. Reckon your slain. Have your bards sing tales of my charity. Then send me hostages to keep your faith. Inisfail has seen bloodshed enough today."

Brecc's head jerked up, his eyes glistening with shock and relief. He cast a pained, sidelong glance at Fergus's head as he rose, then left with his shocking reprieve.

Connor stood in the doorway, the late-day breeze lifting the braids of his hair. His face was flat and controlled. "It is almost done, then." He nodded soberly.

"What is undone? Fergus is dead and Ulster bows to the O'Neill." Again Niall tried to rise; again the raw cleft in his ribs pinioned him. He sank back, groaning.

"The Druids . . ."

"Likely back to Uisneath. Without Fergus to incite them, they'll dare no more against you." Niall hoped . . . as he hoped that Connor would leave them be.

"It was their witchery that wrought this fate." Connor walked to the basket. To Niall's horror, he stroked his hand over Fergus's hair. Connor's eyes wore a strange, other-worldly expression.

Even as Fergus's severed head lay beside him, Connor clung to the innocence of his traitorous son. All their past fights seemed forgotten. The high king had gone mad; he would lay the blame for Magh Rath on Uisneath. He would wreak his cruel justice on Grania.

"Father, the Druids were victims of Fergus's deceit—"

"The necromancers must die."

"Whatever feeble magic they owned was weak and useless against you—surely a king as great as you need have no fear of it." Niall waited, hoping his argument had some sway.

"Once before, I spared one who rose against me." Connor's eyes wandered back to Fergus. "It will not be said I was weak a second time. It is the cross, not the rowan, that stands by my throne. From this day the old faith is outlawed in all of Inisfail. I have called the brehons; the law is made. Those found practicing it will be condemned to die."

Niall struggled onto one elbow, ignoring the knifing pain in his side. "Father, please."

Connor leveled him with wide, flashing eyes. "Will you too betray me? Did the witch ensorcell you? Did you lie when you swore she meant nothing to you?"

Niall could see there was no hope of persuading him; Connor had decided, just as Grania had chosen not to renounce her priestess ways. And now, if Connor found her, she would die for her faith.

"What say you, Niall? Are you with me?" Connor's face was wintry. In all their years together this was the first time Niall had really seen him, this man he'd worshiped since boyhood. And what he saw was cold and unforgiving.

"You are high king. I will do as you bid me. Uncle." Niall's voice was toneless and distant, and at that pained moment both men knew: Connor would never be father to Niall again.

Grania heard the scraw crunch in front of her. She jerked up her head and snatched Isolde from the reed cradle where she lay while Grania had been gathering herbs. "Stay away from me!" Hitching her skirts with one hand, Grania hurtled down the grassy path. The leper scrambled after her.

Grania spared a quick glance back over her shoulder. The woman was gaining on her. Even at a distance, Grania could see her squamous skin, crackling and pocked with dried blood. Soiled yellow linen draped off her, and though the wind worked the opposite way, the woman still gave off a sickening stench. Lepers were usually given food and shelter. But Grania had Isolde, and she could not afford to be generous.

"Grania!"

The familiar voice froze her feet. Grania turned slowly, squinting.

Maeve raised her bandaged fingers to her face and scraped off the calf's blood and rye dough. ''I thought it would be safer at Magh Rath in disguise.''

Grania was faint with relief. She was still recovering from the fever of the druidhect. It had seized her badly since the moment she'd felt Niall take the blade. She slumped down in a limp heap on top of the sedge.

Maeve smeared the bloody pulp off her hands onto the skirt of her *leine*. ''Are you better now than when I left you?''

Grania shrugged, smiling weakly. ''The druidhect still sickens me. Though it denies me all Sight of Niall. It was I, not you, who should have gone to the plain. What is it you know? Tell me.'' She leaned forward with wide, eager eyes.

Maeve pushed the tattered linen hood off her head. Grania's heart sank as she saw the corners of Maeve's eyes sag downward. Her aunt's mouth pursed into a thin, tense seam, and Grania braced for the worst of news.

''What do you know?'' she demanded, near exploding.

''This.'' Maeve reached into a small leather belt satchel and unfolded her fingers. In the middle of her palm, cracked and covered with mire, lay the serpent's egg.

Grania's breath went to ice. She'd spoken to the boy on the battle morn: he'd sworn he'd delivered the dragonstone. Had he lied? Or—the thought vaulted her heart to her throat—had Niall dropped the charm in a fight . . . or in death? Her eyes, veiled with tears, pinned Maeve.

''This? No more? No news of Niall?''

''The egg lay among the field's refuse. I begged it from an O'Neill who would have discarded it. Niall—'' Grania's fingers tore at Maeve's tattered cloak. Maeve paused, carefully mining her words. ''It was said he was wounded.'' Grania let out an anguished moan. ''But I saw no trace of him," Maeve added hopefully. "For two full days I walked the battle plain, turning the faces of the slain to the sky. They lay in the thousands. And though I cannot swear to have seen each man's face, I saw nothing of Niall there."

"Then he lives." Grania sat back, strangely calm.

"Those still alive were taken back to Fort of the Shields."

"Niall is there. He did not die." Grania's eyes glassed over, fixing on some distant, invisible thing. "He did not die," she repeated, smiling and crying softly.

"He is lost to us nevertheless," Maeve answered sadly. "You cannot hope to find him."

"I do," Grania blurted, bolting to her feet. "Why else would I send you to beg news of him? If Niall is alive, I will go to him."

"But the differences still stand between you—"

"What does it matter how God or Goddess is called, whether we take up the sword or the rowan branch? I have run like a desperate child seeking the place that was always within me. With Niall. I belong with him." Grania breathed deeply, trying to still the sobs threatening to bound up from her heaving chest. "The sickness lessens a little every day. Soon Isolde and I can go from Uisneath. To find her father."

"Child." Maeve seized Grania's shoulders gently and caught her eyes. "You cannot *ever* leave the mists. Magh Rath is finished for Fergus, but for us the war still rages. Connor has decreed those among us unwilling to renounce our faith must die for it."

"Then I renounce it," Grania answered, steel infusing her voice. "What good to keep it and live here in misery?"

"And who will believe your tale of conversion? What O'Neill will not think it a ruse to exalt your half-pagan child among them?"

"Niall will believe me."

"*If* he lives. *If* you can find him before Connor finds you."

Niall would protect her; Grania was sure of it. Even if he didn't love her, Niall couldn't kill the mother of his child. If he lived. If she could reach him. A thousand dangerous ifs. She realized Maeve was right and began to cry again.

"Promise me you will not go." Maeve's eyes pleaded with her. Grania looked down at Isolde, so peaceful and small and helpless, and she began to shake. Then, after a long while, she nodded. She could risk her own life, but not the child's. Maeve was right; she could not leave Uisneath.

Maeve took Grania's chin in her hand and forced a blithe smile. "Is Uisneath so very terrible? Once you were happy here."

A sob squeezed out of Grania's chest. She had been happy here, before Niall. Her eyes clung to Isolde's perfect little face. The baby woke and looked up. She was just learning to smile, and she cooed obliviously. Grania pressed a kiss to her hairline. This child, this tiny part of Niall, was all the happiness that would belong to her now.

The mist clotted like slush on Murchad's hooves. Niall had been searching for Uisneath since dawn. He guessed it was late in the day, but there was no sun or moon to mark the hour. In this misty forest, only magic kept time.

That the mist existed at all meant some shred of the druidhect had been saved, that Grania and Isolde might still be safe. His prayer, offered up to a God he was no longer sure of, had been answered.

He doubled his *bratta* over the wound in his side; the cold bit him sharpest there. The binding helped the rib a little, but he had peeled off the poultice once its warmth had gone cold. It would take more than the week he'd rested to heal the wound properly.

Connor's face had gone rigid with fury when he'd seen Niall packing Murchad for the ride. The high king had protested that Niall's wound couldn't bear it. Then he'd forbidden it, for he knew too well where Niall meant to go. But Niall was past obedience; he didn't spend a second thought on his decision to defy Connor. If Grania would have him back, he would do anything. And if she wouldn't have him—a thought that tore at his heart—then he'd go to her anyway, to warn her of Connor's vengeful decree.

What masqueraded as his fosterer's love could no longer hold him. Niall wanted no more of the high crown, of the precious O'Neill honor—these things had gone to ash in his hands. War, which had once increased him, now left him lessened and empty. Only in sparing Fergus had he cast off his shame. But now the place hatred once claimed in him had been filled with misery.

Niall urged Murchad on with a gentle tap of his heels, though a walk was the best they could manage in the fog. Niall's hopes rose at every bend of the trail, every knoll that peeked over the horizon. He cocked his ear for the familiar slap of lake water, but the silence was deafening.

What Niall had known all along now came painfully clear to him: the mists could not be navigated without faith. And he was bereft of it. The fire in his heart had died thrice: when Grania had left him, again on Magh Rath's plain, and finally in the icy detachment he saw in Connor's eyes. Except for his throbbing ribs, he was numb. Pain alone strummed the thin cord of life left in him. That and his hope that he might find Grania.

Now he understood she'd sent the dragonstone to protect him. If he'd been worthier of her trust, if he'd kept it, he might even have been spared the rib wound. He wondered if Fergus too might still be alive. . . . He shook his head, refusing the tears that welled up with embarrassing frequency of late.

The mists were worsening; Niall had no hope of the faith needed to part them. What was there left he could believe in? Only his love for Grania.

He drew a deep, jagged breath. His eyes watered as memories of Grania ghosted back to him. Her skin, soft as new moss, the blinding shine of her hair. He heard her voice, purring to him.

A breeze stirred and Niall looked up, blinking. The mist thinned and sudden sun glittered down, firing the oak leaves. At the clearing's far end, silent and smiling, stood Grania.

Niall slipped off Murchad, hurrying as fast as the wound would allow him, praying she was not a chimera, not some thirsting man's dream. But she kept her form as he moved closer. The mist crowned her head like a halo, and her eyes were as full as a fall moon. Only when he stood straight in front of her could he see she was real, that her face mirrored his own disbelief.

"Grania."

She gasped as Niall kissed her hand and pressed it gently against his cheek. *He was real.* Tears streamed down her face as Niall's hand slid around to her nape. He pulled her close to him, molding her head to his chest. Grania whimpered softly, then pushed back, desperate to see him.

"I thought you'd died in the fight." Her chin quivered as she cinched her arms tight around him. He gasped, wincing; Grania's eyes flew to the bandage, and she fingered it gingerly.

Niall stared at the cracked serpent's egg around her neck. He lifted it up and leaned his mouth to her ear. "I should have trusted you."

"Fergus—is he dead?" She watched Niall's eyes harden at the mention of his fosterling's name. Still he mistrusted her, thought she'd been complicit with his worst enemy. Perhaps she'd misunderstood after all. Perhaps Niall had come only to claim Isolde.

"I could not kill him. It was my fosterling Cuanna who slew Fergus. And Connor who belted his own son's head." Niall's face was an enigma. Grania would have thought this turn of events would elate him, but his eyes were dark and clouded with pain.

"I am Connor's son no more. He will choose another to follow as heir to the high throne."

"Connor disowned you, after the price you've paid to earn his love?"

"I chose to leave him. I've been so misguided. Seeking Connor's love when I could not claim it. Refusing yours when it was mine for the asking."

"What is it you want of me?" Grania's eyes were glistening with fear. This was their final reckoning. If Niall would not have her now, he never would.

"I choose you to be my wife. If you have any love left for me. If it is not too late . . ."

She shook her head, smiling and crying. She pressed light kisses all over his face. When she brought her mouth to his their lips clung softly. She sank into him, letting her pounding heart slow until it beat in time with his. She was afraid to look up, afraid Niall's eyes would disclaim his incredible, wonderful promise. He chanted her name in her ear. Again he kissed her, this time hard, and his breath melded with hers until they drew their air from each other.

Grania's bones surrendered against him. When Niall finally set her back, his eyes combed her face, then sobered suddenly. "Will I be allowed to stay here? After all that has passed between us, am I still welcome at Uisneath?"

Her brows flew up in amazement. "You would stay here, with me?" Grania was struck dumb with the notion. "Uisneath would have you, gladly," she answered, "but your heart is in the world. This is not your place. Nor is it mine. I am Druid. But my blood is also O'Neill. Let me come back to Aileach. . . ."

"Aileach belongs to my brother Cael now. If we return, Connor will kill you."

Grania pressed her finger to Niall's lips. "I have heard of his decree. But if I give him my promise, if I forswear the practice of any magic—"

"I would not ask you to be less than you are."

Grania thought her heart would burst with love for him. "Nor I you," she answered, her eyes adoring him. "I choose my place with you, Niall. Wherever that will be. Come here now," she said, tugging on his hand. "Isolde is with Maeve at the lake—" She stopped, loosening the serpent's egg from her neck. It fell to the sod with a muffled thud. She gave Niall a warm, bidding kiss. "This, what goes between us, this is the true magic," she breathed softly.

Epilogue

Grania pushed off her doeskin slippers with her toes and ran one bare foot down Eithne's flat, furry spine. She smiled sadly; the years had stiffened the wolf's soft coat.

She moved her leg slowly, trying not to wake Audr, who'd fallen asleep nursing. The baby's translucent eyelids flickered with dreams, and her cherub's lips parted on pink, toothless gums, white at the corner with pools of Grania's milk.

The girls and Eithne kept her good company while Niall was with Connor. So too did Aileach, this place that had been so many disparate things to her. It had terrified her the first day she'd seen it, and now, five years later, Aileach had become her home.

After Magh Rath, Grania would not have dared hope for such happiness. But she and Niall had gone to Connor to beg his lenience, and the king, half-mad with grief over losing Niall, had finally allowed, if not blessed, their marriage. Over Niall's protests, he had even restored him as heir to the throne.

Grania had been forced publicly to forswear all magic; but it was a small price to pay, particularly since Uisneath still breathed. Maeve and her sisters were alive—and safe in the mists. And though she now lived as O'Neill, Grania knew Niall loved her however she would be.

She'd even found some peace with her father. He'd come often to Aileach since she'd returned, and though the torn years between them could not be mended, Brian had made a fresh start with Isolde before he died.

Audr shifted against her with a soft sigh, her tiny hand slipping down to rest on the gold cuff, made to match her wedding bracelet, that Niall had given her the day of the second babe's birth. Audr was close to six months now; if she'd been bigger, Grania would have taken her and Isolde to Connor's *feis*. But dust choked the summer roads, and no infant slept well in a chariot. Grania would go to the next fair, three years from now.

Niall would bring them a sampling of the gathering's best, anyway. He never returned home without pockets jammed full of trinkets and tops and hair ribbons. Grania worried he was too doting, that he spoiled the girls. She worried that out of love he'd put them out to fosterage, as his own father had done with Deirdre. She would beg him against it when the time came to decide; she knew she couldn't bear the parting. Finally she had a family, a place, a niche of her own. She would let nothing change that.

The *grianan* door banged open on Isolde. She scampered in, skirts flying, strumming her small harp and singing loudly. Brian lived on in his granddaughter's mellifluous voice. Audr twitched and fussed at the sudden noise.

"Shhh. . . ." Grania cautioned Isolde with a finger to her lips.

Isolde smiled, showing her missing tooth and canting her blond brows slyly. "Did I wake her?" Her look promised she'd keep on trying.

"Not yet." Grania gave her a stern, admonishing stare, which melted into a smile. She could never stay angry at Deirdre's shining blue eyes.

Isolde came with her each week as they tended her aunt's grave. Ossian was gone, but his cross still loomed over Deirdre's tomb. And beneath it, always a surfeit of flowers, especially thick and vibrant in spring. Aileach still mourned Niall's sister. But at sunset Grania sometimes thought she heard Deirdre's laugh, dancing over the dun's wall on the wings of the wind.

Isolde skipped up to her mother, her small face straightening as she saw Grania's grief. "Smile, Mama. Father's coming."

Grania stroked her palm down Isolde's silky blond hair. "I know you wish it. But the *feis* continues through the end of the week. Father won't be home till after that."

"He's coming today," Isolde chirped as if she hadn't heard her mother. She slithered free of Grania, bouncing over the floor rushes and standing on tiptoe to peer out the *grianan* window. "He's bringing a pup for me—just like Eithne—and a red hair bell for you!"

Grania shook her head with an indulgent smile. "And a blue wave from the great eastern sea?"

Isolde spun back to face her, hiding her eyes behind a long strand of plaited hair. "I dreamed it."

It was only the wish of a child lonely for her father. But Isolde believed it, and Grania knew that when Niall didn't come, the girl would be disappointed. As soon as Audr woke, she would ask the backhouse to make Isolde's favorite speckled cake.

The *grianan* door eased open with a crack, then swung

wide. A miniature version of Eithne, all paws and tail, bounded toward them. "Oh, Father!" Isolde scooped up the pup, which wagged and twisted wildly; she was snatched up in turn in a tight hug from Niall.

"What a fine welcome!" He laughed, smacking loud kisses all over Isolde's head.

"The *feis*?" Grania was pleased but surprised. Niall had not left the gathering early before.

"Three days' worth of rain and the tradesmen packed up their wares. I'm glad for it; I missed you." He bent down, Isolde under his arm like a sack of happy flour. He pressed a kiss to Audr's brow, then lifted his mouth, slowly and softly, to Grania's. The sight of him still made her heart sing, even after all the years.

"Here's a present for your patience." Niall held out his fist to her, then, seeing Grania's hands wrapped up with Audr, unfurled it. It was a set of gold hair bells, their centers encrusted with bright red garnets. Grania had never seen anything so beautiful.

"What's that strange smile?" He cocked a quizzical brow at her.

Grania's eyes shifted to Isolde, who was getting an affectionate bath from the wagging pup's tongue. She'd tell Niall later. For now it was enough for her to know: Isolde, the child of their different worlds, had been gifted with the Sight.